The House That War Minister Built

Enjoy

[signature] aidayton @yahoo.com

Andrew Imbrie Dayton

Elahe Talieh Dayton

Octavio Books
Washington, DC

Published by
Octavio Books
Washington, DC
www.octaviobooks.com

Visit www.aidayton.com to find out more about *The House That War Mnister Built and* to communicate with the authors and other readers

We thank Daniel Ladinsky for permission to use the poems, "Love is the Funeral Pyre" and "When I want to Kiss God," From the Penguin publication *The Gift, Poems by Hafiz*, © 1999 Daniel Ladinsky.

Text and cover design by Bookwrights
Cover photo of Gholestan Palace © iStockphoto.com, Amir Niknam Pirzadeh

Printed in the United States

ISBN 978-0-9830958-0-4

To Andy and Frances

Acknowledgments

We thank David Stewart and Rosemary Ahern for critical reads of the manuscript.

Author's note

In 1794 Aga Mohammad Khan was cementing his newly-founded *Qajar* dynasty's control in Iran. At the exact same time, half a world away, George Washington was cementing his federal control of the American colonies under the new Constitution. They acted within hours of one another: George Washington made his point by suppressing the whiskey rebellion. Aga Mohamed Khan made his by suppressing Kerman. George Washington marched troops about rebellious western Pennsylvania and arrested twenty miscreants, who received fines of from five to twenty shillings each, with treason convictions overturned by presidential pardon. Aga Mohammad Khan ordered all the men of Kerman either killed or blinded, and, in a sort of metaphorical revenge for having been castrated by political rivals as a young boy, had a pile of twenty thousand of their detached eyeballs poured at his feet while he sold the women and children into slavery.

In America a man may have at one time a single wife and as many mistresses as he can hide. In Iran he may have at one time four permanent wives, as many temporary wives as he can afford, and assistance from current wives in acquiring new ones – all with the church's blessing.

East and West – night and day. The icons and mores of one may be abhorrences or jokes to the other. Of course, it is the universality of the human heart that bridges these divides: what it seeks everywhere is just to find a place in the world. And that is the story here, wherein the issue of Aga Mohammad Khan's dynasty struggle with the sequelae of its decay.

Cast of major Characters
(in approximate order of appearance)

Nahdeer e'Sepahsalar – War Minister of the *Qajar* dynasty, husband of Nargess

Nargess – War Minister's wife

General Z. – Former aid to War Minister

Vali – Son of War Minister by his first wife.

Tajmah – Daughter of War Minister by Nargess

Zahra – Cousin and laidy's aid to Nargess, wife of Mansour

Mansour – Cousin and major domo of War Minister

Rakshandeh – Wife of Vali

Gholam Ali - Eunuch

Abrahim e'Kashani – Nargess's second husband

Ashraf – Mother of Abrahim

Tahereh – Sister of Abrahim

Afsar – Sister of Abrahim

Golnar – Wife of Abrahim

Masumay – Wife of Abrahim

Javad e'Abasi – Tahreh's son

Nossrat – Friend of Javad

Maryam – Daughter of Rakshandeh by her second husband

Rasheed – Son of Abrahim and Nargess

Morvareed – Wife of Rasheed

Shohreh – Daughter of Rasheed and Morvareed

Pari – Daughter of Abrahim and Nargess

Akhbar – Pari's son

Fahti – Pari's daughter

Saeed – Tajmah's husband

Book One
1929

The House That War Minister Built

*M*any years later, when Nargess had lived one hundred and eight winters and had spent the last week of her life teaching herself to write the words "Help me," she would recall one last time the morning of General Z.'s visit, the morning in 1929, when her husband Nahdeer – whom even she addressed as War Minister – had abandoned her. She would then look back across three quarters of a century, and would recall General Z.'s Ford motorcar idling, the throaty exhaust sounds it made above the dew-stained cobblestones, and the oily smell of its fumes in the chill November morning. And she would finally understand how her life had been a crude marionette play, staged by hands in the background of the events of that morning – hands unseen until the last moments of her existence. Yet, what she would dwell upon most vividly was not that she had wept so shamelessly before General Z. and his officers, but why.

What could an underling like General Z. be thinking, to assemble a party of officers and soldiers before the *hashtee* to War Minister's palace? General Z. was a nobody, a vile and fawning weasel Reza Khan Shah sent to seize the estates of feckless *Qajar*s who had not supported him. War Minister was vital to the Shah, who would still be a peasant in Mazandaran had not War Minister drafted him into his militia. War Minister had raised Reza Khan through the ranks, had made him colonel, had eventually talked the British into having Reza lead the coup that deposed the last *Qajar* shah. (The British refused his own candidacy because of his Russian connections.) After the coup, War Minister had loaned Reza Khan troops to quell the tribal unrest he had caused. Even now, War Minister had put his entire militia under Reza Khan Shah to fight Sheik Khaz'al, the last holdout. In all of Persia no one bowed to the Shah who did not also bow to War Minister. General Z. was dust beneath his feet.

Nargess watched General Z.'s party assemble in the cobblestone courtyard before the single story *birouni* offices at the palace entrance. Charcoal shadows cloaked the officers and men and horses, and the lone motorcar. Nargess could see little in the dark before her. She arched her eyebrows, as if that would bring in more light. General Z.'s black Ford motorcar lurched like a tipped hat and emitted a brief wrenching sound from the springs when he emerged. As he stood stiff-backed on the running board, grasping onto the car with one hand, he greedily inspected War Minister's palace facade. He and the other officers wore flat-topped caps with thin black visors and modern khaki uniforms, having adopted the German uniform style after the abolishment of the Persian Cossack Brigade some eight years earlier. General Z. click-stepped smartly across the courtyard and into the octagonal *hashtee* entrance room outside the *birouni* to announce himself.

General Z. returned to his motorcar and positioned himself stiffly against the front fender, making the motorcar lurch again. Nargess shivered when she saw him look tiredly up at the green veined, white marble pillars, and the carved limestone windows and wrought iron gates, taking in her window. But, he would have no way to see her, masked as she was by the limestone lattice, wrapped in an embroidered blanket against the morning cold. That was as it should be. General Z. was no one to cast eyes upon War Minister's wives in even their most formal dress, certainly not in Nargess's current state of morning dishabille.

And he couldn't have picked a crueler time: a year ago to the day, War Minister's only son, Vali, had died, clutching the cold cobblestones where General Z. and his officers and men now stood. He had vomited his liver out. Reza Khan Shah had attended the funeral.

Oh, why had War Minister left the palace? Several weeks ago he had embarked on a hastily planned motorcar trip. He said it was to inspect his far-flung estates in Mazandaran, Gilan and Kerman. He had not said when he would return.

He would be furious with General Z., would have to put him in his place. It was nothing for War Minister to order a servant's hand severed for the sin of theft; or a cousin banished to the family's crenellated stronghold in Kerman for the sin of ambition (which he regarded as solely his perquisite). If you vexed War Minister, you might very well spend the rest of your days peering through prison bars overlooking the *Dasht e'Lut* (Desert of Lot). No one dared cross War Minister – least of all a *petit fonctionnaire* like General Z., his former clerk.

General Z. kept his left hand in his pocket, and, with the right tapped his swagger stick against his calf. Then he tapped it against the sole of his left boot, which, while craning his neck, he pretended to inspect. He let his monocle dangle, flickering in the pale first light that was just beginning to evanesce from beyond the *Dasht e'Kavir* (Great Salt Desert) to the south.

Nargess could hear the throaty rattling of General Z.'s Ford. The horses' breath smoked in the cold and their backs made steam. The other officers stood beside them in rigid dismount. Nargess could only watch as the scene unfolded. Occasionally the horses flinched, their ironclad hooves echoing clack-clack against the cobblestones. These men feared her husband, feared what they had come to do.

"Oh, why isn't War Minister here?" Nargess said. She spoke nervously to herself. Then she spoke with more authority to her cousin Zahra, who had come to attend her: "Zahra, where are the guards?"

"I didn't see them this morning. Mansour says they've gone off."

"Gone off?" Nargess stifled a gasp. "And nobody said anything? Who sent them off?"

Zahra shrugged as she began to straighten the covers.

Nargess was surprised by Zahra's nonchalance. Zahra's husband, another cousin, Mansour, was major domo and it was his duty to handle such matters, so she told herself there must be a simple explanation. But, Mansour was a dunderhead. No guards was unsettling. Nargess didn't even know they could "go off."

Nargess began to worry. With War Minister gone she had no more power than a child's doll. Neither did anyone else in the palace. Had the Shah turned on his benefactor? Had War Minister taken warning and fled, abandoning them all? No. It was not possible. War Minister had dodged assassins and led armies to battle. He had survived wars. More importantly, he had spies. At any perfidy on the part of Reza Khan Shah, he would rush to his estates and raise more militia with arms from his strong rooms. Maybe that was why he had embarked on his trip. Any minute now War Minister would arrive at the gates of his own palace with troops.

Just then Nargess's eunuch, Gholam Ali, arrived. He pattered across the room on bare feet. Gholam Ali was a natural eunuch, a diminutive Ethiopian, whom War Minister had purchased some twelve years earlier as a young boy. War Minister had acquired him in Kerman, from a Jewish sideshow that charged a single *sanare* to view him from behind a parted curtain, the novelty being his blackness. He had a jolly nature and War Minister employed him every *Noruz* to dance as Hadji-Firooz (a black-faced, red-suited clown) to celebrate the New Year.

"Come, come! Quick, quick, *Khanoum!*" he said in his high-pitched whine. "No time! War Minister wants hurry. The mirror hall…"

"No, no, Gholam Ali," Nargess interrupted. "War Minister's in Gilan…" She tried to explain to Gholam Ali that he had not returned. "Who told you…"

"No! No! War Minister back – late last night – Want you now."

"What…?"

No one had told her of War Minister's return! Why hadn't Zahra told her? She must not have known. Oh, you can't trust anyone. But, Nargess felt a rush of relief: War Minister was in control.

Nargess prepared herself. She was an exceptionally tall woman, a good half a head taller than any man in Tehran. Despite a fair face and well proportioned figure, she had been doomed to spinsterhood by her height. Her only salvation was marrying an older man – a much older man: She was thirty and

War Minister seventy when they married. Now, five years later, she was battling the creeping signs of age. Her hair had started to gray. She masked this with henna washes, but even that could not keep her hair from stiffening. It now made unmanageable lumps beneath her headscarf. Her eyes, a humdrum brown, had lost their youthful sparkle and were straddled by crows' feet. Her pleasures were few. She smoked a traditional water pipe, sewed, embroidered and drank tea with the other women, read from the *Qaran*. She swayed like a tree when she bent over to pull on the clothes her servants brought: black pantaloons tied at the ankles; a simple beige linen shirt; then multiple, short, overlapping starched skirts embroidered in bright colors of purple and green and pink; then over these a maroon velvet vest embroidered with gold thread and miniature pearls; finally, a white linen scarf, which she tied under her chin. She hoped this day would end like any other.

"War Minister will put an end to all this nonsense," Nargess said over her shoulder, starting down the hallway. Her private hallway was paneled in walnut inlaid with pictures of white-flowering dogwood trees and ruby-eyed crows. "And spread word that if ever there's a time for guards to get beatings, this is surely it!"

The great hall to which War Minister had summoned his wife was his favorite room. His great grandfather had laid out the entire palace so that on the morning of *Noruz*, which was also his birthday, the servants could draw wide the massive double bronze doors at the east end of the great second floor hallway and set off a splendid show, celebrating the beginning of his life and the beginning of spring. The green tinged doors towered twice the height of his festooned carriage horses. They creaked like the gates to Salahedin's castle. Embossed with verses from Hafez, they welcomed the rising sun like giant cupped hands. The yellow morning light would spill down the length of the marble hallway, washing the green veined pillars of the verandah and etching the carved relief of the green doors. At the end of the hallway the sun would illumine brilliant gold leaf chrysanthemums carved in bas-relief on the walnut-paneled doors leading to War Minister's private quarters. Along the sides of the hallway led a series of peaked arches of filigreed ivory. You could lose yourself in the vastness of this hall, topped by large, circular clerestory windows of stained glass in dark blue and green geometric designs. The arches, each thrice the height of a man on a horse, framed a series of ceramic scenes from the south of Persia: aqua skies above emerald lawns; turbaned picnickers on silk carpets woven in pink and green with hunting designs; turquoise domes of Isfahan mosques. Surrounding the arches and covering the ceiling, thousands of tiled mirrors cast the light in a sea of sparkles. The finger-sized mirrors, set at angles, were so numerous that, from a distance, they looked as if they had been crushed and splattered against the wall like glitter. You could imagine that if you stroked them carelessly they would scratch your palms like pumice – and draw blood.

It was a hall, it was a house to last a thousand years.

War Minister used this hallway of mirrors for occasions of state and pleasure. Every *Noruz* he would boastfully stride the carpets in the center, tossing gold coins to the children, who pranced in the chill of the newly admitted air. Nargess had once been one of those children, darting across the silken carpets as War Minister alternately clasped his hands to his belly and slipped them into his pockets for coins, filling the hall with his laughter. Nargess and the other children shrieked as they chased the coins, watching them disappear like silverfish behind the sapphire blue French urns lined along the walls. Decorated with gilt fleur-de-lis, the urns engulfed the children like a dark blue forest. The children darted through their shadows, setting them to wobbling on top of the marble floors. They made sonorous reverberations, like prayers echoing through the halls of mosques.

Nargess had not heard from her husband in a month. She hoped that as soon as War Minister had dispensed with General Z. he would quell the domestic spats that had developed in his absence. The other women were twittering about her barrenness (their one child, a daughter, Tajmah, didn't count), his declining interest in her, his expanding penchant for young peasant girls. There were even rumors he was thinking of the impossible, marrying Rakshandeh, the widow of his son, Vali. Worse were the rumors War Minister had instructed Nargess to find him a new wife and was irritated she'd done nothing about it. Any marriage would mean that he would probably relegate Nargess to a distant part of the palace compound with his other living wife, who was now senile. Worst of all was Nargess's knowledge that, with what she knew was the possible exception of War Minister's eye for Rakshandeh, the rumors were all true. But, it was nobody's business to talk about her behind her back. How could War Minister's wife keep order in the *andaroon*, if the others were allowed to show so little respect?

She braced herself.

War Minister was a solid man, short, with a flat, escutcheon-like face and a wide moustache turned down at either end like a painter's brush. His hands were stubby-fingered, pudgy. He held his back ramrod straight. He had a firm paunch. Despite the early hour he was dressed formally: He wore a black fez cap and a black frock coat with pinstriped trousers. His collarless shirt was buttoned at the top. He wore slippers of finely tooled, black Russian leather. He came to a halt with his head projected forward and faced his wife with a terse, disinterested gaze.

Nargess bowed, fretting silently in the pale light. She drew her scarf more tightly around herself. She was surprised to see beads of cold sweat on War Minister's broad forehead. He stared at her – rock-like, immovable, his shoulders as stiff as granite. But, she could see his hands were shaking, even as he held his arms stiffly at his side. Any minute she expected him to explode. She wondered how he would punish General Z. With her, would he be soft, or short tempered? His moods had a way of their own, and he used this trait as one of many calculated tricks to dominate his household, as he had dominated his army.

War Minister broke the gray silence of the mirrored hall with a voice suited to imperatives: "Tell me, my wife, how is our daughter Tajmah?"

It was strange that he would have her attend him so precipitously for such a commonplace – and for a daughter whose existence he had neglected for a good eight months. Had he no concern for the impatient party of officers and men that waited outside?

"Tajmah is well, War Minister."

Then, War Minister asked after his other wife. She had suffered a stroke and, barely aware of her own name, could only move her tongue repetitively, like a parrot, to collect morsels placed into her mouth. War Minister had moved her to the opposite end of the palace, where she snored away in a mildewed, ground floor room – safely ignored. She stood a chilling reminder to Nargess of what her own future was fast becoming in the absence of a male heir and the presence of nubile peasant girls. Barring divine intervention (which she tirelessly sought), she would soon find herself another sexless, heavy-hipped, gray ward of the household, a pet cat – old and shedding on the frayed afghan of her marriage. The other women would be free to ignore her. Her sole consolation would be dwelling in a magnificent palace and belonging to a man as solidly ensconced as a mausoleum. As for his other wife, War Minister had never once enquired after her since her stroke, at least not to Nargess's knowledge. God knew why he was asking after her now.

"She is well, War Minister. I visit her every day. She's still able to take food..."

"And you," he interrupted, "are you with child? Tell me."

Nargess burned with shame at the tack the interview was taking. War Minister had only slept with her a couple of times in the last several months. She feared that he had called her here to chastise her for having done nothing to find him a new wife. Or maybe he was going to announce he had found her replacement on his own. Or maybe he was going to tell her he'd bid one of the other matrons to go wife shopping on his behalf. She could not bear the humiliation of him finding a wife through one of the other women. And she could not bear to do it herself, even though it was her duty. She was too passive to accept it as a perquisite. Other women in her position would take the situation in hand and secure for their husbands a new wife who was young, simple and ignorant – an easy one to manipulate.

"War Minister, it's only eight months since I bore Tajmah," she said, speaking hurriedly. "But, I can find a wet nurse..." She stopped. Her husband knew all this. She wished she could be alone, praying.

His eyes glazed, passed over her shoulder to the emptiness of the hallway before the bronze doors to the veranda. He turned and stepped away from Nargess, towards the closed bronze doors and grasped the railing, which overlooked the marble stairs leading up from the ground floor.

"Oh, War Minister, it's not fair," Nargess said, as it all began to come out in a rush. She was unable to restrain her fears. "Who says I can't have a son? How would they know? They're making it up. How would anyone know? They probably want to hear you're taking another permanent wife. As if..."

"Woman!" War Minister held up his hand. "Stop! I don't have troops to spare for the *andaroon*." He snorted a brief laugh, which made his moustache flap.

"War Minister," she continued, "you're letting them laugh at me. I have to mention it to you…"

"Bah!" War Minister said. He was no longer paying attention to his wife. He was looking over the railing and down the empty staircase. The palest of gray light was just beginning to kiss the stained glass of the clerestory windows and brush the ceiling with muted colors.

"That shit-shoveling oaf! He'd still be in the stables, if it weren't for me..." He turned his head from side to side. He blew air through his lips to mimic the sound of spitting. This made his moustache flap again. "… as if I should grow grass under my feet for him."

The *Qajars* tasted bile at the thought of Reza Khan Shah's family as royalty. Reza Khan had been illiterate and barefoot when first he worked under War Minister. Now, three years into his dynasty, still illiterate (no longer barefoot), he thirsted for an ancient heritage. So, he stole the name Pahlavi (after a medieval form of the Farsi language), forcing the few families rightfully of that name to divest themselves of it – a thoroughly Pahlavi solution.

"British stooges," War Minister continued, "I step on worms like them – And that Z.: he couldn't lead an army across a ditch."

Nargess waited, feeling guilty. She realized the embarrassing rumors that had been spreading throughout the *andaroon* concerning her graying femininity were not a concern for War Minister. The army outside was his concern. Why didn't he just dismiss them? These soldiers had spent their lives parading before him, polishing his boots, pandering for promotions.

Nargess stepped toward War Minister and grasped his elbows, drawing herself to him in the pale light. He remained stiff and silent, but looked up into her eyes. For a brief moment his eyes grew liquid, as if his thoughts drifted to clouds and picnics, or to the times he used to take tea on a silk carpet laid at the edge of his peach orchards in the mountains and watch his young son Vali chase the peasants with the smoking carriage from America. But, then they heard one of General Z.'s horses snort and clack its hooves against the cobblestones. War Minister stiffened and looked away.

"War Minister, did you send for General Z.? Can't you send a messenger to the Shah?"

War Minister gently removed Nargess's hands from their grasp upon his elbows. His cheek flinched in a small bulge, just above his moustache.

"God will be your reward," he said, and then, with a resigned voice so soft it was almost a whisper, "*Allahu akhbar!*"

Then he turned from her and started to march away.

Nargess did not understand what her husband meant. She started down the hall after him. "Nahdeer?" she called, using his given name in desperation.

He waved her away and kept walking. Half way down the hallway he stopped and turned to her: "I never told anyone," he said.

"War Minister?"

"About a new wife – I never said anything to anyone – other than you."

Again they heard a neigh and a clack-clacking of hooves from the courtyard.

War Minister turned towards the direction of the sound. "Bah!" He blew air through his lips in a snort. "Before God, I won't receive them to even touch my hem." Then he turned back towards Nargess: "I will be alone, now."

As Nargess watched him leave her, she felt drawn away by the first distant prayers from the minarets. Electric speakers were a decade away. The prayers were openly human – naked. They sounded like shepherds calling their flocks. Their calls echoed from the hills, reminding her of the smell of hay. She cherished their sadness. It was the sadness for the Martyr Hossein, Mohammed's grandson, betrayed by Mohamed's own subjects, the Calipha – who slew him at Karbala. It was the guilt of Hossein's allies in Kufeh, who failed to fight beside him – guilt pregnant with hope for the return of the absent Imam, who would return to deliver justice at the end of the world. The guilt and sadness in the prayer calls comforted her, like a favorite shawl.

She felt quickening fear as she watched her husband. He was fading along the second floor hallway toward the walnut doors with gilded chrysanthemums. His Russian leather slippers rustled the red Tabriz carpets like brush strokes on the back of a horse. His frock coat and fez cap made a frozen lump of retreating blackness, like coal piled on a barge, coasting stiffly into a fleeing winter night, illuminated by faltering yellow flames from oil lamps. He seemed more ghost than man, now. He disappeared into the shadows beyond the end of the hall.

Nargess tried to convince herself she did not know what lurked in the darkness beyond the end of that corridor. As the sun announced its unwelcoming arrival, she sought solace in prayer.

She began:

In the name of God,
Who is One God:
Mohammed is His prophet.
Ali rules in His place.
God help me to be able to follow His words.
I pray to the God who is kind,
The One who leads me in the right path…

She would normally pray alone in her private chambers, but the hallway was empty of servants and others, and soon the sun would shine above the distant southern desert to illumine the snowy ring of the Alborz Mountains to the north. The sound of prayers distilled into the morning like vapors. Not having her prayer stone with her, she touched her forehead directly to the red brush of the overlapping carpets, inhaling the odors of incense and rosewater and burned esfand seeds that rose from the weave. Behind her spoken words she worried about General Z.'s visit and silently begged God for her husband's safekeeping: yes, a hundred *toumans* a month for food for the poor, on his behalf, in Imam Hossein's name. She made this solemn promise.

After finishing formal prayers Nargess bowed on her knees in silence for a long time, savoring the yellowing half-light of the great hall. Her throat swelled when she finally felt the red of the sun strike the marble steps at the top of the grand staircases, glowing through the clerestory windows. It was as if the burgeoning light heralded the sad calls of *"Allahu akhbar!"* that would rise from minarets to spread the word of War Minister's fate. It could not be, but the calls would soon consume an entire city. Without War Minister she did not know what to do, but she was afraid to follow him and intrude upon him against his wishes.

Nargess called for Gholam-Ali, who she knew would be waiting by the lower steps. But, when Gholam-Ali appeared before her, barefoot even in winter, and bowing, she became unsure why she had called him. For comfort? Almost unthinkingly she bade him go next door and fetch Rakshandeh. Her heart would rather have her bid him fetch her cousin Zahra, but Nargess awkwardly understood she needed something more than comfort, more than someone to hide her jewels should the need arise.

Nargess did not want to admit it, but she envied Rakshandeh. Rakshandeh was a Russian blond, half a dozen years her junior, and of a proper height for a woman. Every time Nargess saw Rakshandeh's hair, she felt a twinge of embarrassment. Rakshandeh's flaxen locks draped her shoulders like a gentle waterfall, caressed her neck like a French silk scarf. Her eyes shocked you with an emerald green stare. She wore European dresses that were subtle, lacy and trim. They clung to the curves of her lithe little body. Rakshandeh smelled darkly of French eau de cologne, and smoked machine made Russian cigarettes from a thin gold case that snapped with a click when she closed it. Had Rakshandeh been born in America, she would have become one of those athletic women in the Western magazines, who, a decade later, would be seen riding bicycles and flying airplanes – with hair cut short and straight like a man's. Rakshandeh made Nargess feel uncomfortable, but she had summoned her because she was the kind of woman who would know how to handle army officers – or would have in her previous life as a cabaret singer; because she was the kind of woman Nargess could never be. Nargess needed Rakshandeh's knowledge of the world beyond the *andaroon*. And Rakshandeh had a duty to War Minister, which meant she had a duty to War Minister's wife. She was obligated to advise her wisely. Nargess felt a sense of relief upon bidding Rakshandeh to her. She was a force, a power, maybe even a savior.

As she waited for Rakshandeh, she heard the sounds of the compound stretching and pulling to life. She smelled the ashes and smoke from the freshly stoked charcoal fires. She could smell cinnamon and mint and saffron and toast from the kitchen. This could have been a day like any other.

When Rakshandeh arrived, Nargess anxiously watched her stride down the long mirrored hallway. As she walked, she leaned forward, cupping her elbows with her hands. This worried Nargess. She had hoped Rakshandeh would adopt her usual defiant stance, one hand boldly on her hip, the other backhandedly waving, as if shaking a cigarette of its ashes.

"Oh, Rakshandeh, who are these people? What do they want?"

Rakshandeh looked at her blankly. "You don't know?"

"Do you know them? Can you make them go away?"

"You really don't know, do you?" Rakshandeh said.

"What?" Nargess said.

"What they want..." Rakshandeh began to say. But, then she stopped, as if feeling compassion for Nargess. After a brief silence she continued, "I'd say it's got more to do with Sheik Khaz'al than anything else." Rakshandeh straightened a bit. "You knew, didn't you? The Shah's put Sheik Khaz'al under house arrest in Tehran?"

"Oh, who bothers over those affairs?" Nargess said. She was annoyed that the conversation seemed to be digressing from what to do about General Z. As far as she was concerned, Sheik Khaz'al was just one more mountain chieftain with ammunition belts over his shoulder, in need of War Minister's quashing. "Anyway, War Minister helped the Shah to suppress Sheik Khaz'al. You remember, he even lent him his militia." When Rakshandeh said nothing in response, Nargess continued, "We'll have peace now, Rakshandeh, dear." It came out sounding weak, catty. She had wanted to say, You might like that for a change, but she bit her tongue. Rakshandeh had frightened the entire *andaroon* with tales of the Shah's police seizing properties, relishing the torrid details: daughters and wives stripped naked before their neighbors, reduced to prostitutes; soldiers with grime under their nails and warts on their knuckles fingering undergarments in search of jewelry. None of the women – least of all Nargess – was in a position to know that the rumored strip searches were a complete fabrication, that the fingering of undergarments was limited to those not otherwise in immediate use, and that, so far, General Z. had seized only two estates. But, they couldn't help but speculate what would happen to them if the Shah became too fond of these entertainments.

"The Shah's not letting War Minister have his militia back," Rakshandeh said. She paused, cocked her head slightly to the side, seemed to bury a co-quettish smirk. "You knew, didn't you?"

Nargess hadn't known. She again began to feel the creeping paralysis she had first felt watching General Z. from her window. She tried to reassure her-self, but was interrupted by the sound of General Z. and his party entering the main hallway downstairs.

"Tell me, Rakshandeh," Nargess began to speak hurriedly now, "for the sake of your father in law and your husband Vali's memory, do you know these army people?"

"No." Rakshandeh spoke firmly. But then, she shrugged and added in a somber tone, "Z.'s a donkey. Mansour will handle him until War Minister is ready. Where is he?"

"He went to prayers. He left word to not be disturbed." Nargess felt some relief in Rakshandeh's reassurance that War Minister would handle Z. But, Rakshandeh had unhinged her with her news about the militia.

As the two women stood there, the glow of morning began to splay through the multi-colored clerestory windows. The warm light spackled gay swaths of red and yellow and blue and green in the glitter of angled mir-rors. Angry voices began to come from the main hall below, by the entrance – men's voices: "War Minister can not see you now," War Minister's major domo, Mansour, said in the distance. "I tell you, please to wait in the *birouni...*"

Then Rakshandeh said to Nargess, "Well, all is God's will."

Nargess was confused. Her heart began to beat quickly when she heard the footsteps of General Z.'s party mounting the grand marble staircase.

She heard Mansour say, "I have sent a servant for War Minister. Prayers are done now…"

But, they were not listening and kept climbing, their boot steps making echoes. Nargess wanted to return to the *andaroon* until War Minister should call for her again, but she was trapped. She needed him to take care of this. This was not the sort of thing women were meant to handle. But, she could scarcely make her legs move. General Z.'s party kept mounting the stairs.

"Oh, Rakshandeh!" she whispered. "What shall we do?"

The boot steps approached the top of the staircases as Nargess retreated, stranding Rakshandeh in the middle of the hallway. Nargess stopped with her back against the gilded chrysanthemums on War Minister's door. She and Rakshandeh drew their scarves over their faces as Mansour appeared at the top of the stairs. His white haired head was retreating backwards awkwardly. She noticed Rakshandeh turn the ring on her left hand so that the turquoise and diamonds were hidden in her palm. Why did she do that? Following Mansour appeared the bobbing, flat-topped military hat of General Z. Then, through the small space in the scarf she held open, Nargess saw General Z.'s clean-shaven jowls drooping, with the monocle now ensconced in the fold of his left eye, it's black tether draped beside the colored ribbons and medals weighted on the breast of his jacket; then the black leather belt and the khaki trousers and the shiny, polished black leather of his boots. General Z. squinted through his monocle.

General Z. was known to consider himself very devout and when he had ascended the stairs and had found himself before two women of obviously high standing, who were not quitting the hallway, he halted – mere steps from Rakshandeh. Averting his eyes, and turning his head toward Gholam-Ali, who had ascended the stairs before them and now stood to the opposite side bowing, he removed his hat and held it formally across his chest.

"*Khanoum*?" General Z. said, averting his eyes to the side and seeming unsure which woman he should address. His monocle glinted. Mansour tried to interpose himself between General Z. and the two women, his back toward Nargess. But, it was hard to block both women, as they were at different angles. General Z. waited in silence.

Nargess's heart beat faster. Her temples throbbed. How could a woman block the march of an army? She wondered if it were her they were after, but that was impossible. Then she wished it were her because War Minister could save her. She heard her own voice fill the hall, but she felt as if she held a mask before her face again and it was the mask that was doing the talking on her behalf. She heard it say, "I am *Khanoum e'Sepahsalar*. War Minister has sent word that he comes to greet you in the birouni." God would forgive her the lie. But, how long would it work?

What happened next remained a haze for Nargess for the next three quarters of a century. The memories would haunt her for ever after, thrumming a distant drumbeat in the background of her conscience, mute throbbing pangs of warning she would heed only too late – after she had witnessed a lifetime of events slip by with scarcely more intervention on her behalf than she would accord leaves fallen on a stream. She kept wondering what she could do. The presence of these men was an affront. If they were here for War Minister, it could not be worse. How could she possibly change the world beyond the *andaroon*? Why was that world encroaching upon her? How could these men be so disrespectful? Where was God to deliver her? Time and time again, through the entire remainder of her life she would replay these questions and events. First with confusion, then with anger, then with despair. Much later she would eventually come to cherish their bitterness like sour fruit, like the defeat of Hossein, the betrayal by Kufeh.

She wept shamelessly before General Z. – not because she could do nothing, but because she was nothing. Her back against the gilded chrysanthemums, her knees buckling, she sensed a light, warm, metallic smell rising in her sinuses. Only her total helplessness blocked this party of the army from their task.

"*Khanoum*," she heard General Z. ask from the other side of her mask, "we have come for War Minister's account records. It is nothing, a mere formality – a polite request, that is all. Would you please bid him forth?"

She wanted to believe this was true. She wanted to rush to Nahdeer, fling open the doors and tell him it was nothing. But then, she felt shame for feeling relief, because she knew this was only the first step in her husband's destruction. That is the way they did things: they did not demolish your house with gun powder; they tunneled under the walls, to let them crumble into the sand.

Then, to Nargess's complete surprise, Rakshandeh threw herself at General Z.'s feet, stretched her arms out in supplication, palms against the carpet, and wept, "My general! Oh my general, save me! I am a poor widow with nothing and they abuse me. I have no husband to protect me, no son, no cousin. They…"

Even more to her surprise, General Z.'s responded haltingly, interrupting, "Rakshandeh? Rakshandeh – this is you?"

Then, there was a dizzying silence. She would never be able to place the silence before, or after, or even properly among the other events in the great hallway of crushed mirrors. But, the silence bore the terrible, utter finality of General Z.'s visit. More vivid than even the silence, though, were the looks on the faces of the officers and men assembled behind the general, the terrible looks that she desperately tried to tear from her memory. The men cocked their heads to the side while their general spoke. They avoided Nargess with their eyes, feigning detached interest in the painted scenes of turbaned picnickers and turquoise mosques framed in filigreed ivory. They adopted an absentminded, if formal pose. Their shoulders slumped falsely; their mouths clenched silently; their brows tightened. Over and over, for almost three quarters of a century, desperately searching for a toehold in the slipstream of existence, Nargess would revisit this look. She would dissect the look, caress it, savor its every bitter nuance. She had seen the same look in the eyes of her father's physician in the last days of her father's dying, in the first year of her marriage, and again in the eyes of the same physician as he attended her mother's death only a year and a half later of the same illness. Indeed, she would not connect these events or the commonality of expressions until the last days of her own life, when she would be teaching herself to write the words, "Help me," on large sheets of children's coloring paper, and would crumple and toss the messages to strangers in the street below. But, as she stood before General Z.'s men, she did immediately recall the most recent time she had seen that look. It was that morning a year ago when the servants had delivered Vali to the courtyard, after the fatal hunting trip: Vali was laid sideways across his saddle, hanging heavily, like a sack of stale rice. On closer inspection he could be seen to breathe in sporadic, heaving gasps. The servants who had accompanied him on the hunt helped him down, but he stumbled and fell. Then the servants stood, watching blankly, while Vali clutched the gray cobblestones and vomited black bile at their feet. War Minister had rushed from his private quarters, arriving in time only to embrace Vali in his final convulsion. Then War Minister seized his cane from Mansour and began furiously beating the servants of the hunting party with it. After the cane broke, Mansour handed him Vali's riding crop and he beat them with that, crying, "You bastards, what have you done? You bastards!" War Minister beat them until the bloodied crop broke. Then he hit them with his fists until he was too weak to lift his arms or curse them any longer. All the while the servants remained silently bowed. They shifted only to avoid blows to the head. When War Minister had become so exhausted that he could strike no longer, he collapsed on the cold cobblestones beside Vali. He took him into his arms and kissed the curly locks of his hair over and over again, shamelessly weeping, "Oh, my son! Oh, my only son! Oh, my son!" While War Minister wailed over Vali's lifeless body and clasped him to his chest, Nargess peered in horror through the carved limestone lattice of her bedroom window, the same lattice through which she would view General Z., not twelve months later, leaning against his throaty automobile while he tapped the soles of his boots with his swagger stick. In the eyes of General Z.'s soldiers, as they averted their faces from her in War Minister's hall of crushed mirrors, she beheld the same looks that she would forever remember on the faces of the humiliated and terrified servants surrounding the dying Vali, and, more shockingly, in the distant face of Rakshandeh, whom Nargess could see witnessing her husband Vali's death from her own latticed window next door – terrible, shameless looks of undenying guilt.

And then, just as Nargess was warning General Z. that he risked War Minister's wrath, came the unforgettable muffle of the gunshot, and the unseen flinch and slump, and then the pungent smells of gunpowder and gun oil and the sweet copper smell of blood as General Z. and his officers and Nargess and Mansour and Gholam Ali and Rakshandeh threw open the paneled doors to War minister's bedroom and there they found the red and white cone of War Minister's brains trailed against the white carved plaster of his bedroom ceiling.

And Nargess was crying, "Oh my God! Oh my God! Oh my God! Oh my God!"

The Lion of Mazandaran

O n the day Vali was born War Minister commanded celebration far and wide. He ordered calls of joy to echo from the minarets of Tehran. He commissioned a jubilant procession of tambourine players to spread word throughout the city. He dispatched messengers on horseback to grand estates in Mazandaran and Gilan and Shiraz and Kerman and even his small estate in Lahijan. From the Caspian to the Persian Gulf, from Kermanshahan to Khorasan, he had it proclaimed: the Lion of Mazandaran was born. And one day the audacious Lion would rule War Minister's lands with wisdom and (less importantly) justice.

It was a plausible proclamation – at least before they came to know Vali. Every morning tens of thousands of peasants in white shirts, rude cloth shoes and black pantaloons prayed daily for the health of War Minister and his family. They grew dates and walnuts and rice for him, and drew whitefish from the Caspian for him, and wove red wool carpets for him, and performed a thousand other tasks to fill the coffers from his bounteous estates. Holding all this together would require a fearsome heir. It was foreordained.

Nargess was only six when Vali was born, but even in her dotage she would recall the festivities as the most splendid of jewel stones set amongst the golden bounty of memories from that time. Red woolen runners were spread along the emerald green lawns to accommodate four hundred guests with *polo* of rice and beans and sweet nuts and beef and lamb and fruit; roast chicken with orange rinds and pistachios; pastries of almonds and chickpeas and rosewater. For her, back then, within the walls of War Minister's compound, life had been a cornucopia.

War Minister spared no expense grooming his audacious Lion. He gave him wet nurses until he was four. He provided tutors and libraries before he could even read and instructed his doctors to prepare exotic herbal concoctions to make him grow strong. He ordered weekly visits from Tehran's most eminent physicians. But, as the Lion feasted upon the cornucopia of attention his father spilled before his knees, the only aspect of his character which grew to the level of audacious was his indolence. Safe within the cocoon of his father's palaces, languidly draped and cushioned, Vali grew comfortably precocious and lackadaisical, the former to his father's pride, the latter to the *andaroon*'s distress. No one dared tell War Minister the developing truth.

the toy rifle and swung it against the rock, bending the barrel a good inch. Then he tossed it overhead into the stream. He turned to the tutor: "Send him back with the women."

Vali retreated with slumped shoulders. He was old enough for War Minister to allow him to throw gold coins to the children at *Noruz*, but he was young enough to allow himself to burst into tears before his older cousin, Nargess, upon his forced return to the *andaroon*. Nargess, aged fourteen at the time, was shocked at the tales she had heard of his performance, and also angry that she was expected to kowtow to this baby. "You deserved it," she said.

War Minister next essayed to develop his son's leadership skills. He took him in a caravan to his estates in distant Kerman, on the very edge of the *Dasht e'Lut*. War Minister began his lesson by remarking on the three cement obelisks marking the entrance to the first of his villages: "You know what they are, my boy?"

Vali shook his head innocently in the negative.

"Thieves."

"You buried their corpses in the obelisks?" Vali asked.

"They weren't corpses when we buried them," War Minister said. Then, seeing total incomprehension in his son's face, he elaborated: "We walled them in alive. It keeps the peasants quiet."

Vali had nightmares that night.

Shortly after, the local major domo nabbed one of the young peasants stealing a silver chalice from a chest in the basement of War Minister's crenellated, mud-walled stronghold. War Minister would not normally order the entirely legal – though admittedly rare – removal of a hand as punishment for theft, but the young man had taken too keen an interest in the constitutional movement and War Minister was livid at being crossed like this in front of his heir, especially after his comments about walling miscreants alive in the obelisks. War Minister seized upon the technicality that this was the young man's third offense. He would make two points: his peasants couldn't steal his silver; and he wasn't going to coddle them with anything like a constitution. The young man's screams frightened Vali. Three days later he visibly shook, when he discovered the body of the young man: Humiliated by no longer possessing a left hand to clean himself after toilet, the young man had hung himself from a slanting date palm in War Minister's garden.

"Hah!" War Minister greeted the news with a snort. "Who tied the knot, I wonder?"

Vali, who still preferred puffing dandelions and picking wildflowers, again burst into tears. And again War Minister seethed. Beads of sweat gathering on his forehead, his moustache trembling, War Minister lectured: "My son, that boy was a mean traitor and a thief. He cursed himself and made my point to the village. Now we can avoid this desert hole at least another five years. We should praise God, not cry."

But, War Minister's instructions in leadership only brought terror to Vali's heart. Almost as intimidating as the young man who lost his hand was the example of War Minister's cousin and major domo, Mansour, later to be husband to Zahra, Nargess's confidant. War Minister conveyed the secret of Mansour's fate to Vali in absolute confidence, threatening to cane his feet if he blabbed. Mansour was famously dull witted, but he had not been born that way. Once, he had been ambitious and had risked backing three caravans at the same time. He committed all of his inheritance and all he could borrow on top of it, and then some. Thieves plundered all three caravans en route. There was speculation a jealous family member had betrayed him, but the truth was never forthcoming and he suffered a nervous collapse. He recovered from this by becoming fervently religious. He would have joined the ranks of the uneducated clerics, shuffling about as foul-robed mullah, proselytizing emaciated peasants from the haunch of a moth eaten donkey, had not War Minister offered him shelter and allowed him to wander harmlessly about the compound, arranging passion plays of the Martyr Imam Hussein's betrayal. To everyone's surprise, Mansour proved to possess a certain meticulousness. Despite his slow-wittedness, War Minister made him his major domo. To keep him happy in this lowly station, War Minister gave him the thirteen year old Zahra, another distant niece.

"You see," War Minister boasted to his son in a letter he had his manservant deliver, "You must assemble subordinates about you wisely. As for a major domo, choose one who keeps the accounts to perfection, but with a mind too limited to cheat."

Vali turned to the manservant who had delivered the sealed message: "Tell War Minister I do not have an answer."

War Minister penned back: "And if all that religiosity doesn't make him honest, it will at least keep him from cheating family."

Vali scrunched his eyebrows and turned away from the message, hurt that his father was so casually dismissing the dimwitted Mansour in whom he placed so much trust. He did not send a reply.

War Minister then visited his rooms in person. He slapped at the curtains with his cane, as was his habit upon entering a room, to make sure no malcontents lurked. Then he bade the servants leave them in private. He grasped Vali by both shoulders and forced the boy to look directly into his eyes.

"Swear to me you will never tell what I am about to tell you – not to any one. Not your wife. Not your cousin. Not your mother in heaven."

Vali first averted his eyes, but War Minister jostled him and made him return his searing glare. He placed Vali's hand on the *Qaran*.

"Swear it! Do you?"

"Yes, War Minister."

"You must either rule or be ruled."

"Yes, sir."

"Which is it? Which do you choose?"

"Rule, sir."

"He was weak," War Minister said. "Mansour – I was the one who tipped off the thieves to his caravans. He was weak. I couldn't have a spineless fool in the family become rich and powerful. Where would we be, then?"

Vali looked up wide-eyed into his father's emotionless face. "You, sir?" he stammered. Then he gulped and continued: "But, Uncle Mansour could have been strong and successful if you hadn't betrayed him!"

"Betray? Bah! If it had been God's will for him to become strong and successful, believe me, he would have. God's will was for me to get to him first."

Vali did not embrace this lesson in Machiavellian statesmanship. Rather, he dreaded that the knowledge threatened him with a fearful liability: he now knew one of his father's dark secrets.

So Vali grew up wistful, obstreperous, obstinate – and timid. By the age of twelve, not long before the arrival of the first motorcar in Persia, Vali had already reduced a minor succession of tutors. The last of these had been a wizened, fastidious bachelor (another distant cousin) with a waxed moustache – twisted like a snake – and a black cylinder hat imported from England. To mask an offensive breath the tutor chewed cloves. He brushed his hair with coconut oil. War Minister made him Vali's personal manservant, hoping the constant attention would nurture his son's ambition.

At the end of the third day Vali rebelled: "You smell like coconuts," he said, in a pique.

The oily tutor, recently returned from training "in the great cities of Europe," boasted he would master his young charge with traditional French discipline and novel Viennese psychology. But, when, with a shaking finger, he threatened to cane Vali's palms for failing to memorize his lessons, he learned what Vali had discovered many tutors earlier: no one dared touch the son of War Minister. That left Viennese psychology, which ended in the tutor allowing himself to be tied to a peach tree by his young charge. The scene was otherwise idyllic, even pastoral – one of those scenes woven in carpets or inlaid in murals showing genteel picnics beneath the shade of elm trees. But, Vali refused to undo the tethers. He rolled on the ground, plucking tufts of grass, tossing them at his tutor, poofing dandelions at him, then laughing...

"Aaarrgh! Vali, dear, I do everything for you..." The tutor struggled now. "... all day long. You are a terribly spoiled child!" Grunting, he begrudgingly realized he would get no assistance from his pupil. "You will come to nothing. I promise it."

Vali stopped rolling on the ground, stood up and scrunched his shoulders. "Silly old man!" he said.

"You brazen brat, I should think you would piss in my hat if I offered it." He worked one hand free, removed his cylinder hat and held it, inverted, before his charge's knees. "There!" he said.

"I would," Vali said.

Only half tethered to the tree now, the tutor eyed the boy. "Eh? You would not. Not this hat! Do you know how much this hat cost?"

"I would too." Vali released his drawstring and lowered his trousers.

"Would not!"

Vali lowered his under shorts.

"You wretched ..."

That the next dawn broke tutor-less neither surprised nor upset the family. They were accustomed to such discontinuities. They remained, however, thoroughly mystified as to why their fastidious cousin had left behind such an exotic and obviously dear hat. Vali declined to satisfy their curiosity on the matter.

Though Vali paid scant attention to the succession of tutors who declared him dissolute, he sadly accepted the judgment with a quiet despair. Even the son of War Minister was not immune to the opinions of others. After dispatching the last of the tutors, he came under his father's direct tutelage again. But, he only made his father stiffen with anger by yawning before the endless procession of generals, envoys and officials that washed past his gaze. This was well before the disbanding of the Cossack Brigade. The Persian generals wore white tunics in the Russian style, with gray lambs wool fez caps emblazoned with the golden emblem of a lion above a sword, roaring before the sun – and black leather riding boots. The foreign envoys wore western style suits; the Persian ministers and bureaucrats black fez caps, mostly with dark, knee-length jackets or frock coats, pressed pinstripe or black trousers, and as often as not, cravats. Vali feigned obedience. He donned the white linen, knee length jacket and dark, pinstriped trousers his father bid him wear to emphasize the family's stature. But, he nodded off at the endless string of announced names. They either bored him with their familiarity, or confused him with their obscurity. They became vague noises, meaningless tethers to a long line of supplicant feet shuffling along his father's carpets. As the affairs of state droned on and Vali's eyelids sagged, his attention wandered to the silver trays stacked with baklava and pistachios and dried apricots and raisins. But, he dared not touch these, lest he ignite his father's rage.

Vali was first roused from this somnolence by stories about rubber-wheeled, self-propelled "smoking carriages," related to him by visiting Belgian railroad engineers. The Belgians and the Germans had been impressed by British successes in constructing a Persian telegraph system and a Persian banking system. It escaped no one's notice that the telegraph system connected the British with their prized colonial possession, India, and that control of the banks afforded them significant control of Persian commerce. So the Belgians and the Germans endeavored to build a railroad system for the Persians. The Belgian emissaries, hosted by War Minister, regaled the family with tales and photographs not only of steam locomotives, but also self-propelled smoking carriages, until Vali decided he just had to have one. He begged his father to buy him one.

So, thanks to Belgian hegemonic ambitions, War Minister imported the first motorcar in Persia. Vali was almost thirteen. War Minister's compound anticipated its arrival with equanimous curiosity, not sure what to expect. But, Hashem knew better. He was the master of War Minister's stables, Vali's one-time riflery tutor. Hashem regarded the advent with justifiable suspicion. War Minister invited Vali to his tent (it was summer), thinking to afford him training in understanding servants.

"Hashem," War Minister said, placing a cube of sugar in his mouth and sipping tea through it, from a lyre-shaped glass. "Hashem, these Americans are going to put you out of business. I have it in good faith." He gave Vali a secretive wink.

"Out of business, my lord? Who?" He messaged his ruddy cheeks and shifted on his feet. He adjusted his soiled turban and fingered his scabbard-like moustache, frowning.

"Ah, Hashem, the brothers of the English."

"My lord, why would the English be angry with me? I am a simple man. I tend your estates in the mountains. I..."

"Americans, Hashem. Americans. They have invented a box that moves by itself, a box with seats for people – that carries a fire in its belly and makes smoke. A steamship for the land, Hashem! Do you see? No horses, no grooms, no stables – no more Hashem!" He waved his arms in feigned excitement.

"I don't think we should trust these Americans, my lord. They are casting an evil eye upon us."

The entire family watched as the smoking carriage from America, through the Belgians, arrived in a great box on a giant wagon, drawn by four horses. With it arrived twenty square metal tins filled with petrol from the new British APOC (Anglo Persian Oil Company) refinery in Abadan, and one frisky Belgian driver, who wore a long white trench coat. Petrol, carriage and driver disappeared forthwith into the stables. By morning the peasants from as many as three villages away had arrived to witness the spectacle of the box that moved by itself.

It was Hashem who started the stampede. He had allowed himself to witness the carriage remove from his stables. The wiry Belgian driver, wearing the heavy leather gloves and the shiny leather goggles, with the flat, circular lenses, and the white trench coat, inserted a crooked handle into the mouth of the carriage. Meanwhile, War Minister and son sat proudly beneath the cloth roof that looked like a black bonnet, War Minister in the seat of honor, Vali in back. The explosions made Hashem shriek. Eyes bulging, he fled the stables. Following him fled the horses, which no one had thought to tether, and then the belching carriage. The shrieking Hashem, the panicking horses, the intrepidly smoking automobile, with War Minister, Vali and the goggled driver seated within, lurched past War Minister's shocked family in an instant. With smoke and backfires the automobile burst into the orchards, terrifying the congregated peasants, bumpily squishing the yellow peaches that they knocked to the ground in panic. Almost faster than the smoking carriage, a rumor spread among the peasants that the fire and smoke heralded the arrival of Satan himself – the return of the absent Imam at the end of the world! Most fled into the depths of the orchard. Some fell to their knees and prayed. In all they trampled half of War Minister's peach crop.

Then War Minister insisted on driving. The peasants gathered at a respectful distance, creeping forward warily, like timid animals, to watch him squeeze his belly behind the wheel. The Belgian driver directed him in faltering Farsi, but War Minister, not to appear helpless before his peasants, dismissed him with a wave. He pushed the transmission lever forward and the lifted the left pedal (instead of pressing it down) sending the automobile into a single solid lurch, followed by a single sharp explosion, and then silence. The peasants murmured. The goggled driver dismounted, inserted the crooked stick into the mouth of the carriage and recranked the engine. War Minister tried to master the directions: advance the spark lever with one hand and increase the hand throttle with the other. But, where was that third hand to cling to the steering wheel? Another lurch. Bang! Then silence. Seeing the ominous threat deflate, Hashem crossed his arms, and from a distance peered through the newly unburdened peach trees, watching his lord learn to drive.

War Minister fumed. "You father's a dog!" he cursed at the Belgian driver, furious that the driver knew how to do something he didn't. The driver, knowing the risks of making War Minister look even worse before family and peasants, pretended to be exhausted from cranking, and threw up his arms. He rested against the fender, panting like a dying donkey. The peasants reapproached – hesitantly – Hashem in the lead. War Minister avoided Hashem's eyes for as long as he could.

"Does my lord want his horse?" Hashem asked, bowing.

"Your lord wants you to crank the engine, Hashem. And don't try to fool me with that asinine bow!"

Hashem surveyed the situation: the sweating, exhausted driver panting on the fender, the crooked stick dangling from the mouth of the box, like a broken machine-made cigarette, the angry red face of his master, who was now back in the passenger seat. At last he spoke: "Yes, my lord tires. I will fetch the horse." He began to march away, slowly, almost methodically.

"Curse you, Hashem!" War Minister called at his back.

"So God wills it," Hashem called over his shoulder. "I am dust beneath thy feet."

Vali began to plead: "War Minister, let me…"

"Hashem will find the horse. I don't…"

"… drive, War Minister…"

"Eh?" War Minister eyed him dubiously. After a brief pause he nodded: "Hah! *Allah* be your guide!"

Vali found his true mettle then. On the first try he advanced the spark, slightly reduced the throttle, pressed forward on the left foot pedal and managed to roll forward enough to reduce the first hard lurch to a series of successive jerks and belches that gave way to a self-sustaining momentum.

"See *Pedar!*" Vali shouted over the noise, so excited that he failed to address his father properly. Abandoning the wary driver, he crookedly pursued Hashem, who broke into a run for the stables. In the excitement the Belgian driver had forgotten instructions on how to stop. So, after a delightful, if brief, chase, Vali crashed the smoking carriage from America into the back of the stables – with impunity, of course.

It took the Belgian driver a solid week to repair the carriage till it could smoke again, and it would take a whole year for new fenders to arrive from America, by which time the second motorcar had arrived in Tehran, a Rolls Royce for the Shah. As for Belgian hegemonic ambitions, only a single Belgian railroad engine was ever imported. It lived out its life on display in central Tehran, lacking tracks of the correct gauge, courtesy of German and the British intercession in designing and laying the tracks.

Within a month of the smoking carriage's arrival, though, Vali had learned everything the Belgian driver could teach him: how to replace the tires and repair the inner tube; how to clean the carburetor; how to straighten the tie rod after hitting a rock; how to harness a team of horses to pull the smoking carriage from the ditch; how to curse in French and Dutch (or, as Vali called it, Belgian); how to remove grime from under his fingernails with a screwdriver. Vali should have left the mundane chores to the driver. He was just another, if more exotic, servant. But, the magnificent contraption fascinated Vali. The Ford gradually succumbed to dents and tears and spent more and more of its time stabled. The proud black bonnet of the smoking carriage from America progressively drooped. War Minister lost interest. The Belgian driver divined his fate and booked passage home. Hashem was vindicated. And Vali became sole master of the automobile.

Vali loved the summer evenings in the Alborz mountains. He loved to meander about the orchards with the smoking carriage, rousting startled peasants from their trysts, blasting them with the aooga horn that arrived with the brand new fenders. High up on a hill, at the edge of the orchards, he could see his father taking tea on an ivory silk carpet spread beside a cherry tree. He imagined how he would appear to his father, his motorcar's yellow headlights delving through the distant twilight like flickering candles. When he tired of rousting the peasants, he would join the assembled family for their nightly feasts.

The feasts were languorous. On hot evenings (which were rare) they ate watermelons and drank sweetened cherry juice. Then they would have yogurt mixed with cucumbers and mint, to which they sometimes added walnuts and raisins. On cooler nights they would supplement these with kabobs, and stews of lamb or chicken. These would be cooked with celery or eggplant or zucchini or string beans with tomatoes. Sometimes they would cook the chicken with cherries and almonds or pistachios. With all of these dishes they served heaps of steaming, crusted saffron rice. The cooking was done on donkey-sized brass braziers, stoked with sparking charcoal fires.

The family would pass the time with jokes, stories and poetry. Eventually they would retire to smoke water pipes in tents the servants had assembled. They smoked tobacco, and, as often as not, opium. They told endless jokes about the apocryphal *Mullah Nasr al-Din* (Lit. "victory of religion"), who, like his mullah companions, loved in life nothing so dearly as a great feast – and indeed thought of little else – and loathed in life nothing so vile as a dog. The most vulgar insult *Mullah* could imagine was being told a dog had pissed on his father's grave. Not surprisingly, everyone's favorite tale was about the dog who soiled *Mullah's* dinner: *One night, Mullah Nasr al-Din and his companion clerics settled down to feast on a mountainous heap of rice and lamb, which awaited them on a platter in the middle of the carpet. As greedy Mullah raised his arm to scoop a generous helping, a shaggy, wet dog jumped on the carpet and shook himself all over the food, and then ran off. Mullah Nasr al-Din, confronting a vexing theological conundrum, halted his arm in mid air. He looked back and forth between his suspended spoon and the defiled dinner. He looked to his fellow mullahs for spiritual guidance and scriptural precedent. They looked back to him. Silently they weighed the pleasures of a sumptuous feast against the sin of defiled consumption. Then Mullah divined a solution: "Aahh!" he said. "Let's hope it's a cat!" "God be praised!" the others agreed. "Now, let us eat!"*

Vali half envied *Mullah's* dubious life of simple greed and ignorance. Though he dared not utter the thought, he grew to emulate it, albeit on a considerably grander scale. As the Great War expanded and parts for the smoking carriage from America became increasingly scarce, Vali abandoned it. He let it collect mouse nests and cobwebs in the stables, while he indulged in more visceral pursuits.

He was becoming a handsome teenager, with dark curly hair like the ancient Persian soldiers carved in stone at Persepolis. Despite his indolence, he developed broad shoulders, the kind that women love, and a lanky, self-assured gait. He was already a full head and a half taller than his father and had adopted the habit of leaning his head forward in conversation to better hear. This bestowed upon him the deceiving air of a tolerant savant, in full control of those surrounding him. Despite this rather commanding presence, he had a cherubic face and a disarmingly boyish smile, both of which better displayed his disposition.

No one dared deny him any pleasure. At an age when the sons of lesser families toiled evenings beside smoking oil lamps studying theology or memorizing poetry, Vali mastered the complexities of opium and sex. Vali knew his father approved of these pleasures as the birthrights of rulers, but he suffered the constant fear of banishment to the Tehran Military Cadet College, should his father decide the indulgences had become excessive – as, indeed, they had. War Minister himself had prepared at the Austrian Military Academy in Tehran. There was no reason (other than a completely unsuitable character) that Vali should not follow a similar path. But, if he imposed the sanction, he would lose its value as a threat. And if he didn't impose the sanction fairly soon, he would simply lose it.

Vali had no one to help him navigate the narrow channel between his father's wrath and indulgence. He had numerous party friends, but they were only interested in amusement and flattery. The sole cousin in whom he could confide was Nargess, six years his senior. He pitied Nargess for being an old maid by her early twenties, but he could understand it. After all, she was embarrassingly tall. Who wanted to mount a stepladder to take his wife into his arms? It was clear even then she would have to be married off as third or fourth wife to a much older man – who didn't mind stepladders. She knew this herself and sought solace in prayer – and in reading the *Qaran*. So if she lacked experience in the world – as, indeed, she did – she was at least morally trustworthy.

After a night of debauchery Vali would rouse himself to take afternoon tea with Nargess in the *andaroon*.

"Vali, dear," she once said, closing her maroon leather-bound *Qaran* on her lap, "you'll be War Minister next. What will you do?"

He placed a large crystal of sugar between his lips and sipped tea from one of Nargess's mother's jewel-encrusted silver tea glasses.

"You pray too much, cousin dear," he said.

"But, seriously, dear cousin, you'll have to some day,"

Vali understood that she meant he would have to start preparing himself. He appreciated her indirectness. He returned to sipping tea. "It's easier for you, cousin," he said, at length, "You don't have to do anything. You can just…" he paused, then continued with a wistful sigh, "… sit. Oh, it's so much easier for a woman."

"Vali, dear, that's not a good sentiment for War Minister's heir." She closed her eyes and enjoyed the warmth of the sunlight that streamed in through the tall window, glad that she would never have to be a Lion of Mazandaran. "Besides," she added, "waiting around's not all so wonderful."

Vali pitied her. He wanted to say something comforting, but didn't know what. He knew that she wanted to believe her life was God's will, but suspected that was of little solace. "Nargess, dear," he said, "someone will be just right…"

She sat forward, opening her eyes. "Oh, Vali, dear, what's going to happen to me? They come and take a look and rush home and I never hear from them again." She referred to the countless squads of reconnoitering matrons who had been dispatched to inspect her on behalf of the eligible young men of various families. "You are lucky, Vali: you will go out and choose."

"Choose?" Vali said. "Since when did War Minister allow anyone to choose? The only choice I have is to avoid him."

"Still, Vali, dear, that's a choice. I don't even have that."

"None of us do, really."

Vali knew he could only postpone the inevitable. Someday responsibility would be thrust upon him, whether he liked it or not.

While he waited, the Bolshevik revolution had delightful consequences for him and his party friends. The Great War, the sweeps through Persia of British, Turkish, Russian and indigenous troops, the conscription of peasants, the consequent decay of irrigation systems and their dependent agriculture, the resulting widespread famines, all appeared to Vali and his retinue as distant stories read in history books or foreign newspapers. The war experience they tasted was the suffering of minor shortages here and there: parts for the smoking carriage from America; cigars from London; quality beef and lamb; fresh fruit. But, opium and local tobacco were plentiful and the famine improved the supply of whores, as young peasant women became increasingly desperate. Deprived of real power by War Minister, most of the men in the family shared in Vali's dissolution, and ingratiatingly promoted it, anticipating his succession. Evenings were an endless series of celebrations till morning and mornings a series of dissipated recoveries till afternoon. Through the early part of the war the parties boasted Russian officers and vodka, the latter secreted through Persian customs controlled by the former. But, the Bolshevik revolution did away with the officers, along with their army and vodka. War Minister regretted the dearth of Russian military. His strategy had been to play one major foreign power against another and he had sided mostly with his northern neighbors, through the granting of oil concessions. Vali regretted only the lost vodka. And he tired of the swarthy peasant women

provided by a mysterious, dark man who wrapped his face in a soiled turban and who wheeled the women up to the compound nightly in a canvas
covered wagon drawn by four horses. He began to spend less time with the
whores and more with the Chinese opium pipe. He floated through the postwar machinations blissfully unaware of the distant Paris Peace Conference
(where the British sidelined the Persian envoys to gain full control of their
oil). In the postwar years of famine and chaos Vali indulged in his pleasures,
oblivious to the schemes of emissaries, foreign and local. He ignored the admonishments of his father, who blustered about the British and about Nosrat
Doleh e'Farmanfarmaian, who had helped sell control of the nation's oil to
the British, and about the venal Ahmad Shah, who was too weak to stop it,
and about the ever lurking British operatives, the communists and the clerics,
all of whom could assassinate anyone at any time. As Vali dallied, his father's
admonishments and exhortations became like the endless shuffling feet, a sea
of threats, plans, meaningless obligations and avoidable burdens. Through
the brassy dissonance he eventually discerned that his father was planning for
him to marry Moulook, daughter of Amir e'Doleh, who was well connected
with the British. He was to have no more choice than his cousin Nargess.

It came to a head on the eve of a projected meeting with a customs agent
from Rasht. War Minister explained to his son that the man was willing to
seek an accommodation: War Minister's protection in return for a cut of the
revenues. It was a fairly mundane matter and War Minister wanted his son to
conclude the deal. Vali figured that, as usual, his father would be too preoccupied with his machinations to remember the conceit of his involvement,
and he let his attention wander to concerns that were, well, more pressing.

That very afternoon one of his uncles had brought him a proposition vast-
ly more titillating than a dowdy customs agent from Rasht: "As blond haired
and blue eyed as the *Bakhtiaris*! I promise you." He winked.

Vali raised a curious eye. Wealthy Russian émigrés had fled the Bolshe-
viks and made their way to Tehran some years earlier. By now many had
depleted the stashes of jewelry they had brought with them, and were desperate. Daughters of these families were not unknown to descend to the less
illustrious pursuits, and were highly prized.

"And we bring you a young one tonight – untouched!" His uncle kissed
the tips of his fingers and thrust his hand forward in the air, as if to fling the
kiss across the room. "Just for you. With breasts like sweet lemons. And a
pedigree better than *Qajar*."

Vali released a long, wistful sigh. "Truly, Uncle? Untouched?" He could
already feel his hand massaging the warm, smooth, tympanic abdomen,
working its way downward…

"Well …" His uncle shrugged his shoulders.

His father interrupted the reverie: "Well?"

"What, War Minister?"

"A customs agent. You can handle it?"

Vali sighed. "Yes, War Minister."

War Minister, skeptical, released a dissatisfied grunt.

That night, with the threat of the Tehran Military Cadet College rummaging about the back rooms of his conscience, Vali drew on the Chinese opium pipe just long enough to feel himself giddily floating backwards, as if he reclined on clouds. He was scarcely prepared for what awaited.

The room was lit only by two candles on sconces flanking a gilt-framed mirror, and a large brass brazier filled with charcoal. The brazier cast a red glow on the carved plaster of the ceiling. The slight acrid smell of the burning charcoal mixed with the scents of rosewater and foreign perfume and the sweet smell of opium. By the brazier, on a series of embroidered pillows lay his special treat, supine, knees together, naked except for necklace and bracelets. Her skin was alabaster, except for the dark spots of her nipples. The hair between her legs was shadowed by her thighs, but Vali could see it was sparse and fair. Her hair flowed sideways in a flaxen wash along the pillow that propped up her head. She kept her face averted from him. He could feel his temples swell and his throat thicken.

"What is your name?" Vali said.

She did not answer.

His heart thumped and he could feel his face flush as he spoke: "*Khanoum*?"

She kept her face averted. "It is not important, sir."

Vali stroked her hair softly, combing it with his fingers. "Turn to me, *Khanoum*." He could feel himself enlarging in his trousers.

When it became evident that she would not face him, he lifted her necklace in his fingers and played with it. The quality stunned Vali. The necklace was a series of egg-shaped stones of the finest Khorasan turquoise, each inlaid with strands of gold, and connected by gold bands, set with alternating sapphires and emeralds. The bracelets matched.

"*Khanoum*," Vali said, caressing the necklace, "you could earn enough by selling these not to be here."

After a long pause, and still averting her face, she answered reluctantly: "He told me I would earn more with them."

Vali understood she referred to the dark man with the soiled turban wrapped about his face. He wondered how a man so low could snare a young woman so precious. Although she kept her face averted, Vali could see her features were angular, intelligent, so unlike the square-faced, soiled peasant girls with heavy eyes and gourd-like noses. Vali now touched her skin with his index finger. Its warmth surprised him. Starting at the center of her neck, he smoothed his finger slowly along the hardness of her breastbone, then along the softness of her abdomen letting it catch lightly on her navel. Her abdomen twitched slightly. Then he drew his finger down. She opened to accommodate him, but he stopped. He did not want to discover she was not ready.

Then he burst within his trousers, surprising himself. He looked to see if she had noticed, but she kept her face averted. This had never happened to him before.

"Who?" he said. "Who told you that?"

She did not answer.

Vali, subsiding, his temples still throbbing, knelt on both knees, as if praying. He lifted her hand and kissed it, and then kissed the bracelet. "*Khanoum*, I will pay for these."

"Please no, my lord."

"I will pay for these every evening and give them back to you every morning and pay for them again every evening – but there must be no one but me."

She did not answer, and in that silence Vali wondered if she was waiting to see his money, wondered if she had any idea who he was. He realized he had been talking to a woman who possessed more purpose and presence than the peasant woman who were the usual fare. And he realized he was smelling a fragrance other than rosewater and incense. It would not be until he had fled to Paris that he would learn it was an expensive brand of French perfume, Cotté. He departed in a flush, still not knowing her name.

❧

Vali's father, red faced and sputtering, thundered into his room and awoke him at lunchtime, beating the drapery with his walking stick.

"You can't even handle a customs agent from Rasht?"

Vali rubbed his eyes, half asleep. "Oh, War Minister, did you need me for that?" He squinted in the painful sunlight leaking past the velvet, embroidered drapes. He spoke dreamily.

"I don't' need you for that. You need you for that."

"Oh, *Pedar...*"

"'War Minister.' Can you remember?"

Vali made a sleepy groan and pulled the linen covered pillows over his eyes.

"Do you have any idea what end you are casting for yourself?"

"Oh *Pedar...*"

"Don't call me *Pedar!*"

"You sleep with whores, War Minister."

Two days later Vali found himself tied to his horse, his wrists secured to his saddle with leather straps, his eyes again aching from the glare of the morning sun, sleepily enroute to the Tehran Military Cadet College accompanied by mounted guards.

"Please, War Minister, I will die there."

"I suppose there could be worse fates," his father answered. He rode fitfully beside his son. At a respectful distance behind them rode two household guards, in black tunics with brown leather belts as wide as outstretched hands, rifles strapped to their backs. Two identical guards rode in advance.

"But, War Minister, I have met the most beautiful woman in the world. I want to marry her. I will do as you say then, War Minister. I promise. She has blond hair like silk, and eyes as blue as turquoise. Then…"

"Eh?" his father interrupted, "I don't think so. Who is the family? What is her name?"

This stymied Vali. He hung his head in silence as they rode along, listening to the clumping of the horses' hooves against the frozen mud, and smelling the sharp smells of frozen grass. As they approached the wrought iron gates at the entrance to the Tehran Military Cadet College, War Minister lectured him on his obligations and reminded him he was intended to take as a first wife Moulook, the daughter of Amir e'Doleh.

"The daughter of Amir e'Doleh is ugly, War Minister. Nargess has said so herself. She should know." Nargess and Vali's great aunt and two of his female cousins had visited Amir e'Doleh's compound to see Moulook for themselves, on behalf of the rest of their family.

His father shrugged: "So, what is an ugly wife? You were born to be a leader of men."

Vali could think of no counter argument. An ugly wife was only a problem the night of the consummation celebration, when you had to deflower her and present a bloody handkerchief to the two families waiting outside the bridal chamber. His father leaned close into him and undid the straps from his wrists, ostensibly to spare both of them the humiliation of his arriving before the plumed commandant a prisoner. Vali tried one last time, pleading with his eyes, searching unsuccessfully to find pity in the implacable face of his father: "Please, War Minister, I'm in love."

His father raised one eyebrow and then let it fall. "Love? – With a woman whose name you do not even know?" He blew air through his lips, making his moustache flap. He turned his horse away. With his back to Vali he flipped the reins against the horse's shoulders to make it move.

Vali watched his father clomp fitfully away into the yellow haze of morning. Then, in the distance, he saw his father turn his horse and clomp back to the iron gates. There his father glared at him silently, moving his eyes angrily from head to toe. Then he turned his horse again, preparing for a second departure. He waited.

No longer looking at his son, but staring off into the yellow light, War Minister spoke dispassionately, "Her eyes are green, my son, not blue."

Vali stared at his father's broad, solid back, as his father flipped the reins and his horse snorted through flapping nostrils and began again to clop away, twitching its braided tail.

"War Minister?"

"She calls herself Rakshandeh."

Vali's sojourn at the iron-gated Tehran Military Cadet College lasted only slightly longer than it took War Minister to realize the college had raised his son's political acumen to the level of knowing who and how much to pay, first for the right to quarter off base, and then for a surrogate to dispense with whatever exams, papers and training had no requirement of immediate, identifiable physical presence. When his father again complained to Vali of his inattention to the nuances of politics, Vali replied hazily, "You mean, there's more?"

War Minister spared his and the plumed commandant's mutual embarrassment by reassigning Vali to the family compound, an assignment which Vali honored mostly in absentia. Hunting was not a sport he took to naturally, given the traumas of his childhood target practice, but he seized upon it as a good excuse for long absences. His military training in marksmanship, however desultory, had made him a favorite guest at hunts – and he loved the natural beauty of the countryside. He certainly enjoyed hunting more than suffering his father's admonishments to prepare for marriage to a proper wife and provide him a proper heir with proper British connections and learn how to deal with frumpy customs agents from Rasht.

Mostly Vali hunted with the men of his own family. But, often, and by his father's arrangement, he joined the sons of Amir e'Doleh, father of his intended. Nahdeer e'Sepahsalar and Amir e'Doleh, each with an eye to the other's international advantages, had boastfully planned the projected union during Vali's internment at the Tehran Military Cadet College. But, rumors not of Vali's dalliance with a whore, but of his besottedness with a Christian, threatened the marriage plans.

"You expect a daughter of Amir e'Doleh to be second wife behind a Christian unwashed ass?" War Minister said. "Don't be foolish, boy! Take the Christian as a temporary wife after she converts, after you marry Moulook. If you don't stand up for yourself, these women will start running your life."

"I will marry only Rakshandeh, War Minister. You cannot stop me. I am old enough now."

"Old enough to raise yourself for worn loins?"

Vali shook at this. Turning bitterly red faced himself he answered, "She has had only me, *Pedar*. Only me. This I know."

War Minister then blew air through his lips, making his moustache flap.

"I shouldn't have to remind you: Amir e'Doleh has sent quite a number to their graves – and for quite a lot less."

℘

Amir e'Doleh was dangerous. He had eliminated his own brother by tethering his wrists behind his back and sitting on his face with a pillow, thereby clarifying his attitude toward sharing power within the family. But, Amir e'Doleh would not dare harm the son of War Minister. War Minister's remonstrances to the contrary were just bluffs – or so Vali hoped.

At every opportunity Vali would flee the threats of impending marriage to seek the pleasures of Rakshandeh. He would leave hunting trips precipitously, feigning illness or fatigue, or would depart for hunting trips early, all as ruses to seek solace with Rakshandeh. He had rented quarters for her in a narrow alley in southern Tehran, and when he arrived he would toss a small satchel of gold coins to the dark figure with the soiled turban wrapped around his face, whom he now considered guard rather than procurer, but who kept his identity, visage and even voice secret. He would rush to Rakshandeh's bedside, always to find her waiting for him as he had first met her, unctuously naked, supine, knees together, nestled in embroidered velvet pillows. He would kneel and offer her gold coins, jewelry, fine silver, anything he could filch from his father. He dully wondered how she could be always ready for him, lying naked all day long for his unscheduled arrivals. But, that was her concern, not his.

"You must wait for me, my pretty."

"Yes," she would promise. "Always."

She would let him run his finger along her as he had the first time. Sometimes he would fondle her breasts. But, as soon as he disrobed he would explode, before he could even kneel between her knees. He would burn in shame as he spilled upon her, or upon himself.

"I am not like this," he would say.

She would not answer.

Then he would finger the turquoise eggs of her necklace and beg her to forgive him. "Please," he would say, in tears now. "Tell me these are mine. Mine alone."

℘

War Minister was adamant. Worse, he was persistent. He and Amir e'Doleh together dispatched messengers on horseback to the four corners of the land with invitations for the wedding. They did not seek Vali's counsel in this endeavor. It would be a late spring wedding. To the reception in his palace War Minister invited a thousand guests. He ordered fresh whitefish from his estates along the Caspian, and gaz from Isfahan. When he heard Amir e'Doleh describe the gifts he would be giving to his daughter, War Minister wired hurriedly to London for gold watches and to Paris for porcelain vases. Though he knew they would never arrive in time, he also knew the telegraph agent would inform Amir e'Doleh – and it was the thought that counted. A month before the wedding he sent to Amir e'Doleh's compound a train of two dozen porters bearing gifts for the bride. A troubadour led the parade through the streets of Tehran, toting a charcoal brazier with pungent esfand seeds to purify the air before them. Immediately there followed eight armed guards on horses festooned with peacock feathers and ostrich plumes, and a horse drawn cart displaying an iron-strapped, strong box secured with a large wax seal. The strongbox protected a mirror tray wrapped in chiffon and bearing jewels. When the gifts arrived the guards would present the tray to Amir e'Doleh's servants and they in turn would carry it off to Moulook for her to select the ones she wanted and return the rest. The strong box also held a trousseau of diamonds and emeralds, the latter symbolizing good luck. The caravan of porters carried wide round trays of silver, hammered and cut into geometric and floral design. These held the parade of presents and were in turn perched atop wooden pallets the porters balanced above their heads. Leading the presents was a chest sized, maroon leather *Qaran* imported from Karbala (where the prophet's grandson Hossein was martyred). Next followed a silk wedding dress embroidered with Japanese pearls, dresses of satin, velvet, chiffon, silk, wool, linen and tulle (and bolts of the same), perfume and incense, imported Yardley cosmetics and a tray carrying just two cones of sugar, to symbolize sweetness. At the end came the crystal candelabras and the gold-framed mirror that would be placed before the bride and groom during the wedding ceremony (to honor a Zoroastrian tradition celebrating light and reflection). A dozen musicians playing sitars, tambourines, flutes and drums pranced before the porters, shepherding the procession along the stone walled streets shaded by bursting green oaks and elms.

The wedding festivities would last a week. On each of the first three days, the women would bathe together at Amir e'Doleh's compound. On the first day, special attendants would remove their facial hairs using twisted threads. On the second day, the women painted their fingernails and toenails and dyed their hair with henna before an evening party for both families. On the third day, the day before the wedding, the women would take massages together wearing white bath towels. Afterwards, the men of the bride's family would bath together wearing red towels.

The wedding ceremony itself would be a private affair, on the fourth day, drawing perhaps fewer than a hundred close family and friends to Amir e'Doleh's palace. The men and women would assemble in two adjoining rooms, separated by a high curtain. On the women's side would be a silk carpet for Moulook, and velvet pillows embroidered with gold and pearls for her to sit upon. Before her would be two crystal candelabras placed beside a facing gilt mirror. Immediately behind her would assemble a half dozen or so women who were considered to have led lives of good fortune. Several of these would hold a large swath of silk above Moulook's head. Others would grind together, above the silk, the two cones of sugar to sweeten the marriage while the remainder sewed stitches in the silk, to symbolically sew shut the mother in law's wagging tongue. Further behind would collect a semicircle of elderly matrons. On the other side of the curtain, with the groom and the men of the two families, the mullah would begin to say the vows. At the end the mullah must ask the bride two times if she wants to marry the groom and she must hang her head in blushing silence. Each time one or two of the other women then must call across the curtain to the mullah, "Please repeat that because this bride is very shy." Then the mullah must ask a third time and the bride responds, "Baleh!" Upon which the women raise ululations and sprinkle upon the bride gold coins and almond candies covered with white sugar and rose water. Then the women hush and cover their faces as the groom is invited to cross through the curtain to the women's side. Only the bride, who is veiled in gauzy silk, and the bride's mother may allow their faces to be seen. The groom then sits beside the bride and places a special wrapped present in her lap, lifts her veil and kisses her. Immediately the women resume their ululations and sprinkle more coins and candies on the bride and groom, who remain seated as the women come forth to give the bride presents. Some leave jewelry wrapped in velvet bags, some adorn the bride with jewels, if they can find space. The groom then returns to the other side of the curtain and the men and women celebrate separately.

On the afternoon of the fifth day, Amir e'Doleh would send Moulook in a big procession to War Minister's compound. There would be two dozen porters carrying the gifts War Minister had previously sent in the earlier procession, and a hundred more porters laden with new gifts from Amir e'Doleh to start his daughter's household. That evening would be the great reception for a thousand guests at War Minister's and then the consummation night. Traditionally newly weds would wait for variable periods of time (sometimes years, more recently, hours) after a wedding ceremony before consummating the marriage, which was supposed to take place when the groom was well enough established for the wife to move into his family's compound. Vali's resources were, of course, unquestioned. At the great reception, while the guests continued to party, the bride and groom would retire to consummate the marriage and shortly thereafter produce a bloodied handkerchief for inspection by elderly representatives of both families. This was to prove to the groom's family the bride was a virgin and to the bride's family the man was a whole man (though if not, he could do the job with a finger). Then the guests would continue feasting through the next morning.

Vali worried as he listened to the plans. He wondered if he should put a stop to it before it went too far. But, then it had gone too far already. In his deepest heart he hoped that none of this would come to pass. All he really wanted was Rakshandeh. But, without his father's money he could not have Rakshandeh and with Rakshandeh he could not have his father's money.

"Vali, dear, you can not put it off for ever," Nargess advised him. They were taking tea together in the orchard. The servants had provided them with a crystal bowl of salted pistachios before withdrawing.

"Oh cousin, I do not care."

"But, you do care, Vali. I can see it. And you don't want to do it, do you? What is in you, cousin, dear? You are so lucky to be marrying."

"War Minister gets what War Minister wants," Vali said. He spoke wistfully, thinking of the day when he would be master and would answer to no one. He sighed. "Oh, if only there weren't so many troubles!"

"You must pray, Vali. 'We are each like a feather in the desert, blown by the wind's whim.'" It was a quote from the Prophet Mohammed, favored by the Sufi poet, Rumi.

Vali pondered it was rather better to be blown towards effortless wealth, pleasure and power, and he really didn't care to be blown elsewhere, thank you. And Nargess might sing a different tune were her wind to land her in the arms of a frumpy customs agent from Rasht.

"Except that War Minister sends this wind," Vali said, "not God."

Nargess shrugged, a little too smugly, Vali thought – and a little too naively. "Wind is wind, my cousin," she said. "And it can blow in many different directions quite quickly."

After a minute or two of resigned silence, as if to dismiss the topic and change to another, Nargess continued her lecture, paraphrasing Rumi:

> The Shah fell in love with a maid in the market.
> The bird of his soul fluttered, so he brought her to him.
> But illness beset her, not joy.
>
> He brought her doctors. He brought her potions.
> But the angabine only made more bile,
> And the almond oil made her dry.
> As if you put water on embers and made fire,
> So did her medicines heal.
>
> The Shah saw no hope; he went to the mosque and prayed.
> He wept to God, and crying fell asleep,
> When a wise man brought gospel:

Someone will come your way from us, who will find the problem.

The doctor talked with her in confidence.
He felt her pulse and talked:
Where are you from?
Tell me about your town?
Who are close to you?
…

When she talked of Samarghand, her pulse quickened, her color
reddened.
Samarghand, the home of her lover, so the doctor knew…

The Shah brought her lover to the castle;
Showered him with jewels and dignity;
Gave his love joy,
So the Shah had her lover poisoned,
And dragged away in secrecy,
And lost her love again to despair.
…

Love of gold is dross, love of beauty sin…

Listening, Vali knew that Nargess had heard about his dalliance with Rakshandeh. But, who had told her? Perhaps one of his male cousins told his wife who passed it on to the rest of the andaroon? It was too delicate a matter for a devout young woman like Nargess to discuss openly with him. So she had given him a signal instead. But, for all her protestations of a Sufi-like acceptance of celebrating life as feathers and leaves blowing where they may, Vali couldn't help but feel that her philosophy was no more weighty than the diaphanous air beneath the feather – and with no real responsibilities other than bearing children, knitting and sewing, she would never have to test her faith; would never even want to. God help her if it ever came to that!

❦

"Wait for me, my pretty," Vali begged again that night, laying an emerald-studded silver urn beside Rakshandeh's alabaster figure draped on the velvet pillows. "Wait for me and we shall have everything together. Moulook will be just a convenience – an inconvenience. We will have each other all the time – all the time that matters. She will be furniture. You will be my true wife." Rakshandeh turned from him. Vali worried he had angered her. "I must be careful," he continued. "War Minister will have me watched."

"Who is she to be so special? I could just sit and embroider all day; tell my servants what to do…"

"You will always be my pretty…"

Rakshandeh turned back to him. She reached out and began to fondle him. "I don't want to be just 'your pretty.'"

Vali could barely feel her hand upon him. He wanted to enter her, but he was too nervous to sustain an erection. He lay beside her and pulled her to him. He spoke in a half whisper. "Wait for me. I promise. We will go to Europe together – Paris, London, Venice. We will spend our lives in cafes."

"I want it all."

"This is nothing," he said. "We will love each other there, morning, noon and night. We will be free."

Rakshandeh lay on her back with her eyes fixed on the ceiling, digesting his words. She began to cry. "No," she said.

He leaned over her and kissed her warmly on the mouth, massaging his hand between her legs, thrusting his tongue between her nibbling lips for what seemed like hours. Periodically he kissed her tears away. When he stopped she would cry again and Vali realized he loved her for her weakness as well as for her brown nipples and paper white skin and flaxen hair and shocking green irises.

"No," she repeated between sobs. She curled into herself. "I'll end up with nothing. You offer me nothing."

"What are you saying?"

Rakshandeh remained silent for a while. She pushed herself away from Vali and turned from him. "It's good for you," she said. "But, what about me? If she is furniture, what will I be?"

Vali reached a hand to her shoulder. "You will be everything to me."

She brushed his hand away. "No."

"Rakshandeh…"

"No. I will be nothing to you. I will be a second piece of furniture, a used carpet…"

"I will marry you. I will arrange it."

Silence settled between them. They heard horses hooves clatter past the door to the small courtyard. They heard a gentle trickle in the water canal as the water keeper diverted water to the street for the evening. Rakshandeh broke the silence: "Then you must come to me on your wedding night – if I am everything to you."

Vali choked. His temples throbbed in the darkness. He and Moulook would be surrounded by family and friends waiting for the bloody handkerchief. "Rakshandeh, how can I? Before a thousand pairs of eyes? This is the daughter of Amir e'Doleh."

"I'm to be your wife? Then it is to me you come on your wedding night."

"Rakshandeh, don't be cross."

"Then don't come – not ever."

"Rakshandeh…"

"Go! Go, and don't come back."

ℭ

Vali wandered across the days toward the wedding in a daze. Approaching it was like riding towards mountains across a desert plain: they were always far away in the vast distance and never closer until one moment you were stumbling upon them. To escort him across this desert, War Minister provided an armed guard, morning, noon and night. He was not only the son of War Minister, but soon also to be the son in law of Amir e'Doleh. He was a very important man, his father explained – a tempting target. But, Vali knew they were to keep him from Rakshandeh. His father had now forbidden him to see her. When he went to the mountains in Mazandaran to hunt, and slept out under the stars, the six guards would sleep in a circle, head to toe, around him. At home, nights, two of them stood guard outside each of his bedroom doors, and another two outside his windows. There seemed no hope of escape. As he got to know them better, he was able to bribe them a couple of times to let him out into the night, but when he arrived at Rakshandeh's residence, her maid would not let him in, with the excuse that her mistress was ill. He did not press the point that he was still paying the rent. Days before the wedding, as the festivities were beginning to encroach on his preferred entertainments, he secreted her a small golden peacock decorated with diamonds, emeralds and rubies. But, Rakshandeh had the maid return it to him, unopened, at the door to the courtyard.

By the second day of the festivities, two days before the wedding ceremony, Vali felt lost. The men from the two families and many of their friends had assembled at Amir e'Doleh's to recite poetry. Vali felt uncomfortable in sharing the company of Moulook's brothers, even though he had hunted with them many times. Their moustaches, though fashionable, seemed like daggers, ready for drawing at the slightest provocation. He knew they were watching him. Vali realized he had crossed the desert and was about to face the mountains. He was restless – restless for Rakshandeh. But, he was trapped, chattering with the men of the two families, suffering them blaring at him meaningless lines of poetry.

He saw no escape other than the Chinese opium pipe. No one would begrudge him this. Grooms were allowed to be nervous. Grooms were allowed to be high. Opium was as plentiful as tobacco. But, he dare not take too much before the disapproving eyes of Amir e'Doleh and his sons, lest they judge him an addict. So before their eyes he only had a few puffs, enough to justify the odor of opium about himself. From time to time he would withdraw to the toilet and inhaled more worrisome quantities.

He imagined Moulook, whatever she looked like, with the gourd nose, gossiping and laughing with her cousins and sisters at the baths, painting her toes with henna, all aflutter like chirping sparrows at her approaching de-flowering. She would have no idea what a man looked like naked. She would blush at the contemplation of it. Vali lusted for the cool rush of Rakshandeh – naked Rakshandeh in a sparsely furnished room.

Vali's temples throbbed as, over the course of two days, he listened to endless Hafez – and more endless Hafez. Then on the day before the wedding ceremony, the men attended the baths together.

Vali panicked. He was surrounded in a closed room. Moulook's brothers flanked him in a wide arch at the end of the pool, three to a side, their voices reverberating from the turquoise tiles. Opposite him sat his fearsome father in law, beside his equally fearsome father – the two most powerful men in Persia, after the Shah. Each tried to best the other with *taarof*, begging the attendants to pour water over the other first, praising each other's children, bowing to each other's stature, recounting each other's victories. Each subtly tried to convey an attitude of confident dominance that breathed unspoken ruthlessness. It seemed an entire nation blocked Vali's escape. Even though the men wore sarongs around their waists, Vali felt naked. Soon he would be naked with Moulook. Everyone would know if he spilled before entering her. But, this had happened only with Rakshandeh. He could always do the job with a finger. But, would Moulook complain. Probably not: she would feel it was her fault. But, if she did complain, he would have to blame her. Her brothers would draw their daggers. But, they were only moustaches. They would pound him with their fists. War Minister would beat him with a belt. It would all become public. He longed for the cool rush of Rakshandeh's loins, the brushy stroke of her hair. He knew the next time he would enter her. He must go to her. This was madness.

He began to sweat. This was normal for the baths, after all. But, his sweat was fear. The others would notice. He might faint. No, no one would notice.

"War Minister, I feel ill," Vali said.

Amir e'Doleh stiffened. He glared at Vali with a tiger-like frown. His moustache twitched downward at either end. The Lion of Mazandaran was meowing. He turned to War Minister for an explanation. Moulook's brothers halted their idle chatter and waited.

It was Amir e'Doleh who acted to resolve the crisis. As Vali arrived before him to pay his respects before departure, Amir e'Doleh placed a hand affectionately on his shoulder.

"Ahhh!" he said, adopting a smile. "You are truly your father's son: the most generous man in all of Tehran – You have hosted us to exhaustion." He slapped Vali warmly on the shoulder. Then he winked. "We will party for real tomorrow! Eh, my new son?"

"*Baleh*!" Vali answered, lamely, glad to have been spared.

The two embraced and kissed on both cheeks. Vali sensed a stiffness in Amir e'Doleh's embrace, but ignored it. As he departed, War Minister snapped his fingers at the guards and they escorted Vali home.

❦

After the baths, War Minister stalked into Vali's bedroom, red faced and sputtering. He beat at the velvet curtains with his walking stick, this time with extra ferocity. Then he strutted back and forth, beating Vali's futon and the embroidered sitting cushions lined against the wall.

"You fool!" he shouted. "How you could be my issue, God will never tell. Amir e'Doleh! Amir e'Doleh's daughter!"

Vali lay prostrate upon his futon, staring up at the carved plaster on the ceiling. "They can take me as I am, *Ped…* War Minister."

"You humiliated me," War Minister shouted. "Before my enemy!"

Vali pondered a moment before answering: "I thought this was all to make him your friend."

War Minister swung his stick against the futon. The thwack made Vali flinch. "He'll be an enemy, again – fast enough."

Vali said nothing.

"And don't think you're running off to your beloved whore. I'll see to that."

"I love her. I'll marry her, I will."

"Oh?" War Minister blew air through his lips to mimic the sound of spitting. His moustache flapped. "Where did you acquire the blood to become a Rashtee!" he said again, as if spitting. He turned his back and departed.

Vali trembled and sweated. With shaking fingers he removed a piece of engraved writing paper and penned a message on it:

"She has had no one but me, *Pedar*."

He sealed the note in an envelope and wrote his father's name on it and entrusted it to one of the guards. Within half an hour he received his father's penned response, also sealed:

"How much do you think it will cost me to pay her off? You can measure her by that."

Vali penned back: "Not everyone is in your employ."

He shortly received his father's penned response: "You are."

Vali penned back: "Then how much are you paying me to show tomorrow? Enough to keep Amir e'Doleh happy? Two thousand *toumans*? Ten? A hundred?"

War Minister penned back: "I'll tell the family you're recovering for to-morrow – or else!"

☾

Vali slipped his guards a package of his best Kabul opium late that night, together with a bottle of Russian vodka, one of the few left in Tehran. When his gifts had taken effect, he offered the guards double what War Minister paid them and slipped off into the night. He had decided to give Rakshandeh the diamond and emerald ring that he had planned to present to Moulook at the ceremony. He would find a substitute somewhere the next day. No one would notice. He stumbled through the walled streets to see Rakshandeh.

Vali broke from his reverie when he arrived at Rakshandeh's house. The carriage for the whores was there, with the dark man wearing the soiled turban. He usually was there when the maid was absent, guarding his treasure. Vali flipped him a gold coin and let himself in through the unlocked courtyard door without knocking, knowing the maid would be absent.

When he entered Rakshandeh's receiving room, he was stopped by noises that immediately horrified and sickened him, noises that seized him with knife-like belly pains. From Rakshandeh's bedroom came the unmistakable sounds of lovemaking at climax: hoarse masculine grunts and thrusts, and Rakshandeh's moaning cries of ecstasy, which Vali recognized immediately for having never elicited them himself.

His head began to swim. He tried to tell himself he was in the wrong house. His bowels loosened. Dropping the diamond and emerald ring, he clutched his stomach and fell to his knees, panting. His brow felt cold and sweaty. He could smell the acrid juices pressing upwards from his stomach. While he remained there, powerless to move, he heard the silence that follows climax, imagined the heavy breathing and the twinned twilight drifting into sleep. But, still he could not move. He could not crawl. He could not stand. He began to retch. Immediately as the dry heaves started, he perceived a commotion in Rakshandeh's bedroom, the silent sounds of bare feet on carpets and pillows. He was still dry heaving when he looked up and saw War Minister emerge from Rakshandeh's door and stand there before him, stark naked. His father's body was speckled with liver spots and covered with thick, curly gray hairs. He approached. This body disgusted Vali. He had never seen another man naked before. And he knew his father was displaying himself to humiliate him yet further. War Minister was holding one of Rakshandeh's embroidered handkerchiefs by his side, not even bothering to cover his groin or his sagging paunch with it. Vali began to vomit uncontrollably now, bringing up sulfurous chunks of the dried peaches from lunch, and burning his nostrils and throat with acrid yellow juices. His father said nothing, but stood beside the vomiting Vali, threatening him with his dangling genitals.

"Oh War Minister," Vali eventually panted between heaves. "War Minister, you pig! You foul pig!"

War Minister dropped the handkerchief he had carried from Rakshandeh's bedroom beside the vomiting Vali. "She sends her love."

As his father returned to the bedroom to dress, Vali summoned the courage to inspect the handkerchief his father had offered. Realizing what was before him he curled up and fell to his side, grasping his knees within his elbows, sobbing uncontrollably, shaking his head, almost in a seizure. On the handkerchief were the red stains of Rakshandeh's blood.

On his way out, fully dressed, cinching his belt, War Minister stood briefly beside his sobbing son. He looked down at him pitilessly. "I pay guards a whole lot more than you – whores, too."

For what seemed an eternity after his father's departure Vali clutched his knees and shook. Dry heaves consumed him. When he had gained enough control to move, he called for Rakshandeh, but she did not answer. He pulled himself along the stone floor and lay his head down before her door. He could smell the dust on the floor and the odors of Rakshandeh's perfume wafting through the crack above the jam.

"Rakshandeh!" he bellowed. "Rakshandeh!" But, he heard no movement within, no response. "Rakshandeh, we can go to Paris. I will take you. We will go forever – Rakshandeh." Still hearing no response, he began to weep. "The two of us, Rakshandeh." He drew his knees up to his chest and clutched them with his arms and continued weeping for close to a quarter of an hour. Then he began to sweat again and breathe more heavily. "Oh, you pig, Rakshandeh! You shitty ass Christian pig! We buy and sell peasant trash like you."

Afterwards, all Vali would remember next was being dragged out the door by the dark man with the soiled turban, hoisted into the whore's wagon and driven home in the silent dark.

❦

The next day, the day of the wedding ceremony, broke warm and sultry. A platoon of gardeners finished gussying up War Minister's gardens, where flagstone paths coursed beneath flowering mimosas. There were grape vines and shaded pools of water lilies, bursting roses of red and pink and white, fragrant lilies, sweet jasmine, tuberoses, pink lotuses, nasturtiums and hollyhocks. The air was laden with honeysuckle. At the back of the gardens the servants had begun to accumulate bundles of wood to make bonfires for cooking large vats of food for the great reception scheduled for the following day.

The men of Vali's family, who were going to accompany him to the ceremony, began to collect. Some were dressed in impeccable European suits. Others wore knee length jackets and shirts buttoned at the collar with no tie. They milled about their coffee and tea and water pipes and cigars, waiting for him. But, Vali was nowhere to be seen.

At first his absence was scarcely noticed. He had been celebrating. He was late to arise from slumber and perform ablutions. It was a relaxed affair, with no fixed schedule – at least for a while. But, Amir e'Doleh would be waiting and soon would become irritated, and begin tapping the table with his fingers. He would become visibly tense as the sun continued its rise with no sign of the groom. Eventually he would send a messenger to War Minister's.

No one wanted all this to happen. But, no one wanted to tell War Minister. As the hour drew near with no sign of Vali, they began to admit to one another there might be a problem and they debated whether to alert War Minister. The women of the family, traveling separately, left in a flotilla of cars and carriages for Amir e'Doleh's, but still no Vali. Finally War Minister himself appeared and asked if they were ready.

☙

When they found Vali, he was still in his room, still guarded by the squad of burly men with wide belts, black tunics and major hangovers. Upon entering, War Minister found his son beneath the bedclothes. He was still dressed in his clothes of the night before. His lay on his side, clutching his knees with his arms. He shook uncontrollably and bubbled spittle out of the corners of his mouth.

Vali heard only a confused onslaught of words, empty words, a sea of anonymous voices swelling beyond his window. Then noises at the door and light breaking through the curtains. His temples hurt as his father made words with his mouth, but he could not understand them. Then his father was beating him with the belt from one of the guards and he was crying pain clutching his knees and the far off noises of people talking like bees, like a waterfall, abruptly ceased. It was an embarrassed sound, now, an awkward sound: hushed voices – then silence.

Vali was sure he heard shrieks from Moulook and tears and women's sharp voices and tap, tap, tap running of women's feet, but that could not be. The women were at Amir e'Doleh's, waiting. And Amir e'Doleh had a lion's frown and his sons would have their dagger moustaches drawn in anger, and red throbbing faces. And then silent men smoking guiltily, because they were there and had nothing else to do. And then day and night merged and succeeded one another, with sliver trays of tea and bread and feta cheese and drawn curtains. A succession of doctors came and went and whispered opinions behind half open doors and gradually Vali perceived he was to be flown to Paris for treatment, which meant he was to be removed for safety – and to spare War Minister's embarrassment.

☙

It took War Minister several weeks to decide what to do and several months to make the arrangements. By late in the fall he had arranged transport to Europe for his son. The morning of Vali's departure, a knee-high mist lifted from the dun colored, frost tinged grass of the airstrip. The carriages and horses waited on a thin skin of frozen mud for the airplane to arrive. They had been waiting since dawn, together with a small detachment of guards War Minister had summoned from the army and another small detachment from the Tehran Military Cadet College, dispatched with the commandant's respects. A small contingent from Amir e'Doleh's family attended as well, invited by War Minister to witness the sorry, neurasthenic condition of his son and, he hoped, pity him and his family rather than demonize them.

Airplanes were still a novelty in 1922, so the women were excited to accompany the men to bid Vali farewell. As if to avoid the real issue, the men gossiped endlessly about the army's recently purchased modern marvel, a steel-framed, 5 passenger, water-cooled, Fokker F IV single winged transport aircraft. War Minister boasted it was capable of a full 67 knots. The technical description meant nothing to the women. They only knew to expect a loud and imposing air machine whose engine was so tall that the pilot had to sit to one side of it, in an exterior seat, separate from the passenger compartment.

It was a confusing scene.

There were squads of women from two families of War Minister. The women wore black *chadors*, and no one seemed to notice the strange woman who appeared out of nowhere at the back of the crowd, just as the first sighting of the airplane drew everyone's attention. The airplane seemed like a gray vulture hanging upon a distant riser. The women of each family thought the strange woman must be a late arrival from one of the other's, if they thought of her at all. In the excitement of seeing an airplane, no one took notice that this woman had arrived unaccompanied. And amidst the great noise and rattling buzz of the airplane, which kept its mammoth, man-tall engine running after it had taxied up from the far end of the airstrip (where it had finished its landing with a quick turn and a single wave from the goggled pilot beside the engine) no one noticed the mysterious woman at the back of the crowd slip out of her chador. She wore a man's military uniform and readily blended in to the scene. She instantly donned a cadet's hat to hide the bun of her hair and marched slowly, deliberately, purposefully down to the opposite end of the airstrip, rifle slung sharply over the right shoulder, the morning sun reflecting from the polished, black visor. The cadets from the college, standing at attention, thought the soldier had been detached from the army squad. The army thought the soldier might be an oddly dressed cadet, some sort of rank they did not recognize. But, the magnificent airplane dominated their thoughts and stole their attention. War Minister briefly noticed the lone marching figure, but only vaguely. He was paying attention to Vali, who was seated in the stretcher chair. They had wrapped him in a white hospital gown, covered him with heavy blankets and strapped him into the stretcher chair with inch wide leather belts. He held his head buried in his chest, as if he slept. Accompanying him were a nurse in a starched white cap – borrowed from the German ambassador – and a monocled physician (also borrowed from the ambassador) with a walking cane, a goatee and a black bag – a grand display of western medical science pressed into emergency service.

"Will he ever be well?" War Minister muttered to Vali's doctor.

The doctor stroked his goatee and answered: "They have the best science in Paris and Vienna. He will come back."

War Minister felt relief. He had had this conversation before, but he needed to hear it again and again. Though he would have preferred Vali's illness to be dissimulation and he was deeply distressed for his son, he believed he had finally broken the back of his son's adolescent dissipation.

War Minister asked for a moment alone with Vali. He whispered into his ear: "You will be better, freed from that whore"

Vali whimpered something incomprehensible.

"My son: Never let yourself be tricked by anyone. Not by fools. Not by whores. Not by whoremongers. Learn from me and be strong."

Several turbaned servants lifted the whimpering Vali from his stretcher chair and strapped him into his passenger seat and loaded his luggage and the white-capped nurse and the monocled physician in beside him. Still no one thought anything of the lone soldier, standing at attention now in the angling yellow light at the far end of the field where the pilot would start his take off run.

It was War Minister who first understood what was about to happen. It came to him in a violent flash. He jumped. He burst into a run down the field behind the taxiing airplane. The pilot swung the airplane around towards the party of waving well-wishers and applied the brakes. He revved up the engine for take off. War Minister saw the plane shudder as he ran towards it. "Stop!" War Minister yelled against the distant noise. But, it was pointless. He saw the soldier lower the rifle. War Minister forced his legs on against the heaving drag of his heavy belly and wildly thumping chest. The pilot released the brakes and the plane inched forward. As War Minister ran on, stumbling and gasping now, he watched the airplane begin its slow rumble towards him, lurching from side to side like a loose saddle on a horse. The pilot, his seat mounted to one side of the engine, could not see the side of his aircraft where the soldier had unlatched the passenger compartment door. The soldier was running beside the airplane as it heaved back and forth in the early stages of acceleration. While War Minister gesticulated impotently, his cries lost in the distant roar of the man-tall engine, the soldier lunged into the open door, feet kicking in the air, miraculously working himself inside.

As the airplane drew closer the pilot waved War Minister away, unaware of the boarding on the other side of his airplane. War Minister veered to the side to let the airplane pass. As the airplane drew abreast, the engine hid him from the pilot's view. As the wingtip passed him, in the dark of the held-open passenger door he saw the shadowed figure crouching against the inside edge of the doorframe. The soldier was peering back at him with a face that was at once shockingly familiar and strangely unrecognizable – with one hand propping open the passenger door against the building rush of air. The soldier removed the military cap and spun it towards War Minister, but the prop wash jerked it backwards. As a flaxen stream of hair burst from the door War Minister confronted the delicate extended finger and the green-eyed stare unmasked: Rakshandeh.

War Minister bent forward with his hands on his knees, panting help-lessly. He watched the plane pass the main crowd, showing him its tail. In an instant the hair and hand were gone and they were airborne, slowly disap-pearing into the desert sun. Then, while he watched, a small object he would only later learn was the soldier's rifle plummeted earthwards from the air-plane.

Lost somewhere between seething anger and curious detachment, War Minister muttered helplessly, to no one, "Son of a bitch!"

Victory of Religion
November 9, 1929

E ven as she fled down the long corridor towards the sound of the muffled gunshot, Nargess felt feverish, as if she were acting behind a pale yellow pane of glass, or on the other side of a mirror and were spying upon herself. She passed through meaningless animated motions without force, without content, without feeling or sound. The wails of the other women were immediate as they flung open the doors and found War Minister slumped at the apex of a cone of blood and brains trailing from the middle of his bed to the ceiling. Her own cry rose with them, distant and unreachable. She was afraid to go near the bed. Afraid to touch the floppy doll that was War Minister. And even then she knew something was wrong but could not say what. Not that War Minister was dead, but that the players before her in the drama were strange and unreal – chimeras in a miasmal dream, an unrealized logic – and flailing somewhere behind it all, the furious masked puppet master.

In shock and disbelief she watched General Z. reinsert his monocle and walk past War Minister's body, over to the cupboard in the adjacent room. He removed the dozen or so leather-bound account books, one by one. His monocle glinted, rocking back and forth slowly as he bent to catch favorable light from the window. Under one arm he kept his swagger stick clamped. With the hand of the other he turned the pages methodically. He perused each ledger stiffly, his eyes moving up and down the lines with suspicion, his sallow jowls oblivious to the shame and grief surrounding him. When he had finished inspecting the account books he handed them to his adjutant, who stacked them smartly under his arm. Then General Z. nodded to Mansour.

"I will need them, my general," Mansour said.

"You will get what you need, Mansour Khan," General Z. said. He tipped his hat and departed.

Nargess scarcely understood the letter, which arrived a week later from the Ministry of Education. It informed her that the newly formed Sub Ministry of the *Vaqfe*, which now controlled large religious donations, had taken title to War Minister's estates and would distribute them to the poor forthwith. The seized estates were listed alphabetically. She would be allowed to keep a tea estate near the Caspian, in Lahijan, for her maintenance, and the Tehran palace, dependent upon full disclosure of the remainder of War Minister's holdings. The letter further informed her that all documents concerning War Minister's oil concession to the Russians were being retained by the Ministry of Justice, in that the concession had been canceled for lack of confirmation by the *Majlis*, and that despite continuing legal challenges in conjunction with foreign powers, the matter was considered closed and there were no documents of any further interest to War Minister's family. Should a decision be made otherwise, the government would contact her at the appropriate time.

Nargess never had time to wonder how General Z. had found the account books so directly, or how the Ministries of Justice and Education knew so readily about the tea estate in Lahijan. The tea estate was one for which War Minister had never kept records, fearing just such a seizure. He owned it through an intermediary. Nargess knew this only because Vali had confided in her after one of War Minister's droning sermons about the precautions he must some day assume. It did not occur to her that it was strange for General Z. to have recognized Mansour as the manager of War Minister's affairs. After all, Mansour was the only male family member present, even if an obviously limited functionary. General Z. would not be expected to address the women about such matters under any circumstances, and in their grief they were clearly beyond approach. She did know enough to feel relief that General Z. had not taken more.

In the months that followed, she cowered deep behind the brittle, tepid window of shock and grief. She dressed entirely in black and secluded herself in darkened chambers. She prayed, morning noon and night – even between scheduled prayers. Her eczema, an affliction which she had kept hidden by artfully draped towels at the baths and which she had confided only to her mother, flared, making her elbows scaled and flaky beyond her worst experience. Three or four times a night she would wake up to massage her elbows. They sometimes left bloody streaks on the bedclothes. She refused to tie her hair into braids and stopped dyeing it with henna washes. The roots grew out gray. She stopped washing. She began to resemble a crazy woman. She developed a sore back and swollen knees from praying. She found solace in this, a source of pride, even: no one could question her piety; no one could doubt her grief. At all hours she silently begged God for forgiveness, for a sign, for guidance on how to make amends. She promised to God an annuity of a hundred *toumans* a month, as a gift to the *Vaqfe*, then two hundred *toumans* a month – if only she could discover her sin. It never occurred to her that such sums were no longer available to her. She searched her heart for a reason that God should have done this to her. She had always been so devoted to prayer and she knew so little of her husband's affairs. Had she not been a good wife?

There was more to her despair than loss. She bore in private the anguish that War Minister had been preparing to replace her. He had needed a male heir and she had not delivered. If one of the peasant girls he had taken in temporary marriage were to have produced a son, then Nargess would be demoted. She had tried so hard to conceive a son: She had strapped eggs around her waist, taken potions, had delivered endless prayers and hoped endless hopes – all to no avail.

War Minister was unpersuaded. When their first child, Tajmah, a daughter, had been born, it had taken him two weeks to acknowledge the birth. Two months after Tajmah's birth, War Minister had sent Nargess a decorous note, having it hand delivered through her eunuch, Gholam Ali. The note instructed her to find him a new permanent wife: "… one of a fair figure, and good breeding, petite feet… and not nearly so tall… one much younger, and succulent … of a sweet disposition… breasts no larger than pomegranates, but not so small as lemons… hips neither slender, like a man's, nor broad, like a cow's… and if a widow, she must have birthed at least one healthy son…" He expected Nargess to dutifully inspect and interview the candidate and had finished the note with one last instruction: "…and this time, one who plays chess."

His parting words to her had been that he had told no one else about her finding a replacement for herself, but she could not know for sure. The same tongues that wagged about War Minister developing a hankering for his widowed daughter in law, Rakshandeh, did not need word from War Minister to read the tea leaves. They needed only look at the facts: Nargess was as barren as the *Dasht e'Lut.*

Her only comfort was the warm reassurance of suffering – the way martyr Imam Hossein had suffered, battling the caliphate – betrayed. Selfish men had defied Mohamed's legacy, had deprived his heirs of their succession. Defeat and betrayal and loss had afflicted Persia for twenty-five hundred years, starting with Alexander the Great and reaching an apotheosis under Genghis Khan. The roses bloomed red for a thousand years with the blood of the Mongols' victims. Sadness was a warm tendril in every Persian heart. Grief succored the Persian soul. It was her turn now.

Loyal Zahra sat with Nargess and held her hand. Shy, serious, bird-like and devout, even at thirteen she had been considered a delightful, unchallenging reward for the dim-but-faithful Mansour. She had been frightened to marry a man so much older and had cried for six weeks upon hearing the news. Although her parents had once quietly harbored ambitions for her higher than wife of a major domo, they were dependent on War Minister and dared not object.

Zahra had the servants bring the infant Tajmah from the nursery to amuse Nargess with her stumbling attempts at walking, as she balanced herself against stools and tables and pillows and reached from one object to another, and as she gradually transitioned from prattle to words. She encouraged Nargess to help her fix ribbons in Tajmah's hair, but Nargess could not summon the strength. She would look at her baby and tears would well in her eyes and she would kneel, wrap her black chador tightly around her shoulders and place her forehead against the prayer stone, first gently, but then force-fully, as if the pain would cleanse her guilt and fend her from the suffering of her child, as if suffering were a greater love than that of a mother for her child. Tajmah's first steps were across the room to her praying mother. She leaned bodily against the bent, black figure and waited. But, Nargess jammed her forehead harder against the prayer stone, ignoring her. Zahra had to lift the infant to give her hugs and kisses as a reward.

At night Zahra would take Nargess's hand and lead her to her bed and sit beside her. Nargess would murmur, "Dear Zahra. How could I live without you?" She would close her eyes and try to sleep. Sometimes, as she drifted off to sleep, she would mumble, "Save me, dear Zahra! What will happen to Tajmah? Where is she?"

"I'm here," Zahra would say. "Always." She would pat Nargess's forearm gently with her bird-like hand.

As Nargess drifted off to sleep, she asked herself how she could thank her beloved Zahra for her loyalty. Then she would feel agonizing pain at the dark memory of what Vali had confided to her long ago: that War Minister had secretly betrayed Mansour's caravans, ruining him and condemning him to servitude. In fitful dreams she would see herself holding a torch to Mansour's hair while he cried, and then she would hear General Z.'s motorcar rattling in the courtyard and his steps echoing on the marble staircase. And she would seek comfort in pain and knowing if she never joined the world it could never hurt her.

Oh Zahra, she would think, how can I ever atone? Truly you are blessed of God. You and Mansour both. Oh, how could I have said nothing for so many years? But, then, what could I have said? And it would have been a far worse sin to betray a husband. Oh, I do trust Vali, but it was then just a rumor. Perhaps War Minister invented the story to torment him. And I was not the one who had sinned. But – Oh Zahra, can you forgive me?

Nargess became ever more deeply secluded in grief and guilt. She scarcely noticed her household's decay.

It was only in the summer, when the cotton fluffers refused their services without prepayment, that Nargess noticed the death-like silence of her household and the signs of inattentiveness in a dwindling staff. The palace had formerly always bustled so. The cotton fluffers were a family who for generations had restuffed the household's futons. A half dozen of them would work the better part of a week. Each had a strong bow, strung with a tight gut string. They would place the cotton from the futons in piles, pinch a tuft at a time and hold it to the bowstring, which they would then pluck in the middle of the tuft. The vibrations would fluff the cotton, one tuft at a time, while the piles of matted cotton slowly transmogrified into puffy mounds. The plucking from the bows rose rhythmically into the air, as if emanating from a strange and wonderful orchestra, a harmony heralding summer. The cotton fluffers had never before demanded prepayment. For as long as Nargess could remember, they would arrive, empty the futons and start plucking. When they had finished, War Minister would order Mansour to pay them generously and from his balcony he would wave to them and deliver the cheerful exhortation: "God bless our mutual wealth and the coming summer!" Few customers were so generous, and so the cotton fluffers gaily provided the latest gossip from among the shopkeepers and small businessmen as they cheerfully discharged their services. But, the summer after War Minister's death, they behaved strangely.

Nargess had noticed their arrival from her apartments. When she failed to hear the music-like strumming, she ventured out of her rooms for the first time, braving War Minister's sitting room balcony in the company of Gholam Ali, to see what had happened to the cotton fluffers. She moved through the halls bent backed and stooped, like a specter. She was surprised to find them sitting cross-legged, motionless and silent before their untouched piles of matted cotton. From the upstairs balcony, the white-turbaned workers, beside piles of matted cotton, looked like a stand of giant, angry mushrooms. They held their arms crossed in defiance.

"Zahra!" she called. "Zahra? She looked around. "Gholam Ali, why are they so cross? Go find out from Zahra. Oh, I can't deal with all this..."

Gholam Ali returned with Mansour, who held his arms crossed before himself, gently grasping his elbows and slumping slightly to one side. He had a sheepish look on his face, and cast his eyes to the side.

"Dear cousin, you should return to bed," he said. "You need rest."

"But, why do they just sit there?" Nargess asked, clasping her own elbows. She wanted to hear the thrumming music evoke the memories of summer.

"They will start soon." He took her gently by the forearm.

Nargess thought silently. She didn't want to intervene. She didn't want to make trouble. She wanted to return to prayers. But, the cotton fluffers were being rude. "No," she said. "They've been an hour already. Where is Zahra?"

"She'll be back soon. Come..."

As Mansour gently led her away Nargess finally understood that War Minister's quarters seemed somehow unfamiliar. "Mansour, where are..." She paused in mid sentence. "He had a pair of gilt bronze swan lamps on his desk – And two gold vases – and there's more. Where are the rest of his things?"

"Zahra asked me to store his valuables. She was afraid General Z. would return to take them – or some of the servants..."

"But, Mansour, the servants would never cross War Min..." she let her voice trail off. "Mansour, where are the guards? War Minister always had guards..."

Mansour shrugged. "No need now, Nargess, dear."

Of course, Nargess thought. But still... All of a sudden she felt extremely tired. "Take me to my rooms," she said. Then, when they were only half way down the corridor: "But, who has War Minister's things? I didn't see his jewelry boxes or his hair brush – and why are the cotton fluffers not working?"

"Dear cousin," Mansour sighed. "They want to be paid first. They emptied the futons and now they're demanding money to continue."

"But... Well, pay them – Can't they wait? They shouldn't have emptied the futons if they weren't going to fluff them. Have they become highway robbers now? Oh, those wretches! Have they forgotten whose house this is? Tell them War Minister will have them flogged..." She caught her self in mid sentence. "Oh, those stone-hearted peasants. They're worse than *bazaari!*" She pondered the situation silently as she opened her door. "Well, pay them, Mansour. But, tell them this is the last time. Tell them we won't be needing their services next year. Can't we find someone else? Oh why does God do this to me?"

Mansour shrugged.

"Well, God shall bring them their reward – in due time. Tell them that – Here, give me the money, I'll tell them..."

"Zahra hasn't gotten back yet," Mansour interrupted.

"Zahra? She has the money? You sent a woman to the bank?"

"No..." Mansour stammered. "No, War Minister's accounts were closed – it's the pawnbroker..."

Nargess felt a stab of fear. She had never given a thought to how to pay for the upkeep of War Minister's compound. Were they pawning her furniture? Had the government seized the accounts Mansour had kept at Bank Melli? The bank had only opened a couple of years before and she didn't think he had put everything there. She really didn't know – except that War Minister had ranted about the dangers of putting money right out where any shah could seize it – as safe as laying meat before a tiger, he had said. But, then the letter from the Ministry of Education had mentioned nothing about War Minister's bank accounts. Oh why was it all so complicated? Why couldn't Mansour explain it to her?

"But, War Minister's things were priceless – you couldn't have needed them to simply pay the cotton fluffers – could you?"

"It's not just the fluffers, cousin, dear," Mansour answered, wringing his hands and opening her door for her.

Of course, Nargess thought. Of course. A whole compound...

"... and it's not just day-to-day things," Mansour continued. "It's Rakshandeh – She's..."

"Rakshandeh?"

"...well..."

"Rakshandeh's what?"

Mansour hunched his shoulders and wrung his hands again. "It's gotten so bad, we can't get credit any more," he said. "Opium. Jewelry and perfume from Paris. Silver. Carpets. Pastries. Parties..."

"Credit? You can't... ? Parties? How is she paying?"

Mansour shrugged. "Tabs in War Minister's name."

"They'll do that? Don't they...?"

"She's gone wild."

"Oh, that's so like her: charging – just like a common laborer – Well, I guess that's what she is – Well, if they require cash in advance from *us*, why are they extending *her* credit?"

Mansour sighed, "I don't understand the *bazaari*. I really don't – it just doesn't make sense." He nodded his head.

Nargess then asked Mansour to explain the accounts, but she had no head for numbers. She asked which antiques they would have to sell each week to pay the bills and he started to explain that it was more complicated than that; that the bills changed with the seasons; and in the spring they had received some rice from Lahijan to sell and they received a constant trickle of funds from the Lahijan tea, but the lamb from Lahijan only came in occasionally; and he didn't know how many repairs would be needed to the palace and which could be put off; and how many people would remain in the household and how many would find jobs elsewhere because not a lot of the Shah's new sycophants had the courage to employ a cousin of War Minister's and, of course, there were antiques and then there were valuables; and that swarthy pawnbroker was being ever more evasive...

Nargess's eyes glazed over. "Well, let's start with the vases: how many porcelain vases do we have and how many do we need to sell?" she asked in exasperation. "I never cared for them much, except for the sapphire ones in the great hall..." She thought with a wistful pang of the times she had raced among them in the hall of crushed mirrors, darting after War Minister's gold coins in the angling light of *Noruz* morning. She recalled how the vases reverberated as she and the other children jostled them, the excitement, the burgeoning of spring, the dark blue forest...

"Well, there are vases – and then there are vases. Some are Chinese, some from Paris, some from the *bazaar* – of course those aren't worth much – I don't know, exactly – and that pawnbroker's always lowering the price. I could go count – I guess – but some are in storage, I'm not sure how many – and there's a leak in the roof above War Minister's apartments so we've closed them off – mostly ..."

It was a dismal list, complicated by developing chaos and decay in the household. Some of the men in the household had left to set up shops in the *bazaar*, a few to take servant positions in the household of the Shah's sycophants. Most just hung around the compound and ate. Mansour found War Minister's old smoking room, beside his bedroom, infested with bats, which had entered through a small break in one of the shutters. So he had the door nailed shut. Then the two nurses who had attended War Minister's senile wife, refused to be servants any longer, and left. Mansour had to replace them with two heavy-browed scullery maids, who were less fastidious about being paid. Catching wind of these events and hearing of Rakshandeh's excesses, the tailors now refused to visit altogether. Even the peasants who sold charcoal from the backs of donkeys would not unload until they had coin in hand. Only the swarthy pawnbroker relished their trade.

Oh, why did God do this to me? Nargess thought. Was it because I kept War Minister's secret from Zahra? What would He have had me do? How can I atone?

"Zahra, what is Rakshandeh doing?" she asked that evening, as Zahra helped her prepare for bed. "Where is everything? The house is empty. Why…"

"Mansour wanted to store everything in the basement," Zahra said. She seated herself on the pillow beside Nargess's futon, her legs extended together to one side, her arms folded. "You needn't worry. We'll take care of it all…"

"Will I have to sell my jewelry? I couldn't bear that. What would I be without it?" Nargess had no head for numbers, but she understood appearances. "I don't' see why I should have to sell my things while that Rakshandeh is throwing money to the river. Can't we do something?"

Zahra answered with resignation: "Do what?"

"I don't know. Can't we have her arrested?"

"Arrested? For what? The *bazaari* don't *have* to give her credit."

"Well, can't we tell them to stop?"

Zahra paused before she answered, "Do you think any of them will listen? They've got the judges on their side now that War Minister's gone. Just pray that General Z. doesn't come back…"

"General Z! Oh, hasn't he had enough?" As soon as Nargess had said this she realized her foolishness. She started to massage her swollen elbows with her hands, wincing at the pain. "Oh, Zahra, look at what I've become: a hideous cripple. Oh how awful. What would I do if anyone ever saw me like this?"

As for the *bazaari*, they were plucking at the carcass of War Minister's estate like vultures and General Z. could return anytime to join them. The merchants feared only that he would interrupt their feast. It had happened to others. The merchants were probably using their influence to keep General Z. at bay for their own benefit. And the Shah wouldn't mind them bringing misfortune to the family of a former rival. It was all so complicated. There was nothing she could do. Nothing to pay for expenses. No one to put Rakshandeh in her place.

"I'm afraid she's got us where she wants us," Zahra said.

"But, why? What does she want? Is she really a Russian spy, Zahra? She must be. That's what they always said. I know. Why else would she do this? Somebody's helping her? But, why, now that War Minister's dead? Wasn't Vali enough? Oh Zahra, how long can we go on like this? What if General Z. comes back?"

Zahra fluffed up Nargess's pillow and pulled back the covers for her. As Nargess closed her eyes, Zahra sat beside her, patting her tousled hair with her bird-like hand.

"Sleep now," Zahra said.

"But, how long, Zahra? What if they take the house? Where could I live? They'd have me fetch tea and sweep for them. I know those types. They take everything from you and call it theirs – even your ancestors."

Zahra sighed and tried to speak very softly, as nonchalantly as possible, as if she were discussing a trivial detail of gardening or sewing: "Mansour says another year or so – maybe more. We will see…"

Nargess sat bolt upright. "Maybe more?" She groaned. She grabbed Zahra's elbow. "Oh Zahra, I can't become an old wrinkled she goat banished to a farm in Lahijan. I would die there. Only a year? Oh please, you must come with me…"

"More than a year," Zahra said. She grasped the arm Nargess used for support and gently pressed Nargess's back down into the futon. "Sleep."

"But, Zahra, I can't do anything. What does Mansour say?"

"Hush."

Nargess closed her eyes and said a prayer of thankfulness for the attentions of Zahra and Mansour. The guilt for what War Minister had done to them weighted heavily upon her. Oh, how could she ever reward them for their blessedness? She would never feel clean without atonement. She would never feel unburdened until she had confessed, and they had gained their reward. She dreamed of General Z.'s boots again. She woke up sweating – and counting how many months remained.

In the morning Gholam Ali wakened Nargess for a breakfast of tea and fresh pita bread with feta cheese and walnuts and fig jam. This simple fare belied the elaborate teacup Nargess held to her lips. It was one of a set of two dozen. They were very rare, crafted of interlaced strands of gold and silver twined into stems with leaves of blue and green and red enamel and flowers of rubies and emeralds. The inserts were deeply carved Czechoslovakian lead crystal. The tea set was as precious to Nargess as her jewelry. She felt guilty for enjoying anything, given her dire circumstances, but this tea set was one of the few amenities remaining, and it reminded her of her mother and her grandmother and she bathed sadly in the luxury, wondering how long it would be before they took that too, and she was reduced to nothing. It had been so easy to think of taking life as it came, being a feather blown happily in the wind – when there was War Minister to command the winds. Facing poverty she now bridled at the injustice of it all, despaired of any hope for a future.

"Gholam Ali," she said sadly, "there's no nothing here anymore. You must go – find someone else. There's nothing left to pay you with."

Gholam Ali remained at attention. "Is *Khanoum* displeased with Gholam Ali?"

"No, Gholam Ali, *Khanoum* is not displeased."

"I will be very good, *Khanoum*."

"Yes. Yes. I know." Nargess sighed. "Here, you will join me." She removed another jeweled teacup from the armoire and poured the concentrated tea into the bottom, placed it on a china saucer with two cubes of sugar, and poured hot water to dilute the concentrated tea. She placed it on the tea table, sliding it gently in Gholam Ali's direction.

"Is the tea bad, *Khanoum*?" Gholam Ali asked, remaining at attention in his bare feet. "I will bring more. Will I scold the cook?"

"No, Gholam Ali. *Khanoum* likes the tea. She wants you to have some."

Gholam Ali remained silently at attention, leaving the offered tea untouched.

"Do you understand, Gholam Ali? Everyone is gone. You must leave too. There is nothing more to pay you with. They may take everything soon. Then where would you be? There won't even be money to buy you food."

"I will stay with *Khanoum*. I will not let them hurt her."

"They have guns, Gholam Ali. Soldiers. Jails. How will you stop them?"

"Poof to their jails! I will not let them hurt *Khanoum*."

Nargess sighed, partly in exasperation, partly in gratitude and mostly in relief.

Then Zahra arrived to join her for breakfast and Nargess bid Gholam Ali wait outside her door while she steeled herself for what she was going to say.

Zahra mentioned that Mansour had put the sapphire colored urns from the great hall into storage. "Who wants them, after all?" she said, offhandedly. "Shall I have Tajmah brought to you?"

Nargess sighed with nostalgia. "We used to chase War Minister's gold coins behind them on *Noruz*. Do you remember, Zahra…? No, I'm too tired for Tajmah."

Zahra shrugged and fell silent. The silence lasted rather longer than usual, until Nargess wondered if Zahra were preparing something awkward. She so feared it would be more bad news, that General Z. was seizing the palace or her valuables. That the last of the cooks had left.

"What is it, Zahra, dear?"

Zahra straightened her back and clasped her hands together and looked to the side. "Time is moving on, Nargess, dear." She shrugged again and began to recite,

> *"If you don't plow the earth, it gets hard,*
> *Nothing grows in it…"*

"Oh no, Zahra. I could never. Just look at me. I have you and Mansour to look after me. I could never do that to War Minister." She closed her eyes and prayed silently, as if to confirm to Zahra the finality of her answer.

But, Zahra persisted. "Nargess, you must. You need someone to look after your affairs. Mansour asked me to make inquiries. I've learned that Karim Mirza e'Tehrani, would be willing. He's descendant of the *Qajars*. He would be proper…"

"No, Zahra. My life…" Nargess stopped in mid sentence. "But, Karim Mirza has four wives already. Surely you don't expect me to become a temporary wife." Her mouth puckered with bitterness, as if she had eaten a rotten betel nut.

Temporary marriages, though a central tenet of Shia Islam, were the last refuge of spinsters and widows, and one of the higher achievements of attractive servant girls in wealthy households. Some husbands treated their temporary wives with the same respect they afforded their permanent wives, especially if they produced male heirs in the absence of any produced by the permanent wives. But, some husbands treated the temporary wives as mere servants. In many cases, temporary marriages were simply a pious nod to bodily urges, with no promise of anything more. Nargess refused to consider the thought of contributing to housework herself and merely existing to satisfy perfunctory urges was no better than prostitution, whatever the greasy mullahs said.

"Ugh! He'd have me sweeping. And what's so special about him? War Minister didn't receive him, after all."

Zahra shrugged again and after a brief silence said, "Nargess, dear, Karim – his first wife has died."

Nargess tremulously raised her eyes to search out Zahra's. "Then I wouldn't be a temporary wife?"

"No."

Nargess lowered her eyes again and considered the proposition while she sipped tea with a crystal of sugar held between her lips. Then she sighed audibly. "No, Zahra. Not now. It's too soon."

There then followed another long period of silence while both munched on the small pieces of fresh pita bread spread with the fig jam.

"You must think about it," Zahra said.

Nargess did think about it. Zahra was right: Tajmah would need a respectable mother and a respectable household. What hope would there be for her if she grew up on a peasant farm? Collecting eggs for breakfast? Nargess took stock of her life reluctantly: her time of mourning was coming to an end; so were her resources. She was getting older, but might still produce children with some luck. She was still *Khanoum e'Sepahsalar*, even if War Minister were deceased. News of War Minister's estates would savage her prospects, but, then, no one would know exactly how much remained to her. Her *Qajar* ancestry still commanded respect. And War Minister's palace remained an imposing, if increasingly precarious, monument. Finally, of course, there remained the issue of her height and her inflamed elbows. These were disastrous defects. Men old enough to put up with these were scarce – dying off, actually.

"It's only a matter of time before General Z. comes back," Zahra said. "And they always know the cruelest time to do it." She did not need to say more.

Added up, Nargess's prospects did not amount to much, but they might do – and they would only dwindle with time. If they seized Lahijan, she would end her days as the impoverished chattel of one of her cousins. Nargess tasted bile at this thought: they would relegate her to a dank, inconvenient room, with mildew on the walls, and expect her to do housework – prepare their tea. They would savor their ascendance over *Khanoum e'Sepahsalar*: aahhh-ing and oooing over how the little princess Tajmah waited on their daughters – those daughters who by rights should be Tajmah's ladies in waiting. Oh, if only War Minister had lived longer! It was all too sordid! Zahra was right. God's will was for her to move on.

Nargess let it be known that her time of mourning was drawing to a close. She was available again. She offered her help to sick relatives. She would sit by their bedsides and nurse them through fevers. Sometimes she left the palace for days at a time when one of her cousins who had departed to set up her own household needed assistance. She even helped the poorer ones with laundry and household chores when they were laid up. She began to feel like a person again, deserving of God.

But, she could not accept Zahra's offer of a new husband, until she had removed the heaviness in her heart for having betrayed her. She did not want to wound Zahra with her knowledge of War Minister's betrayal. She did not want to turn Zahra's love into anger and resentment. But, she could not know peace in her heart until she had bared this injustice.

Nargess clasped her hands in her lap and scrunched her shoulders forward. She cocked her head to the side and looked at the carpet.

"Oh, Zahra, I love you so much."

"Nargess, dear, you are my best friend from forever." Zahra lifted her shoulders and brought the glass of tea to her lips, still in its saucer.

"I would be lost without you – you and Mansour, both," Nargess continued.

"Nargess, dear, you speak as if something will happen between us. We will not leave you."

"Nay, but my heart is sad and I can never rest until you forgive me."

"Nonsense, Nargess, dear! What is there to forgive?"

"I will marry Karim Mirza, if you say it is a good thing to do, but only if you will forgive me. Will you? Will you forgive me?"

"Nargess, what is it? Of course I will forgive you. I will forgive you anything."

"No, Zahra, not me – not only me, at least." Nargess griped her hands tightly now in her lap. She twisted the little linen napkin that had accompanied the tea. She kept her gaze to the side. "War Minister..." She did not want to say what she was going to say. She did not want to hurt her friend. She did not want to speak badly of the deceased. But, she could no longer harbor the gnawing ache. "It was War Minister who betrayed Mansour's caravans. I was just a girl. I didn't know. I..."

"Nonsense," Zahra said. "That's a mean, silly rumor. We've all heard that..."

"Zahra, dear, you must tell Mansour. I haven't the courage. Vali told me. War Minister told him..."

"Vali?"

"...War Minister threatened to cane his feet if he told anyone. He was only a boy..."

"He told Vali? He – Oh – Then..." Zahra's voice trailed off.

Nargess stole a glance at her friend. Zahra preoccupied herself with pouring more tea, avoiding Nargess's eyes. Her hands shook uncharacteristically, causing her to spill some tea on the silver tray. After she had finished pouring her tea, she held the glass in its saucer at waist level. Nargess could see her chin wrinkle and then twitch. She wondered if Zahra were angry. Because of War Minister's act she had ended up married to a bumbling sycophant. Oh Zahra, Nargess thought, please forgive me. I know you are good. I know you will be hurt. But, we pray together. We study the *Qaran* together.

"Oh Zahra – Are you angry with me, Zahra, dear?"

Now Zahra turned to catch Nargess's eye. "War Minister?" She raised the shaking tea glass to her lips, but lowered it without sipping. "War Minister himself told Vali? You're sure of this?"

Nargess nodded yes, aware that her friend was staring at her now. She kept her eyes averted. There was a long pause. Nargess worried Zahra was going to break into tears. "Vali told me after he returned from Paris with Rakshandeh."

"Then it's true?" Zahra spoke in a tissue-thin voice.

Nargess waited, saying nothing.

Zahra's look went far away now. After another silence she returned her gaze to Nargess, and the two looked deeply into one another's trembling eyes. "But, what did *you* do?"

"Oh, Zahra dear, please don't be cross." Nargess reddened. She felt her inflamed elbows. "I didn't tell you…" She didn't have the courage to say more. She sought her friend's eyes to see how she was taking it.

Then, after a long silent pause, Zahra let out a long breath. "Oh Nargess, you were a girl then. You didn't do anything. I wasn't even married to Mansour then, nor you to War Minister." Then she began to speak in a rush: "And you could not betray your husband's secrets. You didn't see it happen. I would never want you to be a rumor-mongering viper, like Rakshandeh. I absolutely won't take steps to forgive you…" Zahra allowed herself a dramatic pause, took a deep breath, and then continued, "…because there is nothing for God or me to forgive!"

Then the two of them burst into tears and embraced until Zahra let Nargess curl up within a blanket upon the futon. While Zahra sat beside her, Nargess fell into a vast and untroubled sleep.

☙

The unburdening of Nargess's conscience by her confession to Zahra was the turning point in the journey of her heart. She knew it would not make the threat of General Z.'s return go away, but she knew she had done God's will and she felt cleansed. She began to sleep through the nights peacefully. Though still adorning herself in black, she began to wash her hair, and then dye it with henna washes to bring color back to the roots that had grown out gray. A few weeks later she began to pluck her eyebrows into well-shaped arches. She lined her eyes with almond charcoal. She now dealt only with the sadness of War Minister's death and the loss of his fortune. She maintained the constancy of her prayers and daily included among them a request for a new husband. She waited and waited for her devoted Zahra to again broach the subject of the arranged marriage with Karim Mirza e'Tehrani, but Zahra had become strangely silent on the issue.

Nargess began to try to learn more about where the money and furniture were going, but Mansour remained endlessly befuddled about what had been stored – and where – how much it would bring. And Rakshandeh was incorrigible. No one could control that viper. Every day a new *bazaar* merchant would arrive demanding payment for one trifle or another, pretending he had not been informed they were no longer responsible for Rakshandeh's bills, or claiming the bill was from before the disclaimers and threatening to bring upon them the wrath of *Allah*. Mansour would scratch his head as he tried to recount the details to Nargess. Nargess never did understand how War Minister could have made dimwitted Mansour head of his personal affairs, but she assumed there must be a vast divide between keeping track of marks in account books and understanding the value of antiques and personal valuables and how to get a good price for them – the difference between a bookkeeper and a businessman. She took to roaming the halls and vacant rooms in between prayers, silently inventorying her remaining possessions. But, each week a few more servants left, along with a silver vase here, a prayer carpet there. The hallways and rooms became progressively bare of portable items. Mansour wanted to start pawning the furniture in Nargess's apartments, but Nargess begged him not to. Appearances would be necessary if she had to entertain the women of Karim Mirza e'Tehrani's family.

"There's a whole basement full," Nargess said. "Why not pawn those antiques first?"

Mansour scratched his head and thought. "We won't have them forever, you know." With his thin white hair combed down over his head like an umbrella and pointed gray beard, his head resembled a confused almond. Nargess wondered if the stress were making him even more befuddled than normal.

Nargess waited in vain for Zahra to notice she was preparing herself to take another husband, but she did not want to ask her directly about Karim Mirza. That would be the way of the grasping lower classes. She expected others to come to her, not the other way around. She was still *Khanoum e'Sepahsalar.*

She began asking Zahra to bring Tajmah to her each morning, so Zahra could watch while she slipped Tajmah small pieces of bread and cheese, and tiny sips of tea. But, Tajmah would not leave Zahra's lap. She nibbled on the offerings only if Zahra took the morsels and put them in Tajmah's mouth herself. Nargess tried having Zahra leave her and Tajmah alone in the room together, but as soon as Zahra rose, Tajmah's chin would quiver, her eyes would tremble and become watery and she would shift her gaze back and forth between the two adults as if demanding to know what they were planning. She would fuss and cling to Zahra, so that Nargess had to pry her arms from around Zahra's knee and hold her, squirming, while Zahra exited. Then Tajmah would scamper to the closed door, where she would collapse in a lump on her tiny bottom and cry for Zahra's return. Nargess eventually relented and returned devotedly to praying, surrendering her daughter to the welcoming arms of Zahra. God must have a purpose in this, she thought, and she must let it happen. And there were so many more pressing things to worry about.

As the anniversary of War Minister's death passed and then several more weeks, Zahra still had not broached the subject of marriage arrangements with Karim Mirza. Now it was Zahra who buried herself in prayer, only to look up at Nargess from time to time and excuse herself for having ignored her. They burned charcoal sparingly and only kept a *korsi* in the smallest rooms through the long nights, as ice accumulated in jagged daggers outside the shuttered windows and knee-high snow suffocated the carpet of leaves, still unraked from the fall. Burning a fire in one of the large ceramic heating stoves was out of the question, because they could scarcely afford wood or charcoal in such quantities. The cold further irritated Nargess's chapped and itching elbows, but she hid them from sight lest word escape that she had a physical defect and ruin her chances of remarrying. She longed for Zahra to complete the arrangements with Karim Mirza, but dared say nothing lest she lower herself. And Zahra, who had formerly so acutely shared her worries about their dwindling finances, seemed oblivious to the future now, unconcerned about the approaching, inevitable poverty. Nargess decided Zahra was just being strong, so she, Nargess, would not succumb to her own fears.

When finally Mansour suggested pawning the jeweled tea set, Nargess knew it was time to ask Zahra to arrange the marriage.

"Dear Nargess, it's only a tea set," Zahra said to her.

"It was my mother's – and her mother's before her. Oh, Zahra, it's more than a tea set. I can't receive the women from Karim Mirza's household in an empty room – his mother and his sisters and his three permanent wives – and two of them have grown daughters. What will they think?"

Zahra scrunched her petite shoulders and looked away.

"Zahra, what is it?"

Zahra's chin shivered and she began to stammer, "They're going to take Lahijan for the *Vaqfe*. Mansour said so."

"No Zahra, they said I could keep it as long as we gave them the records of War Minister's estates. It's all in the letter…"

"They don't believe Mansour. He told them everything. He gave them everything. But, they say he's hiding something."

"No, not Mansour. They don't know him. He could never hide anything from anybody."

"I know, but they're threatening him. The adjutant of the Ministry of the *Vaqfe* has threatened him with arrest." Now Zahra turned to Nargess and looked at her flatly. "He wants a payment."

This was a knife wound. The Shah's functionaries would bleed her to death with bribes and false promises. They would not let her slide into genteel poverty. Petty and low, like all the newly rich, barely a step out of the *bazaar*, they wanted revenge. They would never rest until they had devastated everything and everyone noble and cultivated and genteel. Oh how could such a godless man have become shah? And now they were threatening her through the simple, harmless Mansour. Her insides quivered and stiffened.

"Oh Zahra," Nargess said, grasping her elbow, "if we pay them, they will never stop. They will take everything: the house, the furnishings, my jewels. Then no one will ever marry me. What is going to happen to me?" Nargess then saw Zahra's eyes flash dark and hostile with fear. Immediately she felt the slap of Zahra's silent resentment. "No, Zahra," she said quickly. "I didn't mean we shouldn't pay them – wouldn't pay them. Of course we will pay them – but what will we do next time? How much do they want?"

Zahra breathed a loud sigh of relief. "I don't know, exactly, but Mansour figured the tea set would cover it."

"And that's why you want to sell it?"

Zahra nodded.

"But, there must be something else, dear Zahra. There's a whole store-room downstairs. Why the tea set?"

Zahra shrugged.

"Come, Zahra. We will go down to the storeroom together and choose something else. I will tell Mansour. You can show me which trunks hold what." She slid herself out from under the *korsi* and extended her hand to Zahra. But, Zahra returned the gesture with a blank stare.

"Mansour had the storeroom emptied and sent to his cousin's house. We'll have to wait till his cousin returns from Mazandaran hunting."

Nargess's tongue thickened. She tried to ask why Mansour had moved her belongings outside of the compound, but something scratchy caught in her throat and all she could manage was a rasp. Was it possible Rakshandeh had a hand in this?

Zahra rushed to put her at ease: "Mansour wanted to protect you. He was worried for you. That's all. You can get War Minister's things anytime. He's got them where General Z. will never find them."

Nargess immediately relaxed. The throbbing flew from her face. Oh bless Mansour, she thought silently. She was surprised that someone as slow as Mansour had managed to keep a step ahead of the Shah's cronies in the Ministry of the *Vaqfe*, but her gratitude washed away the weight of her concern – and she certainly wasn't going to express such thoughts to her dear Zahra.

"But, Zahra, I need the tea set to serve the family of Karim Mirza. I can't have them think me a pauper! Can't we wait till your cousin's hunting trip is over? It's one of the few things I can't entertain without."

Now Zahra was not so quick to answer. As Nargess sat down and drew the blanket of the *korsi* back up around her torso, Zahra preoccupied herself with smoothing out the folds in the blanket, to block any further incursions of cold air. Finally she blurted, "Nargess, dear, I don't think it's going to work out with Karim Mirza ..." She paused.

"Zahra?"

"...He withdrew his interest."

"But, Zahra, they haven't even visited yet! Zahra, Why? What will we do?"

Zahra sighed and waited before answering. "I know of another: Abrahim e'Kashani..."

"Abrahim e'Kashani?" The name sounded vaguely familiar, but Nargess couldn't quite place it. "But, what happened with Karim Mirza?"

"... He has only two wives. The best part is no children. He's done quite well..."

"Abrahim e'Kashani: Oh Zahra, I do know that name: He's..." Nargess stopped in mid sentence. She was afraid to think the thoughts that assaulted her. "...*bazaari*?"

"No, cousin, not *bazaari*: he builds houses. He buys up old estates and turns them into houses."

"Oh Zahra, that's worse! He might as well be a common laborer..."

"No, cousin. He's built his own private *bonyad* to build houses. He's made a small fortune..."

"Oh Zahra, *bazaari*, *bazaari*..."

"Nargess, dear..."

"... Who will I talk to?" Nargess thought to herself for a while. Then she said, "All their friends will be shopkeepers. Who will Tajmah marry? Oh, Zahra, it's all so common. How could I?"

"Nargess, dear, you'll be queen there – His other two wives are older – no children in their future. None of them have your ancestry. You've just had Tajmah. You can have another. And I hear he doesn't let any of the women in his household snipe and gossip the way that viper Rakshandeh ruined everything..."

"Why did he back off – Karim Mirza? Please, Zahra, tell me what happened. What did they say?"

Zahra remained silent, working up the courage to tell the truth. "It's your elbows," she said. "Someone told him about your elbows."

Nargess clutched her elbows and gently massaged the pain. It was just the sort of defect that the women of a prospective match scouted for when they came to visit. And Nargess had been so careful to keep them secret. She had never bared her elbows to any woman other than her mother for her whole lifetime – at least since she developed the condition. And none of the women who had long ago visited to scout her out as a prospective bride had ever proposed to return and bathe with her, as was the custom. So, who could have told Karim Mirza about her elbows, and why? Oh it must have been someone who hated her. But, who could hate her besides Rakshandeh, and how could Rakshandeh possibly know a secret shared only with her deceased mother and her beloved Zahra?

"Oh who cares what a shallow person like that does?" Zahra continued. "Who would want to live with someone like that – all he cares about is elbows. Oh, you're so much better off with Abrahim e'Kashani…"

When Zahra stopped talking, Nargess exhaled a resigned sigh. This was God's wish for her. She should pawn her noble blood while Abrahim e'Kashani still wanted to marry a title. And if she acted quickly, as the wife of a wealthy businessman she would have a husband to protect her from the endless seizures and deceptions of the Shah's sycophants. She would be able to hold on to Lahijan and sell the palace, arrive with her own income…

"How much do we pay?" Nargess asked.

"Mansour will take care of it. The pawnbroker has a buyer for the tea set. They want to see it. Mansour says he's offering almost double its value. He only needs it now long enough to show. He's agreed to rent it back to you until you can buy it back, if you need. The buyer's already advanced him the full price so he can take it if you're late buying it back. But, by then, Mansour's cousin will be returned from his hunting trip…"

Nargess's head spun at the complicated arrangement. She had no idea how pawnbrokers worked, so she assumed this was just another grasping *ba-zaari* arrangement. But, she assessed her options simply. She knew the Czech tea set would bring a good price. It was one of the household's most treasured possessions. It was said the Tsar of Russia had possessed the only sister set. She probably had a greater need for the furniture she had stored beside her apartments, to keep the house from looking empty. She hoped there would be enough to bring the palace into shape before the women of Abrahim e'Kashani's family came to visit. They would be easier to impress than a family with royal blood, like Karim Mirza e'Tehrani, but she couldn't have them thinking she was coming to Abrahim barefoot. She vaguely wondered how the pawnbroker's buyer could know about her tea set, but she knew worrying about this was a luxury she could ill afford.

Zahra interrupted her thoughts: "Nargess, dear, there's not much time. General Z. wants the house for himself – well – Mansour doesn't know – but he's hearing rumors. That's how they do it, you know – You wouldn't want Abrahim to lose face."

Nargess understood that it would be as embarrassing for Abrahim to have her arrive barefoot as it would be for her. "And you've arranged it all?" she said.

"Yes, Nargess, dear."

Nargess leaned to the side and grasped Zahra's shoulders, pulling her towards herself, warm with the feeling that someone was fending for her. She kissed her on both cheeks and then a second time on both cheeks. "Oh, Zahra, dear, you and Mansour think of everything. You must live with me at Abrahim e'Kashani's house. You can be my *dame d'honneur*. You can take care of Tajmah; she loves you so."

℘

Immediately after the pawnbroker had packed the tea set and paid Mansour (less the first month's rent to make sure Nargess didn't back out of the deal) Mansour departed to make payment to the adjutant of the Ministry of the *Vaqfe*. Upon his return he, Nargess and Zahra together planned their preparations to receive the women of the household of Abrahim e'Kashani.

Explaining he distrusted the discretion of local laborers, Mansour sent to Lahijan for a dozen male peasants to pose as guards, and their sons, to pose as gardeners. They would not need to work the fields for another six weeks yet and they would welcome the adventure of visiting War Minister's Tehran palace. Zahra and Nargess found the uniforms of War Minister's departed guards and decorated them discretely with additional colored buttons and linen sashes. For Gholam Ali they fashioned a particularly elaborate army uniform, with brass buttons along the lapels and the shoulders. They fitted epaulettes and an ebony-handled ceremonial sword from War Minister's second during the Kermanshah campaign. Gholam Ali being a petite man, they provided layers of quilting inside the refurbished guard's uniform, to add bulk to his stature. Nargess topped it off with an eighteen inch high bonnet of black bear's fur in the shape and size of a truncated watermelon. He would be assigned to guard the last approach to Nargess, wherever she went – an impressive and splendid statement. In thanks to God, Nargess had Zahra prepare a large tray of *halvah* and bread and deliver it to the *Mosque e'Sepahsalar*, which years earlier War Minister had built and donated to the church.

Nargess instructed that she would greet the guests at the end of the hall of mirrors, on a settee from India, covered in gold and red damask. They would position it across the gilded-chrysanthemum doors, blocking them and sending traffic to the turquoise side doors, which led to Nargess's apartments. Under no circumstances were the chrysanthemum doors to be opened, lest the visitors see the bare, water-stained and decaying hallway to War Minister's quarters. Every last stick of furniture was withdrawn from unused rooms and from the storerooms beside Nargess's apartments, to line the parade route, starting at the *hashtee* and ending in Nargess's private apartments. The heavy mahogany doors to the now empty dining and entertaining salons on the ground floor, one on either side of the entrance hallway, were closed. To each door or hallway leading to the abandoned wings or emptied rooms, Nargess assigned two of the peasants from Lahijan, now bedecked in splendid uniforms, to stand at attention, with empty rifles strapped across their backs, and strict orders to maintain silence. Mansour instructed the peasant boys to rake the garden and prune the rose bushes, always within view of the windows from Nargess's apartments. He found the cash to order extra wood and charcoal for the large ceramic heating stoves in the main rooms, and ordered they not be ignited until an hour before the guests arrived.

Nargess polished the tea set, which she kept displayed in a glass armoire in her private sitting room. The pawnbroker had sent word that he would demand all of his money back, plus rent, if even one cut glass insert were so much as scratched, his customer having agreed to wait for delivery only if this guarantee were offered. And he would charge her the value of his lost sale, which was twice what she would get anywhere else for it. Nargess was miffed at this addendum to their supposed agreement, particularly because it was not unknown for the occasional guest at such affairs to deliberately stage an "accident" to judge the response of the hostess, but she had no opportunity to disagree. She developed a simple stratagem: she would take her tea from one of Zahra's straight walled kitchen tea glasses, in plain view of the tea set. They would interpret this as pious – not necessary – a display of true humility that only a devout aristocrat or an impoverished ascetic could muster. Nargess was going to make sure they saw her as the former, not the latter. She planned to shame her guests into declining the opulent glasses as well: while she accepted a simple glass from a tray of simple glasses that would be brought to her, she would scold the servant and offer the visitors to have her pull out the fancy tea set glasses for their tea. She knew they would see this as a game they couldn't win. If they accepted the offer of the fancy tea set, they would look like grasping *bazaari* excited by the opulence. If they declined the fancy set, they would appear nervous and insecure, as if trying to hide their *bazaari* excitement. She congratulated herself on this stratagem. Yes, she might be marrying beneath herself, but these were simple merchant types and, well, *noblesse oblige…*

At the appointed hour, Nargess positioned herself nervously on the red and gold settee before the gilded chrysanthemum doors. She fiddled endlessly with her hair. She could not say so to her beloved Zahra, but the whole affair was tiresome, distasteful. Who were these shopkeepers' wives to judge her? She would be gracious and humble, but God had delivered her to her station in life and it was her duty to command that station with seamless confidence. She would not have a family of business types expecting her to join in their drab pastimes. It must be clear from the very start she would need accommodations for servants and possessions – very well, for her breeding.

She would come with an income of her own, and expected gratitude for that. But, she feared a surprise visit from General Z. The vile adjutant had started grumbling to Mansour that a single woman could not live alone in such a splendid palace. It was not safe. It was not right. Soon he would want another payment, or maybe he would again accompany General Z. without warning, out of spite, to seize what remained. To marry a commoner was humiliating. To arrive at his doorstep barefoot, was unconscionable. Even worse, would be to be rejected as a prospective wife on the basis of poverty.

She wore simple jewelry – bangles of gold and pearls, a necklace of enameled gold, ruby earrings and a turquoise ring. (The very religious considered themselves too pious to take food or drink directly from tableware made of valuable materials, such as silver or gold, or to pray while wearing their jewelry. But, this transcendence of the temporal did not extend to ownership: It was acceptable to wear expensive jewelry while not praying, and to own fancy tea sets. The *Qaran* even celebrated material success and overtly disparaged poverty.) She positioned Gholam Ali, at attention, on the side of the hallway opposite the turquoise doors to her apartments. In front of these she positioned two guards with empty rifles. She prayed no one would notice the absence of the silk carpets and French sapphire blue urns that had once lined the hallway. It seemed so empty to her without these, every footstep a clacking harbinger of her empty future, but the Kashani family would never have qualified to even enter the hallway and thus could not possibly notice the absences. Meanwhile, Zahra staged the entrance. She timed herself to arrive downstairs and greet the guests just as they finished exchanging their heavy, black *chadors* for the light gray ones the servants would provide.

"God show me the way," she prayed. "Let me walk in the path of righteousness."

Abrahim's mother, Ashraf *Khanoum*, led the platoon of matrons on reconnaissance from the household of Abrahim e'Kashani. Ashraf *Khanoum*'s face resembled a steamed cauliflower, with a pale, drooping eggplant for a nose. Well into her eighties, her waist-less body resembled a poorly stuffed bed pillow. Her swollen ankles bulged painfully over her shoes as she lumbered forward. Her hands shook as she gripped a carved ivory cane with her gnarled knuckles. Zahra ingratiatingly kissed Ashraf *Khanoum* on both cheeks and took her by one hand, while one of the daughters, Tahereh, took the other. The two of them led puffing Ashraf *Khanoum* up the marble stairs to the second floor great hall.

Nargess arranged the folds of her chador to appear casual, leisurely, as if she were reading the *Qaran*, while her guests climbed the marble stairs. She was going to set the tone. When Ashraf *Khanoum*, supported by Zahra and Tahereh, appeared at the top of the stairs, Nargess carefully counted three steps. Then she rose and swept down the length of the hall, calling, "*Salaam! Chittori!*" She timed her stride to meet Ashraf *Khanoum* and her family three quarters of the way down the hall, just enough to convey respect, as if apologizing for not having risen immediately upon seeing her, and just enough that she could walk fast to make the rush of air billow her chador like a spring breeze, an effect she aided by holding her arms out to either side in greeting. Gholam Ali marched three steps behind and to her right, dutifully displaying his mountainous bear hat and empty rifle. Nargess beamed as she embraced Ashraf *Khanoum* and kissed her on both cheeks: she was off to a good start.

Every dozen or so steps, assisted now by Nargess on her left and her oldest daughter, Tahereh on her right, Ashraf *Khanoum* would halt, lean on her ivory cane, withdraw a lace handkerchief to wipe her brow, fan herself with a folding red silk Chinese fan, and exclaim, "Oh, my! So many steps! I must rest." She would nod as if faint, and reach out for support – or someplace to sit, if only there was one. She was in obvious awe of her own Herculean efforts, but not above darting glances here and there to make a full accounting, despite her failing eyesight.

Nargess observed that the oldest daughter, Tahereh, held the position of chief acolyte. It was Tahereh who led Ashraf *Khanoum* everywhere by the hand, and who, at the very commencement of her arrival in the great hall, led her to rest on Nargess's red and gold settee by the chrysanthemum doors; Tahereh who deftly guided the mother's hand to just miss the back of the settee as she sat down, so she would tumble into it, shoving the doors ajar. "*Madar*, careful!" she cried. Nargess pretended it was nothing and avoided the mistake of eyeing either Tahereh or the opened slot between the doors, but she noticed with relief the angle made it impossible for Tahereh to peer through the opening onto the crumbling emptiness of War Minister's water-stained, private hallway. She and Gholam Ali stood their ground on the side that did give a view through the open doors, deftly blocking the two cousins who accompanied Ashraf *Khanoum* and the other sister, leaving them the disadvantageous view. Nargess prayed the bats were asleep.

"Oh my!" Ashraf *Khanoum* gasped. She allowed Nargess to lift her hand and pat it. "You young people go on ahead," Ashraf *Khanoum* said." She fussed briefly with her handkerchief; then busily fanned her neck. "Tahereh and I will be along in a minute."

"I wouldn't think of it," Nargess said, patting her hand, playing the gracious host, fully aware that Tahereh and the mother planned to go exploring.

When they had seated Ashraf *Khanoum* on the futon with a full view of the glass armoire, it was Tahereh who exclaimed, "Oh, Nargess, dear, you have such pretty things." Then she asked to hold one of the tea glasses up to her mother's eyes, her mother's eyesight being in serious decline. Nargess was annoyed to see her stratagem circumvented, but she innovated as best she could:

"They were my grandmother's," Nargess said. She held a tea glass up to

Ashraf *Khanoum*'s eyes herself, and compassionately guided her hand to it. "Czech."

When the servant girl brought tea in plain glasses, as instructed, Nargess chided her, saying she had wanted her to serve the guests tea in the Czech glasses, that the simple ones were only for herself and Zahra. She did not get more than three steps towards the armoire before Tahereh protested. Nargess could tell from the slight tremor in her chin that she discerned a test, but was unsure if she would pass. She again beamed inwardly at her small victory, and as they lifted the glasses from the saucers, she said with a sigh, "Thanks to God!" to which they responded in kind.

Nargess summoned forth an endless parade of silver trays bearing tea and baklava and almond cookies and crystal bowls holding persimmons, pomegranates, raisins and oranges – enough for a wedding or an army. Every once in a while she would lead a guest to a window overlooking the rear gardens, ostensibly to share the view or check the weather, but particularly to show her the squad of hardworking gardeners from Lahijan.

Ashraf *Khanoum*'s oldest daughter, Tahereh was tall, slender, languorous. She had deep liquid eyes, smooth brown hair, long, fine fingers, and angular hips that occasionally caught the folds of her chador. Nargess had to adjust to the simplicity of Tahereh's jewelry. Her necklace was a set of gold coins with designs strung along a thin gold chain. She wore only a half dozen bangles on her right wrist; plain turquoise earrings. After all, Tahereh had never been the wife of a War Minister – doubtless not a drop of royal blood. Tahereh's first husband had divorced her many years earlier and her second husband had divorced her about six years ago, after the birth of their son, Javad. No one had been brave enough to give her a third try at wifehood. She shared with the other sister a certain quality of sadness. Of the group, she was the only one to profess an interest in poetry, but her tastes were limited to merely telling fortunes with verses of Hafez, rather than appreciating his spirituality, which transcended religion and had, in the poet's lifetime, often earned him the wrath of the religious authorities. She had little knowledge of Sa'di and Khayam. Nargess calculated that her new life would be a dull one, but she would have Zahra visit often – after all, she'd offered her to be her *dame d'honneur*. Otherwise the conversation of the afternoon dwelled mostly on clothes and babies and cooking and common acquaintances, the last of which were abysmally few.

The younger daughter, Afsar, was more difficult to read. As much as Tahereh was languorous and outgoing, Afsar was mousy, and stiff-backed and top-heavy with watermelon breasts that made her look wearied at the effort of supporting them. She was soft spoken and shy, and had eyes that were perpetually swollen and red. Nargess recognized she would prove dull company. Tahereh was the formidable one.

The two cousins spoke little and stayed in the background, not wanting to intrude, but silently observing.

Nargess fretted when Tahereh described Abrahim's house to her in detail. It seemed as if she were actually boasting it would fail to hold the possessions of a mansion, let alone a palace. It did not matter, she decided. She was prepared to arrive with roomfuls of possessions, to make her point – a small caravan's worth. Feigning surprise at finding her new quarters inadequate for holding her possessions would both emphasize her status and give her a respectable excuse to sell what little she had for cash. Between what she had to pay the pawnbroker in rent for the tea set and what she had handed over to the various *bazaari* for this day's feast, she was desperately strapped. Nargess wondered whether Tahereh's smile at describing Abrahim's house was endearing, condescending, or taunting. Was it some sort of test? Did she know about her circumstances? Whatever the case, Nargess knew it was a smile to fear.

The only truly dangerous moment came late in the afternoon, when Ashraf *Khanoum* began to talk about spending the summer near Tajreesh. Nargess feared the conversation would turn to War Minister's summer estate in the Alborz Mountains, now belonging to the Sub Ministry of the *Vaqfe* in the Ministry of education. She tried to steer the conversation to the cherries and plums of the region, and then to which region produced the best figs, which she hoped would take the conversation hundreds of miles to the south. But, Tahereh, seeming to sense an advantage, launched into a brief discussion of the beauties of Abrahim's summer house in Tajreesh. "It's so unpleasant in Tehran in the summer," Tahereh finished. "Where will you summer, dear Nargess?"

Before Nargess could answer, Ashraf *Khanoum* was overcome by a coughing fit. Tahereh had to thump her mother's back until she hacked something unidentifiable into her handkerchief and secreted it away.

"*Madar*! You shouldn't interrupt nargess." Tahereh said, seeking to return to the subject of Nargess's summer residence.

"Nay, Tahereh dear," Nargess said, countering. "*Khanoum* is a blessing– to us all." Nargess thanked God for her future mother in law's frail health. Then she made a quick prayer, begging forgiveness and amending the gratitude to cover just that one coughing spell.

"Oh my," Ashraf *Khanoum* blurted. She motioned to Tahereh to help fetch her cane and help her rise from the sitting pillow. "Look what I've done, dear! Oh, it's so late. Nargess, dear, you are so gracious, we completely forgot the hour."

Nargess spent the next two weeks in desperate fear. Had Tahereh figured out how poor she was? No, it could not be: how could she know? But, two weeks was much too long to wait. Had Rakshandeh gotten word of the introduction? Was she telling Ashraf *Khanoum* that Nargess was barren, was at best only possessed of a palace because War Minister hadn't yet replaced her with one of his peasant girls? Had she told her that the Shah was only waiting for the cruelest moment to cast her naked into the street to reduce her to the level of a whore? Her bills continued to mount.

Two weeks later Ashraf *Khanoum* sent her a message through Zahra, asking if they could come again for tea and bring sweets.

"Oh Zahra, dear," Nargess sighed, "bless you!"

Zahra accepted her kisses on both cheeks readily.

Nargess delivered another tray of *halvah* and bread to the *Mosque e'Sepahsalar*, and personally delivered it to the head cleric, with her thanks.

The second visit was a replay of the first, except that Nargess had the servants nail a board behind each door leading to anything but a lavishly decorated interior, most especially the walnut doors carved with gilded chrysanthemums leading to War Minister's decaying hallway. And afterwards the peasants from Lahijan departed for home and Nargess returned her grandmother's tea set to the pawnbroker.

❧

But, General Z. was not so cooperative. He waited until Nargess was at her most vulnerable. The morning on the very day before Nargess's wedding, General Z. arrived with several dozen officers and men, this time with a caravan of lorries. They carted off the remaining furniture and searched her trunks of clothes, even her stored undergarments, for hidden jewelry. She was allowed to keep her clothes, a few trunks to store them in, several futons, and whatever jewelry she was wearing at the time of their "inspection," which wasn't much, because they arrived while she was taking breakfast with Zahra – a few gold bangles and one rather massive diamond pendant, which she had merely donned on a whim, imagining before the mirror how she would look in it on the morrow, and which she had hidden upon their arrival. They cleaned out the storeroom in the basement, even removing the pickled preserves, dried fruit and cold-stored melons. General Z. left Mansour with a written eviction order, with twenty-four hours notice.

Just two days earlier, Nargess had spent her last *touman* – and then some – on tailors and hairdressers to ready her for the procession to the house of Abrahim e'Kashani, and musicians to go before her to announce the procession, and porters to follow her, displaying the remaining splendors of War Minister's mansion enroute to his widow's new husband's household. Mansour had arranged for them to work on credit, explaining to Nargess she could pay them when she sold the bulk of her belongings, which she planned to do anyway, once she had impressed Abrahim's waiting family.

Nargess spent the whole night vomiting with fear and self-loathing.

"I can't, Zahra. I can't. How can I face those awful *bazaari* – a pauper? Oh, I promise you they planned it. That awful Tahereh. I know she's in cahoots with that Rakshandeh. How do they know..."

"Nonsense, Nargess dear. Who are they to have such connections? It's just the Shah's sycophants..."

"How could God have made kings out of common thieves, Zahra? Is there no justice? Is there no truth? Zahra, what did I do to deserve this? They're even taking Lahijan. Now I'll have nothing." She grasped the diamond pendant General Z. had allowed her to keep. "Nothing except this..." she blew air through her lips. "Oh, Zahra, how did they even know about Lahijan? They wouldn't dare do this if I were marrying Karim Mirza..."

"Hush now! They can't do anything once you're Abrahim e'Kashani's wife."

"... I might as well go barefoot."

Zahra reached forward and gently lifted Nargess's last diamond pendant and gave it a brief inspection. "Well, nothing would be bad – but this, we'll at least it's something."

By the time Gholam Ali came to knock on her door to wake her for the hairdresser in the morning, Nargess's eyes were swollen and red, as if they had soaked all night in a mustard plaster. Her face was otherwise ashen, her complexion as frail as tissue paper.

"Tell them it's off, Gholam Ali," Nargess wept. "Tell them there's nothing. I'm dead. I've gone away. Tell them to go."

Gholam Ali spike through the closed door: "Yes, yes. The hairdresser comes."

"No, Gholam Ali! No hairdresser. No wedding. I..."

"Yes, yes, I fix it. I fix everything."

Nargess sighed. Gholam Ali was unstoppable. He was right, though. She had to pay the hairdresser anyway. She might as well get it done. She could poison herself afterwards and at least depart the world decently coiffed.

Whatever she did, she had to make peace with God. When she was dressed she spoke to Gholam Ali:

"Gholam Ali, how is Zobeideh?" Zobeideh was a well-known local beggar woman. She'd had four children, all of whom had died in infancy. Bent-backed and afflicted with lice, she spent her days at the *bazaar* entrance, collecting and selling old rags. Nargess had often sent her old clothes at the request of Gholam Ali, who had known her husband through the old side show.

"She gives thanks to God to be alive," Gholam Ali said.

"I want to give her a gift. Will you take it to her for me?"

Somewhat shakily she removed her diamond pendant. Clasping it in the palm of her hand, she handed it to Gholam Ali, who responded with a look of terror.

"No! No, *Khanoum*! She cannot accept that. Not if…"

"Nay, Gholam Ali," Nargess interrupted. "It's not what you think. *Khanoum* will not hurt herself. There's nothing left now. This will fool no one. Here, take it to Zobeideh. It's all I have to give God." She waited while Gholam Ali eyed her skeptically. "God wills it," she said. "He does."

Gholam Ali eyed the pendant suspiciously. Then he eyed Nargess with worry. "Does *Khanoum* promise?"

"*Khanoum* promises."

Zahra held her hand through the hairdresser's visit, and washed her face with warm water. Late in the afternoon she returned to prepare her wedding dress for her but Nargess could not lift herself to get into it.

"I'll send a messenger to Abrahim e'Kashani to tell him it's off," Nargess said. "Call Gholam Ali. I'll have him do it."

"Nay, Nargess. You mustn't."

"Zahra, dear, I have a dozen musicians with drums and tambourines outside waiting, and six dozen porters to parade my belongings before all of Tehran, porters who now have nothing better to do with their day than watch my ruin. Am I supposed to arrive at Abrahim e'Kashani's with the musicians and say, 'Oh, my! Where did those porters go?' No, it's too much. Too, too much."

"Gholam Ali isn't even here, anyway," Zahra said. "He's run off like the others."

"Run off?" Nargess felt a sharp stab. Had Gholam Ali decided the pendant would do better starting a new life for himself rather than one for a beggar woman? "I just saw him this morning."

"I haven't seen him all day," Zahra said. "He's been sneaking out all week as far as I can tell. I knew something was up…"

"But…"

Just then the two of them heard a commotion from the courtyard beyond the *birouni*. There was a great clacking of wooden cartwheels on the cobblestones and people shouting to each other, and above all the unmistakable voice of Gholam Ali calling, "Come, come, *Khanoum*! I fix. Come, come!"

From her window Nargess could see that upon the same cobblestones where General Z. had waited on that fateful morning, where Vali had departed this life at the feet of his father a year before that, now stood Gholam Ali, at attention, in his brass studded uniform and the towering black bear hat, and behind him a caravan of donkey carts loaded with furnishings and finery: porcelain vases, silver urns, velvet-upholstered French empire chairs.

"Good heavens!" cried Nargess. "What is it? What has he done?"

Zahra agreed to go find out and when she returned she seemed flustered. "What is it?" Nargess asked.

"He borrowed it all from the family, he says. All week he ran to every cousin and friend of War Minister he could find calling in favors – all over

Tehran. And what he couldn't get from the owners he had the servants filch. Oh, I wouldn't touch it if I were you. You should send it back. It's hardly the quality for War Minister. Some of it's so tacky..."

"Oh, it will do," Nargess said. "Hurry, Zahra, before the porters leave."

Gholam Ali beamed at attention from the edge of the courtyard as Nargess arrived to witness the transfer of the goods from the donkey carts to the porters. Beside him crouched the beggar woman, Zobeideh, along with a small group of vendors and shopkeepers who had come to see the spectacle. Nargess walked towards Gholam Ali and Zobeideh and stood almost at attention herself, thanking them with a look of tearful relief. "Oh, Gholam Ali, God has been good to me," she said, "through you."

"God smiles upon *Khanoum*," Gholam Ali said.

Then Gholam Ali removed a small rag from his pocket. "A wedding gift for *Khanoum*," he said, extending it to her.

Nargess accepted it with reserve, but she reddened with shock when she opened the rag to find the diamond pendant she had only that morning asked Gholam Ali to give to Zobeideh.

"Nay, Zobeideh, you are too kind. This is a gift for you." She let the pendant dangle, then coiled it into her hand.

"Now Zobeideh gives it to *Khanoum e'Sepahsalar*," Zobeideh said. Zobeideh was missing her front teeth and tried not to part her lips when she smiled, but it was a beaming – if gummy – smile, nevertheless, and she could not keep it from bursting forth fully. "We would be nowhere without War Minister. The honor is Zobeideh's."

Nargess bent over and took Zobeideh's hand, placed the pendant in it and closed Zobeideh's fingers around the pendant. "Now the honor is *Khanoum e'Sepahsalar's*."

❧

Abrahim proved a gentle, likeable man, despite his reputation for severely disapproving of frivolities and dissent. With broad, athletic shoulders and a white, toothy smile punctuated by receding gums, he had a way of clasping his knees as he sat leaning forward, appearing as if he wanted to drink in every word his interlocutor could offer. If not clasping his knees, he was bridging his fingers together in a judicial apse, still with the same wide smile, his head nodded slightly to the side, arching his back forward as if he were taking confession or dispensing Solomonic justice. His bushy, salt and pepper hair and short-trimmed, gray beard added to the judicial appearance. Although he had the shoulders and torso of an aging athlete, he was incongruously slight in the hips, and this gave his overall appearance the shape of a V.

The very first sentence Nargess uttered to him in private was at the end of the celebrations, when they had retired to his quarters: "Abrahim, someone needs to pay the porters."

Abrahim lifted one eyebrow and smiled. "Of course, my pretty." He seated himself on the sitting pillow across from hers. "Whatever you need, Tahereh will get for you. She'll take care of everything. She offered to. She's been so excited to have you join us." He sighed, as if he were pleased with himself for having thought of everything before hand. "As am I."

Nargess wasn't about to spend the rest of her life begging her sister in law for favors. But, she didn't want to play the role of household witch. They had only just struggled through the wedding ceremony. At least, she had struggled. All day she had hidden her tear-swollen eyes and streaked almond charcoal behind a heavy silk veil, a veil that was not strictly called for by the occasion, but which was a convenient excuse, and one that further conveyed her devout disposition. And it gave her a layer of protection from her *bazaari* in-laws. Without that, she was sure, they would discover she had not a single *dinar* to her name.

"I'm sick tonight," was the second thing she said to her new husband in private.

"Of course," he said. He clasped his hands before himself and nodded, as if every bride had her period on her wedding night, like clockwork. He turned down the wick on the oil lamp and went to sleep on his pillow, leaving her the choice of sleeping on his futon or being shown to her own quarters.

Nargess was grateful that he allowed her to remain in his quarters. It looked better for both of them that way.

In the morning, when she was taken to her new apartments for the first time, she cried again. Abrahim's house was on the edge of the fashionable Government Gate district and was quite large by the standards of the day. But, to Nargess, it measured only a bit larger than the dining salon in War Minister's palace. Nargess had three rooms: a bedroom with sitting room, on the ground floor in the older, less ornate part of the compound, in the rear, just beside a small archway that separated the servants' quarters from the main house. There was an additional small adjoining room for Tajmah. Outside her window a water channel led in from the side street along the back of their neighbor's and divided into two channels. One fed into an opening in the side of the house just below her bedroom window and down into a large iron cistern in the basement. The other led to the large cistern pool in the middle of the interior courtyard. Twice each week, water was diverted to the district and flowed through the channels, replenishing both cisterns. Opening onto the neighbor's property, and situated in the rear of Abrahim's house, Nargess's apartments received little direct sun. In fact, that corner of the property was decidedly dank. And though freshly painted, her rooms bore the unquenchable odor of mildew.

Oh, Zahra, Nargess thought, if only you could live here with me to make it bearable, protect me from those in laws. Then she caught herself. But, I must make do, she thought. Surely I can't sink any lower than this.

In the afternoon, Tahereh invited Nargess to lunch with her and the other women, after which she promised a tour of the house.

"Oh, Tajmah is such a dear," Tahereh said, as she led Nargess down the dusty hall with paint that had once been white, but was now yellowed. She had kept Tajmah in her quarters for the wedding night. "I can't wait for you to see her. She's been entertaining us all morning." She opened the door to her sitting room. "There. See how cute she is!"

Nargess shook with anger when she saw the entertainment consisted of Tajmah sweeping Tahereh's rug with a child size broom, back and forth with complete abandon, and with not one whit of interest in the arrival of her mother, while Tahereh's little boy, Javad, sat on the floor, eating bread and cheese.

"She's so comfortable with strangers," Tahereh admired. "You must be a wonderful mother." She turned to Tajmah and spoke: "You can help your *Madar* get the terrace ready for tea, Tajmah dear. Would you like that? Tea outside? On a sunny spring day? Dear?"

Nargess stiffened, but said nothing. It was no coincidence Tahereh had arranged the invitation for the hour of peak daylight streaming in through her comfortably sealed windows with the southern exposure on the third floor. Afsar, the other sister, and Golnar and Masumay, the two other wives, had bright, airy, second and third floor apartments too – all kept toasty warm with iron heating stoves.

Tahereh's most brazen act was to show Ashraf *Khanoum*'s apartments without warning Ashraf *Khanoum*. Her apartments immediately adjoined Abrahim's on the second floor, hogging the preponderance of the southern exposure, with three spacious sitting rooms, each with a direct view onto the French gardens in the interior courtyard in the rear.

"What are you doing?" Ashraf *Khanoum* gasped when Nargess appeared before her in the third sitting room, where she was blindly knitting.

"*Madar*, be polite!" Tahereh said.

"Oh my!" Ashraf *Khanoum* dropped her knitting, mopped her brow with her lace handkerchief and eased herself back into a pillow propped against the plaster wall. She swatted at her neck with the Chinese silk fan. "These rooms aren't yours, dear, you know…"

"*Madar*…"

"It's nothing to me if Abrahim marries again. I'm just a mother. But, well, toss me aside like an old rag…"

"*Madar*…"

"… the ingrate. He'd move me to the cellar, he would. What with all that *Khanoum* this and *Khanoum* that. I won't, you know. Just see: I give away everything I have for him. But, no, my health isn't enough, he wants my apartments too. Just because I'm not a *Qajar*..."

"*Madar*, stop!" Tahereh finally prevailed. "I'm just showing Nargess the house. No one is going to take your quarters. She wanted to see where you lived."

"And give you my love, Ashraf *Khanoum*," Nargess said.

Ashraf *Khanoum* exhaled a suspicious grunt: "Hmmmph!" She settled herself into her pillow like a pug dog – a very large pug dog – a very large and disquieted pug dog. "Hmmmph!" she said again, apparently debating the matter with herself, calming down a bit, wrinkling her nose. "Well, of course she wanted to see my apartments. Who could blame her?" She fanned herself with the Chinese silk fan and thought to herself. Then she spoke again: "But, I'm not going to give them up. She can wait her turn – like anybody else. When I'm dead and gone..."

Nargess took to her bed the rest of the day and refused to come out. She left Tajmah to her fate.

The third sentence she spoke to her new husband in private was, "I'm still sick."

"Of course," he said. He sat cross-legged on the pillow opposite her. He held his hands bridged with his fingertips.

Nargess stood and turned her back towards Abrahim, letting him know it was time for him to let her leave.

He rose and placed his hand on the brass doorknob. "You mustn't make Mother angry," he said. "God didn't give me three wives to make trouble for me."

After Nargess had been sick for a full two weeks, Abrahim understood, and he apologized for his family. He seemed polished in the endeavor.

"Please, my pretty, they want to make amends," he said with a well-practiced tone, hanging his head by her sick bed. "I think they're feeling a bit guilty for having made Mother angry with you."

"I thought it was my fault."

"They were worried I would forget about them." His voice was quiet, smooth, soothing. He spoke with such confidence. "Surely you understand. Patience..."

"Then let them have the cellar," she said, holding up her hand and gesturing to the walls of her sitting room where the mildew was already staining the fresh paint. "See how patient they will be."

Abrahim rose and shrugged. He extended his hand to her. She refused it and remained seated.

"I'll redecorate..." He let out a long, sad, sigh of resignation. "O.K., tell me which one to move," he said guiltily, "and I will switch your place with hers."

Nargess reddened. She rose to her feet, with her head bowed. But, she refused Abrahim's hand. She knew that he knew that she could not accept that offer.

"Come," he said, crooking her elbow with his. "They have a special present for you. The five of them put in together for it. I don't know how they thought of it. We will all take tea in the garden."

The rear salon on the ground floor, where Ashraf *Khanoum*, Tahereh, Afsar, Golnar and Masumay waited, was deathly silent. The silence of guilt, Nargess thought. Abrahim stepped into this minefield with the levity of a ballet dancer, albeit with the physique of an aged and overweight wrestler. Everyone tried to pretend nothing was amiss.

"Nargess, dear," Tahereh spoke first. "Do join us for tea."

Feeling faint, Nargess looked around and saw no preparations, no samovar, no glasses, just a brightly wrapped box.

"We wanted for all of us to get you something special," Tahereh continued, indicating the brightly wrapped box. "We really didn't welcome you very well. We wanted to make up for that." She took Nargess hand and led her to the brightly wrapped present.

Nargess began to gush inwardly at this apology. Delivered before Abrahim and Ashraf *Khanoum*, it must be heartfelt. She began to choke with emotion. But, as she peeled the wrapping paper from the box, which turned out to be a shipping crate, her hands began to tremble. No, she must be mistaken. Protruding from the mounds of straw within the crate were lumpy swatches of linen. She removed a few and placed them on the carpet. Each was about the size of a cantaloupe, irregularly shaped. They looked strangely familiar...

"We wanted to do it just right," Afsar, the other sister, said.

Perhaps it was just the same pawnbroker, Nargess thought. But, no, they were the same size – the same... Blood rushed to her temples. No...

"Open them, my dear," Abrahim said, pleased with the newly forming bonds of friendship he was harboring, the seeds of domestic harmony, marital bliss...

Almost gagging, and with her temples throbbing hotly, Nargess unwrapped her present.

"Oh Abrahim!" she cried. She burst into uncontrollable tears and fled the room. Behind her she left a thoroughly mystified husband, five of his closest female relatives, (each bursting with secret delight) and her grandmother's jeweled Czech tea set.

Queen of the House

A brahim's household overflowed with women he didn't want upset. Almost daily he laid before Nargess a minefield of sensitivities to be navigated, reminding Nargess that one of his sisters or the other suffered an unfortunate life, that he expected her to indulge them because they were husbandless, or their children difficult or they were old or sick or whatever. If it weren't one of his sisters, it was one of his other wives, to pity for being childless, or ill or lonely or old. He expected a big, happy family – demanded it – and if it was going to be assaulted by internal divisions, he didn't want to hear about them. He made it quite clear, or rather, his mother made it quite clear for him, that despite his affable disposition, his sagely clasped hands, his athletically broad, hunched shoulders, his smile as broad an elephant's tusk, he would rid the household of anyone who threatened the peace amongst the inhabitants within, or the peace amongst the extensive network of friends, relatives and neighbors he cultivated without. One misplaced step in the minefield could shred a marriage faster than Abrahim could say divorce.

In fact, it was Zahra who had informed Nargess on one of her frequent visits, that fifteen years earlier Abrahim had divorced Shireen, wife number three, for lying:

"Lying?" Nargess said, a bit shocked and still a bit tearful, alone in her mildewed quarters. "What does Abrahim think his wives and sisters do all day?" It was early in the marriage and she was still "sick" a lot. In fact, she was so often "sick" that Abrahim quipped, "Eh, poor me, my dear: it seems I wooed a wife and wed an illness." He was not smiling.

"But, this was different," Zahra said. "This was serious – worse than hurtful. Shireen heard from her seamstress that she had heard from a friend of hers who was her friend Monir's maid that Monir was always at the doctor's, but – well, never sick. Well, Monir wasn't such a close friend, after all: she had a bigger house, and since her husband had acquired a ministry position she had not once visited Shireen. Putting on airs! So Shireen was quite happy to let the whole world know how it is with women of a certain age and their doctors, after all. Well, I mean, well – Monir wasn't getting what she needed at home, so..."

"Lying?" Nargess said again. "He divorced her for lying? What's the difference between lying and gossiping, pray tell? At least half the time..."

"Three times to the wind: 'I divorce you.' And that's as much as she took with herself. I tell you, he threw her out and paid her fare home and that was it! Because it was worse than gossip lies. It did serious harm – irreparable harm."

Though legal according to religious law, such harsh terms for a divorce were rare and only invoked for the worst, most flagrant, most shocking infidelities – those, of course, that fell short of warranting stoning. Nargess considered such spiteful gossip lies to be beneath her, but she quaked at the cruelty – especially coming from a man whom she had thought to be of such gentle temperament. Nargess shuddered.

Noticing the shudder, Zahra said, "Nay, Nargess, dear, he would never do that to you. You are too pure."

But, Nargess knew she would have to tread lightly around the gossiping – there being such a fine line between gossip and lies. To be safe, she should not mention Afsar's crippled children or Golnar's and Masumay's barrenness, or Tahereh's two divorces. And with stoic silence she would have to recover alone from the gift of her grandmother's tea set and the constant, nagging question of how Abrahim's wives and sisters had found out about it and what they would do next. And on this shaky ground, in the fertile patches between buried mines that could shred a foot or a marriage, Nargess watched helplessly while the wives and sisters of Abrahim e'Kashani doggedly sowed the seeds of her destruction.

Abrahim's start in life had been a shaky one. His mother had enjoyed his gentle demeanor as a child, but suffered great distress to see it blossom into laziness. So she convinced Abrahim's father to enroll him in the Tehran Military Cadet College. In addition to learning how to hold his opium, he did acquire some undeniable discipline, but at every opportunity he would flee home clutching a battered leather valise and his toothbrush, smelling of vodka and opium. His mother would great him with a sob, fanning her sweaty brow with the rectangular fan of woven straw. The violence of recent anti-government riots about the country protesting Muzzafar-edin Shah's continuation of his father's dissolute practices convinced Abrahim's mother of the inadvisability of a military career toughening Abrahim into a man. But, as his only distinguishing talent seemed to be the consumption of large quantities of opium and, increasingly, vodka, with no untoward effects, the alternatives seemed limited. She begged her daughter, Tahereh, to take him in. Tahereh was only a year older than Abrahim, but she was married to a manor lord in Mazandaran, who was a decade their senior, and she became like a mother to him. At Tahereh's pleading, and against his better judgment, her husband gave Abrahim a job managing his lands. Abrahim continued to flee home to his mother, as before (still drunk, but minus the toothbrush), but after a year or so he settled in to his new career under his brother in law and to everyone's surprise, prospered. Even more surprising, he moderated his drinking to a cocktail (or three) per night –a worrisome habit still, but at least trending in a wholesome direction. True, he did trade in the vice of excessive alcohol consumption for gambling; and true, he did subsidize his new vice with periodic loans from his brother in law, but the debt was mounting tolerably slowly and only caused an occasional row between Tahereh and her husband – nothing that would require his departure. The untimely death of Abrahim's father upset this happy equilibrium. Abrahim reverted to heavy drinking and took up with a crowd of ne'er do well locals. Warned by the local gendarmes not to socialize with these ruffians, he was elsewhere when they picked a fight with a local hashish dealer and stabbed him to death. Tahereh and Abrahim heard the news that very same evening, when one of the perpetrators sought refuge in their barn. Tahereh understood local justice and immediately (within minutes, actually) bundled Abrahim off to Tehran, knowing that if he remained in Mazandaran, he would be arrested and imprisoned for at least a year or two before his innocence would be determined, if ever. Tahereh's husband refused to send support to Abrahim because he too feared local justice, so Tahereh, eight months pregnant with her first child, ignited a conflagration of tongue wagging by following Abrahim to Tehran, where she calculated she could better pawn her trousseau to help Abrahim set himself up in their mother's old house, which would have to be sold to pay the father's debts, if something weren't done soon. Tahereh went into early labor when the second pawnbroker confirmed the opinion of the first, that only about a third of the trousseau was real, the rest being merely artful. The money was enough to set Abrahim up in the business of building houses, at which he proved surprisingly adept, but not enough to soothe Tahereh's rage, the extent of which she unwisely conveyed to her husband. Unsurprisingly, in her absence, her husband divorced her (yes, three times to the wind: "I divorce you!") and sent notice, after which he honored his paternal responsibilities by removing to Paris with a cabaret singer barely half his age. Tahereh's life seemed doomed when her first son subsequently died of smallpox. Fortunately, Abrahim enjoyed rapid success in the house building business, and he remained forever grateful to his sister, supporting her until she eventually remarried. She returned to live with him when husband number two divorced her when he discovered, after the birth of their son, Javad, that husband number one had deserted her for a cabaret singer.

Afsar, Abrahim's half sister, had joined Abrahim's household after the death of her husband had left her penniless. Years earlier she had enjoyed the sky-blue days of a blessed marriage to her first cousin. They lived in the old Safavid capital of Isfahan, with his family. It was beautiful. The days were sunny. The air clear. In the breezy evenings they would wander the ancient city, strolling hand in hand along the crystal water channels that coursed along the paved streets. Above them shone the glistening domes of jeweled turquoise. They were surrounded by friends and family and laughter and beauty. Then, about a dozen years ago, she had given birth to a boy afflicted by a congenital spinal condition that led to infection and early death. A family row erupted. Afsar's family blamed the husband's side for the faulty blood. The husband's family blamed the wife's. Although first cousin marriages were traditionally approved, even encouraged, the doctors blamed a consanguineous marriage. Husband blamed wife. Wife blamed husband. And on top of the blame came dire warnings from doctors and family alike not to conceive again. But, they desperately wanted children. This time Afsar gave birth to twins. As doctors and detractors had prophesied, these twins were also afflicted. In sending two, each family pointed out, God had made a particularly blunt statement. This time, by benefit of early diagnosis, the condition left the children litter-bound and incontinent, but alive. Shortly afterwards the husband died, reportedly of typhus, and Afsar inherited his tile factory in Isfahan. When her brother in law offered to manage her share for her, she temporized until she finally calculated she could live in Tehran, closer to her family. Within a year, the brother in law reported "complications," couched in the vaguest of terms and in missives of increasing length and dwindling frequency. Communications gradually diminished, then disappeared, taking the monthly remittances with them. From time to time nosy relatives, returned from Isfahan, would remark upon the continued prosperity of Afsar's brother in law. Afsar would answer, with feigned nonchalance, "Poor him, he does his best. It's so hard to keep up appearances." "Hmmph!" the nosy relative would respond. "Would that God should grant us all such suffering!" Records being what they were and Afsar being a woman, there was no hope of recovering her inheritance. But, she clung to the belief that her brother in law would someday honor his promises and resurrect the remittances. In the meantime, she ignored the persistent rumors that her husband's death had been suicide over the shame of crippled children, and her brother in law's prosperity the price of keeping it secret.

In her youth, Afsar had been beautiful, with striking cheekbones and almond eyes. The last dozen years had reduced her to a moldy relic. She walked slowly, with a painful back. She developed an old woman's cauliflower breasts that seemed to unbalance her, requiring her to stiffen her back to remain upright. Shyly she knitted away her gray days, coughing fraily beside the creaking litters of her twins, smelling faintly of their urine, leaping to her feet at the sound of the postman's bicycle bell, and tilting sadly back upstairs to her apartments when the mail failed to deliver solace or remittance, which it continued remorselessly to do. Her eyes became permanently red and swollen, like harvest moons. There were rumors of a brief relationship with a distant cousin who was a department manager in the city postal service. The two had met when she braved the local bureaucracy to enquire after the fate of the numerous letters and remittances from Isfahan that she was convinced they were continually misdirecting or otherwise failing to deliver. Some in the household reckoned her second visit to the post office was the first time in ten years she had washed herself completely free of the scent of her children. She hired a car and driver to take her to the central post office and arrived back late in the evening, bleary eyed and disheveled. She slept till noon of the following day. But, on subsequent visits she grew careless and overlooked the possibility that her enamored might find distasteful the clinging aroma of her children, as she merely masked it hurriedly with rosewater on the way out the door. The visits to the post office dwindled in duration and frequency. Soon they were downright perfunctory and she returned as primly coiffed as when she had departed. Eventually the visits ceased, replaced by long, wistful sighs exhaled into oblivion over letters that never arrived. Abrahim supported Afsar willingly, and without resentment, but never with the sense of indebtedness he bore towards Tahereh, who was more his mother than Ashraf *Khanoum.*

The two wives, Masumay (number one) and Golnar (number two), led lives much like Afsar's, but with no hopes of mail (or its absence thereof) to sadden their days and no children to scent their romantic longings with urine vapors. In Nargess's eyes they seemed more like grandmothers than wives. For all the physical intimacy they commanded from Abrahim (according to Tahereh), Nargess's regard was rather more accurate than otherwise.

Abrahim was the sole oasis of masculinity in this feminine desert. From dawn to dusk, sisters and aunts collected, first in one sitting room, then in another, then in the receiving room downstairs, then in another private sitting room, endlessly knitting, embroidering, sewing, gossiping, smoking water pipes, directing servants to prepare *polo* for dinner, and sharing tea and light housework – an occasional dusting here, an occasional rearranging of furniture or tea services there, or bringing tea to Abrahim in the afternoon. Daily, Abrahim's sisters, aunts and female cousins migrated about the house like wandering Bedouins – though, being of a sensible nature, they generally camped with only one wife at a time.

Almost every blossom of an utterance in this desert burst from atop a spiny cactus.

When Tahereh expressed sadness for her half sister Afsar's having to suffer the odor of her crippled children because she constantly attended them, everyone understood it to mean, "She really ought to have them washed." Were she to say that they needed washing, it would be interpreted to mean that Afsar had brought it upon herself anyway.

When Afsar voiced admiration that Tahereh's son, Javad, entertained himself alone for so long, she actually meant, either, "It looks like he's the type not to have many friends – like his mother," or "He's a bit girlish, don't you think?" Of course, "He's the image of his father," would have drawn blood.

Once, when Nargess seemed to be in bright spirits, one of the four, (it was Tahereh, but could just as well have been any one of the others), said, "Oh Nargess, dear. It's so good to see you blossom so." She reached forward and touched her forearm affectionately. "It must have been so hard, losing your favorite cousin – and that wife of his, the one he brought back from Paris, what was her name? And then his father only a year later, and then…" Her voice trailed off. The part she omitted was the pernicious one, namely that she had lost her fortune and come to Abrahim's household barefoot. And, of course, there was the unstated scandal of having been widowed by a suicide. It was all delivered disguised as genuine affection, so Nargess could say nothing. The other women who were present knitted on furiously, their heads bowed closely over their work, seemingly oblivious to the attack. But, they relished the sport. More than Bedouins, they resembled geese, feeding tirelessly on every morsel of sadness or blame or weakness that appeared on the well-trod ground for their beaks to peck. The less charitable – or more honest – would describe them as vultures.

Nargess knew God did not want her to stoop to the level of pecking back at these women. After all, they were beyond child bearing and thus stuck with their meager lots. And they were capable of genuine kindness at times. When Nargess was bedridden with a winter fever, even Tahereh would spend nights mopping her brow, feeding her chicken soup, preparing her tea and making eucalyptus vapors, not trusting the competence of the servants. But, as the youngest wife, and one from a respectable family, Nargess was *de facto* (if not *de jure*) head wife and it was expected of her to maintain her position.

She answered Tahereh atonally, as if she were a librarian reading an entry from an encyclopedia to a school child or a mother reading a bed time story to her child, nodding off to sleep herself, "Vali's wife was named Rakshandeh," she said, not missing a stitch of her embroidering. "I heard she was a cabaret singer." She knew this would wound Tahereh by reminding her of her own usurper.

But, Tahereh was not one to quit the field easily: "It was a poisoning, wasn't it?" she said, swaying her torso lithely but uttering the phrases with an atonality to rival Nargess's. To avoid the humiliation of admitting he could not identify, let alone punish, the poisoner, War Minister had spread the story that Vali had died of a stomach infection. Tahereh knew that even these several years after War Minister's death, this secret would be a shame. After all, everyone could see that Nargess had arrived in Abrahim's household more possessed of attitude than assets.

Nargess remained silent, pricking her own needle through the soft mesh of the cotton, realizing the exchange was in danger of growing vicious and not wanting a knock down, drag out, blood scratching cat fight.

But, Tahereh sensed the advantage and went for the jugular: "They never did figure out who did it, did they," she said. And then she switched to a peculiar lilting voice: "I wonder how they knew how to get to him?"

It was this last statement, delivered with the peculiar, high-pitched lilt that made Nargess shudder. Tahereh was implying there had been a traitor in War Minister's household, and if there had been someone who made his enemies privy to his son's whereabouts, then there must have been someone who made them privy to Nargess's reduced circumstances and her tenuous attachment to a priceless, antique Czech tea set. Oh, how did Abrahim's wives know how to cast such hurt and at the same time avoid his punishment? They must to a woman have had brilliant, legal minds, knowing which offense did cross the line and which did not. And how could Tahereh have a connection with Rakshandeh?

"I really wouldn't know," Nargess said, trying hard to speak blandly.

Tahereh decided to twist the knife: "I hear – what's her name? – yes, Rakshandeh – married a wealthy German businessman. Imagine that! All that way from nothing."

Ashraf *Khanoum* maneuvered more directly. She would collapse on a sitting pillow like a camel, all knobby knees and elbows and groaning sounds like collapsing bagpipes. Occasionally she released gas in an embarrassing muffle that everyone pretended not to notice. Then she would lean towards Nargess and spread before the entire gaggle, "You're not getting any younger, you know." Then, by way of apologizing, she would fan her neck, snap shut her Chinese red silk fan and add, "Wait till you're my age, my dear!"

In short, it was a life not much different for Nargess than it had been in War Minister's palace compound, except that the rooms were narrower, the ceilings lower, the servants scarcer, and poetry went unmentioned (except for fortune telling). As for the pecking order, Nargess was rather nearer the bottom than the top.

The one note of sweetness among the dependents of Abrahim was Tahereh's six-year-old boy, Javad. He was curious as to who this interloper might be, this mother who had arrived with a baby daughter, a brilliantly festooned personal guard in a giant bear hat – and a lot of fuss. In the afternoons, after his nap, he would wander into her rooms, seat himself at her feet, while she took tea, and stare. If he had forgotten to beg his mother for some rock candy before visiting the new *Khanoum*, Nargess, he would remain silent and slack-jawed until Nargess pinched his cheek affectionately and gave him a piece herself. Nargess began giving him half glasses of tea. She enjoyed the innocent company, the attention of someone who had no ill intentions, no agenda.

"You must come to me often, my handsome nephew," she said one day. "Every day. You will bring me good luck and someday I will have a son like you and you can teach him big brother things." Then, holding his face gently in both her hands, she quoted a poem by Hafez:

> Your face lifts the lights of a Kingdom,
> Your mind hides All Knowing.
> Whoever your wisdom doubts,
> Will the hen and fish amuse.
>
> If bazaar of man cheats,
> The Eagle leads to rule.
> If sky be rent asunder,
> You restore it to your plan,
>
> So well-written is your fate.
> Give your life,
> It is for man's glory.
> Dig your mind,
> The beauty-red rubies,
> From flaxen field emerge...
>
> Let the porter bring from the springs of ruins,
> Water to cleanse our mien anew.

Javad stared back at her unknowingly, too young to fully understand the words. But, he understood well enough, for he put his arms around her, hugged her, and kissed her on the cheek.

When he left, Nargess wiped a tear from her eye.

The hostile gift of her own jeweled tea set had stung Nargess and forced her into a permanent retreat that lasted years. Abrahim's wives and sisters knew that if Nargess complained to Abrahim about the tea set, she would humiliate herself, appearing whiny and petulant. And those women knew it would be an unceasing torment to Nargess not only to have suffered the insult, but also to be able to say nothing about it, to constantly have to wonder how they knew about it in the first place and to forever fear what they could or would do next, should it so please them. The wives never voiced the sentiment openly, even among themselves, but secretly each hoped this would drive a wedge between Abrahim and Nargess, maybe even big enough to delay consummation of the marriage for a couple of years and take Nargess past the age of child bearing. The stakes were high. The sisters remained torn between wanting their brother to have a male child of his own, and fearing for the lot of themselves and their own children if he did. As for Ashraf *Khanoum*, she just wanted respect. As long as Nargess cloistered herself in devotions, they all felt safe.

Nargess endured as she had accepted the guilt God had cast down upon her earlier in War Minister's death: she withdrew and prayed. Morning, noon and night she prayed –so much that she would become dizzy upon standing and had to hold onto a wall or a doorframe when she rose to her feet. She prayed for herself. She prayed for God to deliver her tormentors from their own demons. She prayed for the poor. She prayed for the sick. She prayed to know the identity of her betrayers, who had told Tahereh about her tea set before she had even contracted to marry Abrahim, who had helped General Z. discover even the most minute of War Minister's holdings, who had led the poisoner to Vali on his hunting trip, who had done who knows what else to her. Soon the repetitive chants comforted, as they had before. They became as the sound of her own pulse – a steady, measured swell and recover, a river of escape from the temporal into the spiritual, a comforting mantle of guilt and suffering.

❦

"Oh Zahra, I know she's behind it – that awful Rakshandeh!" Nargess confided to her friend in the first months of her marriage. "Who else could have told them about the tea set? And who else would have wanted to? And now they're just smirking at me, bowing before me so Abrahim can see, and then laughing about me in their bedrooms. And Abrahim's angry that I won't prepare them tea and that just makes them happier. Anything for peace he wants – just nothing to upset his day. Oh, they're all so mean! Don't they have anything better to do? And now they're having Tajmah sweep carpets for them. She's not even three – Like she's a peasant – Oh, what can I do to put a stop to all this, Zahra dear? It's just so tiresome."

Nargess looked into her friend's alert, brown eyes, searching for an answer.

"Nargess, dear," Zahra said, her hands primly in her lap, "A wife's duty is to her husband first. All else she must endure. It's God's want that…"

Nargess interrupted with a failing sigh, like collapsing bellows. Was no one going to take her side? "But, what's she going to do next," she said, "that Rakshandeh: I know she did her husband Vali in – she's a Russian spy, you know – They wanted to get War Minister's oil. That's why they killed him – Get rid of the son to weaken the father…"

"But, I thought it was Amir e'Doleh," Zahra said, "for humiliating his daughter – and War Minister had already lost the oil concession to the government ten years earlier – I don't think anyone needed to do anything to get his oil, anymore than…"

"What? Oh – Whatever! As if we'll ever know. They always see to that…"

"Nargess, dear, you're the wife of Abrahim e'Kashani, now, not War Minister."

Nargess paused, asking herself what Zahra meant by this. Did she mean she was expecting too much? Or that she was being arrogant? Could Zahra be trying to bring her down? She felt her tongue thicken in her throat, but then she pushed the thought from her mind. No, not Zahra.

"Zahra, dear, could you have Mansour make inquiries? Someone must know."

"Inquiries about what?"

"About how that pawnbroker knew I had my tea set. About how that Tahereh knew about the tea set. About Rakshandeh, and who's she connected with."

Zahra paused. For a moment Nargess thought her friend seemed shaken. Then Zahra eyed the door, as if to make sure it were fully closed. Then she eyed the window, as if to make sure it were fully closed too. "You hadn't heard?"

"Heard? Heard what?"

"Don't tell a soul." She leaned forward conspiratorially and whispered: "Rakshandeh had a temporary marriage with Karim Mirza."

"Ugh!" Nargess said. "Oh, Zahra, how vulgar. I'm so glad I didn't marry him. Imagine competing with h… that! Oh, ugh!"

"Oh, I know what you mean. That awful witch – you know, she was the one who told him about your elbows."

"My elbows? But, Zahra, you had always said she had married a German businessman. Are they still married? How did Rakshandeh know. I never bathed with her. I never bathed with anyone…"

Zahra looked at Nargess blankly before answering: "Well – No, they were just married a month."

"Oh, Zahra, what can I do in this household? There's an army of them and just one me and I have nothing to defend myself with."

"You're the head wife, now," Zahra said. "It doesn't matter if you're the third or the first, you're the young one. You're the one with the future. You have to stand on your word."

"Please ask Mansour – I don't even know how Rakshandeh and Tahereh know each other."

"They don't know each other – I don't think – Stand on your word, Nargess, dear. Do that and they will collapse like paper bags in the rain. Rakshandeh: pshaw! She can make all the schemes she wants. There's nothing she can do to you now."

"Oh bless you, Zahra," Nargess said. "What would I do without you? One day you'll be able to come here and live with me. I promise you. Then you can take care of me for ever."

☙

Abrahim had only just tolerated the arrival of Gholam Ali with Nargess. He had started to explain his house was already filled with as many servants as it could handle, and, furthermore, he scarcely had need of a eunuch to guard such an aged harem. Nargess burst into tears at this, which led him to apologize profusely. The endeavor seemed heartfelt, if well practiced. But, also, he explained, having completed his apology, in his house Gholam Ali would look a bit silly in his brass studded, bear-hatted uniform with a rifle strapped to his back. The fatuity of this last objection being immediately obvious even to Abrahim, he acquiesced in a protracted sigh. "OK, my dear. He can dress like the other servants and live in the servants quarters."

But, Gholam Ali resented the rescission of his recent sartorial splendor. And he resented that no one listened to his complaints that he should not be relegated to a dormitory for common servants. He was head eunuch, after all! And, though he could not say it, he had saved his mistress from humiliation – and on more than one occasion. So, off duty he would divest himself of the black pantaloons and cloth shoes, don his splendid uniform, crown himself with the giant bear hat and seat himself alone on the chair outside the door to his room. Straight backed and imperious, he refused to speak to the other servants. He chanted to himself recitations from the passion play of the Imam Hossein, betrayed by his own, blessed victim of suffering and betrayal. He soon grasped that his reduced status derived from the meager power his mistress commanded at the hands of jealous rivals. So there was no one he could approach to complain. For weeks he wrestled with his quandary: Nargess didn't have the power to provide him the equivalent of the two private rooms that used to be his in War Minister's mansion; Tahereh and the other women had the power he needed, but wanted him to stay right where he was – which was miserable. His only amusement in his off hours was to let the young Javad play with his great bear hat.

At first Gholam Ali limited his displeasure to discretely, but audibly, passing gas before individual members of Abrahim's family, but only when his mistress and everyone else was beyond earshot. Without simultaneous witnesses the act was too embarrassing to permit mention and too egregious to command punishment. But, many a face turned beet red at the behest of Gholam Ali's anus. Nargess remained unaware of his subversive tendencies until later, when she harbored the nagging suspicion that he was expressing his displeasure with Abrahim's household by anonymously flinging large rocks over the wall into Abrahim's gardens.

The first of the flying rocks arrived on a balmy summer evening, while the family was having mint and cucumber *sharbat* in the wisteria-draped pergola in the back of their summer house near Bridge Over Tajreesh. A large crash brought the entire family stampeding to the front. They feared a servant had fallen from a ladder or a rooftop and had broken a leg or snapped a neck.

But, all they found was Gholam Ali presiding over the small, collapsed garden shed, the roof of which had been crushed in by a sizeable, elongated quartz boulder. Turning from staring at the crushed shed and the protruding bristle of rake handles and hoes, Gholam Ali cast a sheepish glance at the onrushing family and, as if on cue, raced to the garden door. He thrust it open, stepped half way into the street, looked right and left and then shook his fist high in the air and cursed, "Don't you come back, now! Hear?"

A moment later Abrahim drew abreast of Gholam Ali.

"Eh!" Gholam Ali said. "He's fast, that one."

Abrahim peered up and down the alley, but found it empty. Towering over Gholam Ali as a mountain over a foothill, Abrahim eyed him in mute challenge. But, Gholam Ali shrugged in mute denial.

The event repeated at intervals throughout the rest of the summer. Abrahim set up watches from time to time, but it always seemed that a day or two after Abrahim would cancel the watch, another boulder would fly through the air and land in the garden, though only occasionally finding an object of sufficient size to make a noticeable noise. The last occurrence surprised a gardener pruning the roses, causing him to let out a fearful whelp. Immediately came curses outside the wall from Gholam Ali, and moments later Abrahim found him there, still shaking his fist and throwing dirt at a long gone assailant.

"Who is he?" Abrahim demanded.

"Gholam Ali didn't see his face, master."

"Look here," Abrahim said, pointing down the walled street, "nothing but walls. Where did he go? Whose house?"

"Gholam Ali gave him a good scare this time," Gholam Ali said. "He won't be back. No sir! Ruin our household."

The announcement of Nargess's pregnancy put a halt to concerns about boulders mysteriously flying over Abrahim's wall and crashing into his garden, and it otherwise put to route the hordes emboldened by Nargess's impoverishment. In the face of her compromised position in Abrahim's household, the need for a male child to solidify power had dawned on Nargess only slowly, and then mostly as a sense of duty. She had decided it was time to stop being sick and start begetting. This had been neither an understanding, nor a realization, nor – God forbid – a calculation of the obvious equation. At least not on her part. It was an expectation, as accepted as morning prayers, as natural as performing ablutions. An almost passive pilgrimage, one might say. Besides, alternative recreation was scarce.

Nargess was too involved in praying to enjoy a sense of victory from her condition. But, she attributed the resulting deep sense of peace to her intense devotions: God had answered her. The arrival of a stillborn child did foster a gleeful, clandestine cackling over the lessening likelihood of her ability to produce a male heir, but the arrival of a healthy male child, Rasheed, two years later, silenced the smoldering unrest.

Nargess allowed Javad to see the new baby when she was well enough recovered from the delivery to readmit him for afternoon tea. But, she was surprised to see the now ten-year-old Javad's chin quiver when he parted the silk netting around baby Rasheed's crib.

"Nay, Javad, dear," she said, with an understanding voice. "Your face still lifts the lights of a kingdom - a special kingdom."

Javad's quivering chin turned to a beaming smile and he let the netting fall back into place.

"Come, Javad, dear. I heard you learned to play chess. You must teach me. We will surprise them – all of them. You and me together."

She felt a part of the family, now – no longer an intruder.

Nargess knew God had answered her prayers when she gave birth to a daughter, Pari, three years after Rasheed. Two children by Abrahim, including a boy, seemed to remove all possible challenge to Nargess. When Abrahim purchased his neighbor's house, knocked down the intervening wall and built a new wing for Nargess and her children, with apartments for Nargess on the third floor, Nargess felt a sense of holy bliss, which she insisted Abrahim honor by building three private pools for her ablutions. They were strictly for her personal use, in her personal garden in her new, personal courtyard below. Tahereh, Afsar, Golnar and Masumay, pool-less, seethed behind smiles of praise and congratulations, for even just a lone male heir was essentially a checkmate (lit. *shah maht*, similar to shah *morte*, hence shah death), and it was hard to inveigh against someone so outwardly devout, so obviously blessed. But, they could always hope for a draw. Ashraf *Khanoum* simply beamed in contentment to witness her son's enlarging family and his enjoyment at tossing a soccer ball against the feet of his first male child. "My!" she would say. "Oh, my!" Then she would continue: "He'll be shah, some day – that Rasheed. Count on it: He will show you how Kashani blood runs."

Abrahim, of course, was the most delighted of all. At tea he would seat himself beside his mother on the bolster and lean his head on her shoulder. She would tap his shoulder. Then she would bless him and tell him how wonderful he was and he would close his eyes and, with broad shoulders, smile.

With a new wing all her own and two children by Abrahim, Nargess smiled too. She wondered if she should stop worrying about Rakshandeh and her schemes and plots. Mansour's inquiries had come to naught. It seemed that she could no longer touch Nargess.

Sadly, it would be the ultimate and unintended consequences of Reza Khan Shah's modernization decrees that would reverse the course of the chess game that had swung in Nargess's favor. Inspired with a national pride in Iran's 2500 year history as a polity, Reza Khan Shah shared with his countrymen a sense of shame for the two millennia of subjugation by foreign powers that succeeded Darius and Cyrus. Most recently it was the British and the Russians, whom the Shah tried to balance by overtures to the Germans. Foreign interest in Iran focused on oil as early as 1901, when Iran granted the British a mere 600 acre concession with a contract that guaranteed Iran a significant share of the oil profits. Following the discovery of oil in 1904, the British ignored their obligations. They hired Persians only into menial positions in the rapidly expanding APOC and cloaked their profits with hidden accounting tricks and fraudulent practices blatant enough to warm the cockles of a financier's heart. By the 1930's the chicanery had advanced to a level shameful even by the standards of an Armenian rug merchant. Reza Khan Shah sought an antidote to the competing Russians and British in bestowing upon his citizenry the imprimatur of modernity: In 1935 he changed the country's name from the biblical "Persia" to "Iran", to invoke the more ancient, Aryan heritage. In the same year he banned men from wearing traditional frock coats and fez caps, in favor of Western garb. But, even adopting Western style hats was not without its perils. The first time the Shah's ministers greeted him publicly after his decree that Western hats only would be worn, there had been a mad rush among the hat makers to churn out British style top hats for ministers. The hatters worked from photographs. They shaped the hats out of metal, which they then covered with soot – the only medium they knew could achieve such a deep, rich, unfathomable black. The reception was outdoors. It rained. The soot washed off the ministers' hats, stained their faces, smirched their starched white shirts, their faces. Furious, the Shah marched along the line of domestic dignitaries assembled to greet him at attention, and, swinging his walking stick, drummed each hat down with an ignominious bonk. Undeterred nevertheless, at the beginning of the following year he encouraged women to enter society beyond hearth and home, and banned them from wearing the chador in public. Police who found women in public wearing traditional garb were ordered to beat the offenders and strip them of the anachronistic outer garment on the spot. Many women welcomed the new found freedoms. But, many others, including Nargess, recoiled. To them, appearing in public without a chador was as scandalous as baring their breasts at prayers. Having a chador removed on the street by a policeman was akin to being stripped naked, even though women wore a full set of clothes underneath. Nargess, and many women like her, chose to remain cloistered within the *andaroon*, rather than appear in public undressed. Consequently, she and women like her became ever more removed from society at large than the woman who welcomed the new freedoms. Nargess began to pepper her prayers of beneficence with invective against a godless, greedy and now shameless shah. While her withdrawal in prayer became increasingly bitter, Tahereh, Afsar, and to a lesser extent, Golnar and Masumay expanded their wanderings into the world outside. Here they could gossip and snipe, away from the spying eyes of servants and relatives. For insight into what was going on in the world, even at the level of family affairs, the women like Nargess, who stayed behind, became ever more dependent upon the women who didn't.

Confident in being the mother of Abrahim's only children, including a son, basking in the consequent ministrations of the entire family, and cloistered in the removed world of the *andaroon*, Nargess made the cardinal mistake of believing the news the other women brought to her. She even entertained with equanimity Tahereh's suggestion that her own son, Javad, might someday make a blessed match for Tajmah, a convenient four years his junior. Tahereh had recently been rebuffed in a similar overture to Mashdi Hossein's wife concerning their third daughter, who was Tajmah's age as well. Mashdi Hossein was their neighbor two blocks away. He was a prosperous shoe merchant at the *bazaar*, with serious political connections. Nargess pitied Tahereh for having suffered such an overt rejection. After all, inquiries at that age for a girl were considered rather tentative. The family of Mashdi Hossein could easily have responded indirectly, could have said all decisions will be made in good time, could even have said their younger daughter was unworthy of such a match or was so ornery they suspected they would have no say in the matter and would never think to inflict her on such a suitable mate. But, Mashdi Hossein's wife had responded with silence. Tahereh felt humiliated. It did not matter that her beloved son Javad was only twelve at the time. When Tahereh subsequently gave Nargess news of Haj'Ali, scion of a famously devout family, Nargess saw no reason to suspect treachery. It was a naïveté that would cost three families dearly.

The women were bathing together, taking turns plucking each other's facial hairs with twisted threads. Tahereh looked over her shoulder to make sure loose-lipped Ashraf *Khanoum* was out of earshot and leaned forward confidentially. "You must swear to tell no one," she whispered to Nargess and Afsar and Golnar and Masumay."

"Tahereh, dear," Golnar said. "What could it be?"

"Haj'Ali, I tell you – that most handsome young man: he's engaged to Mashdi Hossein's oldest daughter." Mashdi Hossein's wife, a soft, plump woman, with the gentle air of a family cat, had treated Nargess very kindly, mopping her brow through several winter fevers. Nargess felt indebted to the family, even though she found them a bit dull, and she retained her surprise at the bluntness with which they had recently rejected Tahereh's nuptial overtures. The older daughter was a supple-haired beauty, innocent, hardly old enough to have stopped playing with dolls, and as pious as the famous family she was about to marry. The upcoming union promised to unite two devout and respectable lines.

"So?" ventured Masumay. "This is no secret."

"It's a secret Haj'Ali has syphilis and won't tell his bride's family." Tahereh finished by lifting her eyebrows and tilting her head.

"No!" there was a collective gasp, lead by Nargess, who was so stunned she dropped her glass.

"Well, I'm not going to tell anyone about it," Tahereh said.

"Pray tell, how do you know?" said Golnar.

Tahereh shrugged and cocked her head. "A little birdie told me." She cast a demure, demi-smile that forced one of her cheeks to bulge and make a dimple.

"No," Nargess ventured. "Not Haj'Ali! He would not lie before God. Especially not to Mashdi Hossein's daughter! She's such a sweet, innocent young thing. God would not permit this..."

"God should choose a messenger, then," Tahereh interrupted. " – from among those whom He most trusts..." She stared at Nargess.

Silence fell as everyone stared at Nargess, who in turn was busy absorbing the spilled tea from the rusty-red geometric designs of the carpet with her handkerchief. Then Nargess stopped and returned the stares. Who could be closer to God than she?

"...Otherwise," Tahereh continued, "Mashdi Hossein's daughter... Well..." She lifted a hand to her shaking forehead in despair, declining to complete the thought.

But, Nargess completed it for her, silently contemplating in her own mind the oozing ulcers that would disfigure a beatific complexion, the black liquid eyes that would turn gray and opaque with blindness... Nargess ran from the room in tears and spent the next two days praying for Mashdi Hossein's daughter. How could God let this happen to such a pretty child?

On the second day, Tahereh let herself into Nargess's bedchamber while she prayed. Tahereh delighted Tajmah with a bag of raspberry sweets, which she doled out to the child one at a time, while she skipped around the room. Nargess declined to interrupt her prayers for Mashdi Hossein's daughter, but Tahereh delivered her message anyway: "It's all very well and good to pray, whatever it is that you are praying for. But, you can do something, you know. I mean *do* something. Surely you believe God means for us to have a hand in life..."

Nargess continued her prayers, periodically leaning forward to place her head upon the prayer stone. But, she lapsed into silence now.

"It wouldn't kill you," Tahereh continued. "If God hears you, he might very well ask you to intervene. Did you ever think of that?"

Nargess maintained her silent praying. Tahereh thrust the whole bag of sweets at Tajmah. "I suppose," she snapped, "that had your cousin Vali been more of a doer, he wouldn't have let them poison him. As far as I can see, your constant prayers are no more than self indulgence."

"Oh, Zahra, dear," Nargess said at their next meeting. "What shall I do? I can't be one to spread rumors." She shuddered at the memory of Rakshandeh and the invidious tales she had spread throughout War Minister's *andaroon*; shuddered at the thought of what Abrahim might do to her if he found out. Widowed by suicide and then divorced, without means, she would be shunned and reviled – despicable. On the other hand, she despaired at the endless dark secrets concealed in War Minister's suicide and Vali's untimely death, and in all the rest of her existence. War Minister's fate made sense: he knew the forces unleashed by a petty tyrant; knew that grasping sycophants would reduce him to beggary to puff up their breasts; knew he was a threat and consequently a target. But, Vali? There was a mystery! Had Amir e'Doleh really instructed his servants to poison Vali on the hunt, out of revenge for his slighted daughter? Had he bribed War Minister's servants to help? Or did the Shah arrange for the poisoning to undermine War Minister and reduce his proud carriage for the final sword thrust through tired shoulders? Both? Were the Russians taking revenge for a lost oil concession? The British removing a threat to a new one? All of these? And what did Tahereh mean by saying Vali let them poison him? How could she know anything? Long past the period of mourning, Nargess felt deeply afflicted with a wanting to know. But, the truth would never be uttered and seemed forever concealed in the dark realm of rumors and whispered secrets. Now Nargess beheld an opportunity to dispel the cruel hurt of secrecy and dishonesty that threatened a virginal innocence resembling her own.

"You must do what God wills," Zahra answered.

"And what is that, Zahra, dear? How will I know?"

"You will know, Nargess, dear. When God tells you, you will know."

Nargess took that to mean yes. She must tell Mashdi Hossein's wife. But, this was daunting. She couldn't just walk over to her and say her daughter was about to contract syphilis from her betrothed, Haj'Ali. The wedding was only weeks away. The mother would doubtless be fantastically busy with the wedding preparations. She would have no opportunity to invite her to her house, or visit hers amidst the hustle and bustle. She would have to waylay her on some pretext, out doors. But, Nargess felt uncomfortable leaving the house. To do so without a chador, or to risk having it publicly stripped from her by the gendarmerie, would mortify her. Based on some judicious spying afforded by Gholam Ali, Nargess arranged a "chance" encounter outside the *Mosque e'Sepahsalar*, which Nargess began with congratulations.

"Nargess, dear, it's so good to see you out. But, you should not look so troubled."

"Baleh," Nargess replied, circumspectly. She grasped her elbows and stared at the cobblestones in the street.

"I'm quite comfortable *sans* chador. It's not so awful. I'm a good deal your senior, you know, dear..."

"I bear a heavier burden," Nargess said sadly, still not looking up.

"Heavens, dear, what? You have wonderful children. Now is a time for rejoicing. Don't be silly! Are you ill?"

"Tell me, if you were given a secret in confidence, would you betray it?"

"Of course not."

"But, what if holding that secret could hurt someone?"

"Well, that *is* different. Ah, you are more devout than any other. You will know what to do, whatever it is. But, Nargess, dear, this is so strange. Enjoy God's blessings. Don't talk of secrets. They bring only unhappiness and worry."

Nargess forced a smile. "Yes, of course."

"Let's forget such talk now. Come help me fit my daughter's wedding dress." She grasped Nargess's elbow and led her to her house.

Nargess suffered the whole of an afternoon taking tea at the house of Mashdi Hossein, watching the seamstress and the mother fuss with the wedding gown. The gay, even bubbly innocence of the bride-to-be weighed heavily upon her as she saw herself the instrument of its imminent pustulous destruction. She could not bring herself to broach the unpleasant subject. Tears came to her eyes when Mashdi Hossein's daughter gave her warm goodbye kisses on each cheek, and then a deep hug, a hug worthy of a close friend or relative, a hug that let Nargess feel against her own bosom the petite bride's child-like breasts.

"You must make a decision," Zahra said when she next visited. "There are only two weeks left."

"Oh, Zahra, how can I?"

"But, how can you not?"

"That's what Tahereh says, and Golnar and Afsar and Masumay. They all insist I say something. But, why can't they do it? What's so special about me? Tahereh's the one who knows all about it. Why can't she? And what if Abrahim finds out? Oh, Zahra, he would have me beaten. He'd divorce me. What then? What would people think?"

"Have you talked to them about it? Abrahim would never punish you for speaking to save a life, especially the life of one so innocent and devout."

Nargess thought for a moment before answering. "Well, no, I haven't discussed it with them. But, it's obvious they expect me to be the one – I just don't understand why."

Zahra paused briefly. "Because only someone so good can be trusted with a message so hurtful, Nargess, dear. If it were I, I could only bear it were I to hear it from you."

Nargess buried her head in her friend's embrace, weeping. "Oh, Zahra, I don't want to hurt anyone. I just want to be left alone. Why can't they just leave me alone? I want to live my life in God and let my children walk in His way. I don't belong with all the sniping and the meanness."

Even Gholam Ali urged her: "Gholam Ali knows," he said.

"Knows what?" Nargess asked.

"Gholam Ali has friends. Haj'Ali Khan is sick. Bad sick. Big hush hush."

"Gholam Ali, why don't your friends tell Mashdi Hossein? Surely they would listen."

"Big trouble, *Khanoum*. Big trouble. Servants shouldn't know."

"You're sure, Gholam Ali? Absolutely sure?"

"Gholam Ali has good friends, *Khanoum*." He paused as if waiting for Nargess to ask him more. Then he continued: "Rakshandeh *Khanoum* is bad, *Khanoum*. Rakshandeh *Khanoum*'s servants – they tell all – they tell you hiding secret of bad sick from Mashdi Hossein Khan's family – you jealous – you want hurt…" Gholam Ali stopped in mid sentence at Nargess's blanching face.

Nargess said nothing, but she knew it, knew Rakshandeh would do anything to undermine her. But, now she had to act, lest everyone believe her ugly rumors.

Again, with Gholam Ali's reconnaissance, Nargess arranged an encounter. But, this time she dispensed with formalities. Without any greeting, she strode up to Mashdi Hossein's wife, grasped her by the elbows and looked deep into her eyes. She wondered if the woman thought her mad.

"Nargess, dear, what is it? Nargess – dear…"

Nargess spoke with a crackly voice, as if she suffered a cold: "I have to tell you. Please, I have to tell you, but don't tell anyone it came from me. Promise me you won't. Haj'Ali has the syphilis."

"What? What? Nargess? Wha…"

"Syphilis," Nargess said again. "Haj'Ali has syphilis!" She squeezed the elbows of Mashdi Hossein's wife. "You must believe me. Don't let him marry your daughter."

Nargess then released the mother's elbows abruptly, turned, and walked away. Her whole body trembled. Her knees wobbled like jelly. She had not been so nervous since the time she had confronted General Z. in War Minister's hall of mirrors. Once home, she refused to leave her chambers, and prayed for a solid week.

The warning seemed to have worked. Nothing more was said of the marriage of Haj'Ali and Mashdi Hossein's daughter, except that at the last minute the wedding had been canceled for reasons unstated, and the two families had become bitter enemies.

"Oh, Zahra," Nargess lamented the very day she heard the wedding had been canceled. "I hope I did the right thing. I couldn't bear to see that innocent young girl infected by that rake. And now they're avoiding me." She looked to her friend to reassure her once again. "I guess I can't blame them." But, to her complete surprise, she encountered an unsettling silence. Eventually she asked, "Zahra, dear, what is it?"

Zahra folded her hands in her lap and waited a moment, her head cocked to one side. Then she started squeezing one hand with the other. "Nargess, are you sure you were right about that– about the syphilis?"

"Zahra!" Nargess's heart skipped a beat. "Of course. No one would ever lie about something so serious. Even the servants knew." Her heart now raced and her face flushed as she again suffered Zahra's silence. "Zahra? Zahra, you said I should tell her."

Zahra released a sigh. "Indeed – I said you should do God's will..."

"Zahra, do you know something?"

"No. I haven't heard anything." Zahra paused; then continued, "I'm sure you were right."

Nargess's face flushed.

Now, whenever she took tea with Tahereh and the other women, Nargess trembled with fear. Any day she expected them to tell her it was a lie, that Tahereh had been mistaken, that she (Nargess) should have waited for someone else to tell, or for someone else to confirm the news before telling Mashdi Hossein's wife. Her sin would be unforgivable. The forces that swirled around her threatened to consume her in fire, drag her down to the level of a Rakshandeh. Then, even prayer would not save her. Had this been a trick planned all along by Tahereh? But, how could Gholam Ali have heard? Could Tahereh have bribed a servant to tell him?

"Strange," Abrahim muttered one evening as they were all seated on the floor for a dinner of lamb, lima beans, yoghurt and rice, "two doors down a marriage blessed by God vanishes and I hear nothing about it until after it's over." He peered up and down the length of the linen runner upon which the food was laid out.

Tahereh, Afsar, Golnar and Masumay concentrated hard on the food, each having suddenly developed a serious appetite, each surreptitiously trying to glimpse the reactions of the others. Nargess began to feel hot.

"I heard it was syphilis," Abrahim continued. He pretended disinterest, but Nargess knew he was prying. She pretended to choke on her food, to hide the reddening in her face. Her elbows scratched sorely against her gray chador and began to throb.

"Mashdi Hossein's daughter?" his mother, *Khanoum* Ashraf said, settling into her fluffy pillow. "Nonsense, dear, She's as close to god as holy can get. Here, dear," she now spoke to Nargess, "drink some water."

"Nay, Mother. Not Mashdi Hossein's daughter. Haj'Ali."

"Well, shame on him!" Ashraf *Khanoum* said. "That poor innocent girl!"

"Yes," Abrahim said. "Shame on him if he really has it."

"I thought you said he has the syphilis. Well, what is it? Does he or doesn't he?"

"I don't know," Abrahim said, "but I intend to find out."

"Well, if you don't know, why are you bringing it up now?"

"I'm bringing it up now, Mother, because I want to know who told Mashdi Hossein's wife that Haj'Ali has syphilis. – I have known Mashdi Hossein since we were children – Haj'Ali's father as well. We all played hide and seek in the stalls of the *Bazaar*. They loan me money for my business. Now Haj'Ali gets the syphilis and that's why they called off the wedding and no one tells me anything about it?" He put down his spoon and crossed his arms. "Something's not right here."

"Nonsense," his mother said. "They're always putting on airs anyway – pious this, pious that..."

"It's not nonsense. They would have told me. Why didn't they tell me?"

"Well, they did tell you, dear. You said it was the syphilis."

"I didn't say *they* told me."

"Well, somebody must have. Who was it?"

"Never you mind who it was."

"Well, if you're going to be so secretive about it, don't come to me with it."

"Because if they learned about it from anyone other than my family, they would have told me about it. That's why. What I can't figure out is how would any of you know? How would any of you even suspect he had syphilis?"

"Don't be silly, dear. I know nothing about it. And neither do any of us." She turned to Tahereh: "Do we, dear?"

"Nay, *Khanoum*," Tahereh said. "I haven't heard a thing."

Golnar now commented on the garlic she had pickled in vinegar seven years earlier, saying that it would probably be ready next summer. Afsar said it would take at least another five years and they had better start putting up some more for the future. The conversation then devolved to favored pickling techniques, favorite stalls in the *bazaar* and the ages of various children of various friends and then where they would take their next picnic in the mountains until finally Abrahim interrupted:

"Yes, that's all very well and good, but heaven help anyone who's been lying to me." His voice swelled like a giant balloon. "If I ever find they live under this roof I'll put a stop to it, I can tell you that! And don't think I won't find out. I'll ask Haj'Ali myself, if I have to. Their doctor is a good friend of mine. I'll ask him..."

"Oh Zahra," Nargess confided a few days later, "I know it's going to be a lie. That syphilis: Abrahim says it's not true. He's going to ask Haj'Ali's doctor. What am I going to do? What if Mashdi Hossein's wife tells Abrahim that I told her? I have to tell him. I have to tell him that Tahereh put me up to it."

"He'll be furious with you, Nargess, dear. That's no excuse – if you're wrong – he'll throw you out..."

"But, what shall I do, Zahra? – I can't do any more."

"Pray, dear. Pray that he never discovers the truth."

"But, she'll surely tell him – Mashdi Hossein's wife."

"Pray that she's too humiliated to tell him anything. Pray that he's too embarrassed to ask. Pray they're too embarrassed to admit they learned this from anyone else. If it's true, they look foolish for having to hear it from you. If it's not, they look foolish for believing you. That's your only hope."

"But, what if Tahereh tells? Or Golnar or Masumay?"

"Then Pray that Haj'Ali really has syphilis."

And Nargess did. For days she prayed and cowered in fear that some-one would tell Abrahim that she had been the one to tell Mashdi Hossein's wife; that Abrahim would thrust before her face a letter from Haj'Ali's doctor declaring him fit and healthy and uninfected; that the two families would despise her; that Abrahim would divorce her; or almost worse, that Tahereh and Golnar and Masumay would forever hold the secret over her and turn her into their chattel.

It was not long before Abrahim found out:

"I knew it!" he cried, throwing open the front door and storming into the front hallway on a bright spring afternoon, when the narcissus blossoms in the garden outside were at their yellow peak and the household doors and windows had been opened wide to admit the moist, earthen, sunlit smells of the season. "Pray that I never..."

"Abrahim!" Ashraf *Khanoum* yelled back. She grasped the carved walnut newel post at the second floor landing with a shaky, gnarled hand. "Abrahim, don't yell like that!" Using two hands to hold the railing, she ventured first one foot, then the other onto the uppermost step and began to work herself painfully down the dark, high-ceilinged stairwell to her distressed son. "At least if you're going to yell like a peasant, do it when the windows are closed."

"Who told Mashdi Hossein's family that Haj'Ali has syphilis?" Abrahim was still yelling. "It was a match blessed by God. If anyone ever proves any-thing – that we – that..."

"Well, it's a good thing they did," Ashraf *Khanoum* said with a harrumph. She stopped her treacherous climb down the stairs and fanned herself briefly while she spoke: "Haj'Ali's entirely too full of himself anyway – if you ask me."

By this point, the other women had assembled, Nargess from the garden in back of the house, the other four from their quarters upstairs. Abrahim raised his arms and looked up at the second floor landing, where Golnar and Tahereh and Masumay and Afsar had congregated in conspiratorial silence.

"Well?" he said angrily.

Ashraf *Khanoum*, resumed her climb down the stairs. She blew air through her lips, making them flap once, like a horse. "What makes you think any of us knows anything about it? I've heard what you've heard…" She stopped speaking in mid sentence but continued her painful crawl down the stairs.

Golnar and Tahereh and Afsar and Masumay stood awkwardly together on the second floor landing. Nargess, at the foot of the stairs, folded her arms and held her elbows with her hands. Except for the creaking of the stairs as Ashraf *Khanoum* worked her way down, there was complete silence. Nargess was afraid to look at Tahereh, lest Abrahim discern her complicity. She presented to him a blank, questioning face and drew relief from the fact that he only looked up the stairs at the women on the landing, not at her.

Abrahim let his arms drop, as if in defeat. But, he still spoke with anger in his voice: "No, you haven't heard what I've heard." He cocked his head to the side. "I have it from Haj'Ali's physician himself that he's not infected with the syphilis – or anything else, for that matter – other than grief that you…"

"Then, ask *him* who told her family. Or ask the family."

Abrahim looked at his mother askance. "…I can hardly do that, mother." He was not yelling now. He was on the defensive.

"Well, it doesn't bother you to come around here accusing us, does it! If you really want an answer, go ask them. Just stop blaming everyone. You know I'm too old for this…"

Finally Ashraf *Khanoum* gained the bottom step, where she remained so that she would be eye to eye with her son.

Abrahim spoke with a voice that sounded like air rushing out of a balloon. It was a rushed voice, still angry, but quiet, as if defeated: "They could destroy me, you know. I don't care if you are my sister or my mother or my wife, if I ever find out one of you spread this lie, I'll throw you out on the street – all of you if I have to. I'll have your feet beaten in the square. I swear on the *Qaran*. Pray to *Allah* I never find out who did it!"

Watching Abrahim stalk back out of the front door and slam it behind him, Nargess experienced relief only briefly: Abrahim had been staring the whole time at Tahereh and Golnar and Masumay and Afsar, not at her. But, after the door slammed, Tahereh had immediately and silently caught Nargess's eye and did not relinquish her stare until Nargess turned away in shame. Tahereh knew why. Golnar and Masumay and Afsar knew why. Nargess knew why. Excepting Ashraf *Khanoum*, they all knew why: if any one of them confessed, they would all be punished together. They were all of them, to a woman, irrevocably mired in the conspiracy – and now no one of them was above any other. Tahereh had prevailed.

And Nargess suffered the burden of an additional worry: whoever it was who was plotting against her within Abrahim's household, was plotting with Rakshandeh.

Javad in Love
September 6, 1946

I t was a bright summer day, a year after the peace, a splendid day for painting. Javad was a man now – no longer a boy, no longer a student. He lifted his chin, drew his shoulders back, projected his chest forward, and admired his moustache in the gilded hall mirror of his Uncle Abrahim's house. Yes, he thought, his aunt Nargess was right: it was his time; time for his face to lift the lights of a kingdom; time to be the Eagle.

❧

Javad had watched helplessly as his uncle Abrahim's health failed during the war. Javad was struggling through law school. The Rashidian brothers, two *bazaari* who bedecked themselves in gold and jewels from British bribes, informed the occupying British authorities that Abrahim was dangerously pro-German. The best way to defuse the threat, they successfully argued, was to commandeer his rental properties "for the war effort" – which meant conveying them to themselves and a few select friends at one tenth their war-depressed value. The authorities were happy to oblige.

The British did nothing to allay popular resentment for actions such as seizing the assets of innocent citizens like Abrahim. They had been manipulating Iran for centuries and to the thinly veiled crime of stealing oil, they now added the theft of rice, wheat and votes. Exiling Reza Khan Shah to Johannesburg for having briefly canceled the oil concession ten years earlier, and for coddling up to the Axis powers, they purged Tehran of German agents (most of whom fled to the gregarious but traitorous *Qasgahi* tribe in the south, who sold them – literally – back to the government when the tides of war reversed). The British pretended that Reza Khan's replacement, his son Mohamed Reza, had been chosen to bring enlightened reform. It was a reasonably credible assertion – to the gullible – given the cruel despotism of the father, and that Mohamed Reza had been educated at Le Rosey, an exclusive Swiss boarding school. But, what they didn't say was that they couldn't find anyone else foolish enough to accept the throne, because whoever did would be in thrall to Ambassador Bullard, who wielded the real power. Knowing Iranians despised their dark skinned neighbors, Bullard had already made a point of posting high-turbaned Indian guards in front of the embassy compound on Ferdowsi Avenue, ordering them to strike any passing Iranians with their batons. Bullard preached capitalism and paid below cost for wheat and rice (while the communist Russians paid fair market). Bullard ignored the starvation the commandeering caused, and reasoned that the local primitives could forage. Bullard preached democracy and fixed elections. Bullard preached justice and allowed Russian death squads to scour Tehran for former White Russian supporters. Bullard encouraged schemers to collaborate and rewarded them with their countrymen's gold.

Amid all this, Abrahim's house building business had dwindled to almost nothing. After the Rashidian brothers had absconded with most of his wealth, he'd had to pawn his wives' jewelry at war-distressed prices. Despite his reduced circumstances though, he still spoiled his young son Rasheed with imported English bicycles and gold coins from the *bazaar*. He bought his daughter, Pari, imported dolls and almond pastries from the best bakers in the city. He bought his wives bolts of expensive cloth and custom made shoes.

Even though Abrahim was only in his late fifties, these extravagances gave rise to rumors that his mind was going – or at least his will to live. But, no one had the courage to intervene. It was not that they feared Abrahim, who was gregarious and generous to a fault. It was just that no one could conceive of the family without him as head of it. Better to live with endless feminine squabbles, petty rivalries and rapidly depleting coffers than to live with nothing at all. And if he was spoiling his children and squandering his fortune, those were his rights.

Javad felt grateful that his uncle Abrahim had supported him through law school during these deprivations. And he felt considerable guilt. The hope to repay his uncle weighed heavily upon him, and he vowed that when the time came he would become protector to the family – yea, even champion. When finally he took his place in the world, he would take Abrahim and his family with him.

℧

Pondering the morrow, Javad drew in a deep breath to savor the morning. He adjusted his coal blue beret to a jaunty angle. He decided he would stick with the beret instead of switching to the straw hat that was like the one Monet wore, and straightened the round, horn-rimmed glasses on the bridge of his nose, where he had carefully cultivated two bridge marks. Then he pressed smooth the horizontal blue stripes of his collarless cotton shirt. The shirt was a favorite of his for being almost identical to the shirts worn by Venetian gondoliers. He picked up the rattling, maple wood box of paints smelling of turpentine – and then the creaking ash wood easel and finally his round, tinned copper lunch pail. But, then he discovered he had no hand free to put the canvas under his arm and he'd forgotten his book, so he put everything down to start over. He debated whether to pick up the lunch pail first and then put the canvas under that arm, or start with the canvas. He started with the canvas; then the book. But, it was awkward to pick up the other things while crouching, so he put the canvas and book down. He checked himself once more in the mirror, readjusted the glasses, stroked his upper lip with his index finger, and decided the moustache was a success. It went well, he thought, with the dark blue beret and the bookish glasses with their thick, non-corrective lenses. His choice of clothes was his own personal synthesis of photographs of painters like Matisse and Picasso he had seen in copies of foreign journals purchased on occasion from the booksellers by the university – asking his friends to translate the captions.

Then, with a fatalistic pang, he recalled his thirteenth birthday, almost ten years earlier. His cousin Pari had just been born and he was feeling the acute loss of Abrahim's attentions. His mother, Tahereh, had planted a big kiss on the top of his head.

"Oh, how that face will make women faint!" she said.

It was his Aunt Afsar's comment that had wounded: "Eh, that it will!"

The years had failed to erase that. Well, he thought in defense, his Aunt Afsar hadn't expected him to last a month in law school either. Neither had anyone else, for that matter, even the dean – except for his Aunt Nargess: she seemed to be the only supportive member of the family. It was Aunt Nargess who had allowed Abrahim to pawn her jewelry after Javad's first term in law school, to slip the dean "a little something to see Javad through," which was a source of great embarrassment to Javad, and entirely unnecessary, he thought – well, largely unnecessary.

But, his Aunt Nargess had been very comforting at the time: "It's nothing, Javad, dear," she said, when he came to thank her. He was blushing. She lifted her hand to his face. "You will find a place for yourself in the world, you of the beauty-red ruby. You are truly the Eagle now that you've grown to be a man."

Her words touched him. Since age ten he had been eclipsed by Abrahim and Nargess's son, Rasheed – a brat of a boy. By dint of Rasheed's birth, Javad had become an outsider. Once heir apparent, he had now become ward, the lowly son of a divorced mother living on her brother's charity. That little nose-picker Rasheed got the lavish birthday parties, the soccer balls imported from Italy, the nuanced inquiries from *bazaari* matrons interested in marriage contracts for their young daughters fifteen and twenty years down the road, the fawning attention of shopkeepers and family members seeking to ingratiate themselves with Abrahim. The birth of Rasheed's sister, Pari, three years later, had only sealed Javad's fate. He did not hold it against them, but instead of being cute kids, they were pests. Rasheed was a conniving brat, large for his age, continually sneaking into Javad's rooms and rifling his drawers for sweets and spare change and then swearing to god before his mother,

Javad's aunt, that he'd done nothing of the sort. As Abrahim's oldest son, his word went unquestioned and Javad learned to keep sweets and change in his pockets during waking hours and under his pillow at night. Pari was a sad little case, always in tears outside her mother's closed doors – or pouting. Javad understood how Pari felt, though: *Khanoum* Nargess had produced a male heir for Abrahim and she seemed to regard that as the end of her duties. Her daughter by War Minister, Tajmah, got what little mother-daughter time Nargess could muster – probably because she was her mother's last tether to her days as royalty. Javad had lost something because of those kids. But, he never lost the gratitude he felt towards their mother for being so kind to him. His obligations were heartfelt and numerous.

Javad decided to first pick up the pail and the book and then put the canvas under one arm and then the easel under the other and then, finally, crouch to pick up the paint box. But, before he could get started, his mother, Tahereh, appeared in the mirror. Her long dark hair and the way she craned her neck forward always reminded him of a vulture. Her hair, which had been a very deep chestnut brown – almost black – before the war, now had a reddish hue from the henna washes she used to cover the gray. He pitied her for what he only partly understood: that she was a veteran of household skirmishes with the other women, skirmishes in a contest she was bound to ultimately lose because she was sister, not wife to the family patriarch.

She gave him a silent look, a worrying look. She was a good three inches shorter than he. He turned around so she could inspect him from the front. He wondered if she still disapproved of the horn-rimmed glasses and the beret. He had started wearing them at sixteen. He was probably the only man in Tehran, in all Iran, for that matter, to get himself up so – particularly with that shirt. Well, he was a year out of law school now, wasn't he? Old enough to wear what he wanted. And soon – tomorrow, actually – he would be married… well, that surprise was his business. He would wire his mother from Tabriz.

He wondered if she were going to admonish him, tell him to try to concentrate this time, to just get something on the canvas, start with a few lines, a sketch, worry about colors later, or maybe forget about the whole thing, go back to the office. After all, the canvas and paint set had occupied his office for a year and his bedroom for four years before that, without significant issue – without any issue at all, actually, other than smudged jumbles. Or maybe she was just giving him that silent look that said she needed more from him, that his friends were earning good money, launching careers of power, that she would rather see him wearing a suit and tie than a beret and glasses – that his habit of bringing home stray animals was – well, not seemly for a man. Instead, she reached up and removed his cap, combed the thick brush strokes of his mussed hair with her fingers, replaced his cap at a more conservative angle and brushed his shoulders.

"We could get you a drawing instructor," she said.

"Do you have to treat me like I'm Pari and Rasheed's age, mother? Besides, where's the artistry in doing it by rote?"

"Well, watch the lamp with the easel on your way out," she said. "You know how your Aunt Afsar worries so about you and that easel swinging around..."

"MOTH-ER!" Javad said. "PLE-EASE?"

His mother hesitated, then said, "Alright, shall I get the door?"

"What, without Aunt Afsar's permission?"

When his mother had left him, he picked up the lunch pail and the book and the canvas and the easel and the box of paints in the order planned and, with one parting nod to his moustache in the mirror, turned towards the front door.

The easel creaked gaily as it swung around behind him with the accuracy of an American baseball star and swatted the hall lamp off its rosewood pedestal. Javad stopped and listened to see if any in the household had heard the embarrassingly sharp sound of marble lamp greeting marble floor. If they hadn't seen him do it, they couldn't prove anything. He could always return later and blame it on Rasheed. Fortunately, everyone seemed to be out back in the garden, so they betrayed no notice of either the sound of marble cracking or Javad sneaking like a cat burglar to the back of the kitchen to find the broom and dustpan to clean up the lamp – and a mop to clean up the oil that had leaked from the lunch pail spilled in the rush. His mother had filled the pail with *kufteh*, a grapefruit sized meatball with a plum in the center. *Kufteh* did not hold the cooking juices well. Next time he would ask for dolmeh (grape leaves stuffed with rice and meat). They were more self-contained, but he would miss the sweet plum in the center of the *kufteh*. On the other hand, he had to admit, it was a bit tiresome to work through the bland meat and stuffing to get to it. And next time – well, soon everything would be different. He would show them all. He would make his Aunt Nargess proud. He would show that love conquers all. After cleaning up the mess he stole upstairs and retrieved the change from under his pillow to keep it from the little snitch, Rasheed.

Loaded up once again, Javad found he couldn't unlatch the front door without putting down at least the easel and the box of paints. But, just then, his aunt Afsar, with her eyes swollen and faintly pomegranate-red, appeared. She was like an apparition at the bottom of the spiral staircases that flanked the entrance. She smelled faintly of urine from the diapers of her crippled twins, who still inhabited their upstairs room in litters. He wondered where she came from, why his mother tolerated her and her constant sniping. She opened the door for him. He mused whether her mountainous breasts put her at risk for toppling over. The thought of those aged breasts made him queasy. Then he chuckled to himself, wondering if she had to walk extra carefully to avoid toppling, if the extra work in holding those tired water melons up gave her backaches. He wouldn't mind meeting a girl his age like that – though, undeflated. He didn't think that his fiancée, Maryam, had breasts that imposing, though he was hard pressed to remember, having not seen her since he was sixteen, and even then having only seen her twice – and briefly at that. Tomorrow he would know for sure. He would meet her in Tabriz and marry her and then he would wire the news back to his family and together he and Maryam would give their money to the masses and devote their lives to purity. He clunked and rattled as he squeezed through the opening – wondering if he should have picked up his stash of hard candy when he had retrieved his change.

"Javad, dear," his aunt said, "you don't have to experience all of life's pleasures in one transcendent moment."

"Auntie, dear?"

She pointed to the book. "You know, I've heard in England they have magicians called ventriloquists, who talk and drink at the same time. But, I don't think anyone can read and paint together – and see clients."

Javad stared back at her with a feeling of helplessness. Why did they always get back to the clients?

He put down the easel and box of paints and handed her the book of poems with his newly freed hand. Then he loaded up again, walked out into the sunlight, and proceeded down the street, clattering at each step like a vendor's donkey loaded to the sky with cooking pots.

"Finish it and I'll buy it," his Aunt Afsar called after him, in a surprisingly contrite voice. Then she added, "Start it, even, and I'll buy it."

Javad was glad he had told no one (other than his friend, Nossrat) about his plans for the morrow. Five years he had waited. Finally, he was going to wed his fiancée, Maryam, who was the daughter of his distant aunt, Rakshandeh. No sense in letting his family in on it. They were tiresome about things like that. They hadn't spoken to Aunt Rakshandeh in years. He just couldn't face another family squabble, endure more conspiracy theories. There would be countless admonishments: Maryam's mother was a Russian spy; a German spy; a British spy (they didn't mistrust the Americans yet); she worked for British collaborators during the war; she was bent on destroying Nargess, Abrahim, every last *Qajar*... There were some things he did know were best avoided in life. That came with being a lawyer, after all.

Javad had decided he would spend the day painting the *Sheikh Hadi Saga Khuneh*, a shrine where, twenty-three years earlier, an enraged crowd had stoned to death the hapless American vice consul, Robert Imbrie. You weren't supposed to paint sacred subjects, but Javad was above others: he was a rebel; he belonged to the *Tudeh* (masses party, overtly identified with the international Communist Party only after the successes of Maoist forces in China at the end of the decade); he was an intellectual. The history made painting the shrine interesting. Javad had always meant to become a painter. For several years now he had lugged his paints and easel about town with an eye towards the picturesque. He took pride in letting his heart pulse to the beat of life's adventures. But, when he tried to reduce his feelings to line and color, he always stalled, facing a great blank of mind – and of canvas, as his aunts would observe. Nevertheless, he was not one to quit. And who knows, with a little luck he might just become the next Omar Khayam, philosopher, poet, mathematician, astronomer – and seducer of women! And the canvasses really weren't blank, just unfinished. His aunts exaggerated so. Someday he would become a judge. He just knew it. And when he did, he would show his paintings to celebrate, and they would sell out to the older families of Tehran, the intelligentsia, and they would ask for copies of his first book of poems. *Bazaaris*, like his Uncle Abrahim and his scheming aunts, would not understand, really. But, he would make them respect that the learned of the land had come to pay homage to Javad, legal scholar, judge, artist, poet... Someday they would lay rose petals on his grave to celebrate his birthday, as they did for Hafez. And while he was at it, he would become a great leader, bearded and wise, like Cyrus the Great, who had risen from his mother's destitute exile to defeat his grandfather, the fabulously wealthy Croesus, and seize control of the empire in 546 BC. In the meantime he would settle for just escaping the prying of his aunts.

In resignation he recited to himself from Ferdowsi,

> *"Strong will be whoever has knowledge,*
> *From wisdom, the heart of the old is full..."*

And then from the poet Sa'di:

> *"If a man be an artist,*
> *The art speaks, not the man.*
> ...
> *Wisdom is in the spirit,*
> *And needs no herald..."*

One day, soon he would be old and wise and his art would speak for itself.

Shortly he found his way to the *Sheikh Hadi Saga Khuneh* shrine. Robert Imbrie had been of Scottish Presbyterian clergy stock, *via* New Jersey – and consequently of scant import, despite being an American vice consul – though Javad knew little of that. He did know enough to feel sorry for

Imbrie, though. A local crowd attacked him, way back in 1924, ostensibly for trying to photograph the faithful as they prayed and also ostensibly for having poisoned the local well at the behest of the *Baha'is*, a splinter sect of Islam promoted by the British. But, everyone knew the British had plotted to stir the crowd's anger against Imbrie, to burn the meddling fingers of the naïve Americans and chase them away from upsetting the renegotiation of the British oil concession to Britain's advantage. The event made the New York Times in America. The ploy worked.

As Javad set up the easel and canvas by a low wall where he could sit, he noticed a kitten licking its paw across the street. He reminded himself to ignore it. The last thing he needed was for one of his aunt's friends to report back that he was befriending stray animals again. It had been a tendency of his since childhood – like wetting the bed, his aunts said. But, one outgrows wetting the bed. He opened the paint box and removed the pallet from the lid and started squeezing colors onto the pallet. They looked like parrot-colored bird droppings. Would that he had the parrots to go with them! He enjoyed the turpentine smell, which lent an earthiness to the venture. Not sure how to start, he leaned back and removed the forks from their eyelets on the lunch pail. Then he opened the top compartment, which held flat bread, scallions, radishes and feta cheese. After that he opened the bottom to get the *kufteh*. The kitten seemed to be watching him with insouciant eyes between paw licks. After an hour or so the day grew suffocating. His shirt stuck to his chest. Sweat smeared the thick, non-correcting lenses of his glasses. He regretted having opted for the blue beret over the cooler straw hat in the manner of Monet. He still had nothing on canvas other than some pale blue sky smudges. He loved skies. Loved blue. Loved turquoise. Of all of Iran's cities, he loved Isfahan the best, for it's jeweled turquoise domes cast against cloudless skies. He loosened his collar. He tried mixing a few of the colors. He pulled the brow of his beret down to see if that would work…

Soon he was spending his time watching the kitten that had been hiding in the shade of a lamppost all morning long. He had tried to ignore it at first. After all, he was a lawyer. On one hand, what harm could there be in watching this one for a while? On the other hand, when was he going to become serious? He concentrated on ignoring the kitten. He tried mixing different combinations of colors again and made a few khaki-colored strokes to outline the buildings. But, his attention soon retreated from the pallet to the kitten. It was the color of English marmalade. It seemed to be spending an awful lot of time licking one paw. Was it wounded? He had noticed the kitten was limping. He suspected it had cut its paw, or gotten a thorn or a splinter. Soon he had lured the kitten into his lap by letting it lick the juice from the *kufteh*, which he swabbed from the side of the enameled lunch pail with his finger. He knew he should forget about the kitten, should return his attention to the still blank canvas which yawned before him in the lingering heat, but he couldn't. He wished he had not succumbed to his aunt Afsar, and had brought his poetry book. He could ignore the kitten if he had some good poems to read. He tried to remember what his fiancée, Maryam, looked like. It was hard. He had not seen her for five years.

By late afternoon, when the heat was just breaking, he had returned to his uncle's house with an empty lunch pail, a full stomach, a wounded kitten and an incoherent canvas. His mother met him at the door with a silent sigh. In vain she searched his eyes. These days she would settle for gainful employment. Even just employment would suit her. Then she tried to shepherd him to his room before the other women loosed their barbs. But, Afsar had lain in ambush all afternoon.

"Javad, dear," Afsar said, "you must be exhausted. Do come have tea with us and show us your *chef-d'oeuvre*."

"Tomorrow, Auntie," he said. Javad was practiced in the art of avoiding his aunts – especially when they spoke French.

Then Afsar said, "Oh my! Tahereh, dear – your son is such a sweet young man..."

Golnar, Abrahim's second wife, completed the accolade: " Another kitten!"

Javad escaped down the hall to his mother's quarters, grateful no one had remarked on the absence of the hall lamp.

❦

The next morning, excited by his plans to set off that day for Tabriz to finally meet his fiancée, Maryam, Javad seated himself on a folding chair outside the front door to his Uncle Abrahim's compound. He wanted to enjoy the shade in the street before the sun beat it away, and to catch his friend, Nossrat, before his family would pounce on him. Sipping mint *sharbat*, leaning back in the folding chair, he admired the sign on the crumbling stucco wall beside the front door to his uncle's compound:

> Javad e'Abasi:
> Advocate at Law

Javad recalled first affixing the sign to the wall. It was a tenuous triumph. It had been over a year ago, between the German and Japanese surrenders, when he had just graduated from law school. He had asked his uncle to help him rent an office near the Ministry of Justice, but his uncle had little money to spare.

Or so his uncle said. Because his uncle had also said, "Eh, Javad, you get a client, I'll rent you an office – right near the Ministry. I'll rent the whole blessed Ministry – buy it, even!"

Javad looked up at the sign and admired the weatherproof black enamel. The raised lettering had cost extra, and the real gold leaf had been downright exorbitant, but, being a lawyer with an eye to becoming a judge was like being a prince with an eye to becoming king, and, well, if you had to have a palace of thick marble to make your father's subjects take you seriously, well, then, you just had to – even if you did have to beg your uncle's servants to loan you the money for it. Plenty of sovereigns had stooped lower. The sign had hung for a year. Any day now it would start to pay him back in clients and fund his imminent marriage.

He decided to wait for his friend, Nossrat, in his office. They had agreed to meet in the morning and depart that very afternoon for Tabriz, but Javad still had not told his family – not even his mother, Tahereh. And Nossrat could be an echo head at times.

He found Gholam Ali seated in the hallway. When Javad was six, Gholam Ali had arrived with Aunt Nargess and his own grand uniform with brass buttons and a giant, black bear hat that was almost big enough for Javad to crawl inside. A decade and a half later, Gholam Ali still donned various incarnations of this uniform. When not engaged in productive endeavors – which meant always – he squatted like an ancient gilded toad on a simple cedar stool in the main hallway, a sort of splendid living counterpoint to the hallway decorations – a human potted palm, if you will. It was summer, so, not expecting company, Gholam Ali had unbuttoned the uniform, placed the giant bear hat on the floor beside his stool, and had piled on the other side the quilted stuffing he needed to provide the uniform an imposing stature. Bent to the side, snoring, his undershirt visible, his uniform no longer puffed up by the quilting, Gholam Ali looked like a deflated tire. Javad nudged Gholam Ali awake and instructed him to show Nossrat to his office when he arrived. Gholam Ali nodded and returned to sleep.

Javad loved his office. It was his bedroom, but he kept the trunks with his clothes and futon in his mother's closets. He had furnished the office with an expansive walnut desk and matching file cabinets – all brand new. He had backed the desk up against the window and in front of it had placed two soft, stuffed leather chairs in a respectable chestnut brown. He paid to have the walls fitted with ceiling-high, ornate cherry shelves, which he filled with a motley assortment of dusty tomes. The bookseller had assured him that they were important works in German, French and English. At the end of the room he had a small table supporting a sturdy professional typewriter. It was almost the size of an oven. Once a week he paid to have a professional typist attend to his correspondence, but so far it had been entirely typing practice and oiling the machine. On his desk he displayed his uncle's elaborate English Meerschaum pipe (with permission) on a small carved rosewood stand, opposite a photograph of himself patiently studying one of his tomes and smoking said pipe, with the Eiffel tower visible through a window in the background. Neither he nor the Tehran studio photographer had understood that the tome was in German, or that Javad was reading it upside down. Underneath the desk Javad had concealed an electric buzzer connected to a small button he had had an electrician install just beneath the sign at the front door. He had assembled the scullery maid and the cook to admire the capital improvements their loans had subsidized and enlisted Gholam Ali to stand outside the front door to the compound and press the buzzer button.

"My!" the cook said to the scullery maid. "Mr. Javad: a genius, he be!"

"Eh, sure enough!" the maid agreed.

After he had finished buzzing, Gholam Ali made his own inspection and begged Javad Khan to have the photographer come and take a picture of him standing at attention in the background while Javad Khan sat at his imposing desk studying one of his weighty volumes upside down. Shortly thereafter, Javad and Pari invented the game of sneaking outside and pressing the buzzer to roust their older cousin from his rooms and make him answer the door, squealing in delight when they greeted him in surprise.

As he prepared for the trip to Tabriz, Javad imagined himself one of those gentleman explorers from England or America or Norway, assembling what he would need for an arctic expedition while he barked orders at his office staff, readying them for his absence. Ahhhh, a staff! He rolled his dress shoes up in tissue paper and then his best European style suit, with broad stripes and padded shoulders, and placed them in the bottom of his hiker's backpack. On the same hangar with it was a white shirt and a paisley tie in a dark, muted green. He would have his dress clothes pressed in Tabriz and make a grand impression for his betrothed Maryam.

Allah be praised! He could scarcely believe they were finally marrying. For five years (well, four and a half); they had furtively exchanged some fifty odd notes at clandestine meetings of the *Tudeh* party – the notes concealed in a *Qaran*. Javad attended the meetings religiously, Maryam never. He always found the note-bearing *Qaran* waiting for him on the back bench and he replaced her note with his. He had only met Maryam twice. The first time he and other schoolboys had been spying on her through a crack in the wall of her father's house when she discovered them and he fled. The second time he had responded to the first of the notes, though this first one had been concealed in the hat he had lost the time he had been caught spying and which had been miraculously left for him outside Abrahim's gate not a fortnight later – and fortuitously discovered and delivered to him by his Aunt Zahra on one of her occasional visits to the household. Through the secretive notes that had ensued over the years, they had promised each other to abandon the pretentious foibles of the petty bourgeoisie and donate their lives to the *Tudeh* party, give their money to the masses. They had agreed on that. And then... Ahhh... his thoughts stumbled..

Money... He hadn't really worked through that part of it – well, at least not in detail. Maryam had never really specified how much she expected him to bring to Tabriz. She had said a lot. But, what did that mean? Maybe Nossrat would know.

He wrapped the Meerschaum pipe in several pairs of socks and put it in a side pocket. Smart of the efficient British to smoke something so much more portable than those old fashioned water pipes so beloved by his backward countrymen. They were like smoking a British water closet. Into the neighboring pocket he slipped a silver hip flask he had bought off the pawnbroker, who had told him it was how stylish British and Americans carried their whiskey. Nossrat had promised to take him to an Armenian liquor store that carried the best brands. Then he packed two hair brushes, an extra comb, two tooth brushes, two bottles of tooth powder, two extra pairs of shoes, seven sets of underwear, seven extra pairs of socks, three shirts, two traveling suits, a kilogram bag of shelled walnuts, a bag of dried peaches, a half kilogram of feta cheese wrapped in wax paper, a stack of wafer bread wrapped in cotton, a pad of rolled, dried fruit, a pouch of American tobacco for the Meerschaum, four small boxes of matches, a magnetic compass, a cotton raincoat and the leather bound *Qaran* that for four and a half years had secreted notes between himself and his beloved Maryam. In the side he slipped the address in Tabriz Maryam had given him. On the top he placed a box of Isfahan gaz – a special gift for Maryam – double wrapped in wax paper to seal in the flour used to pack the candies and keep them from sticking to one another. He was beginning to cinch this all up when his mother entered.

Tahereh cast a defeated glance at the hiker's backpack on the grand mahogany desk, beside the pile of freshly sharpened pencils, the neat stack of blank note pads, the carefully centered silver and ivory inkwell with its matching blotter, the photograph of him studying upside down in Paris, and the empty rack for the Meerschaum. She craned her neck forward, but Javad calculated she could not see the dress clothes.

"Oh, Javad, dear, I hope you're not getting into that *Tudeh* Party again. It's no end of trouble."

Her fears were not unfounded. Since the end of the war, while the British and Russians had been jockeying for control of Iran, the *Tudeh* Party had been promoting illegal strikes. The northwest province of Azarbaijan (whose capital, Tabriz, was Javad's destination today) and the southern provinces were in various stages of revolt, backed respectively by the Russians and the British. Javad's participation in a *Tudeh*-Party-backed, student sit in demonstration at the *Majlis* building several months earlier had been disarmingly free of consequences: The students just walked in to the *Majlis* chamber past bored guards and the guards let them stay there till they got bored delivering speeches to themselves. Ever since then his Uncle Abrahim and his mother had refused him an allowance, which act had a more devastating effect on the fortunes of the scullery maid and the cook than on those of Javad, so acute was his financial acumen.

"I'll be in Tabriz a few weeks."

"There's fighting. And you have your business to take care of here."

"I'll take care of it, Mother."

The business was getting his Aunt Nargess's jewelry out of hock before that donkey of a pawnbroker sold it. Ever since his uncle had pawned her jewelry she had been flitting about the house like a mother hen without an egg to brood. Given that she had been so supportive, Javad was surprised by this development. It deepened his guilt.

Abrahim was just now turning his house building business around, but things were still shaky. His business had failed during the war because no one was building houses, and he could not get government contracts because of lingering suspicions over false allegations made by the nefarious Rashidian brothers.

"You know what it means to your Uncle Abrahim," Tahereh said.

Javad understood both meanings to this. He knew that Abrahim remained ever grateful to Tahereh for pawning her first marriage to help him through his early, and entirely innocent brush with justice. And Javad knew his mother had prevailed upon his uncle to hire him to complete the transaction of retrieving his Aunt Nargess's jewelry:

"Why do I need a lawyer to get them back?" Abrahim had said. "All's I need do is walk the cash in the door. I've got a paper for the jewelry. I don't need crutches anymore..."

"It would be a start for him," Tahereh had said, "a way to get known. Please, dear brother."

"OK," Abrahim had relented. Then he turned to Javad: "But, it doesn't count toward the office, eh!"

୧

Javad had come to know Nossrat at the meetings of the *Tudeh* Party. Although Nossrat was a useful friend – his Man Friday – and Javad needed him as much for advice as for help, Javad bickered with him all the way to the pawnbroker's. Javad wanted to dispense with his obligations to Abrahim concerning retrieving his aunt's jewelry from the pawnbroker and then to depart for Tabriz so he could be there a day early.

"What do you mean you didn't bring any money?" Javad said. "How are we going to eat in Tabriz? We've only enough for the ride."

"We can eat with the masses," Nossrat said. He was a towering giant of sorts, thin as a beanpole. He walked with a perpetual list, as he so frequently had to bend over to lend an ear to his classmates. His gait was more like a giraffe's swaying than a stooped shuffle. To fit within the confines of the droshky he had to bring his knees up almost to his chest. He looked as if he were used to living without food for varying periods of time.

"We're supposed to bring something to give them – funds, money, aid…"

"Well, you've got the dried fruit roll – and the peaches and walnuts and…"

"And what are we going to eat on the trip? Did your brother pack something for us?"

Nossrat shrugged. "My brother just promised his car. That not enough?"

"Eh, don't look at me," Javad said. "I've got to give what I've got to the *Tudeh*. Maryam said so."

"How much did she say?"

Javad debated whether to answer his friend. In one pocket was a bulging wad of *toumans* wrapped in a paper for the jewelry. Abrahim had counted them out to the *dinar* for him to retrieve his aunt's jewelry. In the other pocket was a mere ten *toumans*. Javad had pried that from the cook, documenting his solvency by letting her witness his professional typist clacking away at the alphabet.

"Enough," Javad said. Then he felt embarrassed at having been so short with his friend, and embarrassed that Maryam had simply instructed him to bring a lot of money, but had never said how much was a lot. "Ten *toumans*," he added.

"Ten *toumans*!" Nossrat shouted. He grew agitated, ignoring Javad's waving at him to be more discrete. "Why, that won't even feed a chicken for a week. They're hardly going to accept that…"

Now Javad wished he had said nothing. He'd have to listen to Nossrat complain about his ten *toumans* for a whole trip and make him feel embarrassed for having to borrow his brother's car. He decided upon silence. He needed quiet to rehearse what he would say to the pawnbroker.

But, Nossrat was not to be quieted: "Why did you bring the backpack?" he asked. "You could have left it at home and picked it up when we returned."

Javad thought for a moment.

"I don't want to wake the family," Javad said. "Besides, where's the car? We're supposed to leave this afternoon."

"You'll have to wake them when you bring your aunt's jewelry back, won't you? And if you don't like waiting for the car, you don't have to use it. My brother will have it back together tomorrow morning…"

"Tomorrow morning?" Javad cried. "I'm getting married tomorrow. What happened to today?"

Nossrat shrugged.

"Look!" Javad said. "I'll just take care of everything. Alright?"

Nossrat grew silent and Javad perceived he was feeling hurt. But, he had a more important matter on his mind: the pawnbroker.

While Nossrat waited in the droshky, Javad entered the pawnshop. He strode boldly past the dusty rows of violins, *tars*, drums, radios, vases, hand tools, hair curlers, irons, antique chairs, enameled pots, pressure-fed oil lamps and decorated mantelpiece clocks. He placed the paper on the glass display counter, smoothed it out with his fingers, cited the exact amount due, and laid on the counter beside it the thick wad of *toumans* his uncle had so carefully counted.

"For Abrahim e'Kashani."

The pawnbroker peered up at him through wire-rimmed glasses. Behind him two gas lights illumined the back of the store with flickering yellow. He stroked his bald pate, scratched his gray tufts of hair, removed his glasses. "Eh," the pawnbroker said, "I'm closed."

"Closed?" Javad said. "I know better than that."

"I'm closed."

Javad was annoyed at the firmness of his speech. "What do you mean, closed?" Javad said. "How did I get in here, then?"

The pawnbroker said nothing.

"OK," Javad said. "I see. You're closed. I'll wait, then. But, that's one heck of a late lunch."

"Closed for the day."

"For the day! I should say not. You take that money and give me back the jewelry."

The pawnbroker shrugged his shoulders. "That's not enough."

"What do you mean, not enough?" Javad said. "I've calculated it out exactly."

"You'll need interest through another day."

"Why you thief!" Javad sputtered. "Interest by the day? I should say not. It doesn't work that way." He broke into a sweat. "I'll come back tomorrow with the police. See if I don't."

The pawnbroker held the paper up to the light as if to read it more carefully. "Eh, so – these, I think I've sold."

"Sold?" Javad said. "That..." He pointed to the locked glass showcase counter between them. "They're right there. See?"

"They're sold, I said."

"I'll have you know I'm an attorney at law."

"Those are on layaway, then."

Now Javad grew silent in panic. When he spoke it was with a tremor. "Layaway?"

"Lady made a deposit on them."

Javad pulled his handkerchief out of his breast pocket and wiped his temples and his forehead. He chewed his upper lip. "Well, you're just going to have to give her deposit back."

"No. You've got to pay me her deposit first. Then you get to buy your jewelry back – at full price. Your aunt's, isn't it? Lady gets her deposit back, you get your aunt's jewelry back."

Javad hesitated. Something seemed fishy. Was the deposit extra, or included? He didn't want to ask because he knew the pawnbroker would say extra. He turned and looked down the long corridor and out through the dusty panes of the arched window where Nossrat and the droshky waited. He didn't want Nossrat to get impatient and come in after him to see this interchange. "How much?" he said quickly.

The pawnbroker shuffled back behind a desk stuffed with papers stacked on spindles and old pipes and jewelers loupes. He brought out a large leather bound account book and made a show of paging through it. "I'd say..." He looked up at Javad. "... three hundred *toumans*."

"Three..." Javad choked. He didn't want to lose a sum that big. But, he couldn't lose his aunt's jewelry. Not on his first paying job. "Well, you better give me a paper for it." He looked over his shoulder again to see if Nossrat were getting impatient.

The pawnbroker threw up his arms. "A paper he asks! The man wants a paper for reversing a layaway deposit? Who does that, I ask you?" Then he made a show of calming himself down. "Phew!" He brushed imaginary sweat from his brow, imaginary dust from his sleeves. "I guess they didn't' teach you much in that law school of yours about pawnshops. Ever been in one?"

Javad nodded no.

"Eh, I didn't think so!"

Then Javad had a legal inspiration: "Hey, I thought you were closed."

The pawnbroker shrugged. " 'Closed,' he says! Suit yourself! Don't look at me if lady snaps them up 'fore you get back."

Javad let out a frustrated burst of air through his clenched teeth. "Wait a minute! Wait a minute! Here..." Hurrying, he picked up the wad of *toumans*. His hands shaking despite his effort to be methodical, he counted out three hundred into a messy pile. "But, I'll be back in the morning. First thing."

"I'm closed."

"Closed?" Javad cried. "Are you ever open?"

"Tomorrow's the Sabbath. Day after tomorrow, I open."

Javad struggled to fit the depleted wad of *toumans* back in his pocket. He struggled to keep his chin from twitching. He wanted to shout. He wanted to call this ugly little man a thief. But then, there might be another charge, some sort of deposit tax for pawnbrokers, an extra charge for attorneys. And then there was the issue of how he was going to get more money from his uncle Abrahim.

The pawnbroker saw his trembling. He slapped the account book shut on his three hundred *touman* deposit. "Don't worry, young man," he said, grasping his arm like a grandfather and escorting him towards the front. "For you, I'll charge just one day's extra interest. You have my word on it."

☙

By late morning on the day after the visit to the pawnbroker, Nossrat and Javad got hold of Nossrat's brother's Jeep. Javad calculated they could make Tabriz by early evening, which would make Maryam wait only a half day at most. Only an hour outside of Tehran, suffocating in the heat and having raised clouds of dust that stretched back for miles beneath the assault of the sun, Nossrat's brother's Jeep belched a braying gasp of steam. Nossrat and Javad released the latches on either side and peered under the hood. The engine rushed at them with the odors of steam and burned rubber and oil and a labyrinth of wires and tubes like a burned out radio.

Nossrat bent bravely over the engine. "I think that's the condenser," he said.

"Well, it's *your* brother's Jeep," Javad said.

"Yeah, well it's your fiancée we're going to meet. If she doesn't leave you over a ten *touman* dowry."

Javad thought silently for a while. "I think it's overheated," he said. He reached towards the steaming radiator cap with the rag they had used to polish the Jeep earlier in the morning.

"Hey! Don't do that!"

"Why not?" Javad started to twist. "Here..."

The steam exploded beneath the cap and hurtled it against the hood, where it made a sharp bong and deflected, like a champagne cork, into the tall grass of the field.

"...Aaah!" Javad had already cried, while the cap hurtled away. He jerked his hand away from the steam. "Father burn!"

"Now you've done it – I told you."

"You fix it then! Father burn! Father burn..." He jumped up and down, shaking his hand as if that would cool the burn. "... Father burn!" A little while later, when he had calmed down and had had bandaged his blistered hand with a white handkerchief, he sighed, "Now what?"

Nossrat shrugged.

"And where's that radiator cap?"

"There's a tea shop back down the road," Nossrat said. "We could get water there."

"That was twenty kilometers ago. Remember?"

"Oh..."

For another hour, they sat in the diminishing shadow of the dead Jeep to escape the blistering heat, leaning back against the tires to await help. They gazed at the mountains in the sweltering distance. Ahead of them, to the north of Qazvin, lay the mountains that held the fabled eleventh century castle of Hassan Sabbah, the "Old Man of the Mountain," leader of the Ismaili sect. Hassan Sabbah kidnapped young men, drugged them and let them awake in his castle, surrounded by voluptuous, willing maidens. They believed they had tasted the true paradise and enrolled in his army to get more. They would (and did) do anything to regain paradise: torture, fight to the death, murder. The word "assassin" derived from the steady supply of hashish Hassan Sabbah supplied them. As Javad daydreamed what it might be like to awaken in Hassan Sabbah's castle, he watched several shepherds herd a large flock of sheep in from the distance. They had first appeared against the far horizon like a mirage that floated inwards over the course of an hour. The shepherds and their scattered flock raised only a gentle, waist high cloud of dust, which settled softly behind them like a fleece.

He felt a great sense of peace and recalled a poem by Rumi:

> God, this smiling beauty-rose you have entrusted me,
> I pray you, hide from jealous eyes of weeds.
> As I lie yet far away, shield her body, soul.
>
> Spring wind, when you air her house,
> Bring greetings to her for me.
> Tender from that supple hair so dark,
> Prepare her room,
> And don't destroy her heart.
>
> Whoever fears the pain of being in love,
> He doesn't earn her lips, her face, her step.
> ...
> Glory be to beauty-sound and song.

After Javad explained the problem to the shepherds they filled the radiator from their leather water sacks and then made tea in a small kettle. Javad then provided bread and feta cheese and they all shared tea and cheese and bread and Javad's spiced tobacco –taking turns shading themselves as best they could in the disappearing shadow of the Jeep. This was what Javad loved about the country, the vast distances that ended in mountains, the helpfulness of shepherds and farmers. They had recovered quickly since the war, during which they had suffered severe famine as their crops were commandeered. But, only a year later these shepherds were sharing their meager stores with him. Even if he had nothing, they would have shared their tea and filled his radiator. If only rulers had the grace of peasants, he thought. He vowed to see that happen. He vowed that his paintings would one day capture the nobility of peasants in the honesty of nature. He wanted to paint the turquoise domes of Isfahan. He wanted to paint the sea of wild poppies at the foot of Mount Damavand. They bloomed early in the spring, when the grass was fresh, and made a froth of red against the verdant green, blowing in waves before the wind. It was the most beautiful sight in all of Iran.

… The nightingale sits among roses.

…

The rose comes to the sweet-mouthed bud…

They searched the surrounding field on their hands and knees until they retrieved Nossrat's brother's Jeep's radiator cap.

"It's just going to boil over again," Nossrat said, waving goodbye to the shepherds.

"You got any better ideas?" Javad said. He raised his handkerchief-wrapped hand and waved too. It looked like a flag of surrender.

Nossrat shrugged.

"Then, just let me take care of it!" Javad said.

The two sat in the shade growing beside the Jeep as they watched the shepherds disappear silently into the distance. The angling afternoon light reminded Javad of the Russian airplanes he had seen at the beginning of the war, the very day he had met Maryam the second time, in response to her first note to him. The airplanes too had been silent in the vast distance, then high overhead, glinting in the early morning sun as they had angled and turned. After the first ones had gone, there had rained down about him the many fluttering pieces of paper warning Russian troops were coming to protect the people from Hitler. Then another set of airplanes had come and turned, also glinting silently in the distance. As they were disappearing, Javad heard the heavy thuds of their bombs by the rail center.

Javad climbed into the driver's seat. Then, remembering his hand, he said to Nossrat, "You drive."

By that evening, as they entered Qazvin, which was a quarter of the way to Tabriz, after stopping at their fourth tea house of the day, they were scarcely talking civilly. Javad retained enough tact not to mention Nossrat's low background (his grandparents had been farmers, his parents shoemakers in a dusty village southeast of Tehran) and Nossrat reciprocated by avoiding the issue of Javad's fiancée whom neither he nor his classmates nor Javad had laid eyes upon in at least several years, and whose mother, Rakshandeh, by Javad's own admission was at the very least a suspicious sort.

"Did your brother give us this car to get rid of it?" Javad asked the fifth time the engine boiled over. "You know: take it outside of Tehran and kill it somewhere, so he doesn't have to pay to have it hauled?"

"I think he knew the bus fare was your dowry."

"He could have just had it towed away, you know – saved us the trouble. It wouldn't have been that dear. Maryam's going to kill me." The mere thought gave his heart a pang of guilt. The last time he had seen her was four and a half years ago, when he had responded to the invitation in the first note she had sent. He had shown up at the indicated time, but the entire street was silent and shuttered. It was the day he had watched the silent Russian airplanes bomb Tehran. He had knocked on Maryam's father's door. When Maryam answered, she seemed to not recognize him and then, when he confessed his love for her, she became angry and insisted he go away. He had not laid eyes on Maryam since. She sent him another note, in reconciliation, some weeks later, inviting him to the first clandestine meeting, but she had been quite short with him in the note, accusing him of arriving without notice. She had shown she could be feisty, and he could only imagine what she was going to say, now that he was late for their wedding – four and a half years later.

In Qazvin, they asked around and begged for more water until they found, at the end of a row of dusty shops, a mechanic who delivered last rites to the Jeep and offered them a used American Chevrolet that had just come into his possession.

"I don't know about you," Nossrat said, "but I'm walking to Tabriz. My brother isn't going to pay for a new car. Not now. Not never. I don't care what was wrong with the Jeep. And you owe my brother a new Jeep. You could at least…"

"It isn't new," Javad said. "It's at least eight years old. …"

"And so's the Chevy. I'll take the bus, thank you."

"You want me to arrive at my wedding in a bus, with peasants and goats and chickens? We're already going to be late…"

"Well, how're we going to pay for it?"

Javad pondered the question silently. He hadn't told Nossrat about his abortive dealings with the pawnbroker the previous day. "I could borrow against the jewelry money."

"Jewelry? Your mother's trousseau? This car mechanic's not going to take jewelry…"

"I've got the money."

"…not at any fair…" Nossrat stopped in mid sentence. "I thought you gave it to the pawnbroker."

"Just let me take care of it, eh!"

For the next hour they drank the mechanic's tea, exchanged compliments with him and bickered over the price. Finally they stood up and bowed in agreement, Javad not being able to shake with his bandaged right hand. Javad peeled off the bulk of the wad of *toumans* in his left pocket.

"At last," Javad said, breathing a sigh of relief. "We're off. Have to be in Tabriz by tonight. Now, the keys, if you please, good sir!"

"Eh!" the mechanic said, scrunching the money into a leather purse. He picked up a greasy wrench and started fingering a row of oil stained wooden parts drawers stacked against the wall like an apothecary's. "Not tonight, my friend. But, I'll have it running for you in the morning – first thing."

Now Javad began to redden.

"Bring the *Qaran*," the mechanic said, tugging his pointed gray beard. "I'll swear to it!"

"We're paying you enough to buy the whole car factory and have it shipped to Tehran," Nossrat said. "And the road to go with it. Surely it should run…"

"You want your dead Jeep back?" the mechanic said. "May God protect its soul. You can have it." He pulled the wad of *toumans* from his soiled purse and held them towards Javad. "Here, take it back. Take it all back, good sir. Never let it be said I have dishonored a guest in my own house. Your Jeep too. Please! Before God I will serve you."

Javad gulped. He scratched one thigh with the hand that hadn't been scalded. "No," he said. "Keep it. Please. I am your slave."

"Oh that was smart," Nossrat said when they were alone.

"Well, he's not charging for putting us up the night, is he?"

"And what happened to your mother's jewelry?"

"Will you let me take care of it? Nothing."

"I thought that's why we stopped back at your uncle's place." Nossrat then stooped over, looked deeply into his friend's averted eyes and sighed: "*Eh*, you didn't tell them – No, I don't think so – did you? No…"

There was an awkward silence, as Javad tried hard to stare away from his friend's eyes.

Then Javad spoke: "Nonsense!" he said. He waved Nossrat away with his bandaged hand. "I'm going to return it all – just as soon as we get back. Besides, I've hardly scratched it."

❦

By noon the next day Nossrat and Javad were in view of Mt. Sahand, about 40 km south of Tabriz, when the Chevrolet too succumbed, jetting a streaming gray cloud out through the front grill.

"Father burn!" Javad cursed.

"Don't look at me," Nossrat said. "My brother didn't lend you this one."

"Yeah," Javad said, "and your brother didn't tell us his one didn't work, either." He jumped out and kicked the front fender. "Does every car you drive boil over, Nossrat?"

"Hey, that's not steam!" Nossrat shouted.

All of a sudden, Javad realized he was smelling smoke. "Father burn!" he said. "Quick, get the water!"

Javad burned the fingers on his other hand trying to unlatch the hood. Desperately he and Nossrat squirted water in through the front grill. Javad had to hold the water bag with his forearms, both hands now disabled. But, the water just billowed back in a flash of steam. So next he had Nossrat pour water on the front of the top of the hood, the idea being to cool it enough to lift it. But, that too only made more steam and sent the water bubbling and gurgling along the surface of the hood and off to the side where it fell to wet the sand. Soon orange flames were gushing out the front grill and around the edges of the hood. Their hopes of snuffing out the fire dashed – and their water supply exhausted – they helplessly watched the paint blister and blacken.

Suddenly, the realization came: "Father burn!" Javad shouted. "Our stuff!"

The fire had burst into the passenger compartment. The Chevy was a modern design, with a lockable trunk, and Javad had left the keys in the ignition – now engulfed in flames. Nossrat was able to pull his valise out of the rear seat of the passenger compartment, but Javad could only watch helplessly as a billowing orange fire made clouds of black smoke that twirled into the blazing blue sky. The fire quickly increased in size and ferocity until finally it engulfed the Chevy entirely, Javad's backpack locked safely in the trunk.

Neither one spoke to the other as they watched the Chevy burn itself up over the course of the next hour.

So this is what it's like when machines burn, Javad thought. He had always wondered about that, listening to news stories during the war. Abrahim would officiate, opening the walnut cabinet doors to preside over the short-wave receiver with its yellow-lighted dials, black knobs and glowing red tubes that could only be seen by peering through the pressboard grill in back. They listened to Radio Berlin, and then the BBC. It had been great theater: Nazi troops in polished leather reducing countries in days; buzzing night raids over London and Berlin; fleets of gray steel huddled on dark seas, desperate races to avoid wolf packs; flashes and thunder in the night; screams of men burning; submarines lurking; insane German ministers seizing fighter aircraft and defecting to England. Europe was so exotic! And the mayhem was all so clean, marred only by the squeals and blips of the radio as Abrahim adjusted the frequency knob. Real things burning – like their car – were considerably less romantic.

When the chassis had cooled, Javad retrieved the remnants of his belongings: a melted hip flask, several pairs of shoe soles charred beyond recognition and his Uncle Abrahim's soot-smeared Meerschaum pipe, now with only a charcoal stub where the stem had once been. He borrowed a white kerchief from Nossrat to bandage his other hand, so that he now looked like a hospital patient.

"Well," Nossrat said, "now what?" He leered at his friend. "Was the money in the backpack?"

Javad's heart skipped a beat. Breathlessly he felt his left pocket with the back of his bandaged hand. "No," he said. "My pocket." Nossrat started to say something, but Javad shot him an angry glare: "Don't say it; just don't!"

Beside the charred skeleton of Javad's newly acquired American Chevrolet they waited for help. This time there wasn't a hope of even diminishing shadows. Late in the afternoon, with the heat at its suffocating peak, a peasant appeared in the distance, approaching with mountainous slowness. He was walking down the road from ahead, leading a donkey and cart by the hand. They figured he was returning from having sold his goods in the market in Tabriz. The crude, weather-beaten cart listed as it creaked along, as if it were loaded to the sky with a superabundance of goods and produce, but it was empty.

"Give us a lift to Tabriz?" Javad asked when the peasant drew up.

"Going the other way, sir," the peasant said.

"Listen, I'll pay you – to turn around."

"Got business at Mt. Sahand," the peasant said. "Collecting honey." He stopped to inspect the wreckage.

For a brief moment Javad let his thoughts wander to the pleasures of honey from Mt. Sahand. It was the most famous honey in all Iran, with a unique, floral aroma. His Aunt Nargess had specially ordered some for his fourteenth birthday. The whole room filled with the fragrance of the honey as soon as it was opened. A neighbor even came over to ask what kind of perfume he was smelling. He envied the peasant his job. Then he returned to reality.

"Please," Javad said. "I'm getting married in Tabriz. My fiancée's waiting. I'm already a day late. I don't know what will happen if I don't get there tonight. I haven't seen her in four and a half years and…"

Nossrat pinched Javad's elbow and nodded to be quiet. This peasant seemed a shrewd sort.

"… Stop pinching my elbow, Nossrat, will you!" Javad looked imploringly at the peasant. "Well?"

"Sell you the rig," the peasant said.

"Sell me? You said you had work."

The peasant shrugged: "Yup, I guess I do." He flicked his whip gently at the donkey's rump and pulled him forward by the halter.

"No, wait!" Javad said. "Here. How much? Nossrat, get my money out of my pocket."

"He burned his hands," Nossrat explained as he pulled the wad of *toumans* from Javad's pocket.

"I didn't say nothing," the peasant said.

"How much?" Javad said.

The peasant thought carefully. He stared up at the sky and seemed to be calculating. Javad wondered if he were calculating, or just imagining what might sound like a good sum.

"Five hundred *toumans*," the peasant said.

"Five hundred! God forgive you! Why, you never saw that much in a lifetime. That donkey's not worth fifty. I could buy a car for that."

"Kind sir," the peasant said. "If you see a car here, please to buy it. I will help you, even."

"He's crazy," Nossrat said.

The peasant now scratched his head and thought for a while. "Eh, I tell you what," he said. "I can hardly abandon a man to his suffering, not before God, not on his wedding day. I make a gift to your bride: four fifty."

"Let's get out of here," Nossrat said.

"Father burn!" Javad said.

The peasant snapped the whip against the rump of his donkey. "She's your bride, good sir, not mine."

"Alright! Alright," Javad said. "Nossrat, pay him!"

"That doesn't leave much for Maryam, Javad."

"It's more than I was going to give her two days ago."

"OK! OK!"

They let the peasant watch them as they mounted the cart, Nossrat with the halter rope held loosely. Nossrat flipped the halter rope against the donkey's flank, and pulled it gently to the side, reaching out as far as he could to make the animal turn. But, nothing happened.

"What do I have to do, pay extra for the whip?" Javad said.

The peasant surrendered the whip to Nossrat with a nod and then warned, "I wouldn't do that, sir."

"Afraid he'll break into a walk, eh?" Javad said. "We'll take our chances, thank you."

"Sit in the cart, sir," the peasant said. "I wouldn't sit in the cart."

"What, you're telling me the cart will boil over too? You get it from my friend's brother?"

"He don't like a load – not just yet, at least. Needs to rest a bit first..."

Javad glared back at him in the angling light, stunned.

"He 'don't like a load?'" Javad said. "Do you think I bought him for a picnic? Just how much of a vacation does this animal need?"

The peasant shrugged. "He'll be right in a bit."

"In a bit? Hum up, you animal!" Javad motioned to Nossrat to crack the whip onto the donkey's rump. "We'll see what he 'don't like,'" Javad called back to the peasant, who turned and continued his journey. "Take my car, if *you* like. Key's in the ignition." He turned back to Nossrat. "'Don't like a load just yet.' Does he think I bought his donkey so I could spend the night walking it to Tabriz? Peasant cunning!"

"Well," Nossrat ventured, "he was walking it himself, you know."

Now Javad began to feel his temples throbbing, a choking in his throat. He had to get to Tabriz tonight. What would Maryam do if he were another day late? And now he had nothing to wear except the handkerchiefs wrapping his hands making him a burned cripple, and the clothes on his back, which were raunchy with the smells of grease and burned rubber – and now donkey.

"Ugh!" Javad grunted. "What do they feed these things, beans? Do you suppose it will stop before we get to town?"

"Well, you don't have to watch it, Javad," Nossrat said. "And you don't have to announce it."

"Well, it is kind of hard to avoid," Javad said, "what with being right there in front of you – Ugh! There comes another…" Javad turned his head.

After about five kilometers the donkey started breathing heavily, with a dry, raspy sound. A white froth had dried around its mouth. Javad made Nossrat beat its rump for another two kilometers or so before it quit. Except that it didn't just quit, it rolled onto its side, almost pulling the cart over with it, released a pitiful braying gasp, and selflessly expired..

"Father burn!" Javad said, not quite grasping the significance of the animal's having stopped breathing. "Nossrat, get down and pull it."

"You get down and pull it."

Javad held up his bandaged hands.

"OK," Nossrat said. "But, you walk too."

Late that night they pulled in to Tabriz. By moonlight Nossrat led Javad past an endless series of low, mud walled houses to the house of a friend of his cousin's who had a small barn on the very outskirts.

"What do we need a barn for, Nossrat? We left the donkey back there."

"The way we smell, I don't think they'll let us inside."

Nossrat and Javad had no sooner settled into the two free stalls in Nossrat's cousin's friend's barn than Nossrat volunteered to fetch some brandy from another friend.

"It's after midnight," Javad said, protesting faintly. "How will you find him awake? Besides, I can't stay awake another minute."

"He's a very special friend," Nossrat said. "Besides, it's your wedding eve."

"How much?" Javad asked.

"I don't know. But, it is after midnight."

Javad, his hands still bandaged, let Nossrat take the wad of *toumans* and immediately regretted it. He realized he didn't know where Nossrat lived and Nossrat was not the type to be wedded to a city by a job or any kind of profession, and that was not an inconsiderable sum still left. Nervous, Javad sat alone in the barn, listening to the quiet breathing of two donkeys in adjacent stalls. His eyes began to feel watery with the hay. He began to sweat. What bothered him most was the fear that he would never see his friend again – or the money. Becoming a protector was going to be a long haul.

An hour later, Nossrat returned with two bottles of brandy, two women and precious little change. Javad couldn't see them in the dark, but the women smelled strongly of garlic and armpits. And from their throaty voices, they didn't sound all that young.

"I don't know about this, Nossrat," Javad said.

"Ladies," Nossrat said, "my friend takes his first wife tomorrow – permanent wife, that is. We must show him a good time – make sure he is prepared."

"Nossrat – my hands – I can't..."

"My friend, not to worry. This little one will do everything for you."

It seemed no time at all that Javad, nauseous with brandy, naked except for the handkerchiefs – his hands white-bandaged and red-throbbing, lying uselessly beside him – passed off to sleep amidst the fragrant smells of animal excrements and human lovemaking, with the nagging disappointment that his very first experience had been a good deal more crusty and more watery and considerably less tight than he had had theretofore imagined.

"Well," Nossrat said, as, spent, they drifted off to sleep, "tomorrow's the big day."

The next morning they bathed with water from the animal trough. Javad's hands still required wrapping so the best he could do (and the most he would allow) was to have Nossrat splash water on him. Nossrat took the last of Javad's aunt's jewelry money and returned with a used suit (without shirt) and a hired droshky, which he had festooned with white flowers.

Javad released a sigh of despair when Nossrat pulled the suit onto him. The arms and legs were only slightly short, but the jacket pinned his shoulders back so that he felt like a trussed chicken.

"Short notice," Nossrat said. "Really..."

Javad was too tired to object. He decided to just let Nossrat lead him through the day.

"Look smart!" Nossrat called smartly to the droshky driver, when they emerged from the barnyard. "Here comes the groom."

"Eh?" the driver said, incredulous. "This some kind of joke you boys be playing?"

"Not so, my dear," Nossrat said as he helped Javad into his seat. "His bride awaits."

"Where to?" the driver said.

Javad looked blankly at Nossrat, too tired to bemoan his fate: "It's in my pack – the address..."

"In the trunk?" Nossrat said. "Oye!"

"Somewhere on the esplanade by the lake. I don't remember the family's name."

Now Nossrat sighed. After a pause he recovered: "To the esplanade, then, good sir."

"Don't work past noon," the driver said. "Lest your pocket gets deeper all of a sudden."

With that they set off for downtown Tabriz to the long, paved, tree shaded esplanade by the lake, Javad dressed smartly in a borrowed suit two sizes too small, both hands bandaged, sweating profusely into his soiled shirt.

By the time the driver abandoned them at noon, they had knocked on several dozen doors, eliciting everything from outright laughter to enraged shouts. Nossrat found enough change in his pockets to buy them each a paper cone of salted walnuts. As they sat in the blaze of noon, beneath the shade of a dappled elm, Nossrat holding his own cone while he popped walnuts into Javad's mouth, they were approached by a servant woman – a washerwoman from the looks of her.

"Are you Javad e'Abasi?" the old woman said, after eyeing him suspiciously for a good minute and a half.

Javad perked up. "Maryam's with you?" he asked.

"Eh?"

"I am," Javad said, unable to mask his excitement. "I am Javad e'Abasi. Oh, indeed I am. Bless you, my dear, I am!"

"Here," the woman said. "Your Aunt what stayed with us left you this." She extended him what would prove to be the last note he would ever receive from his beloved. He had to hold it between his two bandaged hands as if they were giant fingerless pincers. "Can't say as I blame her," the woman continued, obviously tiring of her charge.

Nossrat opened the letter and held it up for Javad to read. It proved dismally simple:

"Please do not write any more. M."

Javad looked up at the washerwoman with a long, tired sigh. "What did she look like, good woman?"

"Your Aunt? A woman..."

"Her daughter."

"Twern't no daughter, young man – not one what I seen."

After the washer woman left, Nossrat and Javad sat for another hour together, staring into the hot sun as it began to lower across the river.

Finally Nossrat broke the silence: "I'm sorry about the car, Javad. I guess if my brother hadn't been so stingy you'd be married by now."

"I guess," Javad said.

Another hour passed and Javad spoke again: "I don't know why she had to get her mother to do it. She could have told me in person. I'd give anything to see her again – just to see what she's like – even if she just got mad at me – to hear her voice. I mean, she was always so understanding in her notes…"

"You never saw her once? Not even once?" As he spoke, Nossrat was fingering the note, which he was still holding for Javad in his pocket.

"…like she knew me inside out. Well…" Javad mumbled. "… sort of. I mean once – twice – I mean the first time it wasn't really meeting." He was too embarrassed to tell Nossrat how he and his school mates had climbed a mason's platform by the wall at her father's house to try to catch a glimpse of her naked, and how they had made the platform collapse, falling onto a pile of stones for repairing the wall. His schoolmates had fled with his bicycle, leaving him stranded, and Maryam had laughed at him from her window before warning him that her father was racing downstairs after him… "… but she kept sending me these notes and they were so beautifully written and she promised to marry me if I met her in Tabriz and brought money so she could help the masses…"

"Kind of mean of her, though – don't you think?" Nossrat said. He pulled the letter out of his pocket and began to reread it to himself. "I mean, she'd waited all those years. What was another day or two?"

"I guess," Javad said. Then he recalled how strange was the arrival of the first note. He lost his painter's cap in the rubble pile at Maryam's father's house. His Aunt Zahra found it leaning against the outside front door to the garden when she came to visit and had handed it to him. Minutes later he found the note secreted inside the hatband. All the other notes arrived in a small *Qaran*.

"Hey! Wait a minute!" Nossrat exclaimed. "Javad, look at this here! Look at the date!" He held up the note for Javad to see.

Javad looked over. "What about it?"

"It's three days ago. Javad, she wrote this before we even left Tehran!"

Javad read and reread the date, growing first excited, then angry, so that his temples throbbed. Then he reverted to sad resignation. "So – does it make any difference, Nossrat…?"

"It isn't the car's fault…" Nossrat said. He stopped in mid sentence, understanding his sense of relief could hardly extend to his friend. "…or anything else…"

Javad lapsed into silence with a sigh.

"Well," Nossrat said at length, "it could have been worse."

"I don't think so," Javad said.

"At least you finally got your money to the masses."

Book Two
1982

The Fields of Khoramshar
May 14, 1982

omewhere far away, on the distant side of the Zagros Mountains, wheat fields wafted beneath a yellow sun – fields stroked by little fingers, small hands, tentative feet – ripped by jagged treads, steel shards. From her father Abrahim's house in Tehran Pari struggled to not imagine the fields. She had seen them in Khoramshar as a young girl, when they were still unspoiled. They had visited relatives there after World War II. She was forty-four now, her mother, Nargess, eighty-eight. They were in the second year of fighting Iraq.

Pari had grown up watching her country sold to the West. Many of those selling were the classmates of her older cousin, Javad, who at fifty-seven was still unmarried and still unemployed. A mere six years after the Japanese surrender (five years after Javad's disastrous elopement), Pari had watched Javad try to make a name for himself warning that the foreign powers would never accept Prime Minister Mossadegh's nationalizing of the oil, and would only use the event to abrogate Iran's contractual rights to AIOC profits from foreign subsidiaries, and that the AIOC probably hoped for just such a scenario so the West could take complete control of Iranian oil... He tried to start a newspaper to publicize his ideas, but the sole stack of flyers it produced sat undisturbed on his magnificent walnut desk in his bedroom office upstairs, still gathering dust thirty years after being abandoned when his two lectures attracted only two attendees. His only audience had been Pari, a thirteen-year-old girl at the time – and she had found it all so confusing. The family was embarrassed. Friends simply laughed. It was sad, Pari thought, but Javad had been right: In 1953 the CIA staged a "popular uprising," replete with Rashidian brothers and hired mobs. The uprising placed a multinational cartel in control of Iran's oil. For the next twenty-five years the American-backed Mohamed Reza Shah clung to his throne by torture, arbitrary imprisonment, corruption and cheap oil – until Khomeini toppled him in 1979. A year later the Americans coaxed Iraq to invade.

And that's why her son Akhbar would be sweeping mines at the front.

Was there no place on Earth for them, Pari thought – no place not polluted by oil and power and death? Akhbar was the scion, the grandson of Abrahim. He could have a normal life, could finish school, become an engineer, have a family, build things… But, the mullahs would put an end to that – mullahs and their holy war for oil.

The fields would be at the front. Akhbar would be in them, near them, past them – somewhere. Akhbar. Her face reddened with anger. Her heart choked with despair. Akhbar was only twelve, almost the same age she had been when Mossadegh had made his power grab – an age when she still played with dolls and listened to her uncle Javad. In all of their brutalities, at least, the Shah and the Americans and the British before them had left the children alone. But, not the mullahs. Akhbar would be with her and not wandering the far side of a distant mountain range, tethered to unknown peasant boys, were it not for the mullahs – and not for her very own brother, Rasheed. Ugly Rasheed had proved no better than the Shah's sycophants, who had lined their pockets with bribes and plundered the country – except they were better businessmen. Rasheed, at forty-seven was a furniture salesman.

She could imagine the *basiji* children in the fields: they were too young, too frail for war; but even the youngest and frailest could clear mines; Khomeini's clerics gave them plastic keys, which they instructed would open the gates of heaven for the children when they were martyred. They told the older ones – thirteen and up – young virgins awaited them there. The army officers then tied them waist to waist in lines of 20 or so, each with one hand on the shoulder of his neighbor and the other clutching the little brass colored plastic key, while the children silently prayed, "God is great. God, protect me. God, take my soul…" over and over again. They were safe with the little plastic, brass colored keys to heaven, stamping the minefields with their feet beneath the turquoise skies and white-puffed clouds. They rubbed the keys between thumb and forefinger with confidence. At the corner of each key remained a prickly stub, where the mullahs had broken them off from the stringers – like the parts to a model airplane. You could see the seam from the two halves of the mold, where frail fins of plastic extruded still. Most of the children were peasants, so it did not matter the keys to heaven were shabbily built. Most everything in Iran was. The Shah had vainly tried to spend the country's oil profits on development: schools and factories. But, somehow the funds were always siphoned into private pockets (including his own), leaving Iranian industry burdened with obsolete, used equipment purchased for the price of new (and then some). The plastic keys were done efficiently, however: it was said they had been custom manufactured in Taiwan, as a lot of five hundred thousand.

The clerics were proud of their little plastic, brass colored keys, proud of their peasant children, many as young as 10, few older than 16, proud of their own ingenuity and self-sacrifice: these were the paths to righteousness that avenged centuries of outside oppressors. In two world wars Iran had been ravaged by troops from Turkey, Britain, Russia, America, the Soviet Union and

Germany. When Mossadegh had avenged these indignities by taking back the oil, Britain had crippled Iran with an international embargo. A powerless Iran watched helplessly as the Americans took control of the oil under the guise of a multinational cartel and then sought to whitewash the whole affair a decade later with a land reform program that only further impoverished the country. Eventually the tables turned in 1973, when it was the oil producers who crippled the West. Again Javad was a lone – and ignored – voice of insight: he pointed out to the few who would listen to a forty-eight year old, unemployed lawyer, that the 1973 embargo wasn't led by OPEC so much as the multinational oil cartel, whose member corporations – still Western owned – were the real beneficiaries of the price hike. OPEC, an organization of foreign countries, however, proved a convenient scapegoat for an effete President Carter to avoid angering the oil companies. So he dubbed it the "OPEC" oil embargo. The Iranians in the street didn't care: to them it was victory, revenge – the West now bending to them. Only six years later they would be debating endlessly whether it was they who got rid of the Shah because he was corrupt and oppressive, or the Americans who got rid of him because he had backed OPEC. In either case, it had all led to the invasion by Iraq and now the mullahs had vowed this was *jihad* and no Jew, American, Sadam would ever again disdain the scorpion's sting. Later in the war the mullahs would reward the families of the more heroic martyrs with photographs of the remains of other heroic martyrs who had predeceased them – apparently believing they deserved more than plastic keys to heaven.

Three days earlier, only hours after Akhbar had disappeared, Pari's brother Rasheed – an oily centipede if ever there was one – had said nothing, only, "He's gone."

"Father burn! Rasheed, why didn't you stop him?" She was breathless. "You're my own brother – How could you be so – unholy?"

"I guess you'd say I've no monopoly on that."

"You!" She shook visibly. "You…"

"Since when did you wait for my blessing – for anyone's blessing?"

"…and you did nothing? You'll still do nothing?"

"What, get to the front before he does?" Rasheed busied himself with removing his soiled, sweat-stained jacket and placing it on the newel post. Then he unknotted his knit woolen tie and hung it over the jacket. "He's just bluffing," he said. "Soon as he discovers from his Uncle Javad I've one less mouth to feed he'll come right back. Count on it."

Pari was thumbing her amber worry beads one at a time as she watched her brother. Her face burned as he turned towards her. He had a waxy sneer. Behind him was the cracked and water stained plaster on the ceiling, sagging. Rasheed was "head of the family," but as far as Pari could see, he'd done nothing to earn it – even less to honor it. He'd ruined Tajmah's wedding at the time of the Mossadegh oil crisis, getting drunk at the celebration and insulting her groom, Saeed. Only eighteen at the time and already pegged as irascible and feckless, Rasheed was jealous of Saeed being the son of a famous jurist, jealous of Saeed being a brilliant law student, jealous that his half sister's husband would become head of the family. The next day he'd burst into tears. He'd kicked and fussed and begged for a wife until the family found him Morvareed, the daughter of one of War Minister's old servants, recommended by Nargess's cousin Zahra. While other young men studied law or started businesses. Rasheed stayed home and drank vodka, with the indulgence of his father, Abrahim. When Abrahim died around the time of the American president Kennedy's land reform in the early 1960s, Rasheed, at twenty-six, found himself with no skills and even less interest in acquiring any. His only talent was filching pocketable antiques from the house and selling them for alcohol and cigarettes, which led rather naturally to his employment in a seedy furniture shop in south Tehran. He was only head of the family because Tajmah and Saeed had fled to America at the very start of Khomeini's revolution.

"You like these mullahs, don't you?" Pari said. "You think Akhbar's in good hands with them?"

"If life's so important to you, you could 'like' a mullah – or two. They're the ones with all the clout now – or all the money, if that's what you prefer." He started up the stairs, still looking at her. "I didn't do this, OK?" he said, turning his face towards the stairs. And then he spoke angrily: "And I'm not his mother."

It was always her fault. Everything was her fault. It was the whole family's mantra – Rasheed, Nargess, Tajmah, even the crippled twins, now in their late fifties. Only Tajmah's husband, Saeed, spared Pari blame – but of course that was a different story. Pari had never been the perfect goodie two shoes daughter. She "had a reputation."

"You mean, for instance, I should like Mullah Abol Fazl?" Pari said. "Is that what you mean? You and Mother? Marry the pig-mullah Abol Fazl? Me vomiting on him isn't clear enough? Sometimes I think you've forgotten you and Morvareed have a daughter, Rasheed. Do you remember her? Shohreh? Of course, she's a famous folksinger, so you don't have to worry anymore." Pari felt mean invoking the tragedy of Shohreh, Rasheed's daughter. She had gone blind seven years ago, after being raped by unknown assailants at the age of sixteen, just before her career as a folksinger had taken off. Rumors abounded connecting members of the royal family with the rape, which occurred during a drugs party at one of the royal palaces. The public knew nothing for sure. Nothing was ever proven. Nothing went to court. That's the way justice had worked under the Shah. The story actually furthered Shohreh's success: innocence betrayed by fate, triumphant in the end. It made a touching tale.

Saeed had pitched in after the rape and had used his government contacts to help Shohreh's career as a folksinger, to help her find a life, but Rasheed only hated him the more for it. If Rasheed weren't going to help Pari find her son, Akhbar, she could at least rub his nose in the guilt he should feel for not having been enough of a father to prevent the tragedy, and for not declining to profit from the wages of the success it engendered.

Pari wondered why these tragedies kept descending upon the family. Why couldn't a beautiful, gifted girl like Shohreh have met a wonderful man at the party – a rising intellectual, an engineer or a rising politician who would share a modern life with her, worship her? Was it too much to ask?

Pari's Mother, Nargess, had, in a despair of her own, once tried to arrange a marriage between Pari and Abol Fazl, at the time an impoverished divinity student. It was only society's increasingly Western tilt that allowed Pari to scotch the deal on the grounds of utter repulsion – a fact she did not conceal. Abol Fazl was embittered against the family as a result, but neither modesty nor defeatism tempered his subsequent ascent of the clerical monkey bars. In Friday prayers he had become a vocal champion of traditional mores, of which the act of polygamy, through the sacrament of temporary marriage, seemed his most cherished. Through the intercession of Abol Fazl, God had discreetly bestowed rewards upon a number of worthy pilgrims. God had been particularly busy since the revolution, because Abol Fazl, now powerful, had wisely used up only three of the four slots allotted for permanent wives. This encouraged a substantial train of hopeful supplicants to vie either for discreet favors, or for the coveted fourth slot – if only they could please him first as a temp. The occasional pregnancy seemed a small price for freeing a cousin from prison, or saving a brother's life, or a raffle ticket to the holy sepulcher. The church would see to the support of the child, the treatments for gonorrhea. Only the truly devout were eligible. Abol Fazl had a very big turban.

Rasheed held his right hand on the banister and turned again towards his sister. "For a start, yes!"

"Do you even remember what a greasy, ignorant pig he was? Him and his fat farmer family – that's the kind of marital bliss you'd wish upon me?"

Rasheed held his arms above his head: "He's Khalkali's right hand man. Ayatollah Khomeini's protégé. You could do worse."

"He has a price, you know."

"Yes," Rasheed said. "Piety."

"Right, Rasheed, piety. I'd forgotten that."

"Apparently." He turned and started to lunge up the stairs, taking them two at a time.

In the three days since, as far as she knew, Rasheed had done nothing to discover the whereabouts of Akhbar; had done nothing to determine if he'd been shipped to the front; had done nothing to find out if he'd made good on his threats to join the *basij* so that the mullahs could show him the way to martyrdom.

☙

With her free hand Pari nervously combed her fingers backwards through her hair, over and over again. She wore her hair short cropped, layered and dyed blond in the American style, but the dark roots were beginning to grow out as the war had made luxuries either unavailable or unacceptable. She wondered how Rasheed could be so callous. Here her son, Akhbar, had just run away to the *basij* and Rasheed's concern was to settle old scores. Could he imagine her despair? Of course, according to him, he'd been suffering a lifetime of her despair and there was no need to make this a special occasion. She suspected he wouldn't behave much differently had it been his daughter, Shohreh, blind or not blind, famous or not famous. She wondered if Saeed could help. He was in America, but he should still have some contacts. Would he be embarrassed to take her call? Would Tajmah let him?

She imagined the lines of children combing the fields, small hands, small feet, brushing the wheat, hundreds of child prayers rising to heaven, Akhbar's with them. In yellow fatigues and white bandanas inscribed with red prayers they would winnow the khaki-colored fields. Above them clouds would scud, white puffs in a turquoise sky. And the army would crouch behind the children and their child prayers. And then, somewhere would snap a sharp crack and flash and puff of dirt smoke and spray of rocks and copper-smelling blood, as if spurted from an atomizer, and pulverized body parts and shredded clothes. And then – what? What did one end of the line of children do when the other tripped what the army had sent them to? Did they freeze – in shock – tethered to the bleeding stumps of their comrade? Did they burst into tears and confusion, furiously rubbing their little plastic keys to heaven and reciting their boy prayers? Did they flee back to the clerics, snot-nosed and dragging limp torsos, abandoning splintered feet? Or did they untie themselves first? Was there even anything left of any single one of them besides shredded limbs and burst torsos? Thoughtful mullahs issued them heavy overcoats to keep the body parts together in order to facilitate identification. Did the army bring up the rear, profiting from their progress? Did the soldiers even let the survivors retreat? Did the clerics cinch together the remaining children with the remnants of blood-splattered ropes and send them, vacant-stared and shaking, back to clear more mines? Or did they comfort the shivering boy-veterans and send them home? How deep was their need for martyrs?

Oh, God, why had Akhbar chosen death in the fields? Pari thought. Was this his role in God's universe, his place on Earth? Were they as a family to do no more than this, find no more than this?

"God forgive me. Please, God, forgive me. Only please, return to me Akhbar."

Pari sat alone on the Tabriz carpet in the empty receiving salon of her father Abrahim's house, holding her elbows. She was waiting for news to come. She was waiting for Rasheed to return. She was waiting for her older cousin Javad, though she didn't expect much from him, certainly not if his errands led him past one of his favorite cafes, where he would languidly propound on legal intricacies and pretend he had clients. She thought with revulsion of Abol Fazl. She thanked God she had spurned the arranged marriage with him over two decades ago. She had never heard from him since, but had witnessed his recent rise with dismay – and disgust. She twisted her handkerchief back and forth into untied knots. Despite having never suffered the touch of a shod foot, the carpet was showing its age, with uneven brown splotches that looked like the burlap bags used for Basmati rice. There were white patches on the faded plaster walls – where gilded mirrors had once hung.

She had gone to the police three days earlier, immediately upon hearing Akhbar had volunteered, but the *pasdaran* (Khomeini's religious police) were hanging all over them. The police captain, dressed smartly in a starched navy blue uniform, had cordially admitted her to his private office. He had seated her on a creaking wooden chair before his mottled, gray metal desk, which in turn huddled beneath a picture of an angry, frowning Khomeini. The worn rubber desktop supported a sixties-vintage telephone that looked like a black Maria, a triangular beaten metal ashtray, a stack of impeccably sharpened pencils and a varnished wooden tray for mail. Folded neatly on top of the desk was a copy of a local newspaper, with a picture of Abol Fazl. Pari had seen the paper earlier in the morning. There was a story about Abol Fazl preaching the Islamic virtues of family and sexual abstinence for women (outside of the context of permanent or temporary marriage, of course). Through the overpowering odor of stale cigarette smoke Pari smelled urine and deodorant cakes from the washrooms. She would have refused the offer of tea more than the three times dictated by the conventions of *taarof*, had she not been so worried about offending the captain. The captain had no sooner snapped his fingers for the clerk to bring them tea than the *pasdaran* had stepped in, two of them, no older than sixteen, each with a pious, scraggly beard. One stood behind her, smoking a long *Bahman* cigarette, the other behind the police captain, fingering a cardboard bound *Qaran*. She felt nervous, not being able to see the two of them at the same time. She saw the captain glance back and forth between herself and the *pasdaran* behind her. Grasping the two sides of the chador to make sure she displayed nothing sacrilegious, she had to hold her head forward and her gaze downward. She felt as if she were bowing at their feet.

"*Khanoum*," the *pasdaran* behind the captain said, "your hair!"

Pari brushed the offending strands back inside her chador. "I apologize, sir." She bowed further forward. "*Allah* be praised. It is covered, now."

The *pasdaran* glanced at his compatriot standing behind her.

"*Khanoum*," the captain said, clasping the arm rests and sitting straight-backed in his squeaking spring chair, "it's a war now. What can I do?" He shrugged his shoulders. He leaned his head to the side.

"It was only this morning, sir. Would he not still be in Tehran?"

"*Khanoum*," the *pasdaran* behind her said, "is this not something your son wanted?"

Pari turned her head while clasping the chador tightly around her hair. "He's only a child, sir." It annoyed her to be beholden to a boy the age of her daughter Fahti – and uneducated at that. But, she tried hard to sound plaintive, not angry. "He's only twelve." She turned back to the captain. "You know the *Mosque e'Zenab*, my captain. They were recruiting there Friday. Surely you could make inquiries. He would have gone to them."

"Well, I suppose…" the captain began to answer.

"*Khanoum*…" The *pasdaran* interrupted before pausing. His tone of voice indicated disapproval. "Satan is not picking his nose."

Pari bowed her head to the side. "Yes, my good sir," she said. "But, surely mere inquiries would not cause any delays." She waited in silence for a response. She heard the clock ticking on the wall behind her, opposite Khomeini's angry portrait.

"*Khanoum*," the *pasdaran* said, "you have already come here dressed disrespectfully." He paused for effect.

"Sir, it was a mistake. A mistake for which I apologize. Nothing was meant…"

"You should be very careful," he continued, as if she had no right to speak, "what is a delay and what isn't; what serves God and what serves Satan. We once betrayed the prophet's grandson, we should not betray him again. Bless Hossein!" He paused again for effect, as if he awaited her answer, or the chance to pounce on her. But, no answer was forthcoming.

"Brother, she is a mother," the captain said in a quiet voice, breaking the impasse. "It is only for the love of her son. Surely you…"

"Praise to God, your son will be a man, *Khanoum*!" the *pasdaran* interrupted. "He will revel in the blood of martyrdom and you shall be blessed and proud before God in your suffering."

Now Pari began to weep. She did not want to think of Akhbar in the fields – Akhbar in death. "Please," she whispered. Then she grew silent again.

"Please," the captain said to the *pasdaran*, breaking the silence. He still sat straight-backed, but held one hand in his lap. "She meant no disrespect. Do you not have mothers of your own?"

The *pasdaran* behind him walked over to the window and spread his hands on the sill, looking out at the sun-baked street, where merchants were pedaling by, their goods stacked high on unwieldy bicycles. "Did you know the man who led the coup against Mossadegh was a CIA agent?" he said. "Did you know he was the grandson of the American president Roosevelt? We learned this from the nest of spies. America is everywhere against us. Now they are with Iraq. I have two brothers who went to heaven defending Abadan. They were hardly older than your son. What is the difference between your son's mother and any other? What, I ask you, is the difference between pulling a soldier away from the front and opening the line for the enemy? Both are counterrevolutionary acts, are they not? Either one serves the purpose of the enemy."

Pari began to choke with fear. *Pasdaran* talking about counterrevolutionary acts were dangerous. They could arrest her. God knows what they could do to her. So many women had been raped and mutilated in Khomeini's prisons – even while obviously pregnant – just as they had been in the Shah's. She began to weep uncontrollably. "Please," she said. "I want my son. I only want my son. Please, only my son. My only son…"

After Pari had repeated this for a while, the *pasdaran* behind her, barely old enough to support a beard, said, "I remember you, *Khanoum*. You're related to Shohreh e'Kashani, no?" Pari's heart began to beat with hope. Her niece, Shohreh was a living martyr. The Khomeini regime celebrated her as a symbol of the of Pahlavi oppression. "And you have a daughter," the *pasdaran* continued, "Fahti? Stay home with your daughter, Fahti, and thank *Allah* she is alive. Thank *Allah* she has not suffered like her cousin Shohreh e'Kashani. Home is where women belong. I don't want to have to give you this advice again."

"*Khanoum*," the captain said gently, after the *pasdaran* had departed. "There's nothing I can do." He got up and opened the door to see if the *pasdaran* were listening on the other side. "I will try to make inquiries," he said quietly. "But, I make no promises. There's a war. Things are difficult. We all must make sacrifices." He opened the door again for another look. "We all must do what we can to help."

"Thank you, my captain."

"He may be at the front already, or on his way. It's a dangerous time. Don't make trouble for yourself." He paused, waiting for her to gather herself and leave, but Pari curled herself forward and withdrew her face into the black folds of her chador. "This *pasdaran* – I know him," the captain said. "He has been very hurt by the loss of his brothers. He did not mean to be so cruel about…" He paused, not wanting to say martyrs. "It helped that he recognized you as Shohreh e'Kashani's aunt."

"God's will," she said.

"Yes," he said. "God's will."

Sitting now, three days later, in the receiving salon of her father Abrahim's house, Pari wondered if she should telephone Saeed in America. He had always known what to do. She imagined Saeed, with his rakish moustache, wrapping his arm around her, telling her who to call, what to say, who to hire, what to pay – Saeed who slept in the snow. Then he would be combing his fingers backwards through her wheat-colored hair, soothing her, comforting her, reassuring her, and then he would be stroking her... But, she had had to marry fumble-thumbed Mahmoud and that was Saeed's fault – and Saeed's doing. Everything had come from Saeed's doing. Saeed who'd fled to America. Saeed had been a help, a comfort to Shohreh. Why couldn't he do that for her? If he had to help anybody, it was her. God forbid that any one of the centuries of doddering bodies that haunted her father's house would help her now any more now than they had then. Oily Rasheed had his hand in it, too. Did any one of them care about her child? Their own flesh and blood? Their grandson, nephew, cousin who was barely twelve? They were content with blame: first Fahti, her daughter, hopelessly strange; now Akhbar, her youngest, volunteering for death; she and her children were cursed – would seal the family fate with their curses. And now Saeed was safe in America with his wife Tajmah, her half sister – and she, Pari, was abandoned in Tehran with Rasheed in a mausoleum of octogenarians – and their forsaken progeny, of which she was one.

ℭ

"Does Tajmah know?" she had asked Saeed at Mehrabad airport, before he and Tajmah departed for America. That had been three years ago. Amongst the exchanged embraces of dozens of family well wishers beneath the large portrait of Mohamed Reza Shah, which workmen were just then replacing with an even larger portrait of Khomeini and his angry glare, their cheek-to-cheek kiss – sister in law to brother in law – had gone unnoticed, indistinguishable from the spare corridor of parting embraces exchanged between women in anonymous black *chadors* and nervous men in Western business suits with newly grown beards. "Oh, Saeed, what will I do without you?" she whispered with a furtive glance at the others. "Promise me you'll come back. Call! I beg of you. I need you..."

Saeed snapped shut his Louis Vuitton valise, kissed Rasheed's daughter, Shohreh, also cheek-to-cheek, and then filed across the tarmac and up the stairs into the waiting airplane without comment. Only Rasheed had cast him an angry stare.

But, that wasn't important now, she thought. Akhbar was important. Her insides churned to think of it. Her stomach tautened. It was always this way: her children, Fahti and Akhbar, needed and she could not help. Had she had a mother to show her anything different? All her mother had ever done was pray and spin conspiracy theories about who was cheating whom. Pari wished she could find such solace in prayer. When Pari's children needed her, it was always when something else was happening. How could she solve their lives and hers? Maybe her daughter, Fahti, had made the right choice, had tossed herself willingly into the abyss of tending to her grandmother Nargess, anemic and frail in her grandmother's airless third floor apartments while other girls her age squealed in their basements to tapes of the Rolling Stones and Pink Floyd, hiding from the *pasdaran* – and soon Akhbar – she knew it… She would change - if only she could get Akhbar back. It was too late for Fahti, but not Akhbar. She promised God she would return to the path of righteousness. No more wandering. If she had been lost, she whispered to God, it was only because Saeed had not loved her. Please, was there not room in His heart for that? Could He help her find The Way? Was there no place on Earth for her? But then, what kind of god was there? The one that her mother, Nargess worshipped? The imaginary one that populated Tehran with legions of spies and undermining aunts, like Rakshandeh, who Nargess insisted still stirred a witches' brew against her? The one that tore children to pieces in His Name? The one whose clerics, like Abol Fazl, now paraded about in their chauffeured Mercedes limousines, the abandoned sex toys of the Shah's corrupt ministers and Savaki torturers? Pari wanted to believe Akhbar was safe in the fields of wheat, prayed he was in the fields of wheat that didn't have mines, prayed that he stroked the fields with his boy's hands, safely – scraped the nourishing kernels gently to his lips – touched the sun-dappled sky clouds. She prayed that something good would come – something less harsh than the sharp rocks of the blistering desert, or the snake-infested reeds of the marshes. But, she had no way of knowing. And, now, all she could do was wait – and hope – and hope not…

Pari heard the floorboards creak upstairs as her mother, Nargess, rocked back and forth in prayer. Her mother was in her late eighties and weighed next to nothing. In the adjacent room, Pari's daughter, Fahti, prayed as well – echoing the faint creaks of the grandmother. At an age when her hips and breasts should be swelling, Fahti had come to weigh scarcely more than her grandmother. Had somebody told her? Had she counted? Pari waited until she calculated her mother had finished the final prayer. Afterwards her mother would meditate and Pari could talk to her.

"You must make her eat," her mother said.

"Akhbar is gone," Pari said. "He ran away to the army."

"I know that. I'm talking about Fahti."

"I know that," Pari said. Her mother did not want to discuss Akhbar. That was the way it always was: Pari had to feel her way around every hurtful subject with her mother. And her mother would just sit there, her arms crossed inside the gray chador, staring at the pale shadows on the bare walls, her back to the window – ignoring her – praying. Or she would blame Pari. What else had she ever offered her in her life? Oh why had Saeed fled to America without her? Oh why could she not be her half sister, Tajmah?

"What does Rasheed say?"

"Rasheed? You want to know what Rasheed says, Mother? 'Akhbar's gone.' That's what Rasheed says. And you need his permission to ask Aunt Zahra?"

"And what can Zahra's husband, Mansour, do that an Abol Fazl can't?"

Pari was taken aback. She knew her mother had little knowledge of the world outside, but she couldn't have avoided the rumors about Abol Fazl. "I don't think he'd find me 'pious' enough for his favors, Mother –"

"Posh! None of that's true, those lies…"

"I vomit on those mullahs!"

"… He's a good man." There was a pause. "Yes, dear. We remember." Nargess looked away. "Those are all just ugly rumors from the royalists and the British…"

"Is that what you want of me, Mother? Abol Fazl? Well, don't worry. I'm not in his holiness's holy *Qaran*."

"No, I guess you wouldn't be."

"And not worthy enough to bother Rasheed about, either."

"Well, he is head of the family now – when I think of how hard he works – the sacrifices – and a blind daughter – and what respect do you show? Huh! You've certainly had your fun. He comes home so tired…"

"Please, Mother! I know: shah, or war minister or prime minister – he could be anything he wanted. But, he's a furniture salesman in a mall – and that was all before Shohreh – and I didn't make him any of that…"

"… Rasheed didn't have the opportunities Javad had. He had to support the twins and after Abrahim died…"

"… It's Akhbar, now. Not Rasheed or Javad or the twins or even Baba. It's Akhbar…"

"Shhh!" Pari's mother held her finger to her lips. "You'll upset Fahti."

"Fahti knows," Pari said tersely. "And she knows Rasheed doesn't care about you or me or …"

"Don't say that!"

"It's Akhbar. Do you understand? Akhbar…"

"You don't care about Fahti!" She paused. "You always did put fun before family…"

Pari crossed her arms and craned forward so that her elbows rested on the shiny knees of her American blue jeans.

"What?" the grandmother said and paused again.

Pari knew her western clothes annoyed her mother, but she was too upset to care. She tried to curl within herself. She wanted to become very small. So small that she could hide in a crack like a snail and no one could ever find her. Her hair fell forward around her eyes but she was too afraid to comb it back with her fingers. "Please, just tell me what you want of me," she said.

"Rasheed will make inquiries. He'll take care of it…"

"Everybody's making inquiries, Mother. Even Javad is making inquiries. I need Akhbar, not inquiries…"

"… Why just last week Rasheed sold a dinette set to Alavi. His was Khomeini's driver in France. Javad said so. The minister himself! One call…"

"Mother…" Pari didn't finish. She listened mutely as her mother droned on. It annoyed her that Khomeini's pious sycophants were now helping themselves to the luxuries from the countries they so despised – and in the middle of a war – and she could no longer afford those luxuries herself. It annoyed her that her mother failed to see Rasheed for the petty sales assistant he was. Hadn't it been enough that he'd ruined Tajmah's wedding? And then begging them to find him a wife! A boy only eighteen! And shouting insults at Saeed in front of the wedding guests – So who would be surprised the only woman who would give herself to him would be that scheming Egyptian opportunist, Morvareed? The tragedy of Shohreh should be no surprise, with parents like that. No wonder her mother's friends never visited anymore. Even after Abrahim had to add to his permanent employ two *dash* (thugs) from the *bazaar* to control Rasheed's tantrums, Rasheed was still "the future head of the family." Why should Pari expect anything different now? Oily Rasheed and his angry sneer. Oily Rasheed pocketing the few rials Shohreh still earned singing. Saeed had tried to help Shohreh out of compassion for her being stuck with Rasheed and Morvareed for parents, but there was only so much he could do – and even less he could do from his refuge in America. But, would their mother admit this? No, if there were indiscretions for Nargess to criticize, they were always Pari's. And Pari was expected to be no better than wet loins to serve the hallowed lust of a power mad mullah. Of course, to her mother, Nargess, it was a long overdue marriage – safe – holy – as if it were even a remote possibility.

Her mother, as if reading her thoughts, said, "You're not so holy as to rinse the prayer rug."

Pari began weeping softly. "It always comes to that, doesn't it? Not so holy. Did it ever occur to you I just want Akhbar back? Or that I want Rasheed to stop pretending he's doing something? Or that I want you to stop blaming me? Or that asking Aunt Zahra's husband, Mansour, for help isn't as disgusting as that pig-dog Ayatollah Abol Fazl? Or that maybe, if God wanted to, He could show that He loves me – just once?"

Nargess looked off to the side, avoiding Pari's eyes. Her face became very sad. "I wanted things too – when I was young. I wanted a son for War Minister. I wanted peace. I wanted to be holy – blessed by the eyes of God. I wanted a family to find a life for itself." She paused, then spoke again: "You would receive more from God if you followed the prophet's ways…"

"He's keeping another house, you know, with Morvareed – Rasheed. They just keep the apartments here for show. They think no one will know. Dr. *Masoudi* told me. She heard through one of her patients, whose daughter used to sing with Shohreh. Mother, half the time he's selling the antiques and half the time he's just moving them over to his private house. What's going to happen to us when he's done?"

"After the war, Pari, as soon as it's over he'll – well – go out on his own – start his own shop…"

"On his own? Mother, he's forty-seven!"

"… He's just using those shop owners while business is bad. Why with his contacts…"

"Using his daughter Shohreh is more like it."

"… and he knows a good price – he looks after Shohreh – of course Shohreh needs help. He says they hardly pay her anything now – but his own mother, his own sister, he would never – he's head of the family – he would n…" Nargess stopped when her granddaughter, Fahti, opened the door. "Fahti, dear," she said.

Fahti said, "You're fighting."

She stood motionless, thin as paper, pale. Her black, high-collared dress with white buttons dangled from her shoulders as if carelessly hung from a hook, as if the frail, sloped, boney-hipped body inside were a skeleton of sticks. Her eyes stared vacantly from hollow shadows within the doorframe, against which she leaned. The two braids of her hair were unraveled.

"It's nothing, dear," Pari said. "You must rest."

Fahti opened an empty stare towards her mother, as if she wanted something, expected nothing. Her mother raised her eyebrows briefly and then cast her glance down again upon the carpet. Fahti hung her head to the side "No," she said, nodding. It was almost a gasp, ever so faint. Then after a pause she said, "I don't feel so well, Mother."

"It's nothing," the grandmother, said. "At your age – you're only fourteen – and you hardly eat. As soon as you eat you'll…"

"Mother, stop!" Pari raised her head reluctantly to catch her daughter's eye. "Your grandmother…" She paused and looked away.

"I do so understand," the grandmother said. "It's all very natural…"

"Mother, please…"

"… She's had a great shock. You should teach her respect for her grandmother."

"Leave her be," Pari said.

Fahti hung her head forward. "I will pray for Akhbar," she said. She closed the door.

"You could be a mother to her," the grandmother said. "What do you expect?"

Pari recoiled, as if she had been slapped. Her face throbbed red. She stopped breathing. "It's not what you think…"

"No?"

"… Did I have a husband anywhere to help me? Did I even have a mother to give *me* as much time as her prayers…?"

"You had a husband…"

"… Is there anyone to help me? Fahti?"

"… well, once." Nargess concentrated on smoothing out some wrinkles the gray patterned chador made on her thighs. "I'm just the grandmother. I don't take responsibility…"

"How was I supposed to know?" Pari wrung her hands. "Is that what you think? I'm a bad wife and a bad mother and that's why my husband, Mahmoud, drank and I'm supposed to throw myself to the first offer of support that will take me?"

"Well, you didn't have to marry Mahmoud," Nargess said. "You could have had – anyone…" She became silent. "…except for…" Then she said, "I loved you so – Pari dear, you were so beautiful, any man would have begged for you, but…" She didn't finish the sentence.

"But, what, Mother? I didn't marry till I was thirty? I'm too proud to ask my dear cousin Zahra help me get my grandson back? I shouldn't have dishonored my parents by refusing to marry an ignorant mullah…?"

Now Nargess drew her gray chador about herself and turned away. "That's not the way it is at all – the way you said it."

"… I can't sing – No? – I did listen to you, Mother: You said Zahra's husband, your own cousin Mansour, was a friend of Ayatollah Khomeini. He can't snap his fingers and make them return your grandson for you? Isn't this the Islamic rule you prayed for? Aren't these the holy mullahs who have come to save us from the Great Satan?"

Nargess grew quiet. She drew within herself, hunched her shoulders, hung her head. She spoke, haltingly, almost fearfully: "You don't know what it was like, Pari. The Pahlavis took everything – They were army thugs – peasants, really – no better than animals. I wasn't asking for anything other than to be left alone to pray – to honor God, to raise an honorable family – but they made every servant become a spy. Look what they did to Shohreh. Do you think Rasheed can ever forget that?"

"Yes, Mother, that's what's so awful, isn't it? Rasheed is the one who has to forget. What about Shohreh? What about the rest of us who thought maybe we could have lives too and that's the lesson we get?"

"Well, of course Shohreh…" Nargess paused again.

"It's always you first, isn't it? Mother first, then son – then anybody…"

"That's not true. She's not been well – Zahra. I don't want to be a bother – She's not well enough…"

"Nonsense. She's fit as a fiddle – well enough to dance at Roya's wedding last week. Well enough for her and Mansour to get chauffeured out and about in their Mercedes – Gucci shoes, Channel shopping bag, chador and all. Just not well enough for her beloved cousin to ask her for her grandson…"

"Well, I wasn't there. I wasn't invited."

"You were too. I gave you Roya's card myself."

"Huh…" Nargess paused. She thought quietly to herself. She had never understood why it was Zahra who had to tell her that Javad had been seeing Rakshandeh's daughter, Maryam; how Zahra had been the one to know that Javad had sought to elope with her and had been abandoned on the alter. Poor Javad had been so crushed, he never married. He'd even confessed to her recently that he'd never heard what happened to Maryam – never really understood why she had left. She just disappeared. Now, Zahra had no time for her. She was too important, now. "It used to be the officials were your friends, you know. But, under the Shah they got so uppity – lining their pockets with phony contracts – and now they live in palaces – the Americans helped them. At least we've gotten rid of the Americans. And then they had to take away the prophet, to make it all respectable. Religion was 'backward,' they said – but not Christianity, of course – as if we're some sort of primitives throwing spears in the forest…"

"We are primitives throwing spears, Mother! At least that's what the mullahs are making us. Women can't be lawyers now, or engineers or any kind of doctor other than pediatrician or gynecologist. I grew up under the Pahlavis, Mother. I never knew which of my schoolmates were spies either. I still don't. But, at least I could be whatever I wanted to be. You know, they still run Evin Prison – torture chambers and all. Of course, it's all in the name of God now. You should be happy with that. *Allah* and his boy veterans, *Allah* and his saintly prostitutes…"

"Bah! You never studied to become any lawyer or doctor that I know of – At least they follow the prophet's way – I don't remember you studying to become a mother either, for that matter."

"… and don't forget *Allah* who won't help Akhbar. Do you really believe God wants Akhbar to die for his fat mullahs, the ones with the Mercedes limousines now? If you won't go to Aunt Zahra, why not Aunt Rakshandeh? Her husband imports half the army's ammunition. They have the connections…"

"Hmmph!" the mother said. "You expect me to kiss that hand? She only married this one a year ago –at her age! And then a wealthy *bazaari* before that – and a minister before that and that German spy – I haven't heard from them – either of them – That Rakshandeh was a Russian spy – I know – CIA – British – still out to get me – How else could she get a husband at her age?

– Posh!" She stopped speaking and remained silent for a long while. Then she spoke: "She was just a cabaret singer, you know."

Now Pari spoke in a very tired voice: "What have you got to hide from the Russians, Mother? Or the British – or the CIA?" Pari put one hand on her hip and assumed a posture of defiance. "You have something they want? Royal blood?" She held one hand upwardly outstretched. "Tell me, Mother, what do you even have that you want? You don't have anything, Mother – period!"

Her mother turned towards her, crossed her arms and glared with a face that was gray and wrinkled, like fish scales: "I have God. Khomeini's brought us that, at least. And I can say that's more than Rakshandeh, or even Zahra – with her fumble-brained husband – have. Have they even been to visit me once, now that they have chauffeurs and Mercedes? They would all too well like to forget who I am."

Now Pari spoke with anger: "Of course: you're the mother of Rasheed, who drives a Pacon."

"Yes, the mother of Rasheed!" Nargess said, with emphasis. "And the mother of Tajmah whose daughter is a doctor in America and whose husband Saeed is a legal scholar – and..."

"And the mother of Pari, who is cursed and whose children are cursed because I stayed and took care of my mother. I'm a curse to my family, Mother. Say it!"

"Huh!" Nargess shrugged. She turned away. "You never earned a curse for taking care of anybody I know – God knows – Such a modern woman..."

"Yes, Mother: a modern woman who doesn't want her son blown up for a plastic key to heaven, and for a bunch of fat stupid mullahs to get fatter and stupider, scratching their testicles and asking for silk handkerchiefs to do it with."

❦

There was nothing for Pari to do. She waited for Rasheed to return for lunch, waited for Fahti to get out of bed after praying – wondered how Fahti would get well enough to return to school.. After a while she began to feel the sticky heat of morning. She brushed a strand of hair to the side and worried the perspiration on her temple would cause her makeup to streak. She would remove to the coolness of the basement, where there was the small aqua colored, tiled sitting room with a hexagonal pool and a fountain in the middle, but she feared she would miss the chance to talk with Rasheed before he became preoccupied with his lunch. She tried not to think of the building heat. She prayed for a breeze in Khoramshar, to comfort her son. Then she tried not to think of Abol Fazl – or of Akhbar and the clerics and the fields. Please, *Allah* forgive me! She tried to remind herself Sadam was threatening to bomb

Tehran and she was neither the only mother of a twelve-year-old volunteer nor the only widow dependent on an overweening brother and slated for a marriage of convenience.

But, none of this would have happened if Saeed were with her. She could feel his strong arms around her, longed for *the brush of his moustache across the taut skin of her abdomen, the sticky dark of the last night of* Ramadan *almost thirty years ago and her girl's heart beating on the roof:*

> *Ask for wine,*
> *Cast flowers about.*
> *For what do you long?*
>
> ...
>
> *Take the rose garden,*
> *Wine as your friend,*
> *Take those lips,*
> *Kiss this face...*

... she thought.

The weeks after Saeed had moved in had throbbed with miasmal sublimation. By having gone through the wedding ceremony, Saeed had contracted to marry Tajmah, but they were going to postpone the consummation until Saeed finished law school. Saeed should have then taken Tajmah to live in his father's household and consummate the marriage there, but he had moved into Abrahim's household shortly after the contract –claiming illness. After his "recovery" he complained that his stepmother had turned his father against him once she had born him a son and he begged to stay. Immediately he and Pari had begun exchanging stolen glances. They were innocent glances, furtive glances... she did not know... she did not know... At first she thought she imagined it. Then he would turn from her when their eyes met and she knew it was guilt – hoped it was guilt – because she felt guilt too...

> *Drink blossoms, scent,*
> *Fern dance to rose,*
> *To gain her your heart.*
>
> *Sky and Earth birth your smile,*
> *Oh, beautiful flower,*
> *For what do you long?*

... Was this the way it would be with men? In her grandmother's generation, women were only allowed visits from men who were close relatives. Sons in law had often been married to baby sisters in law to circumvent these strictures. The marriages had been mere formalities, of course – conveniences to permit

families to congregate. Could this be why? The only other young men she had known as a girl were cousins – and her odious brother, Rasheed. She and Saeed had touched fingers one morning as he passed her a plate of bread. She felt a rush in her chest. Her body tingled. She felt a quiver in her groin. She looked away; pretended nothing had happened. But, she could not dismiss her thrusting heart. She was only fifteen. A man could marry four permanent wives, but not two sisters. She had no hope. Her older sister, Tajmah, had been lucky to marry for love. Always she was the lucky one. Everybody said so. Maybe it was fantasy. She began to blush crimson when her eyes met Saeed's. She would look away. She would not let herself do this. She was imagining it. It could not be. She would lie awake, pretending to be asleep, bursting, dreaming Saeed would take her in the dark...

> *Flute cry of hearts wrest,*
> *All lovers bewail...*
>
> *O're Sky and Earth unite...*
>
> *Close, my secret to my pain,*
> *Ear and eye n'ere alight.*
> *Love's fire lives in the reed,*
> *And boils in the wine.*

Had he moved into her father's house because of her? He had seen her at the first wedding ceremony, the contract – could not seem to take his eyes off of her. She wondered if anyone else had noticed. She wondered if anyone else saw her face burning whenever he spoke to her now. Then Ramadan had rushed upon them. They fasted during the days, but celebrated after sundown with roast lamb kabob and baklava. Every night was a party in a different house. And then had come the last night. There was utter silence on the roof. Tinny pings from the courtyard, far away where the others were having breakfast before the final fast... she was sleeping in, alone, hoping against hope, her body bursting in the dark. And...

> *... I stand mute*
> *With the agony of wishing ...*

...then the quiet on the roof began to throb. In sticky silence her heart beat beneath the jasmine and honeysuckle. She was not alone. A mosquito buzzed above a sea of crickets below – Saeed's bare feet silent on the roof of dried mud – her eyes closed– waiting – his hand gripping her mouth as he slipped within the mosquito net and soon there was no need for his hand on her mouth as he kissed her and stroked her all over. She did not want it to ever stop: her older sister's fiancée, and she, only fifteen, untouched and imagining anything, and he anything... Downstairs in the courtyard the others talked – talked about the

prime minister, Mossadegh, and oil and the British embargo and the inflation and food shortages. It had been only weeks before the American CIA would hire mobs through the bazaari Rashidian brothers – to stage a coup against the elected government of Prime Minister Mossadegh. Mossadegh had been trying to force the British to honor their side of shamefully lopsided contracts they had bribed Persian officials to sign – and getting nowhere. It was all about force. It was always about force. And who could be more forceful than Saeed who slept in the snow and fixed her throbbing with his eyes and forced himself upon her in the dark? And what was a night and a day of fasting if ...

The two had lain afterwards feeling each other's wetness, his head buried in her neck, his hand on one breast, his hot breath above the other...

> *Mussed hair, smiling lips, drunk;*
> *Torn blouse, wine cup held...*

Saeed recited the lines from Hafez in a whisper and then they lay there, thick with the jasmine and honeysuckle and the guilt and the crickets and the lone mosquito and the metallic sounds of breakfast in the distance.

How did you know? she thought. How did you know...?

Later, they descended separately, with separate excuses, hoping to be forgotten in the incessant buzz about the British blockading exports of Persian oil and driving the nation bankrupt. (They did not know then about the Americans.) With deep suspicion, Rasheed had torn at her throughout the whole of the blazing day with a razor stare, glaring eyes, throbbing temples, the veins in his neck distended. Yet he said nothing, for it was just after Rasheed had ruined Tajmah's wedding and his father, Abrahim, had hired the dash from the bazaar to control his tantrums. And Pari wondered if she looked any different now, if she walked differently, if Rasheed had been in the welling shadows, hidden by the crickets; if she had not heard his voice at breakfast in the courtyard below – if maybe she had dreamed everything and nothing was changed and it had all been her imagination...

"Rasheed, what have you heard?" Pari said. Rasheed had hardly had time to close the front door behind himself and remove his suit jacket. It was brown, in a herringbone pattern. A loose thread hung from one cuff and the two elbows were worn smooth. The collar was oily and darkened from perspiration, like a brown paper bag stained by grease. Sweat stains shaped like cut melons spread beneath the arms of his shirt.

Rasheed said nothing. Striding towards the basement stairs, he flung his jacket across the newel post, wafting the warm odor of his body against Pari's face.

"Rasheed?"

"There's nothing new, OK? There's nothing since yesterday or the day before or the day before that." He started downstairs to the basement, where lunch awaited. He was a towering man and whenever he descended stairs it was more a lunge than a descent.

"Rasheed!" Pari said, following him down the stairs. "Mother said you'd call Aunt Rakshandeh and Aunt Zahra."

"Tell Mother I'm here for lunch..." He grasped the railing and turned backwards, stopping briefly. "She said nothing of the sort."

"Rasheed!"

"I've been asking everyone I can call. OK? Mother doesn't even talk to Aunt Rakshandeh. She'd have her thrown in prison if she thought she could get it done. They don't like me tying up their phone, you know – those *bazaari*. I have mouths to feed, speaking of which, where's our cousin Javad?" He started chewing a radish while he leaned forward to select a scallion and break off a corner of bread for dipping yogurt.

"He's checking with his clients, he said. You could wait for Mother and the others, you know."

"Javad? Clients? In the next world maybe. Tell Mother I don't have long – busy day." Rasheed had wondrous hair. It curled and puffed out before his forehead like a sail. From time to time between bites he bunched it back with his fingers, as if it were a black fleece.

"Akhbar's your nephew, Rasheed. Does that mean anything?"

Rasheed stopped chewing. He placed the piece of bread, which he had just dipped in yogurt, down on the plate before him. He rested his forearms on his knees and glared, his mouth agape. "I'm doing what I can," he said. He started to chew again.

Just then their mother, Nargess, began creaking down the stairs to the basement to join them. Two adversaries at once was more than Pari could handle. And, with her luck, Afsar and Masumay would creak downstairs and join them as well.

"Well, if you tire of reaping as I sow, dear sister, you're certainly well ready for an older profession..." He rose to his feet. "...and in a different kind of house. Ah, Mother, dear!" He kissed Nargess on both cheeks.

"Rasheed, dear. You work too hard. You really must take some time off – those horrid people – Well, now I have you for lunch at least."

❦

Pari burned in silence. She thought about Saeed. He could take her away from all this. Bring Akhbar back. No one blamed Saeed. No one ever blamed Saeed. There would have been no others had it not been for him.

> My love for you is a thousand hearts,
> Each to a tendril of your hair.

A thousand are the paths I seek,
My life for a scent of Bliss,
To open the door and wish…

Oh God, what caraff gurgles like wine,
Frothing in my blood,
Lifts beauty-song to lips…

On winter nights Saeed would sleep outside in the courtyard in a billowy, green canvas sleeping bag, with a flap he pulled over his head when it snowed. He refused the warmth of the korsi *lest it "weaken" him. This engendered giggles of envy amongst Tajmah's friends. Tajmah was so proud. So little did they know! Or maybe they knew. Maybe they even expected it. For breakfast he would have a swallow of French brandy and a set of Belgian chocolate truffles. Then a cigar. A man with such distinctive tastes could hardly confine his appetites to the culinary.*

Pari was of the generation that came of age after World War II. She was fifteen at the time of the CIA staged coup against Mossadegh in 1953. She was in her early twenties at the time of the land reform forced upon Iran by the American president, Kennedy.

In the American view of history, Kennedy's land reform was a deliberately lit backfire intended to interdict the onrushing flames of communism. And backfire it did indeed: what shah would not be delighted at the prospect of seizing more lands from fractious vassals? Only a decade earlier, Mohammed Reza Shah had tasted the joys of recovering the land his father, Reza Khan, had appropriated. The government had seized these lands when the British forced the father's abdication during the war because of his pro-German sympathies and (more importantly) his upstart hubris concerning control of his country's oil. But, under the eyes of the Americans, Mohammed Reza – with consternation – had been obliged to turn the newly-reseized lands over to the peasants – well, some of the lands. Neither a bright nor forceful man, he had reveled in the added power gained by the consequent destruction of rivals from amongst the feudal landlords. But, Mohamed Reza Shah was even more naïve than President Kennedy. Celebrating their newfound wealth, the rural peasants traded their plots for television sets and emerging opportunities in urban poverty. Meanwhile the clergy fumed over the loss of church lands and the impoverishment of their major benefactors, the feudal landlords. Ever holy, ever dutiful, ever loyal to the *Allah*, they reclassified the sin of land reform: they elevated it to an anti-Islamic crime of the highest order. The mullahs carried the newfound tenets of their faith to the dispossessed, now-urban, unemployed peasants, and coaxed their smoldering poverty into the open flames of political unrest. Mohammed Reza Shah largely ended this era by expelling Khomeini, after admonishing him with an exemplary, if tidy, beating in Tehran.

In the Iranian view of history, Kennedy's land reform was a shrewd fostering of popular unrest to destabilize the Shah's government, making him ever more dependent on Western aid and arms sales to help him build an army to keep himself in power. And, of course, this support depended on an unimpeded flow of cheap oil. That Khomeini was subjected to a tidy beating, rather than an assassination, was an obvious nod to the American masters, who wanted to continue their ongoing support of Khomeini as an additional choke leash for their puppy, the Shah.

This was also the era that saw the first appearance of oil wealth in the population, and the consequent debut of an educated middle class. To be sure, the flow was a mere trickle – even by the sixties – particularly in comparison to the obscene geyser it became during the seventies. But, together with continued Western reforms pushed by the Shah and the drift of the upper classes away from the stricter Islamic virtues, it fostered a loosening of traditional mores. By the fifties, young women would openly party with young men to the sounds of Elvis and later on, the Shirelles. By the sixties they were wearing blue jeans and miniskirts, dancing to the Beatles and the Rolling Stones and vibing with the Doors and Dylan. By the seventies, the occasional peasant might still be throwing stones at young women prancing in white tennis skirts to the sounds of disco, but usually the gendarmes quickly hustled the offenders away. Recidivists they referred to the dreaded SAVAK. This was also the era during which foreign meddling in Iran once again peaked, this time under American influence and the exigencies of the Cold War.

So Saeed first slipping his hand between Pari's legs to rustle her bump only slightly preceded the West doing the same to Iran at large, and adhered to centuries of precedent on point – this time under the aegis of American fingers. Pari had no perspective on this, of course. At fifteen, this was just the way it was – and the natural renunciation of her mother's endless prayers and domestic devotions. Sadly, however, though she acquired the mores that came from the West, she never benefited from the money: Abrahim's business had barely recovered from the ravages of the war when the British led embargo drove it into an unrecoverable tailspin. And Rasheed was hardly suited by temperament or ability to rise from the ashes.

Pari had never known when to expect Saeed. On hot afternoons that first summer, before they had removed to the country to escape the heat, she would announce she was retiring for a nap if the family were going out. She would leave her door ajar and recline on her bed in her nightgown, her temples throbbing, her perfumed breasts aflame. She would strain for the slightest sounds of creaking floorboards or padding feet and listen to the street vendors while the servants slept.

"Melons! Melons! I sell melons," the vendors' calls would echo.

"*Toot*! My *toot* are as tasty as *toot* from Harad."

"Ice. Ice. Nice ice in a trice!" They would sing their chants in rhyme.

On very still days, when the silk drapes slumped and languished in the heat, Pari could hear the lone clop clop of the vendors' donkeys on the cobblestones. She would drowse off... sometimes she would be woken by the sound of Saeed's footsteps...

> The day of separation and the night of parting are done,
> Fortune's good book calls me the distance crossed.
> The fall of pain and suffering to spring has run.
> Let Hope's morning draw the curtain's mystery,
> Bespeak the night is o're.
> From now my heart leaves light to utter dusk,
> As I attained the sun, and all the haze is cleared.
> Long night's unrest and soul's despair,
> The cherished of my love have fled,
> I can't believe the story's suffering trimmed,
> Succumbed to the shadow of my heart.
> Oh, Steward, may your cellar always brim,
> By your wisdom all distant misery depart.

... sometimes she would be woken by his mouth on her lips and his hand beneath her nightgown. She longed to lie with him after these encounters, stroking the hair on his chest, nuzzling his clean-shaven cheek with her nose, breathing the aroma of his Monsieur de Roche cologne. But, he seemed to always choose the riskiest opportunities, escaping through the rear door of her bedroom, or withdrawing behind the ebony dressing screen, as her mother turned the handle to the front door of her bedroom. It was almost as if he wanted everyone to know.

"Oh, Saeed," Pari would whisper out of earshot of the others, "can't we slip away some afternoon? Just the two of us?"

"Pari, dear, you have school," he would answer.

"No one will know." Then she would sigh.

They would sit with the family beneath the shade of the willow tree by the dripping cool of the cistern pool centered in the rear courtyard, longing for each other. The family would wander along the garden at the edge – Tajmah, Afsar, Masumay, and Nargess and (before his illness) Abrahim – to inspect the roses and jasmine. Saeed and Pari would recline beneath the willow tree, Pari in her school uniform, a gray tunic with a white collar, and Saeed in his Italian silk suit and Bally wingtips. Pari would have her knees pressed together, her legs crossed, her arms demurely in her lap, the dark braid of her hair hanging behind her to her waist. Saeed would stroke his moustache stoically. They would sip mint *sharbat* (mint, sugar and vinegar in water), watch the family with feigned nonchalance, and pretend to discuss the weather. When Pari would refill Saeed's glass, he would momentarily interlace the tips of his fingers with hers when she passed it to him, sending a rush through her breasts. But, the two of them acted outwardly as if it were just the quotidian transfer of a beverage. They took care not to be overheard by the crippled twins who remained unattended in their room above.

Only Rasheed seemed suspicious. He followed Pari everywhere, dragging the two *dash* along as if they were guarding her, not him. In the afternoons, he and his entourage would escort her home from school, following her along the cobblestone streets past the two story shops and houses, like trotting sheep dogs. And when Rasheed wasn't following Pari, he was following Saeed; the only exception being when he knew Tajmah would be with one or the other, or both, and preferably with others as well.

Pari complained to her father, Abrahim: "Isn't it enough he ruined Tajmah's wedding? If he wants to ruin mine too he could at least let me get one first."

"Pari, dear," Abrahim said, "he'll be head of the family soon." He moved to embrace his daughter with his expansive reach and wide smile, but she twisted away.

"My brother's a creep, Baba."

Abrahim smiled. "All brothers are creeps. Especially older ones."

"The others don't have to have watch dogs."

❧

Through the summer and fall Pari and Saeed only had opportunity to exchange furtive glances. Tajmah noticed nothing. She occupied her days shopping for fabrics. She wore pleated skirts and crocheted sweaters, the same as she saw in the French and German magazines. In the evenings, she would sing traditional songs she heard on the radio. Everything pointed to her being a blissful newlywed. No one noticed anything. Indeed, there was nothing much to notice, so close was Rasheed. Once Pari had returned to school, she lost all hope of ever finding time alone with Saeed. She grew desperate. But, in the coldest months of the winter she found her chance. On moonless nights she would wait for the others to fall asleep and then, knowing no one would ever expect her to be about in such forbidding weather and knowing that her sister, Tajmah, was too prissy to sleep with Saeed out in the courtyard, she would sneak downstairs barefoot, dressed only in her cotton nightgown, and – her feet aching – pick her way across the icy blackness of the courtyard to plunge into the warmth of Saeed's canvas sleeping bag. There, after she stopped shivering, she made ferocious love amid the mingled scents of mildew and sweat and brandy and Monsieur de Roche cologne.

Until a night late in February when Saeed drew tight the drawstring of his sleeping bag and refused to let her enter.

"You mustn't come any more," he whispered. His voice was hoarse, strained.

"Saeed, no one will know. I promise."

"Tajmah…"

"Tajmah?" Pari's heart caught in her throat and she did not even know she was shivering as she bent over, squatting on her bare feet on the frozen stone of the courtyard, tugging at the rough, canvas flap of the sleeping bag.

"It's not right," Saeed whispered.

"Tajmah?"

"Go – before you catch cold."

"How much does Tajmah know? Saeed, tell me!"

"She doesn't know anything. That foolish woman – She's pregnant."

Pari felt her face inflame. A gust of wind sent cold chills along her shoulders and legs and rattled one of the shutters to the twin's room. "Saeed, Saeed…"

"You must go, now."

"… Saeed, what does it matter?"

Saeed turned his back to her.

Pari began to weep. "So why was it right then, but not now? Saeed ?" She pushed at the sleeping bag. "Saeed?"

"Go away! I don't love you."

"You do," she said. But, Saeed had drawn back the flap and she was talking to the cold, lumpy canvas.

"I never loved you. Go now, before you make more trouble!"

Now she was crouching in the frigid wind and trembling. Her feet ached and she worried they would freeze to the stone. Tears were forming icicles on her eyelashes. "Before I make more trouble?" She had little hope Saeed would hear her against the noise of the wind, but she dared not raise her voice. "Before I make more trouble? What about you, Saeed?" She pushed at him through the canvas sleeping bag. "What about you making trouble?" But, Saeed had turned his back on her inside the sleeping bag and he did not answer. Bitterly she repeated this mantra as she wandered, shivering, back through the blackness of the frozen courtyard and then upstairs to her room. Once there she continued repeating to herself, over and over again, "What about you, Saeed? What about you…"

In the weeks that followed into spring all she could think about was getting Saeed back. But, in the absence of his cooperation, it was again impossible even to have time alone with him. Her classmates were giggling about

first dates and boys and American dances and movie stars and the ha
algebra teacher just graduated from Princeton and she had nothin;
Nothing else to think about. Her attention wandered from English
and geometry until the teachers at the Lycée started sending notes
her mother.

"Huh! Those snippety French prunes," her mother said upon rea
letters. "What would they know? Geometry! I'd like to see one of thos
toads raise a family – Nuns! Uggh!" Having dismissed the issue, she
to her prayers, leaving Pari free.

Late in the spring of 1954, Tajmah had a miscarriage just bef
moved to Tajreesh, in the foothills north of Tehran, for the summer.
always took a house there to escape the heat. Tajreesh had a reput
beautiful violets (the Persian violets of Shemiran) and even more
women. The *Qajar* princes made the latter famous by taking so man
as wives. When the Pahlavis started building summer palaces ther
advantage of the cool mountain air, Tajreesh became a stylish subut
sought after by the newly rich poseurs.

Saeed now slept on a futon at Tajmah's feet, to comfort her, and F
doned all hope. After a fortnight in bed Tajmah began to recover an
(Tajmah, Saeed, Pari and even Rasheed and his guard dogs and his
wife, Morvareed) went out together. Sometimes they would hike al
leading up to the mountains along carpets of pine needles, picking
from the sea of Persian violets by the paths and exchanging them
another, Rasheed taking up the rear to better catch any indiscretic
often they would frequent the Bridge Over Tajreesh, which, thoug
cally a bridge over the Tajreesh River, was really an expansive aspl
surrounded by one and two story shops, with somewhere underne:
progressively depleted by upstream diversions of its waters into the
ident shah's multiplying gardens. It was a popular meeting place fo
and newlyweds. Every summer afternoon was a fair, with vendors s
strips of grilled lamb liver, chunks of grilled kidneys, testicles and h
salted walnuts, ice cream, grilled corn. The newlyweds would wal
in hand, searching for friends and gossip. The students and othe
rieds would search for someone to wander hand in hand with. The
a maze of wandering, with cars parked all about, their radios bl:
ambled along with the others, desolate with abandoned hopes of e
ing to Saeed alone. He and Tajmah walked arm in arm, every bit th
newlyweds. And, everywhere they were followed by Rasheed and
Morvareed, and the protective *dash*.

That's when Pari met the first of the "others." He called himself I
and when Pari first saw him, he stood out amongst the drab crov
other young men wore dark jackets and pressed pants. Hooshan;

ewly imported American blue jeans with a brown belt and a cowboy buckle. olled up in the left sleeve of his white t-shirt he kept an American Winston igarette box (filled with domestic *Zar* cigarettes). He was clean-shaven and is hair was freshly oiled and slicked into ruffles. He appeared to have mod-led himself after the new American movie star, James Dean. With a cigarette ngling downwards from his lips, he leaned, bow legged, against the hood f a turquoise blue American Chevrolet coupe with white seats. He and Pari ared at one another as she walked past. He nodded. She turned away. Then ne doubled back on the premise of buying a cone of salted walnuts, and with-1 a matter of days they were arranging trysts on family outings, whenever ney frequented the same environs.

Until a cloud-dappled afternoon with shafts of yellow sun piercing the ky, when Saeed returned to her. Only this time she struggled and he had to eep his hand on her mouth. She locked her ankles. He jammed his knees etween hers, one at a time, and forced her legs open. She, tried to twist away, ut when he entered her, it was with an ease that surprised both of them.

"Damn you!" Pari said when he had done with her and lay still, pant-1g, with all his weight pressing on her, his head hanging over her shoulder. Damn you!"

Saeed said nothing for a long time. Then he fell asleep on top of her until he pushed him off to the side and he woke and said, "You're embarrassing veryone with that creep."

"He's better than you are."

"He's a gardener's son – using you. He's making a fool of you."

"And you aren't?"

"Have you ever seen him lean against the same car twice at Bridge Over 'ajreesh? No. Let me tell you why: He waits till the owners leave and then he truts around polishing the mirror while they're gone. Has he taken you driv-1g yet? Have you ever seen him drive one of those cars? Any car? Even once?"

Pari tried to slap him, but it was awkward from the side and he caught er hand in the air. This time when he made love to her she did not resist. But, he wept all the way through and turned her back to him when he finished.

"Go away, now!" she said. "You got what you wanted."

"Maybe," he answered. "Maybe not."

Saeed continued to force himself on Pari through the summer, until Iooshang disappeared, the new object of Rasheed's attentions. Then Saeed ecame unavailable, as before, until they were back beneath the yellowing rillow tree in the fall, watching the others amble about the gardens along the ourtyard's edge.

"Saeed," she said.

He did not answer.

"Is that the way it is?" Pari said. "Hooshang's gone so you don't need me anymore?"

"It's not that."

"What, then?"

"Tajmah's pregnant again."

"Father burn, Saeed!" Then Pari forced a smile as Nargess and Afsar glanced her way. She wanted to ask what Tajmah's being anything had to do with her, but she couldn't speak in front of the others. And Tajmah chose just that minute to announce her pregnancy to everyone. Pari's time with Saeed became lost in the congratulations.

❧

Over the next several months, Pari became suspicious that she was becoming the object of burgeoning gossip. Her parents became obsessively oppressive. They threatened her with curfews and grounding. She ignored them. She walked to parties on her own, escaping the occasional servant her father, Abrahim, assigned to trail her. She refused to tell them when she would return – even where she was going, though it never took them very long to find out from one neighbor or cousin or friend. She began enjoying a dribbling succession of distant male cousins and their friends collecting around her at these parties. They would offer her cigarettes and look over their shoulders before they sneaked off to a balcony or closet to pour themselves scotch and then return. Once in a while the braver of these would offer her some, which required her to join them for the clandestine pouring. More likely than not, she would linger with them after they filled the glass. She enjoyed the privacy and the simple intimacies. The stuffy quiet. The adventure. The filling of the gnawing emptiness inside her, an answer to an aching search for she knew not what... The young men always spoke so kindly. They made her feel like somebody, not just an object to be ordered about. They were so undemanding. At first she would allow only kisses. She had read in the American magazines that was acceptable, not even risqué. Then she was letting them touch her breasts while they kissed, and then her legs. She would let them rub their hands between her knees, but if they moved upwards, she would push them away and straighten her clothes. Then she would remain with them in the bathroom or closet chatting with an increasingly bleary voice. Or she would just let herself out the door and rejoin the party, with a parting glance of longing that was intended to be noticed.

After about a year of these private intimacies becoming more heated and serious, with dwindling attention to straightening clothes and mussed hair, Rasheed began to figure out her routine well enough to end her encounters by precipitous and unannounced arrivals, face red, neck veins throbbing. Her friends knew about the *dash* that accompanied him, and knew there were thus limits to his threats. But, they also knew there was a threshold they were better off not approaching. So they would divert his search to another room and knock on the bathroom or closet door when Rasheed had stamped around the corner. Pari would emerge and feign innocence, or she would just depart, before Rasheed returned to the room.

But, in those moments of private intimacies, Pari was thinking of Saeed. She would fantasize that the kind words and impassioned kisses came from Saeed. After three or four glasses of scotch she could almost believe the touches truly were Saeed's. And when she grew tired of pretending and pushed the ardent suitor away, she would pine silently, only half ignoring the attentions newly lavished upon her. These were young men who were engineers and doctors and civil servants. They seemed so prim and proper in their dark cotton suits, which were increasingly imported from England, so witty and animated. They tried hard to be chic and worldly, with Ray-Ban Wayfarer dark glasses, even indoors and at night, and freshly laundered white shirts – which their mothers ironed for them. Sometimes they wore Lacoste tennis shirts with the little green alligators under their suit jackets. But, not a one of them could rival Saeed with his rakish moustache that scratched her abdomen, and not a one of them mentioned marriage – just romance, which meant sex. And starting with the first of these, Pari, who now dyed her hair blond and declined water for her scotch, and smoked *Homa* cigarettes (to the dismay of her mother, Nargess and her now ailing father, Abrahim, the two of whom tirelessly, but fruitlessly, tried to arrange marriages for her) learned that Tajmah's state of gravidity had nothing to do with Saeed's interest in her, or lack thereof. No sooner would Pari graduate one of these *amoroso* from secluded fondling to serious trysting than Saeed would steal back into her bed, uninvited. Then, somehow, Rasheed would suspect the new lover and contribute to the serenade in his own, inimitable vernacular, after which Saeed would ignore her again.

Saeed no longer bothered with excuses, once he had become father to a little girl in 1955. Expecting a boy, he had refused to visit the hospital after the delivery. He had threatened Tajmah that, if necessary, he would take a second wife to obtain a male child – this despite his residing in her father's house. Under Pahlavi-sponsored modernization, polygamy had been discouraged, but it had come to be regarded only as passé, not as immoral. To many of the educated classes, eager to shuck any appearance of backwardness, it had become an avowedly embarrassing relic. But, it remained legal, and a generation of men despaired of emulating the machismo of their fathers and grandfathers, who, like War Minister, had been wont to instruct their current wives to find them additional ones – under pain of punishment. And if they reached the limit of four permanent wives, they had recourse to an unlimited number of temporary ones. All of these outlets fell under the aegis of the church. There would be no Moslem bastards – not in Shia. So Saeed was merely being insensitive, if just tolerably so. Saeed was a brilliant law student and would be a judge some day. Saeed was the bright hope of the family. No one ever blamed Saeed.

♋

It was during this time Nargess and Abrahim made their last attempt at arranging a marriage for their wayward young daughter. This was when they introduced the young cleric-in-training, Abol Fazl. Abrahim was failing by this point. He needed help getting up from his chair. Walking was difficult. He had to lean ahead and then, stooped forward, shuffle to catch up with himself. He had a bamboo cane with a gnarled walnut handle, but it didn't work well. He had trouble remembering things, difficulty sleeping, suffered long periods of sadness. It was only because of his failing powers and declining savings that Nargess could get him to agree to a shabby candidate from the divinity school.

Pari was astounded. She arrived home late from an afternoon party, sweaty and disheveled from another sultry dalliance in a stuffy closet, barely able to walk – and desperately nauseous. She found Abol Fazl seated in the receiving salon, with her mother and father. Had he not been accompanied by his own parents, two porcine, stiff-necked farmers from the south, Pari would never have guessed such a visit would have been arranged without giving her prior notice. Certainly *she* wasn't going to prepare *them* tea. And compared to the clean-shaven, slick young men she dated, Abol Fazl was a dud. He was greasy, with pimples, and had thick, strongly refracting glasses. Though neglecting to shave was considered pious, she thought it made him look downright foolish. He wore a white turban and a gray robe with a black vestment on top, and cotton-topped shoes that looked like a peasant's.

Abol Fazl took one look at his candidate, assumed merely virginal modesty, and pledged his undying support.

"And which number will I be?" Pari asked. Sweating, she fought back the swelling waves of nausea. She needed to get to a bathroom quickly.

Abol Fazl gave her a quizzical look.

"Which wife will I be?" She choked briefly, as the contents of her stomach pressed upwards.

"I am not married, *Khanoum*."

"Well after me..." She swayed in mid speech, unsure how much longer she could hold herself. "... how many?"

"Pari!" Nargess spoke sharply.

Abol Fazl held his fingers together and bowed his head briefly. *"Allah's* will is *Allah*'s will, *Khanoum*," he said. "He is the answer to your search." He was eager to prove his divine authority.

That's when Pari projectile-vomited all over Abol Fazl in a giant, satisfying spurt.

"Oh, poor *Allah*!" Pari said, recovering. "He just couldn't help Himself." Then she passed out.

"You're whipping Baba into the grave," Rasheed said, after Abol Fazl and his parents had fled. "He can't handle things any more. Do you care about that? Do you have any recollection of the Prophet's teachings? And before a man of the turban!"

"He can always appoint two *dash* to guard me, if he wants. But, if I were him, I'd be more worried about what my eldest son was doing with my money."

"Not letting Saeed get his fingers in it, that's what. – I don't have the heart to tell Baba one tenth of what you're up to."

"Better Saeed than your hook nosed Egyptian, Morvareed Six-Fingers." (Six-Fingers was the nickname of a famous gangster in the 1940s). "What happened to Baba's rental house in Government Gate?"

"I'm head of the family now. Don't get smart with me!"

"You'll be head of the family when you don't have two three hundred pound nannies padding about after you day in and day out…"

"Yeah, well you'll be the first to know about it when they're gone."

"Try it! Just try it! See what you get away with when Saeed becomes a judge. Tajmah and I aren't going to be your servants – in this life, or any other."

"Why don't you take one of your slime squirts for a husband and stop making us miserable? Like you're too good for the doctor Mother found from Isfahan last month so she wouldn't have to pack you off with a mangy divinity clown."

"Go away, Rasheed! Just go away!"

"OK, maybe I can go all the way to China. I bet guys *there* haven't heard yet. The only ones left, I reckon…"

❦

Not long after, on an early summer afternoon, Pari was drowsing off – again dreaming of Saeed with her door ajar, imagining the scent of jasmine and honeysuckle and honey from Mt. Sahand, while the family had gone out. The air was hot and still and the vendors were calling from the street. She sensed a faint, abortive creak in the floorboards. Half asleep on her back she bent one leg to the side, wrapped her arms about herself, and pulled her nightgown just above her knees. She murmured a dreamy, indulgent, only half calculated sigh, and closed her eyes to wait. But, nothing happened. There were no more creaks. No padding of bare feet. No hand or lips to caress her. She waited in the still heat. The silk curtains hung limply. The house was as quiet as a mausoleum – too quiet.

"Saeed?" she sighed dreamily, still half asleep. It was more a groan of pleasure than a sigh. "Saeed – is that you?"

"You whore!" Rasheed bellowed from the hallway, his voice like an enraged bull's. "You whore! You slut!"

"Aiyee!"

Rasheed burst through the door, slamming it backwards into the wall. "My own sister!" Rasheed's face was red. The veins in his neck throbbed. Sweat glistened on his forehead. "Your own sister's husband! How could you?"

Pari screamed again. She clutched the bedclothes around about her neck and retreated on her back to the head of the bed. She screamed and screamed and screamed for the *dash*.

Rasheed towered in the doorframe, consumed by a red rage. Like an animal he lunged towards Pari and reached for her forearm while he held one fist in the air, threatening. Pari pulled her arm away before he could catch it. Rasheed knelt on the bed and reached for her again, keeping the one arm in the air, ready. He started to shake her, cursing. While they struggled the two *dash* burst through the door. One of them grabbed Rasheed's fist in mid air. The other wrestled him into a full nelson while Pari screamed and Rasheed cursed.

"Wait till I tell Baba!" Rasheed shouted. He struggled to free his arms. By standing up he was able to lift the *dash* who held his head in a full nelson off the floor. He grunted. But, before he could throw him over his head, the other *dash* pulled the two of them away backwards from the bed.

"You donkey!" Pari screamed. "You donkey! You were spying on me, you donkey! You were spying on me naked. I'll tell Baba! I'll tell Morvareed! My own brother!"

"Go ahead!" Rasheed shouted. He was releasing dry spittle from the corner of his mouth. The *dash* were now pinning him back up against the wall with their shoulders, unsure of what to do. He was their boss's son, after all. "Tell Baba and Tajmah why you were hanging around naked for Saeed. I know it. I saw it. You can't lie your way out of this one. You slut..."

"What Saeed? What Saeed? Do you see Saeed? Look for him, you father dog!"

"You think I don't know? You think everyone doesn't know?"

The row continued until the rest of the family returned from their cousin's lunch party, whereupon the shouting match moved to the receiving salon downstairs.

"She's a slut!" Rasheed yelled. "The whole family knows it. The whole city!"

"Saeed was with us!" Abrahim yelled back, raising both arms in the air, as if he wanted to expand into a mountain. But, he no longer had the immense confidence that he once had. The gesture now was more one of an old man pleading. "The whole time he was with us. How could you believe it? How could you say it?"

Pari was red eyed with tears. Saeed stood with his back straight, as if at attention, grinding his teeth. He held his right hand on his belt. Sweat stained his starched collar and he loosened his silk paisley tie. The two beefy *dash* stood immediately behind the inflamed Rasheed, ready to jump him at the slightest physical indiscretion. Behind Saeed Tajmah sat primly, straight-backed in a gilt French chair. She wore a white silk blouse, a calf length gray skirt, white bobby socks, black flat shoes and turquoise earrings. She held her knees together, with her legs angled to the side. She held her white-gloved hands together in her lap. Her face, lips cherry red with lipstick, was as rigid and inflectionless as her girdle. She could have stepped right out of an American magazine of the late 1950s. But, there was perspiration on her upper lip and she only ineffectually hid this by occasionally feigning a sneeze into an embroidered handkerchief. She too held her jaw tight.

"I know what you're up to," Rasheed shouted.

Saeed said nothing. He held his hand on his belt. He glared back at Rasheed. His moustache twitched. Then, still clenching his teeth, he spoke derisively: "I think you made your point at the wedding..." He waved his free hand towards the two *dash*. "In your eloquent vernacular."

Pari ran crying from the room. With uncharacteristic deference, Saeed waited the better part of a year before helping himself once more to his sister in law. This time the causative paramour walked, talked and danced like Elvis.

❧

Pari was still burning in silence over Akhbar enlisting in the *basij*, and Rasheed was just finishing his lunch, when their cousin Javad returned and raised a ruckus. Almost ten years Rasheed's senior, Javad was his polar opposite. Tall and slender, he wore natty, tapered Italian suits with sharp shoulders that made his upper body look like a V. His hair was gray and impeccably styled, his fingernails manicured, his English shoes polished to a mirror shine, his belt of fine-tooled Moroccan leather, his tie of French silk. He could easily pass as a representative to The Hague, a post he discussed obsessively. He knew exactly what he would do, once he got there, he said. He was just waiting for the right opportunity.

Rasheed's comments on his elder cousin's style were less optimistic: "Yep, all's he needs now is a client to go with those outfits – OK, maybe even a job – any day now, just you wait!"

"I've found him," Javad called as he swung open the front door. "I've found Akhbar."

Pari rushed forward and grabbed his lapels. "Oh, please, Javad, where? Where?" she said, breathless. "You saw him? Please! Please!"

Just as she said this, though, they all heard a distant "THWUMP!" thunder above the rooftops of the city – the explosion rattled their windows. Reflexively they stopped to listen for another. There had been endless rumors about pending Iraqi rocket attacks and air raids. Everyone was jittery.

"*Mosque e'Zenab*," Javad said, recovering from the surprise of the distant blast. He displayed a sense of pride in his voice. He held his chest high, as if addressing the court at The Hague with a clinching legal argument. It seemed there would be no more explosions. "No," Javad continued. "I didn't see him. My sources..."

Then they heard sirens and stopped again to listen. First the sirens came from one direction. Then from numerous others.

Rasheed emerged at the top of the basement stairs. Masumay and Afsar were creaking down the paired spiral staircases at the front, one on each staircase, emerging from behind the carved trelliswork.

"Oh, Javad," Pari said, "why didn't you call?"

"Ahmad Mirza told me himself. I didn't have time to get back to the office. He's a client of mine..."

Rasheed raised his eyebrows: "Ahmad Mirza? Office? Client?"

"Oh Rasheed!" Pari said. "Javad, where is he now? Where's Akhbar?"

"Mirza's been a client of mine forever – *Mosque e'Zenab*."

"I meant a paying client," Rasheed said.

"Stop it, Rasheed!" Pari said. "Drive us in the Pacon – Please!"

"We're supposed to go to the basement," Afsar was saying. "They warned us the Iraqis would do this." She had arrived at the bottom of the staircase and was still balancing herself, stooped over, with one hand on the railing. "Nargess, dear, stay downstairs!" she called. "We're coming down. Someone get Shohreh. Fahti, dear, come with us..."

"Hurry, Rasheed!" Pari said. "Aunt Afsar, they've found Akhbar. We have to go out."

"They bus them to the front every afternoon –" Javad said, "about now."

❧

The rusting red Pacon, hot with the smells of stale dust and burned oil, clattered and creaked and rattled and lurched as they made speed through a plague of potholes for the first several blocks on the way to the *Mosque e'Zenab*. Then the traffic grew close and congested and they slowed. A whining ambulance passed them on the left, moving against the opposite traffic, forcing a line of oncoming cars to the side. Now stopped, they could hear numerous sirens ahead, the up and down ones from ambulances, the constant ones from the fire engines. With the sun beating down on them they hung outside the open windows to see ahead.

About twenty cars in front of them the *Pasdaran* had set up a checkpoint. Sixteen year olds wielding scraggly beards, green army fatigues and AK47s were not letting anyone through.

"We must be near where the bomb hit," Rasheed said.

"Talk to them, Rasheed, "Pari said. "They'll listen to you."

Rasheed worked his way past the line of fuming cars, with Pari walking just behind him. She drew the folds of her black chador almost completely around her face, to make sure to give no offence.

"Please," Rasheed said to the *Pasdaran*, "this is my honored sister. Her son is a volunteer. She wants to see him before he goes to the front."

"No one gets through," one of the *Pasdaran*, apparently the leader, answered. "There's been a bombing. Where is her son, sir?"

"*Mosque e'Zenab*."

The head *Pasdaran* exchanged worried looks with the others.

"The bomb went off near the mosque, *Khanoum*. It may not be safe."

Pari's heart began to race when she heard this. "Near the mosque? Please, sir." She opened the chador slightly to view the *Pasdaran*. "He's my only son. Only twelve. He is very brave." Then she choked, "Where near the mosque?"

"The *Pasdaran* shrugged. "We don't know."

"Oh please, he may be hurt."

Then Rasheed spoke: "For the sake of the revolution, kind sirs, let us pass – I beg of you."

There followed a moment of silence. The *Pasdaran* looked back and forth at one another. Finally the leader nodded to the others and said to Pari, "*Allah* be with you, *Khanoum*. And with your son." He motioned them to return to the car. When they passed through he saluted and called, "*Allahu akhbar!*"

Two blocks from the mosque they first sensed the smell of burning rubber. The crowd became thick, blocking the way.

"Oh, please, Rasheed," Pari said. "Please hurry. She was leaning forward from the back seat into the front, to get a better view through the bug-streaked and filmy windshield. Her face was aflame.

Rasheed honked. A few heads turned and that was all. The pedestrians were ignoring the honks from civilian cars and parted only for wailing ambulances and fire engines.

"We'll have to go on foot," Rasheed said.

Pari could barely stand in the burning sun. She had to brace herself with one hand on the blazing hood of the Pacon. She began to feel faint and asked Rasheed to hold her elbow.

"I can't go," she said.

"Here," Rasheed said. "Javad, take her elbow."

"No," she said. "I can't. I know it's him."

"No," Rasheed said. "What are the chances? That's ridiculous."

"Really," Javad said, bracing her. "Rasheed's right."

"No."

"Yes. Come on!"

Rasheed and Javad each took an elbow and walked Pari forward through the crowd. They were on a gentle slope downhill from the mosque, and the water from the fire engines was washing down the street, steaming up from the heat of the pavement where it passed in a thin film across the occasional flat spots.

"What happened?" Rasheed asked a shopkeeper standing in his doorway, surveying the crowd from before his display case of cigarettes and bottles of vinegar and combs and chewing gum and an infinity of miscellaneous other sundries.

"They bombed the mosque, I think," he said. "A rocket..."

"No," a passer by said. He was dressed in a short-sleeved shirt and khaki pants and resembled an American archaeologist. "They bombed the electrical station across the square. Do you have a radio? A terrorist..."

"What good will that do?"

"Do you hear that, Pari?" Rasheed said. "It's the electrical station, not the mosque."

"No," another passerby said. He was a tall, dark skinned man with three teeth missing and a moth-eaten gray beard. "They missed the electrical station and hit the mosque."

They could not see the square for the mass of onlookers before them. But, they could see the mosque above their heads, towering in the distance against the bright clouds – apparently intact. As they drew close, they sensed a sharp, acrid smell like firecrackers, in addition to the overpowering stench of burned rubber and paint. At the edge of the crowd they could see the square filled with chaos. On the far side they saw a line of ambulances with flashing lights and open doors. Two were just driving off with sirens wailing. In the middle of the wide square between the mosque and the turquoise tiled entrance pool, the bomb had left a shallow crater the size of a car. The blast had cracked the wall of the entrance pool in several places and water was steadily rushing out through the cracks and across the square, partially filling the shallow crater where it seemed to drain somewhere underground. Bodies were strewn about the hot stones of the square. Some had doctors and ambulance personnel hanging over them, some had been abandoned, obviously dead; some were being comforted by strangers, awaiting medical help. Well back from the edge of the crater were a bus and several cars, still smoldering, all crumpled by the blast. The flaming bus was bent in the middle like a puckered bread tin. The fire engine crews were just finishing hosing down the burning automobiles and were dragging their hoses over to the bus, which belched forth dirty, orange, lava colored flames. The flames twisted into enormous, black, rolling clouds of sooty smoke.

"Oh my God!" Pari said when she saw the incinerating bus. "I know it's his bus. I know it's his bus. A school bus. How could they hit a school bus?" She let out a wretched wail: "Aiyeee! Aiyeee! Rasheed, make it stop. Make it stop! *Madar! Madar!*" Her cries were lost in the noise of the sirens and the crying of the wounded.

Rasheed grabbed the arm of a blue-jacketed policeman who was holding back the crowd. "Who was on the bus," he said. "Was there anyone on the bus?"

"I don't know," he answered. "I... Keep back, now!"

"Were there children on the bus? Any children?"

"I don't know. There were busses scheduled to take volunteers to the front this afternoon. That's all I know."

"Oh Rasheed, make it stop! Akhbar! Akhbar! God, forgive me, Akhbar!"

They pulled Pari away and made her return to the house. If they were going to get any news, it would be at home. Fahti would need her mother. Surely someone would call. No one at the scene had seemed to know anything for sure. Afsar and Masumay and Nargess melted together into a gray lump of silent tears in the receiving salon. Fahti joined them on the side. Pari withdrew to her room and pulled the curtains shut. Rasheed and Javad sat tensely on pillows against the wall, with the black telephone on the floor between them. First one cousin telephoned, asking them if they knew anything about the mosque bombing. Then word spread rapidly. Cousin after friend after cousin called for news. Then they came over to console them. By evening the house was bursting with relatives and friends. The power went out and they lit candles. It was as quiet as a mausoleum, excepting solely the sounds of hushed weeping and Javad's and Rasheed's voices working the telephone.

Until midnight, when the telephone rang and Javad answered: "Yes – yes – Yes it is – I see – Yes, I see – Thank you, sir – Yes – Thank you – Thank you." He hung up the phone. "Akhbar wasn't on the bus," he announced. "Somebody tell Pari. Quick! He wasn't on the bus – I'll tell her." He raced to Pari's darkened room and shook her awake. "Pari dear. He's alive. He wasn't on the bus. Do you hear me? Ahmad Mirza obtained the *basij* lists. They bussed him out two days ago. He's alive, Pari! He's at the front!"

Pari groaned as she heard the cries of thanks to God from the cousins and friends still assembled downstairs. The women raised a great ululation, as if they were celebrating a wedding. "Oh Javad," Pari said, shifting in the darkness of her room. "The front? Oh, God forbid! Oh, dear God, not the front! Not Akhbar. No, Javad, not the front. Oh, God – Oh, God… Oh, God… he should have been on the bus."

❧

The next morning, at breakfast, Rasheed was angry again. In deference to the wrenching emotions of the previous, day he seemed to be trying to contain himself. But, with Rasheed the effort was always problematic. The whole family was present. Javad sat straight backed, his jacket removed, the corner of a napkin tucked under his chin to protect his blue silk tie and starched white shirt. Afsar, Masumay and Nargess sat opposite Javad, a huddled gray herd of lumpy octogenarians, their faces like potatoes. They chewed silently. Pari wore her blue jeans from the previous day and a starched white linen, high collared shirt with ruffles on the sleeves, collar and front. Rasheed wore his sweat stained brown suit and a wrinkled white shirt that billowed over his belt in folds, honoring his paunch. Fahti, having not dressed for the day, was still in her nightgown and had covered herself with a gray chador.

"I should have known," Rasheed grumbled, "Javad – clients…"

"Stop, Rasheed," Pari said.

"Mirza promised me," Javad said. He was winding the middle of three buttons on his stainless steel Rolex chronometer. "It's not my fault."

"If I had a cousin like yours, Javad, maybe I could buy me a Rolex." Rasheed said this while he was rolling feta cheese with walnuts and fig jam inside a piece of flat bread.

"Rasheed!" Pari said.

"I just want to know how he gets so dandified on my *dinar*. That's all. Italian suits, French ties…"

"Let it go, can't you? Can't we just find Akhbar?"

"Seems to me we've had enough letting go in this family. God's curse…"

"Is it my fault my fault Akhbar ran away to the army? You could have stopped him, Rasheed. You could have just grabbed him and said no – a boy half your size…"

"Yes, blame Rasheed," her mother said, "who has to do everything for everybody…"

"Don't drag me into this," Rasheed said. He wiped his mouth with the back of his hand. "I'm not Akhbar's father." Then, after a tense pause he added with anger, "I'm not Fahti's father either. If I had been, you wouldn't see us in this fix."

Pari's heart began to pound in anger. Her temples began to throb. "What are you trying to say, Rasheed? Isn't Javad enough this morning? Isn't my life enough? Akhbar at the front? What more do you want? You want me to be blind too? Hold a cup in the street for you?"

"Well, I guess we wouldn't have this fix either, if it weren't for Fahti's father. You know..."

Pari threw her tea into Rasheed's face. "Will you stop?" As she said this, Fahti rose abruptly and stumbled out of the room and up the stairs, crying. "Did you have to?" Pari demanded. "Did you have to in front of her? What kind of animal are you?"

"A working animal..." Rasheed said, but he was interrupted by Pari's brisk departure.

Pari ran up the stairs after her daughter. She found her at the foot of her bed, a bundle of bones, collapsed thinly, limp in her chador. She was holding her elbows with her hands, burying her head in her own chest and leaning against the bedpost, crying.

"What did I do Mother? What did I do?"

"Rasheed hates everybody – he hates himself."

"But, it isn't just Rasheed: it's Aunt Afsar and Aunt Masumay. And *Khanoum*. They sit there like cows and he does whatever he wants. Afsar and Masumay love it, like if he gets polite to us they'll be on the out – Fat chance!" Her voice was frail, tissue thin, as insubstantial as falling leaves.

"They're old," Pari said.

"Rasheed isn't old." Fahti spoke with her eyes closed. She nudged her face against the bedpost, burying her eyes in the flowers carved in relief. "It wasn't my fault."

Pari winced. She thought for a minute before speaking. She watched her daughter. Fahti started to rub her eyes back and forth against the walnut bedpost, strongly enough to cause discomfort, but not pain.

"Fahti?"

Fahti didn't answer at first. Then she spoke softly: "*Khanoum* says you might get married again. She says you might be able to get Akhbar back. Is that true?"

"I don't know, Fahti."

"Is that the way it works?"

Pari shrugged.

"They all know – don't they?"

"No one knows."

"Then why does Akhbar want to kill himself?"

"Fahti," Pari said in a tone that sounded without purpose. "The mullahs got to him. They made him run to the front..."

"And they gave him a plastic key? I thought only peasants fell for that. He could have used a straight razor. He would have known that much..."

"Akhbar survived the bus. God is with him. He'll be alright. He'll come home..." Pari reached forward and smoothed her daughter's hair to the side of her face. "... a hero."

"And when he does?" Fahti cried softly. Then she paused. "Will he hate me? You?"

"He's only thirteen, Fahti dear – learning..."

"Mother, did you?"

"...Please, Fahti..."

"Did you...?"

"Please, Fahti – don't..."

☙

Downstairs, in the basement room, Javad was saying, "I hate that cousin – Rasheed..."

Pari emerged at the foot of the basement steps.

"Pari, dear," Afsar interrupted Javad. "Rasheed's gone out."

"... as if he'd care for anyone who didn't lay a *touman* in his hand. What kind of clients does he have, after all..."

"Did Rasheed say anything?" Pari said.

"Say anything? His high and mightiness? – a snake charmer's..."

"He's gone to see your Aunt Zahra's husband, Mansour." Afsar said. "He knows Khomeini and all the *basij* leaders..."

"Mother let him?"

"She's gone out. She doesn't know. She's gone out with Fahti."

"The high and mighty furniture clerk fears the wrath of his octogenarian mother..."

"Javad, dear," Afsar said, "he's doing his best." Then she turned knowingly towards Pari. "We all must – as we can."

"Mother and Fahti...?"

"Well, I could have gone if I'd known Aunt Nargess wouldn't have a fit," Javad said. "They're so important now – what with Khomeini and all – better a lawyer than a store clerk and sweat stains under his arms – Of course, maybe they'll just feel better – helping the downtrodden – God's will..."

Pari was mystified that Rasheed was helping, mystified that Fahti and her mother had gone out. But then, in the end, maybe Rasheed was going to honor his responsibilities as head of the family – one way or another. At this point she didn't care why or how, as long as somebody got Akhbar back.

"Well," Javad said, "as the Turks say, 'beware of Greeks bearing gifts!'"

☙

Pari spent the morning in the cool of the aqua-tiled basement room, listening to the fountain gurgle, avoiding the sticky heat above. Rasheed returned early and joined her in the basement. The two were alone. Rasheed seemed strangely quiet. Pari hardly knew how to talk to him without the interruptions of dinner and family. The noise from the fountain dominated the room.

"Did you get the note?" Rasheed asked.

"What note?"

"I left a note for you with Afsar."

"She said you'd gone out – to see Aunt Zahra and Uncle Mansour."

"Yes." Rasheed nodded his head briefly up and down. Even sitting cross-legged on the floor, his hefty torso made him tower above his sister. But, his ever-present rage seemed hidden, softened somehow.

"Are Mother and Fahti still out? What's happened, Rasheed? Have you heard something? Akhbar?"

"Nothing," Rasheed said. Then he let out a long sigh before speaking again. "I talked with Aunt Zahra's husband, Mansour. He can't find Akhbar." Rasheed combed his fingers backwards through the sail of his hair.

"Did he try?"

"He's been trying for two days now."

"I didn't know he knew."

"I told him the day after Akhbar volunteered."

"Why didn't you tell me? Nobody told me."

Rasheed shrugged.

"What is it?"

"Mansour got an audience with Ayatollah Khomeini."

"Khomeini! He went that far? He'll help?"

"Just a couple of minutes. Khomeini knew of Mansour. He handed the affair off to his subordinate."

"So what did he say? Rasheed, where's Akhbar?"

Rasheed shifted uncomfortably. "You need an audience first."

"An audience? They've got Akhbar's name. What does Khomeini need another audience for?"

"Not Khomeini." Rasheed paused. He sighed again. "Abol Fazl."

Pari recoiled. "You're not serious, are you? That grease-dog ignoramus?"

Rasheed shrugged. "He's got the power now – power enough."

"I'd as soon marry a peasant. He's worse than a peasant..."

"You should hope he offers marriage..."

Pari looked at her brother's eyes, but he kept them averted. Her stomach began to churn. "That's all you think of me, Rasheed?"

"What I think of you is Akhbar's lucky you got an audience."

Pari was stunned. Tears began to form in her eyes. She realized the whole household must know about this. Otherwise she and Rasheed would not have this time alone. Afsar and Masumay would have arranged it. Her mother would know, or the others had sent her out and she would find out very soon. That's why Fahti had been sent out with her grandmother. All across Tehran, cousins would soon be nodding their heads in smug shame: Pari was reaping the ugly harvest she had sown: God's retribution.

"Did you tell Fahti, Rasheed?"

"I don't know what Fahti knows."

"You could have waited, you know. I could have told her."

"You're forty-four years old. That's what I know. And Baba left his business in a mess and you've got two children to raise…"

"Your wife, Morvareed, seems to dress well enough."

"… and maybe only one." Rasheed shrugged again after a pause. "Do you want me to show you the records?"

Pari knew Rasheed was bluffing. He would show her what records he wanted her to see and nothing more. She wouldn't understand them anyway.

They heard muted sirens in the distance.

"I know about the house, Rasheed. How about settling for a tour?"

"I have a lot of people to support," he said blandly, bereft of his usual venom, and immune to his sister's. "I'm trying to turn the corner in the furniture business."

"By marrying me off to *Mullah Nasr al-Din*?"

"I want you for once in your life to be practical."

"You mean, be a prostitute."

"It's only that if you let some shit-ass Christian tell you it is. What do they know about us? It's our faith, not theirs." He paused for a long time, then spoke: "You think no one in Christendom ever married for comfort? For necessity? They all marry for love? They're all God's children and Mohamed's followers tend a flock of hookers and pimps?"

"Where's your faith, Rasheed? Did it keep Shohreh from going blind? If you'd been any kind of a father you'd never have let her go to a party like that – you and Morvareed…"

"Well, she's not clearing mines at the front," Rasheed said. "I can tell you that – OK? I don't know when you got so uppity. It certainly wasn't before you had Fahti. We can all count, you know. Your husband, Mahmoud, could tell you that – if he hadn't drunk himself to death. I guess he finally figured out how to count too – Or maybe Saeed taught him, just to be mean." Then Rasheed rose heavily to his feet. "And don't think Fahti can't count either."

Pari began to sweat in the dampness of the basement. She watched Rasheed depart, nervous. He was going upstairs to take some lunch in the kitchen before returning to work. She clasped her hands together in her lap, rubbing one inside the other, tying them in a useless knot of writhing. Abol

Fazl was a peasant. He probably never bathed. His breath would smell of stale food in the crevices of his teeth. For the rest of her life she would have to endure him on top of her, sweating – and that was if she were lucky. And if she complained, ever, he could throw her out by just saying three times, "I divorce you." She wouldn't even have to witness the event. He could speak the words to himself and throw her belongings on the stoop.

There was no one for her to talk to. The whole family in Tehran would take Rasheed's side – surely already had. They were mostly the older generation and all her life they had resented her, blamed her. All her friends were in America. Saeed was in America. Oh, why couldn't Saeed make it all go away? He would know what to do. He had helped her niece Shohreh get her career started – had redoubled those efforts after the tragic rape. Surely he could use his contacts to help her now. He must have some friends left somewhere in the government. In the waning days of the Shah, after many years as a high judge, he had been appointed Chief Attorney for the Department of Energy. It was a last ditch attempt to clean house and fill the administration with men known to be incorruptible and brilliant. The attempt had failed and now any association with the Shah's government risked imprisonment and most likely death, but surely there must be some who would remember Saeed's impeccable honesty. Everyone around them had been filling their pockets with kickbacks and bribes, but not Saeed. The Minister of Utilities, a close cousin of the Shah, under a mandate to provide electricity throughout the country, had pushed through an ambitious program to import new generators from Italy. They proved to be faulty and constantly in need of repairs. Word leaked out the generators were not new, but used ones purchased for the price of new, with the Italians splitting the excess profits with the minister. At the time Saeed had just been promoted from high judge to Chief Attorney for the Department of Energy, which bore ultimate responsibility. When the investigation he launched began to close in on the Shah's cousin, other ministers began to visit Saeed regularly. Flower arrangements would arrive throughout the day, and filled the house with their fragrance. A line of limousines with police escorts formed at their door. There were whispers about land grants and Swiss bank accounts, but every impeccably coiffed, manicured, pedicured, chauffeured visitor in a thousand dollar, perfectly pressed, pinstriped suit departed fuming. Saeed rebuffed all offers. It wasn't that he calculated the offers were intended to ensnare him in the web of corruption, dooming him under pain of discovery to eternal slavery to the Shah if he stayed, or facilitating the permanency of exile – albeit a gilded one – should he escape. He wouldn't have any of it, because it was simply not right. His own father had been a strict judge, orphaned at fifteen and banished to divinity school in Najaf by a stepmother eager to have her brothers confiscate her deceased husband's wealth, away from the watchful eyes of the rightful heir. After twenty years of training in exile, under full scholarship, Saeed's father had returned to his home town of Tabriz, (walking the entire seven hundred kilometers beside the others in the caravan, who could afford camels). Immediately upon his arrival, without stopping to slake his thirst at the fountain, or wash his calloused, feet, or wait for a lamb to be sacrificed, he marched into the office of the local judge, picked him up bodily, and hurled him into the street. He then declared himself judge. For ever after he refused to suffer the foolish or the unjust, a habit he passed to his son. At nights and early before sunrise, during the waning days of the Shah, Saeed could be heard pacing back and forth in his room, sick with fear, riddled with anxiety. The Shah would dally only so long with bribes before he turned to assassination. The promotion to Chief Attorney of the Department of Energy had been part of a last ditch, delaying tactic to postpone the investigation and buy credibility for the regime. Fortunately for Saeed, before he could abandon the carrot for the stick, the Shah had fled the country and his government had collapsed – on the very night in January of 1979 when Saeed caught a flight to visit his daughter and wife in America. An aide to a former cabinet official had shortly thereafter mailed Saeed a tape of a cabinet meeting in which the long time prime minister and sycophant, Hoveida, had complained that they could not dispense with the obstructive, unbribable Saeed Tabrizi "like a piece of Kleenex." The recording could prove exculpatory, were Saeed ever charged. But, when the Western press published pictures of the refrigerated bodies of Hoveida and other powerful ministers and generals, green beneath the fluorescent lights of the morgue, and dressed only in their white Jockey shorts, Saeed knew there would be no return from America, and no gilding to the cage of his exile. But, surely someone in power would know all this, respect all this. Countless times Saeed had brokered the freedom of their distant cousin, Ali, who was a rabble-rouser and Khomeini supporter, and who had continually suffered arrest and jail under the Shah. Ali was powerful now. He could help. Surely there would be others Saeed could contact.

But, would Saeed help? She never knew what to expect from him – or when. In the middle of her affair with the Elvis wannabe, on a family trip to the Caspian (*sans* Elvis), he had grabbed her on the sandy path between the men's and women's changing huts. His one look deep into her eyes made her melt. He pulled her (you could hardly call it pulling from the resistance she gave) into the tall grass of a nearby ravine. With the voices of the others drawing near, he had pulled the crotch of her swimsuit to the side and entered her. He finished only moments after she had lowered the top. They lay there panting silently, listening to the voices of the others, who began calling for them. She made her way to the women's hut by a back path and emerged for the others to see when they drew close. She said she had seen Saeed climb the hillock to the neighboring beach. Then for months he pretended he hardly knew her.

She resigned herself to his indifference with the scant, despairing comfort that he was different than she:

...the whole business of love is to drown in the sea...

Her fate, to be a lover.

She wondered if Tajmah guessed at the encounter and if Saeed were reacting by behaving so coldly. Many years later, when the whole family had accompanied Saeed to a conference on international law at the United Nations, in New York, he had taken her again. Saeed and Tajmah had a suite adjoining Pari and Mahmoud's at the Ritz. While the others were out, Saeed slipped away from the conference and into Pari's shower. They had soaped each other, made wild love – dripping wet – on the velvet bed cover and had soaped each other clean again. For months after he hardly spoke to her.

The first time she had gotten into trouble had been in 1960, early during the first year of President Kennedy's land reform. It was the 10th day of *Moharam, Ashura,* when the devout males would parade through the streets, flailing themselves bloody with sharp chains to commemorate the death at Karbala of Mohamed's grandson, Hussein, betrayed by Mohamed's followers. Saeed was due to fly back from Istanbul that morning. Normally the whole family would greet him at the airport. But, Nargess was too devout to miss the procession and she talked Golnar and Masumay and Afsar and Tahereh into joining her, which meant Abrahim and Rasheed and Tajmah and the whole family would accompany them. Even the crippled twins would go, carried on litters by servants. The house would be empty. After the parade they were scheduled to help their cousins serve a feast to the poor. Saeed could take a taxi. Pari claimed illness and slept in. Dreaming of the night on the roof on the last day of *Ramadan,* seven years earlier, only weeks before the CIA coup that toppled Mossadegh, she lay still in the languid heat of the empty house, aflame. Would Saeed come? Would he know? With the whole house empty, could they lie together afterward, running their hands over each other's nakedness? She did not know how he knew, but while she waited for him, her whole body perfumed and bursting, he dropped his bags by the spiral staircases and hearing no answer to his calls, clomped up the stairs to her room. He didn't undress. He made love to her with his suit on, finished and departed. But, it was enough. And he ignored her for the next two months. Until Pari visited him in chambers (he was a judge, now) and told him she was pregnant.

Standing before her in his black robe he asked, rather foolishly, "Who did it?"

She slapped him.

As he held one arm up to fend off another attack and nursed the red welt developing on his cheek, he asked the more sensible question: "Does anyone know?"

At great risk to both of them, Saeed arranged for a doctor and no one ever found out. But, six years later, again confronting the same bad fortune, Pari was not so acquiescent: "You're just going to toss me away again, Saeed? There's a child inside me, Saeed. A daughter. A son. I'm almost thirty. How long is going to be like this? I have a right. Your child has a right…"

Within a fortnight Pari consummated an arranged marriage with Saeed's handsome, if dim witted, cousin Mahmoud, who had a year earlier arrived from Tabriz, to be his apprentice. Saeed bribed a doctor to calculate a late due date. Seven months later he bribed him again to put the newborn Fahti in seclusion in an oxygen tent in the army hospital, with no visitors (and particularly no aunts, female cousins, sisters or sisters in law or grandmothers to remark on the unexpectedly large size for a premature birth). The doctor agreed, but refused to actually turn on the oxygen, for fear of causing blindness, even though the child really wasn't premature. No one was fooled, of course, excepting Mahmoud. The arrangements provided plausible deniability for all. So they went unchallenged.

Would Saeed help her now? After all, he would hardly welcome the notion that this was even indirectly his fault. But, if he did not act out of guilt, he might out of pride. Saeed seldom shied at showing Rasheed he was the god of the family, if not the titular head.

Pari choked with despair when the operator said she would have to wait two days for an appointment for a long distance call to America. "You don't understand," she said to the operator. "I don't have two days. My son could be dead in two days." The operator hung up with a brusque click. Now Pari sweated alone in a house made quiet by the collusion of most of the rest of its inhabitants. Rasheed was still asleep. Her mother and Fahti were still out. So were Afsar and Masumay. It was as if the whole world waited for her to make a decision and no one was going to help her make it. With a sense of dread she slowly worked her way up the two flights of creaking stairs to her bedroom. Her shoulders slouched. She searched her trunks until she found a pair of thick nylon stockings. She put on blunt toed, black leather shoes, which were more like boots than shoes. They were sensible shoes, the kind that the nuns wore at the Lycée, the kind that her mother and aunts wore. Then she put on a white, high collared shirt, like the ones she had worn as a schoolgirl. She tied a simple gray scarf around her hair, to be doubly sure of obeying the public dress code for women, and then her best black chador. She slowly descended the stairs and seated herself on a futon pillow in the receiving salon on the ground floor. There she waited silently for Rasheed. When Rasheed emerged from his afternoon nap he halted his rush down the stairs the moment he saw his waiting sister.

"Are you going somewhere?" he asked.

"You're taking me to Abol Fazl," she said.

❦

Abol Fazl had taken residence in the sprawling grounds of an estate that had formerly belonged to the Shah's private banker. It had been said the banker would write three checks for the Shah, and then one for himself. Since the Shah had stolen all his wealth from the country anyway, no one complained. So *Allah* blessed the property's seizure. The entire site was surrounded by a two meter high mud brick wall, topped by gabled flagstones, each the size of a kitchen table. There were two entrances to the site. Ministers were received through the Pasteur St. entrance, beside the gates to wealthy houses. Peasants and other tiresome supplicants were received through the Martyr Ali Akhbar St. entrance, beside a row of car repair shops and barbers. The approaches for two blocks all around were controlled by *pasdaran* who manned small, chest high sandbag bunkers, armed with AK47 rifles. Access to the holy sepulcher was not to be taken lightly.

It seemed their visit was expected. When Rasheed identified himself and his sister, they were directed to the Martyr Ali Akhbar St. entrance. Rasheed was told to wait in the car while Pari was escorted to a waiting room in the old garage of the estate. Here she found a seat on one of the hard plywood benches, of which there were six rows. The room was packed with sweating taxi drivers and tradesmen, construction workers in muddied boots, peasant families from the country with live chickens tied by their feet. The room emptied and the yellow evening sun filtering through the shade trees climbed the far wall before it became Pari's turn. Informed that Abol Fazl had removed for the evening to the main building, she was escorted down a winding marble path through gardens of rosebushes and peacocks and fountains, and finally into the mansion proper; then down a long mirrored hall and through a set of carved mahogany double doors. There Abol Fazl awaited her at the end of a long French Empire room, with gilt chairs, ceiling-high mirrors, creamy Isfahan carpets laid wall to wall, and a series of French doors along one side, opening onto a terrace that in turn overlooked the peacock gardens.

Abol Fazl, without turban, sat at the far end of the room, signing papers behind a massive desk of carved wood, decorated in ivory and ormolu. He was exchanging hushed words and documents with a bowing assistant, while Pari waited at the door with her escort, a young divinity student in cloth shoes who admonished her to wait in silence. Abol Fazl dismissed his assistant and looked up blankly, signaling the divinity student to approach with his charge. He read the file card the divinity student handed him.

"Ah!" he exclaimed, rising, "Pari, dear! It's been so long. Please…" He motioned her to sit in a spindly French chair of a style that matched the desk. "How is your dear mother? How are you?" He snapped his fingers for the divinity student to fetch them tea.

"Mother is well. She suffers the war and old age."

Abol Fazl seated himself behind his massive desk. He leaned back in his chair. He drew his pleated white shawl around his shoulders. "As do we all," he said.

"Yes."

"God's will."

"Yes."

"God's will, we shall prevail." Abol Fazl placed the fingertips of one hand against those of the other as he leaned back. He bowed his head forward. "And you?" he said.

"Sir, my son has gone to war. He ran away. He's only twelve. He joined the *basij*…"

Abol Fazl kept his fingertips together as Pari spoke plaintively. He kept his head bowed and his eyes gazing beneath them. From time to time he nodded as she finished the story.

"…I have only one son, sir."

"Yes," Abol Fazl said gently.

Tears formed in Pari's eyes. "Please, I can't lose my only son. He's the last of his family."

"This one…" he raised his eyes. "His name?"

"Akhbar," Pari said.

"Akhbar is a hero. You should be proud, my child."

"I seek no pride, sir. Only my child's life."

"You are not the only mother of a *jihadi*," Abol Fazl said, staring at her until she lowered her eyes. "Do you realize we have to pay men now to take extra wives; so many husbands and fathers have been lost to Sadam. I myself have three wives."

"Yes, sir."

"Do you know that's why we have four wives? Always, our men are being martyred by our enemies, since the dawn of Islam – since the dawn of history. Women must be protected and shielded to make babies, and boys to become men. The Westerners do not want that. They want us to become their slaves, to become weak and dependent, so they can steal our oil to make themselves strong. That's why they raise our enemies against us. When they built the oil refinery in Abadan over sixty years ago, they only hired us as cheap labor. They kept all the trained positions for British. Even our brightest engineers they would not train or promote – they knew what would happen when we learned how much they were stealing and didn't need them any more."

Pari had no answer to Abol Fazl's growing passion. She decided, out of fear, to say nothing.

After a silent pause Abol Fazl asked her, "You want me to bring your son back from the front?"

Pari kept her head bowed in silence, not sure if it was safe to admit this.

"And you," Abol Fazl continued, "do you have someone to take care of you? Is your husband alive?"

Pari shook her head.

"A brother?"

"He works in a furniture store. He supports my mother and my two aunts and me and my daughter and..."

Abol Fazl thought silently for a long time, staring over his opposed fingertips down the length of the ornate room, past Pari. "I promised your mother and father I would take you as a wife," he said at last. "Will you come to me?"

Pari turned beet red. She desperately feared she would not be able to speak. She dared not risk his anger by hesitating. She hardly believed she uttered the word that came from her mouth, so much did it sound like a gurgle: "Yes..." she said, "... sir."

"Today is Monday," he said. "Come to me..." He fingered through the pages of his calendar absentmindedly, as if he were making an appointment with his manicurist. "...Thursday. Yes, Thursday there's an opening..."

Just then the divinity student returned, entering through a side door with a small silver tray and two glasses of tea.

"No need, Ali," Abol Fazl said. "*Khanoum e'Kashani* is on her way out."

♟

"Saeed!" Pari let her voice burst into the phone. "Saeed!" There was an echo, as if she were talking down a long well. Then she heard a noticeable click. During the Shah's reign she had learned this meant the *savaki* were listening. She expected no less from Khomeini. "It's me – Pari."

"Pari, dear," Saeed exclaimed. "How wonderful to hear your voice! You must come join us. Tajmah is right here. She's dying to talk to you..."

"Saeed – No!"

But, the next voice on the phone was Tajmah's. Tajmah had always been suspicious about Saeed and Pari, especially after Rasheed's outburst. But, she never knew – not for sure. Tajmah was suspicious of everything, everybody. It was easier to be that way than to find out the actual truth. Tajmah was avoiding sensitive subjects. She talked about the weather and shopping and her daughter's new boyfriend, a doctor too. Then she asked after Nargess and Afsar and Masumay and, reluctantly, Rasheed. Finally she asked about Akhbar and Fahti.

"Akhbar's run away to the *basij*. He's at the front. Please, is there anything you can do – Saeed?"

There was a long silence at the other end, and then muffled voices. Then Saeed's voice came on the line: "Pari, dear, I don't know this crowd. Can't you call Ali? He owes me."

"Ali won't return my calls."

Saeed let out a sigh of resignation.

Pari began to weep. She wanted to tell him about being forced to visit Abol Fazl, her mother's plans for a strategic marriage, Rasheed stealing antiques and constantly degrading her, the ever present threat of the *pasdaran*, the complete and utter absence of hope for her or her family in Iran, but she burned at the shame of it all. "Saeed…" she said. "Saeed…" She choked. "Saeed…"

"Pari, dear," Saeed said, "We're late for lunch with friends."

*

The following night Pari was directed to the Pasteur St. entrance. The same divinity student delivered her to Abol Fazl's private chambers, which were dominated by a huge German four post bed, with heavy, curtains hanging around all four sides, the curtains on each side parted by red velvet cords tied around the middle.

With the divinity student as witness, Abol Fazl had Pari kneel beside him and delivered the vows.

Abol Fazl, remaining standing, bade her undress herself before him, reaching to stop her hand when she reached for the light switch. Then he waited while she obliged.

"Everything," he said, when she stopped prematurely.

Then he undressed himself before her while she averted her eyes to the side. But, he made her remove his stained under shorts, which required her to kneel before his flabby paunch. Then he told her to touch him. When he was ready, he had her lie back on the bed. She felt the contents of her stomach churning against her throat. He grabbed her head with both hands and forced his face upon hers. There were large buildups of tarter on his teeth. His breath was foul and smelled of garlic and stale cumin. His eyes were intense. He started kissing her on the mouth. His beard scratched her face like a scrub brush. It was moist, and still had particles of food from his dinner. Pari tried to turn away again, but he wouldn't let her. He forced himself on her, causing her pain. It was taking him forever. He sweated and slobbered. After he climaxed, he fell into a lump on top of her. He was like a sack of rice, except that he was puffing heavily and dripping sweat.

Pari waited for him to fall asleep, but he surprised her by getting up and dressing himself. She pulled one of the velvet curtains in front of her and sat up, with her legs over the side, staring vacantly at the wall, avoiding his eyes.

"God's will, *Khanoum*," he said.

She said nothing.

"I've sent word to the front. I may hear by tomorrow – maybe the day after." He waited for her response, but she remained silent, clutching the velvet curtain to hide herself.

Then she spoke: "I'm having my things sent over tomorrow. Where will my quarters be?"

Abol Fazl raised his eyebrows. "*Khanoum*?"

"My quarters: where will I stay?"

"*Khanoum*..." He clasped his hands and adopted a pious slouch. "*Khanoum*, stay here tonight. I will have my driver take you home in the morning. *Khanoum*, it seems you misunderstand. This is a temporary marriage, not a permanent one."

Pari choked. She recovered quickly, but she was beyond shock, beyond shame, beyond even caring. She felt nauseous. She stared wanly at the wall and then, her voice as frail as tissue, she stammered: "Yes – Yes, I see." With her eyes she followed the gilt edges of the wall panels for a while. Then she spoke again: "Then I will go now."

"As you wish, *Khanoum*."

Once home, she knew she was too weak to wash herself, but she stumbled upstairs to the bathroom anyway. She tried to vomit into the toilet hole, but all that happened was that her chest fluttered and her temples throbbed. Then she noticed a brown paper bag on the sink, with her name on it in blue marker ink. She recognized the handwriting as Morvareed's. Inside she found two plastic bottles of pills from the pharmacist, each with directions and Morvareed's name. One read "ampicillin," the other "erythromycin."

Blind Justice
Monday, November 3, 1997

A s Iran Air flight 2506 from Frankfurt approached Tehran's Mehrabad Airport the airplane began to lurch in the rough winds above the Zagros Mountains. Saeed began to sweat. He felt nauseous. He'd been away from Iran for eighteen years, hiding in America. He did not know what to expect.

"They're too cheap to turn on the air conditioning," he said to Tajmah. He really didn't expect a reply. "Take your money – make you sick."

He'd become accustomed to a naïve culture during his absence: Reagan selling missiles to Iran and mustard gas to Iraq, and Clinton propositioning Paula Jones – high crimes and misdemeanors ending in mild censure; thieving televangelists Jim and Tammy Bakker sent to country club jail or second marriages; don't-ask-don't-tell In Iran they executed you for imaginary slights to the Prophet, even if you were a foreign author. In Iran, even eight years after Khomeini, every third citizen was a religious spy happy to have your genitals burned in Evin prison. He'd been told that it was safe to return, that they weren't arresting former regime members anymore – barring major crimes. Khatami was busy painting a smiley face on Iran. But, you never knew what really went on in the minds of mullahs. And then, he added the thought to himself: if they have minds.

"It's winter," Tajmah said, hunching her shoulders, dismissing her husband's complaints about nausea and turbulence. She removed a chestnut brown Gucci leather wallet from a cobalt blue, Christian Dior purse, both in her possession now for twenty of the forty-four years of their marriage – and substantially better preserved. The purse and wallet were both crinkled and worn at the corners. Except for a few pieces of jewelry they were all that remained of her life before exile in America, where they had moved from house in posh, suburban Main Line Philadelphia to cheap apartment in suburban Main Line to seedy apartment in Upper Darby, just west of the city. She had nursed the purse and wallet for the eighteen years, storing them boxed in tissue paper, liberating them only for weddings, funerals and dinner with her daughter's American in laws. From the wallet she removed a knotted piece of Kleenex to clean her bifocals. The tattered Kleenex left a trail of lint on the glass, but she didn't notice. Then she folded the Kleenex back into a compact square the size of her thumb, daubed carefully with it at the edges of her lips to make sure there were no traces of excess lipstick, wedged it back into a small compartment in her wallet and returned the wallet to her purse.

She was anxious about visiting a family she hardly knew anymore. Anxious lest they discover that she was wife to a man who was bitter and impoverished. Anxious that her dreary half-sister, Pari, would try to rekindle the romance she'd had with Saeed early in her marriage. As far as Tajmah was concerned Pari had earned the gray life she endured, pattering about after an anemic daughter and a self-obsessed mother, what with trying to steal her husband and all right from under the cat's whiskers: Pari deserved her older brother Rasheed. Tajmah had heard he had not improved over the years, rather, had gotten worse.

Saeed began to twist in his seat, as if he were scanning the horizon. "It's too hot. Too hot when they're jiggling around like this. Why don't they turn on the air? Father burn! Ten thousand kilometers and they can't give you air. Bunch of mullahs. I'm calling the stewardess."

"Don't you dare!" Tajmah hissed.

Saeed punched the stewardess button. "There! Tell me what to…"

Tajmah reached up towards Saeed's stewardess button but fumbled, as she couldn't figure out how to turn it off. Then Saeed punched her stewardess button too. She tried to swat his hand away, but was too late. She reddened. "Why did you do that? Do you ever think of anybody other than yourself?" She turned and stared out the window. They awaited the stewardess in silence.

"I think you have a very nice job," Saeed said to the stewardess as she bent over him to flip the call buttons off. He admired what he could of the curve of her breasts. Inches from his nose, he thought. What would happen if he just reached up and cupped one? "Maybe you could hire me too, to turn off everyone's air and chatter in the galley…"

"Saeed!"

"…while we suffocate."

Then Tajmah looked up at the stewardess. "He's sick. It's bumpy." She wanted to say her husband deserved her indulgence, being a former Chief Attorney for the Department of Energy of Iran, and being now unemployed for eighteen years in America, having been fired from every job he could get fellow expatriates to spot him – selling insurance, selling groceries, selling Tupperware, desk clerk…

"Sir, do you need an air comfort bag?" the stewardess said.

"You mean a vomit bag, dear? Were I can throw up that offal you call lunch? I don't need a bag. I just need some air." Saeed made a motion as if he were going for his wallet. "Should I pay you extra for it…"

"Saeed!"

"… You can put it on my card. – See this vent here?" Saeed was on a roll. He pointed to the thumb sized round ball with the knurled nozzle. "Make that work and then you can go back and chitter-chatter with your friends."

The stewardess made a show of fumbling with the vent, even though the pilot had announced at the beginning of the flight that none of the vents in the airplane were working. "I guess I'll have to have it fixed by the ground crew, sir," she said.

"Yes, I think that's very good. Have them bring it around to my hotel in the morning when they're done."

As the stewardess departed, working her way forwards up the aisle, Saeed stared at the smooth bulges where her long tunic coat pressed against her buttocks and tried to ignore his wife's prattle:

"Do you have to embarrass me? We're not even there yet. And why did you say we're staying in a hotel? My mother's house isn't good enough for you…?"

"I don't see why she should know our plans."

"My mother?"

"No. That perky stewardess."

"You said you had the tape," Tajmah said. "What are you worried about?"

"Besides, it's Rasheed's house now, isn't it?" Saeed said. "And Morvareed's – that Egyptian hook nose – And you don't have to go around reminding people Prime Minister Hoveida knew me personally – even if he is recorded cursing God he couldn't bribe me."

"I wasn't reminding – I just said you said you have the tape. You don't have anything to worry about. I didn't say anything…"

Saeed lost track of what she was saying and wiped sweat from each temple with the fingers of his right hand and each time wiped his fingers on his pant leg.

"I hope you're not going to act like that in front of my family," Tajmah said.

"Why? Your mother's a hundred and one. She probably can't see her own nose. And Rasheed's still pushing dinette sets for Jews, isn't he? When he's not filching your family heirlooms. Is there anything left? And then there's Pari who sent her only son off to blow up mines for the mullahs and somehow figured out how to ruin her daughter, Fahti, to boot – without even letting her out of the house…"

Then neither was hearing the other:

Tajmah:	Saeed:
"Stop it! It wasn't Pari's fault. You know that better than anyone. And don't think I don't know you know I know. You think you can fool everyone…"	"…and of course there's Javad e'Abasi, attorney at law – who's never found a client or a wife in seventy years. It's you Kashanis who aren't good enough – butchers. Land swindlers. *Bazaari*…"

They both stopped in mid sentence and succumbed to another embittered silence. It was familiar territory.

Then Tajmah broke: "Yes, dear, you never touched *bazaari* silver when you ate off of it."

This, of course, was an insult. It was the bride who should move in with the groom's family, not the other way around. But, Saeed was only half paying attention now. He was watching the buttocks of the stewardess as she chatted with the other stewardess in the forward galley. Her fanny stuck out into the aisle and stretched against the frock coat as she bent over and delved into the nether regions of the galley. "Yes," Saeed said, sounding absentminded. "Well, you don't have it any more, do you?"

"No," Tajmah answered, "and neither do you. But, it was good enough to get you out from under your stepmother."

"Well, you don't have to tell the whole world we might need the tape and you don't have to tell every street vendor where I'm staying and how my stepmother cheated my family. You just chit chat about the weather with your family and the other women when we get there. Can you remember that? I'll take care of getting my retirement salary."

"I'm sure you will, dear," Tajmah said, "just like you got the air turned back on."

☙

Saeed wondered when his wife had become so shrill. She certainly hadn't started out that way. He began to think of what it had been like back then. When he had married Tajmah, she dressed and deported herself like the Jackie Kennedy they would see some seven or eight years later in the television news and in copies of Life Magazine that some of their more Americanized friends kept around their houses: prim; demure; elegantly coiffed. Tajmah wore wide hats with flowers, trim skirts and fitted jackets, white gloves (for formal occasions). Black flats. An entirely unnecessary girdle. She would sit quietly with her hands in her lap flattening her skirt, her knees pressed together to the side, her back straight, dutifully repeating the French phrases he had been hired to teach her. Back then he couldn't have imagined Tajmah Kashani sitting in anything other than a gilded, French Empire chair. Of course the Kashanis had certainly opened their fist the day of his wedding in 1953: red-faced Rasheed – only eighteen – shouting curses at him in front of the other guests. Calling him a gigolo and a philanderer and a shabby, money-grubbing opportunist. Worst of all, Rasheed accused, Saeed had sent cheap flowers. Saeed's father, having only seen such crude behavior in his courtroom – and that only by peasants – a judge who had trekked the seven hundred kilometers from divinity school in Najaf to Tabriz on foot to bodily eject the corrupt incumbent judge who had overseen the transfer of his father's (Saeed's grandfather's) estates to his stepmother, bypassing him in his absence, this judge and founder of an independent newspaper, who had led the constitutional movement against the *Qajars* and who had braved a consequent assassination attempt on the road to Tabriz and whom even the Pahalavi shahs had feared, withdrew to the adjoining study, closed the door and, in a stranger *bazaari*'s house, burst into tears like a woman at the abuse of his eldest son – his favorite of favorites. Saeed had weathered the onslaught with a straight-backed, rigid, glaring silence, wondering if he should strike Rasheed with his fist. But, if he did, he would be forever under the thumb of his new in laws. If he slapped him, it might be viewed as a challenge to an out and out fight, which would similarly weaken his standing – especially if he lost, which was likely. He may have been one to sleep nights in a canvas sleeping bag outside in the snow, and used to having Belgian chocolates with a swig of brandy for breakfast, but he had always been slight of frame, even before that passel of scheming British doctors had removed half his stomach and with it his wallet – or rather, his father in law's wallet. His only other choice would have been to storm out in a huff, which would either have left him beholden to Tajmah's family for having insulted them, were he to eventually return, or would have returned him to the mercies of his failing father's household, where he would be vassal to a scheming stepmother, if he didn't. When Tajmah collapsed, weeping, he breathed a sigh of relief. He had an excuse now to avoid any difficult decisions by comforting her. Some of the guests wrestled Rasheed to the ground, gagged and bound him, and carried him off to his bedroom. They'd made excuses: "He's drunk." "He's only eighteen." "He can't handle his liquor." The wedding continued, but in almost silence – and not without a certain sense of relief, because Iranian weddings were obligated to produce at least one major family fight. They were, in this sense, ritualized passion plays. Obligatorily, everyone spent the rest of the afternoon and evening raptly inspecting details in their footwear. After the wedding, Rasheed begged and pestered and nagged and whined and sobbed for a bride of his own, until, finally, the family found him a young, artless Arab through Nargess's old friend, her cousin Zahra, whose testimony supporting the good name of the family had sealed the deal. The girl's grandfather had been one of War Minister's servants. There had been considerable embarrassment amongst the family at having a tarnished scion marry a servant girl who wasn't even pregnant, but Nargess trusted so strongly in her old friend Zahra. Now, it seemed to Saeed, that every minute of every day Tajmah bristled with a desire to avenge the wedding fight, as if he, not her half brother Rasheed, had been the offender. Just his luck for marrying beneath himself!

Now he was slipping into Tehran to try and take advantage of the recent thaw under Khatami to appear in person and claim his retirement salary. He wasn't looking forward to the visit. Staying with his wife's family worried him. Pari had called him relentlessly while he was in America – several times a year, always asking for something. Somehow she blamed him for everything – her son Akhbar volunteering for Khomeini's *basij*, her daughter, Fahti at thirty still moping about the house like an invalid – and expected him to make amends.

None of them understood how he suffered in America, where his friends had escaped with millions in Swiss bank accounts. They would invite him to their Bryn Mawr mansions (where their children studied to variously become doctors, drug addicts and Wall Street managing directors); but, he had no bribe money, had escaped with nothing but two suitcases of clothes, family photographs, and Monsieur de Roche cologne. Since then he had suffered an endless parade of diminutive, American-community-college-educated slick-squirts who somehow thought themselves qualified to supervise a former Chief Attorney of the Department of Energy peddling their wares. And he was going to be caught between Tajmah's family wanting to impress him with *taarof* and wanting him to rescue them from their dismal suffering under the cloud of a vengeful and mindless theocracy. As for the business of obtaining his retirement salary, with luck, he would just face bureaucrats who were lazy and incompetent, but who would cause him no problems other than delays. If he kept his head down he could outwait them. As he had patiently explained to Tajmah, who, to his frustration, was just a housewife, and not experienced in the ways of the world, they must avoid any fight at all with the ignorant peasants who ran the government. Most of them had never even traveled outside Iran, let alone studied abroad. Trained by sheep for careers that needed sheepskins, as he was wont to quip. His tenure as Chief Attorney of the Department of Energy had been a brief enough appointment that after eighteen years no one, particularly the peasant mullahs, would remember him. If only he could portray himself as a pitiable pensioner, deprived of all means, a former government functionary who simply wanted to receive his hard earned and desperately needed government pension. With luck, he would wait in a line of supplicants carrying chickens and bags of bread, and his case would be assigned to an official who had spent his youth carrying water from the village well – someone who had only a vague notion of what a Chief Attorney was. Of course, you wouldn't expect a line like that for former Ministry of Justice employees, but he could still hope.

"Try to remember," Saeed whispered when they stood up to remove their luggage from the overhead. "Our situation requires delicacy. We're just here to visit family. Don't attract attention."

"Yes, dear," Tajmah said, scrunching her nose sideways. "You started nicely."

❧

Saeed expected to pass customs with no more trouble than a breeze blowing through a meadow. It turned out to be more like the air through the airplane's vent nozzle. The Iranian Affairs Office in Washington had said nothing when he went to renew his birth certificate and obtain his passport. They seemed to not recognize him, not have him on any lists. The birth certificate was renewed within two weeks, the passport issued a few days later. The family on both sides of the world buzzed with excitement upon hearing how quickly it had gone for him. It had seemed so easy – too easy. Others had had their applications lost, sometimes repeatedly for years. But, the recent election of Khatami had softened the harsh stance of the clerics. Saeed's hopes seemed almost realized when he watched Tajmah admitted without incident. But, as he watched her collect her passport from the agent and pass through the turnstile, he noticed the agent nod imperceptibly to the guard at the far end of the corridor. Had he really seen this? Or had he just imagined it? Saeed choked. He thought of waiting to see if Tajmah passed the guard too without incident. But, what could he do if she didn't? Any hesitation on his part would just make them more suspicious. He began to sweat. His hand trembled as he handed his passport to the agent.

"Bad flight?" the agent asked.

Saeed started to speak, but his throat was dry and it made a rasping sound. He swallowed, and then forced himself: "I'm not used to it..." he said, trying to make himself sound like a man of humble origins, "... airplanes." Then he craned his neck to see if Tajmah had cleared the guard while the agent said something he couldn't quite hear.

After Tajmah had cleared the guard, Saeed tuned back to the agent.

"Sir?" the agent said.

"Family. We're here to visit family." Saeed was sweating profusely now.

"What you do for a living – I asked you what you do for a living."

"Retired. I mean lawyer. Retired lawyer..." He worried this made him sound too high powered. "...I translate things."

The agent nodded very noticeably to the guard this time. He then asked

Saeed for his birth certificate and withdrew through a doorway at the opposite end of the linoleum-floored hallway, asking Saeed to wait.

Saeed's collar was soaked now. He tried to not look at the armed guard, but every time he did, he found the guard staring at him with suspicious eyes – his eyebrows as thick as paintbrushes and his beard of biblical proportions. It was hard to ignore someone carrying an AK47. He tried leaning on one elbow to appear nonchalant, but the ledge was as high as his chest and he felt it made him look presumptuous – even dandified. The fluorescent light above him buzzed. The light flickered. The light and the tiles on the walls and the linoleum on the floor were all green – prison green. He tried holding his hands together, but that made him feel unctuous – a supplicant. He tried loosening his collar button, but worried that it made him look guilty. He tried buttoning his collar, but it choked him and made his temples feel distended. He worried he would look red-faced, as if hiding something. He tried not to look at the guard…

"Mr. Tabrizi?" The agent had reoccupied the booth. "You can retrieve your passport and birth certificate when you depart."

Saeed stared at him in terror. He dared not object lest he inflame their suspicions. But, if he didn't say anything, they would assume he knew they knew he was guilty. And what would he do if they refused to return his documents? If he didn't say something quickly it would look bad – incriminating. But, how could he identify himself at the Ministry of Justice to claim his pension with no birth certificate? The latter thought, he decided, offered the least prejudicial approach:

"Please, I go to the Ministry tomorrow to get my pension. How will I identify myself? I'm sure you can understand, a working man like yourself – just like me…"

"*Baleh!*" the agent said. He leaned forward confidentially and spoke in a hushed voice, "Of course, my brother, I understand." He winked, then straightened his back and announced, "Next!"

❧

"I knew it," Tajmah said. "I told you to be careful…"

"Please," Saeed said. "Don't start. Not here…"

"…The CIA turned you in." Tajmah was not to be dissuaded. "I told you…"

As they worked their way to the pick up area, Saeed ignored the remainder of his wife's patter. It predictably visited the CIA backing the Khomeini revolution, the CIA planting a spy in the house next to theirs in Philadelphia, the CIA putting rust into their water there, and very nearly would have ended in the CIA cutting the power to their house in Philadelphia that winter, to cause their pipes to burst, to make them take out a home equity loan, because they couldn't afford to make the repairs, because they hadn't paid the insurance company in two years, had not the seizing of Saeed's documents offered a more handy outlet. But, it was better to let her rattle on than have her launch into him about keeping his eyes off of her younger sister, Pari. As if eyes were the problem. Huh! His own father had maintained a harem of four permanent wives, together with a smattering of temporary ones – including at least several servant girls. Who was Tajmah to complain? He remembered one evening in particular, at his father's knee, while his father smoked opium: The major domo stormed into his quarters twisting the tip of his moustache in a frenzy. His father had secretly given identical emerald rings to each of his four permanent wives (Islam dictated they all be treated equally), telling each one in private she was the most special and shouldn't tell the others lest they become jealous. Of course, the secret had lasted all of an afternoon. Then, Armageddon: silk shredded, feathers flying, hair pulling, silver trays clanging, pillows torn, peacocks squawking – even fisticuffs. The chief eunuch had relayed word of the fracas to the major domo. The major domo raced to his master: "My lord! My lord! Come quick! Your wives. They fight. They tear each other to pieces! Come! Come! What to do?" Saeed's father leaned back on his pillow. He drew a draught from the opium pipe. He lifted a hand lazily into the air, waved the hand backwards: "Eh," he said, "let them fight." Maybe it would have been different if Tajmah had had a career. But, a housewife? Well, she could just bite her tongue and behave. It served her mother, Nargess, well enough.

Saeed was dismayed by the family waiting behind the glass barrier to greet him at the pick up area. From the generally shabby and rumpled state of their clothes, Saeed guessed they had all come in one car and were all still living on Rasheed's income. This meant that Saeed would have to hire a taxi. Rude of them, he thought. But, Saeed was truly shocked at how they had all aged. He was forgetting that he himself looked like a wizened turtle now.

Rasheed waved a kind of salute above a sideways-twisted smile that under any other circumstances would be regarded as only a hairsbreadth away from sneer. As heavy-chested and imposing as a mountain, he still balanced a beautiful mound of hair on his head like a cresting wave. Only now it was the color of a frothing whitecap. He still walked as if at every step he were heaving his shoulders through a crowd of footballers. Rasheed's wife, Morvareed, was still dark and shrunken within her shoulders, with a stiffly bowlegged, ape-like carriage, as if she harbored a turd in her underwear. She held her hands before herself, one thumb rubbing the palm of the other hand – secretive, scheming, opaque. Saeed calculated it was going to take some effort to ignore the two of them.

Javad, straight backed, with the puckered face of a seventy-year-old and a preciously thin head of hair as white as powder snow, wore an impeccably pressed, dark blue suit and blue paisley silk tie – both threadbare. He nodded from the distance in a kind of imperial, though slightly befuddled bow, like a door hanging ajar.

Most shocking of all was Pari, who, he figured, must now be almost sixty (and definitely not young, even to his sixty-eight-year-old eyes). She was unrecognizable. Though her waist had only slightly thickened, her hips had widened and sagged to resemble a soggy loaf of bread. Her once silky, dyed blond hair was now masked with an unconvincing rust color, and betrayed gray roots. Her cheap makeup flaked and cracked into lines like dried earth in a parking lot. Her once delicate and prancing gait was heavy, deliberate and stooped. Her eyes were as tremulous as a basset hound's. Her daughter Fahti, though, whom Pari draped with a protective arm, was even sadder. She had always been frail. When he'd fled abroad she'd been twelve, and already young in her development, still completely flat chested and overly concerned with dolls and stuffed animals – and terribly, terribly shy. Now she was a svelte, languid, milky woman of almost thirty, with smooth, dark hair that flowed across her shoulders, as if she had just emerged from the shower, a slightly chiseled yet delicate brow. But, her eyes stared into nowhere – and that was his fault. Did she know that during his eighteen-year sojourn in America he had never even once asked for a picture of her? Did she know enough to be hurt by that?

Saeed felt both guilt and desire when he embraced Shohreh. Shohreh had remained beautiful and feminine and young, if you can call thirty-eight young, which at sixty-eight he certainly did. She was a handsome woman, with high cheekbones. Despite her black frock coat over pants, he could see her figure was still firm, still trim – still the kind of figure you would see on American television. Would she think him too old now? He couldn't help thinking what it would be like to be alone with her, away from the others, taking her to himself, caressing her, away from all the memories – but then there was the guilt. He was afraid to look at her eyes. Afraid to look at their aimless wandering. When she was sixteen he was the one who had arranged her invitation to the royals' party. True, he had been forced into it. And they had said it would be a proper affair, a formal affair. How could he have known? When he thought of the royals who had raped her, he was glad for the precious few of them the revolution had caught, tortured and executed. And he hated himself again, as he had hated himself on and off his whole life, because he knew he had previously heard rumors about the royals and their drugs parties – young women beaten and raped and lucky if the royals felt like buying their silence. As a lawyer he'd been sickened by justice under the Shah. If there was anything in life he regretted – and there was a lot – it was sending sixteen-year-old Shohreh to that party. Afterwards the doctors had never been able to find anything wrong with her, but she had never regained her sight. Hysterical blindness they said, or maybe one of the blows to her head. But, what could he have done? He hadn't been there, hadn't been invited. And now she was still blind, still a tragic victim, still a folksinger, if in name only, and, unfortunately, still Rasheed's neglected daughter.

He wondered if his face showed the rush of blood.

"I know what you're thinking," Tajmah muttered in the taxi. She puffed air through her lips to mock him.

Saeed stared at her blankly. "What?"

"Shohreh."

"Shohreh? She's a handsome woman."

"You'd like that, wouldn't you? Don't think that I don't know."

"What's to know? There's nothing to know."

"Just you try something with her, dear: I'll make sure she knows all about you and her aunt, Pari. Yes. Just you see if I don't! And just you see how long I stick around! It's not as if you've got a pension for me to live on, you know – and in America I get half…"

Saeed thought for a moment. It might not after all be such a bad trade. Half didn't come to much. Even all didn't come to much. And Tajmah only had suspicions, he was sure. She was just guessing about him and Pari. True, she would have heard rumors. But, *in flagrante*? No. Tajmah too strongly reviled her overbearing younger half brother, Rasheed, to give credence to his angry outbursts. And if she really believed any of that, she would have left long ago. Of course, she had nowhere to go. But, that was her problem, wasn't it? And what did he care what she believed? Women were a tiresome lot of work.

"And besides," Tajmah continued, "you should be thinking of what you can do to help Fahti. She's sick – just coming out of a breakdown – on medication of some sort."

"And that's my fault, I suppose?" Saeed said, angrily.

Tajmah retreated into equally angry silence.

Saeed was shocked at the Tehran he saw pass by the taxi window. There were still vendors selling roasted beets, liver kabobs, melon seeds. But, everything had become so shabby. Tehran now looked more like Trenton than the Tehran he had known. The walls of the houses were decayed and the windows covered with gray grime. Broken panes had been repaired with cardboard and plywood. Even the main thoroughfares were plagued by potholes the size of dead cats. Smog clung to the streets in clouds. The oily pollutants stung his eyes and made him feel nauseous. He couldn't breathe. When he had left, Tehran had bustled with cosmopolitan chic: Women on the streets wore Gucci shoes and crisp, thigh length dresses in red and green and gold from Paris and Milan, and Chanel sunglasses. They let their hair flow openly, styled in the latest Parisian fashions. They shopped in stainless steel and glass fronted stores as imposing as banks and as chic as any Christian Dior in New York or London or Geneva. Now, all the women in the streets covered their hair with scarves, though, taking advantage of a recent relaxation, many had adopted sufficiently brief Western style scarves to allow stray locks to protrude. And most daintily held folded handkerchiefs to their noses in vain attempts to clarify the air they breathed. But, absolutely gone were skirts. Most noticeable of all: the streets were a sea of black, with only a scattered flotsam of bobbing scarves in muted colors. It was like looking at life through a 1950's television, all in black and white. Women wore either full-length dresses, or *chadors*, or full-length pants with tunic coats, like the stewardesses on Iran Air, but none were colored. The only exceptions were occasional bright scarves. To Saeed's eyes they all looked like grandmothers, an entire nation of penguin women sixty-five and older – even though he knew the post-Iraq-war baby boom had swelled the ranks of the young. But, what could he say? He had cut a dashing figure as a young man, sporting a sharp moustache like the American movie star, Clark Gable. Now, he himself looked like a turtle, with a bald head and short tufts of close-clipped white hair around the crown, and a drooping nose. His moustache had taken on the appearance of a toothbrush more familiar with polishing silver than teeth. His skin was greenish yellow. He wished he could return to Tehran's oil-fired splendor of the 1970s, and to himself as the young man he had been in the 1950s. He thought to himself that Tehran's rampant unemployment and decaying façade and even his own decline into old age would have been a small price to pay to rid the country of the tortures and imprisonments and beatings of the Pahlavis, but the mullahs had succeeded in rescuing the country from the oppressions of one regime, only to replace them with those of their own. He did not know how intimately he was just about to experience this.

℃

By the next morning, frustrated at dealing with the Ministry staff, Saeed had almost forgotten the man whom he had noticed staring at him in the taxi line at Mehrabad the previous day. It was a driver from several taxis behind his in the orange line of vehicles. He had looked away abruptly when Saeed stared back. This thoroughly startled Saeed. General Ferdowsi? he had thought vaguely. No, it couldn't be. Driving a taxi? Not General Ferdowsi. But, then it was better than appearing in *Newsweek* in your white Jockey briefs, stacked under green fluorescent lights beside your similarly disposed colleagues – a set of cover photographs that had made the entire Iranian diaspora quiver at the knees. It was hard to tell, though, because this man was heavier and older than Ferdowsi, and bald. False or real, the sighting brought back a flood of loose memories: *clean-clipped Ferdowsi in crisp uniform showing him the photostats and saying, "I'm sure you would agree there could be no harm – just a little 'quid pro quo,' eh? Your niece Shohreh is a young woman now, really..."*

"She's only sixteen. She's only a girl..."

Ferdowsi shrugged. "Mr. Tabrizi, I would look at it more as a way for her to move up in the world. She's a born performer... All she needs is to be noticed. Why, with this, she could have a future – with the right help, of course..."

"You crut. I know what they do at parties like that."

And later Shohreh trembling and doe-eyed, her girl's hair unbraided in a liquid flow of gentle swells: "You won't be there? Why, Uncle? Why?" And afterwards weeping...

Until the flood had ebbed into the drone of Tajmah's prattle back-dropped by the whine of airplanes: "I hope you're going to behave yourself."

In response Saeed had said, "I'll behave as well as your brother, Rasheed," which, as Tajmah knew, gave him wide license.

But, when Saeed left the Justice Ministry the next morning and took the first taxi in line, the recognition had hit him like a slap in the face. Before he could even give directions, the driver, slumped heavily in his seat, spoke to him in a familiar, oily voice: "To the Department of Registry?"

Saeed froze. His mouth became dry. "Eh?" he ventured. It sounded like a croak. "You know? Ferdowsi?"

"Avenue, sir? Ferdowsi Avenue?"

Saeed then spoke in a tremble: "Ferdowsi? Is this you?" He tried to view the driver from the side, but he couldn't tell if it were Ferdowsi or not. He could see the same mouse-gray winter coat he had seen on the taxi driver at the airport, the same lumpy girth, a pair of blue, reflective dark glasses, but no more. The driver remained facing forward. He had set the rearview mirror so that Saeed could not see his face. Saeed had only met him a half dozen or so times, and that was almost twenty years ago. It wasn't as if they had been friends. Certainly not friends.

The driver didn't answer at first, but pulled into the traffic. Then he broke the silence: "Of course, if you have to go somewhere else for your birth certificate – the bus station, then? Train? Mehrabad?"

"Eh?"

"Sir?"

"How did you know I needed a birth certificate?" Saeed was panicking. "What do you want from me?"

"Your clothes, sir."

Saeed shrieked: "You want my clothes?"

"Nay," the driver said, with a stainless-steel laugh, briefly relinquishing the steering wheel to hold his hands up in mock despair, and by doing so sending a brief shudder of fear along Saeed's spine. New York's traffic was a murmuring brook compared to the category IV rapids of Tehran's. "You see, sir, I figure I'm a student of human nature, I am. Everyone who worked for the government is now coming back from abroad to get their salaries, what with Khatami and all. But, they need a birth certificate – first stop their Ministry. They get told to get a birth certificate. Next stop, the Department of Registry." He stopped, as if that explained it all.

"Father dog. Do you know who I am?"

"Your suit, eh, it's American – I can tell a kilo away – so I figured you were just coming back – So, to the Registry – Is that …"

"Here, stop the car!" Saeed shouted. "Stop the car now! Here will do. I'll get out now. I'll walk. How much do I owe you?"

The driver came to an angry, screeching halt. "Lost me my place in line, you did."

"How much?" Saeed shouted. He started to extricate himself from the taxi and removed his wallet. He wanted to get a look at the man's face. "Here, I'll pay you double. Are you Ferdowsi?"

"Bah!" the driver said, like a curse. "Next time, pay me double for a real fare!"

Before Saeed could close the door and peer around into the front, the driver gunned the motor and popped the clutch, screeching off into the oil fumes of traffic as fast as he had stopped, the rear door swinging to the side like a broken wing. He had almost knocked Saeed over. Half way down the block the orange vehicle came to another screeching halt. The driver reached over the seat to slam the door shut, motioned through the rear window with his thumb, and then gunned again into the traffic before turning down a side street.

"Father burn!" Saeed cursed. But then, he had second thoughts. Had it really been Ferdowsi? He knew his name, didn't he? Or did he? He had said it – but only once. Or was it his imagination? He had denied it when challenged – well, avoided it, really. But, that could have been a trick, Ferdowsi playing dumb. Ferdowsi would have known Saeed was from Tabriz. But, that was back then. He wouldn't remember after almost twenty years and a revolution, wouldn't have access to the government files. "Father burn!"

Ferdowsi was not a man Saeed had ever thought he could forget. Thank God he'd been home all evening with Rasheed that night twenty years earlier when Ferdowsi's aide had called them to the hospital, where they'd taken Shohreh after the drugs party at the palace:

A week before the party Ferdowsi had scheduled an appointment at Saeed's ministry office to discuss a planned waterfront development project at Bandar e'Pahlavi – a project from which the Shah's cousin would skim millions.

"You pig!" Saeed had shouted, causing an awkward looking Ferdowsi to twist over his shoulder to make sure the door to the office was closed before he

had even seated himself. Saeed slammed a law book down on his plaza-sized walnut desk. "Where is your shame? We finally get real oil money and what do you do with it? You roll it in wads and burn it in Paris and Geneva and Monaco. We need dams, my general, not waterfront construction for luxury hotels in swamps. We need schools, not country roads to nowhere, made out of chicken fat. You people should go to jail for what you do. And now you expect me to go in on it with you? Father dog!"

He had always denied requests to put his department's stamp of approval on one pork project or another when they fell into his jurisdiction. He was famous for it. He knew his shouts would make his secretary wince in the adjacent office, but he drew only forlorn pleasure from knowing her gossip about him dressing down a functionary of the Shah's would enhance his stature. Always there was a relative or friend of the Shah's involved in these projects. They appeared from the dark, like mushrooms on shit. And they were always threatening to smear him with it. Saeed would waken nights in a sweat. He would pace the darkened hallways in fear. It was only a matter of time. He had hoped they would remove him by transfer. He had prayed for a post abroad. But, that would be if he were lucky. Imprisonment, torture, "accidental" death – he would never know till it happened. What kept him going was the memory of his father, a massive man who had stared down wild-faced adversaries with clenched teeth. Armed by justice he had confronted scimitars, muskets, daggers – never once had flinched. Living up to his father's reputation had kept Saeed from acquiescing to the corrupt. But, today Ferdowsi would get to him, and he knew it. He just didn't know how.

Ignoring Saeed's outburst, Ferdowsi seated himself with deliberation and crossed one leg over the other. Then he spoke quietly, with confidence: "I have some photostats…"

"Show them to God, for all I care," Saeed said. He was only half shouting now. "Let Him sign a release for the funds! Shah's cousin… Will you stop anywhere, my general?"

Ferdowsi, his general's crisp hat balanced sharply on his knee, blazed at him in angry silence for a full minute. Then he said with surprising gentleness, "You're fully aware of the implications?"

"You think the Chief Attorney for the Department of Energy wouldn't be?" Saeed said. "I make the implications – my general." He spit it out with a sneer.

General Ferdowsi stared emptily at him for another full minute. Then he exhaled a controlled sigh through his military lips. "Well, I think you may want to take a look at these – to better visualize the 'implications.'" He plopped three curling photostats on Saeed's desk. "You see, it's a bit of a different affair, this time, Mr. Tabrizi."

Saeed picked up the photostats and began to examine them. "So what?" he said, eyeing them like a croupier, "You have copies of my bank records. I have nothing to hide."

"Page three would seem to contradict that, Mr. Tabrizi." He waited while Saeed obliged. "You can explain that rather large deposit – from just this morning?"

"This isn't mine. I haven't even seen this – you could never prove anything in court..."

Ferdowsi interrupted Saeed with a self-satisfied snort. "We have a signed statement from the bank president these are accurate..."

"I never authorized any deposit. I have no idea where it came from."

"... and we have a signed statement from Purushahni that it's a bribe for authorizing funds for his construction firm to start developing Bandar e'Pahlavi – that you had him deposit the funds directly..."

Saeed knew that once he succumbed there would be no end – no end of bribery, no end of blackmail. "You liar!" he spat. "You think Purushahni would incriminate himself by vouching for your forged bank records? I don't think so. His construction firm isn't even connected with your precious Shah's cousin's plans."

Ferdowsi leaned back further into his chair, still straight backed. "Yes – very unfortunate for him..."

"... I don't even have that money in my account. You know that."

"... but, of course, he's no longer with us – It's there – if you call the bank..."

"What do you mean, 'no longer with us?'"

Ferdowsi shrugged, tilted his head to the side, said nothing.

Saeed now figured Purushahni's body would show up somewhere in the marshes or the sewers or moldering in a shabby apartment in South Tehran with needle sticks up and down its arm and a bullet – or two – in his brain – a suicide, they would call it. They'd done it before often enough.

"You can't call two bullets in the brain a suicide, General Ferdowsi – even in a Pahlavi court."

Ferdowsi shrugged again, gaining the upper hand. "I'd be more worried about what the Pahlavi courts would call that deposit, Mr. Tabrizi. Even if it was on speculation – which I'm sure even a skilled jurist such as yourself would never want to have to prove in a 'Pahlavi court'..."

While Ferdowsi talked, Saeed's shoulders stiffened. "Do you believe in God, my general?" He forced himself to keep from stammering.

Ferdowsi was continuing, as if he hadn't heard a word: "... They would keep you out of jail, Mr. Tabrizi. You know that."

"As long as it suited them."

Ferdowsi pursed his lips and nodded. "All you need do is keep quiet about..." He paused, shrugged, then continued. "God willing, we might not even need you to sign a release for Bandar e'Pahlavi..."

"God willing," Saeed with a sneer. Inside he was trembling.

"... You could take a brief leave – designate a deputy with sign off authority – all of this..." He reached forward and tapped the photostats. "... would just disappear. We could make that happen, you know."

Saeed knew there was nothing he could say even if he wanted to.

Ferdowsi clasped his right knee with two hands and leaned comfortably back in the red leather chair, and then changed the subject as casually as if he were asking for a second cup of tea: "I came, actually, on another matter..." He allowed himself a confidant pause to drive home his newly acquired dominance. "... as well."

Saeed vainly tried to mask the dread with which he now regarded Ferdowsi. They'd falsified his bank records, murdered a competing businessman. God knows what they would do to him. "I never said I'd granted you your first wish, my dear general." It was a bluff, but it sounded more convincing than he had expected. He'd regained a bit of an upper hand.

"It concerns your niece." Ferdowsi again spoke as if nothing Saeed said made any difference.

Saeed wondered if Ferdowsi were going to threaten harm to his family. "My niece? Which niece? What do you want with my niece?"

"The singer – the folksinger..."

"Shohreh? Shohreh e'Kashani?"

"Your interest in her – yes, Shohreh e'Kashani – has been, shall we say, noticed..."

"She's talented. I've been helping her get gigs." Then Saeed changed to a dismissive tone: "My interest in her is in helping my wife's family, my general – only that." God knows, the family needed every penny it could scrounge up these days, he thought to himself. They should be on their knees giving thanks.

Ferdowsi nodded sideways. "Of course."

"She'll go all the way if given the chance," Saeed said. "What does this have to do with anything?"

"The Shah's cousin saw her perform at a wedding."

Saeed now felt an angry throbbing in his temples. This cousin of the Shah's, who thought nothing of murder and blackmail, was not someone he wanted to notice anyone in his family, let alone his young niece. And she was a beauty, no doubt about it.

Ferdowsi continued: "There's a party this Saturday. He would like to invite her – get to know her."

"If he wants to hire her for a gig, I could arrange a chaperone. I'm sure..."

"I mean alone," Ferdowsi said. "As a guest – at the party – not really 'alone' – but no need for a chaperone. I'm sure you would agree there could be no harm – just a little 'quid pro quo,' eh? Your niece Shohreh is a young woman now, really..."

Saeed reddened. "She's only sixteen. She's only a girl..."

Ferdowsi shrugged. "Mr. Tabrizi, I would look at it more as a way for her to move up in the world. Her performances... All she needs is to be noticed. Why, with this, she could have a future – with the right help, of course..."

"You crut. I know what they do at parties like that."

Ferdowsi thought silently to himself for a while. Then he spoke: "We'll call it a deal, then. I'll send a matron to take her to Charles Jordan for shoes and a purse. Afterwards she'll take her to Princess Ashraf's private seamstress for the dress. You just need to make her available – no need to get the parents involved, if you know what I mean. Eh?"

"So, you'd just barge into her life like that, general?" Saeed said. "Just like that? A young girl?"

"Yes – it is an honor for her."

Astonished, angry, Saeed stared at Ferdowsi. "You think it that?" he said. "Yes, I believe you do. You certainly would."

Ferdowsi shrugged, holding his palms outwards. Then he rose and approached the door. "Is there anything else?" Ferdowsi said, placing his hand on the doorknob, so that he had to talk over his shoulder.

"Yes, my general, there is: Tell the Shah's cousin he can stick Bandar e'Pahlavi up his ass."

Ferdowsi turned the doorknob, opened the door and replied in an even-tempered tone: "Yes, I see. Well, you'll have to arrange things. I'll send someone around day after tomorrow. And we'll arrange for you to join the delegation to Beijing." He nodded politely to Saeed's secretary and then pulled the door closed behind himself.

All that night and well into the next morning, Saeed had paced back and forth in his bedroom. Were they threatening his niece now to threaten his daughter later? She was studying abroad, but they could get to her if they wanted. Were they bluffing about Purushahni? His body might not be discovered for some weeks. If he gave them their waterfront project would they spare him Shohreh? If he gave them Shohreh, would they spare him the waterfront project? Maybe their intentions were honorable – at least concerning Shohreh. But, then, why was the invitation bundled with blackmail? Still, it could be a way to get her a real career, with real money – an escape from the crumbling detritus of the Kashanis, the lost Qajar valor – even if it were only through the frail tendril of Shohreh's grandmother, Nargess Khanoum. If he gave them the waterfront project, it would be illegal. They would have him on that forever. If he gave them only Shohreh, it wouldn't be illegal – at least, not technically. And it wouldn't necessarily even be wrong. It wouldn't be his fault, whatever happened. Somewhere along the line the royals had to bear responsibility. Somewhere there had to be courts and justice. And maybe nothing would happen – nothing at all.

But, a week later Ferdowsi had called him to the hospital.

"I didn't know, Mr. Tabrizi. Believe me, I didn't know..."

"If you didn't know, how is it I did?" Saeed interrupted. "Is the Shah's cousin really worth it? His sister, the Princess, too?"

"The Princess Ashraf was elsewhere. She has witnesses. So does the Shah's cousin."

"And you, my general? You delivered the invitation. Your aide drove my young niece there You called us to the hospital. You – who is here, now."

"I have witnesses too."

"Of course – No doubt the same ones as Princess Ashraf and the Shah's cousin."

"Yes, Mr. Tabrizi, and all evening you were with your young niece's parents, which I find is hard to believe an accident. Are you any different from me?"

And the worst memory of all was Shohreh trembling and doe-eyed, her girl's hair unbraided and done up like Audrey Hepburn's in a liquid flow of gentle swells, and as he moved to close the limousine door behind her she said, "You won't be there? Why, Uncle? Why?" And afterwards he heard her weeping in her hospital room and he could not enter and had to call her father Rasheed who assumed the police had called Saeed first because he was a prominent lawyer...

❦

And now, twenty years later, Ferdowsi was stalking him again. He knew it. First at Mehrabad Airport, then in the taxi outside the ministry. Was it because Ferdowsi had to lay low? That was doubtful. He had to be well known to the regime, on every list there was. Did he know something damaging to them? Was that how he survived? Whatever it was had to be safe in a vault in Switzerland. But, they would have hanged him anyway. No, more likely the regime simply didn't care any more. He must know something about Saeed, though. But, there was nothing he hadn't already tried, when he was in power under the Shah. This was a game. A game that had to start with rattling him.

It was in Tabriz, at a café along the lakefront esplanade, after a fruitless struggle with the bureaucrats at the local Office of the Registry for Azerbaijan over his birth certificate, that Ferdowsi finally caught up with him. Saeed had stopped in the café to warm his feet and cool his nerves. He had just ordered tea and pastries. He was watching the snow fall gently against the limestone sill of the café's high arched window, rubbing his temples.

"On you, my friend, – came the voice. It loomed out of the shadows of the mostly empty café. – I'm sure you won't mind."

"I don't need your games, my general," Saeed said. "It is my general, is it not?"

"Thank you, I'd love to join you." Ferdowsi seated himself beside Saeed, so they could share the view, Ferdowsi's ample shoulder to Saeed's frail one. Ferdowsi motioned to the waiter: "Same as my friend here – we'll double up on his bill."

"That's one hell of a taxi fare, my general, Tehran to Tabriz – I fly, myself."

Ferdowsi shrugged, his shoulders pressing tightly against his suit jacket, straining against his top shirt button. "You have a nice life."

"On the other hand," Saeed continued, "given Iran Air, I can't blame your fare. Nice for you, though. You driving them back as well?" He thought to himself quietly for a moment and then added, "They do have nice stewardesses, though, eh? Dumb, but nice. Wouldn't it have been easier to find me in Tehran, my general?"

"I thought it better for us to meet here, away from your family – if you know what I mean," Ferdowsi said. He clasped a pair of beefy-knuckled, hairy-backed hands together in his lap, the fingers intertwined. "It couldn't be very good for anyone to have Shohreh see me with you – your wife either – or your sister in law, Pari..."

"I see you still have the Shah's regime's habit of making cruel jokes and false accusations."

"Well, stick to your own," Ferdowsi said, not missing a beat. Now it was Ferdowsi's turn to remain silent. Then his turn to add, almost as an afterthought: "You always did fly close to home, eh!"

"What do you want, Ferdowsi?"

Ferdowsi continued as if he had heard nothing: "Shohreh was a nice girl. I remember. As gentle as a kitten. Hair like silk..."

Saeed stiffened. He didn't like where this was going.

"... She could have had a nice career as a singer if the Shah had lasted." Ferdowsi placed a sugar cube between his teeth, poured tea into the saucer and sipped it through the sugar. He effected the entire operation with the delicacy of a ballet dancer, despite the enormity of his hands, which engulfed the frail saucer like a giant lobster claw. Then he continued: "Abol Fazl doesn't think she's blind."

"And why is that important?"

"I don't know," Ferdowsi said. "Maybe he thinks she saw something she shouldn't have. Maybe he wants her to see his grand turban..."

"He could bed better than a retired blind folksinger without having her see again. Does he need his victims to watch? Or is he just worried antibiotics don't work on blind people?"

Ferdowsi shrugged: "Not my concern, Mr. Tabrizi. Neither that, nor your birth certificate. As for me, I get paid, I do what they ask."

"I won't ask you how you got Abol Fazl to employ you, my general – or why. Though I salute you for it. But, why this? And, why now, my general – twenty years later?"

"If she's blind, she wasn't born that way," Ferdowsi said.

"The way you beat her, are you surprised?"

"I wasn't there, you remember."

"Of course, the Shah's cousin beat her."

"He wasn't there."

"The Princess Ashraf? A lesbo thing?"

"She wasn't there either."

"Of course, of course, no one was," Saeed said. He blew air through his lips. "Witnesses." Then he added, "A drunken orgy in an empty palace room with one innocent, lascivious sixteen year old girl who was no longer a virgin, beating herself senseless for the pure pleasure of it..."

"Wise of her to wake up blind, don't you think?" Ferdowsi stroked his chin, staring out the high arched window where the snow was accumulating in drifts. "As if she had legal advice from –" He paused. "– well – if not someone very knowledgeable in the law, then – maybe – God?" He leaned forward and peered into Saeed's eyes. "Eh?"

Saeed paused and sipped tea from his saucer. "God delivers strange mercies, my general – wisdom not the least of them."

"She's still amnesiac too, I take it?"

Saeed raised his arms in a gesture of despair: "Does it matter? The royal kennels are empty now, general – going on twenty years. You're not going to tell me the blessed Abol Fazl used to scratch fleas under the table with them – a dog bowl of champagne and caviar with the Shah's twin sister before a little rutting? A little sniffing under the clerical hem that got out of hand? And now he's worried the famous folksinger, Shohreh e'Kashani, will wake up and remember – two decades later...?"

"Now, now," Ferdowsi said, "water under the bridge."

"... No, Abol Fazl is a dog, but not that much of a dog. At least not a stupid enough dog to have raised his leg with the royals. One thing I'll hand the clergy: none of them were ever that dumb. And that's saying something – for a class that raised stupidity to an art form..." Saeed paused, while Ferdowsi said nothing. Then he continued: "What have you come to confess to me, my general?"

Ferdowsi drained the last of his tea directly from the glass, finished the last square of *baklava*, licked his fingers, wiped them dry with the dainty laced napkin, and rose heavily to his feet. He placed his thick hand warmly on Saeed's shoulder and made a brief half-bow. "My friend," he said, "when it is time, you will be the one to confess to me."

&

his own daughter's age. No demands. No pouts. Just her youthfully rounded features, breasts that pointed upwards, and her chestnut brown, almost black hair like a silken river upon the pillow. He had forgotten the feel of hair like that, like Pari's twenty years earlier. Shohreh was a simple girl – scarcely younger than his daughter. Kiss for an afternoon... her limbs uplifted, lips, breasts, thighs as taut as leather... She would talk of algebra tests and tennis teams and disco from America. But, they had stayed on the terrace and sipped ice tea after she sang and Saeed had never known if she would go upstairs with him, if she wanted to go upstairs with him and had never known if she could even imagine sharing the longing...

And it all ended before he would ever know with that crut Ferdowsi and his waterfront project at Bandar e'Pahlavi and his invitation for Shohreh from the Shah's cousin and her weeping in an all-expenses-paid hospital room as Saeed called her father in shame...

"Saeed?"

"Shohreh, dear. I am here. Over here."

She made her way to him through the shadows with her hands held ajar, in the way of the blind, cautious of a violation of the familiar pattern of tables and trays and carpets and lamps – even though these were mostly gone now, and had been for many years. She held her hands not unlike the way young women walk, paddling the air with her palms, except that she moved hers more cautiously.

"Would you like tea?" she said. She did not touch him. "The others have gone out."

"I caught an early flight."

"Did you get your birth certificate?"

"They said to come back. Maybe next week."

"That's the way it is now."

"Yes."

"Mullahs – all of them, peasants."

"Yes."

They sat in shadowed, awkward silence, each suspecting what the other was thinking, neither knowing what was safe. Saeed was afraid to look at her. He watched her eyes. They wandered indifferently, blankly, gazing at nothing. After a long silence she closed them. She began to cry. Saeed scrunched within himself. He did not know what to say. He was afraid to say it.

"I didn't know," Saeed said. "Shohreh, I didn't..."

"I know."

Saeed wanted to love her. He wanted to caress her, reach out to her, take her to him, hold her head to his chest. But, he could not do that to her, give her hope. Could not do that to her, blind and alone.

"They said it would just be a party," he said. "Just a party..."

"I know."

"… a chance for you…"

"I know."

"… a chance to meet a better sort. Who would you have ever met in this house?…"

"I know. I know. I know…"

They hid from one another within the shadows, the cherished silence of bare walls, the distant calls of occasional street vendors, the constant buzz of motorcycles like mosquitoes, and automobiles rattling like dump trucks. They each feared the return of the family with a dread like sagging plaster. They wanted to reach to one another, but couldn't. Wanted to go forward, couldn't go backward.

"Shohreh, dear, I couldn't write – Your parents would have read my letters. They would have gotten the wrong idea…"

"I know," she said.

"I wanted to come back and help. I kept waiting for a time – but those mullahs… It's not what you think, in America. You're all alone there. These dirty old women sit by themselves in their rooms, watching television all day with their pets. Dogs, they kiss. Cats, they kiss – but children? Never once have I seen a father kiss a son. They're afraid they'll look like homosexuals. You know, they even have pet cemeteries there. I'd come back here and live if it weren't for those father-dog mullahs…"

"There's been a man coming around," Shohreh said, "asking about you. Asking …"

"A man? Who? When?"

"… strange questions… for several weeks now, but never when the others are here – as if he's watching us or something…"

"Ferdowsi?" Saeed said.

"I thought it was a made up name," Shohreh said, nodding. "You know him? He asked if you were ever …" She paused, then continued: "… *mujahedin*…"

"Bah! The crut! The Chief Attorney for the Department of Energy a *mujahedin*? I don't think so…"

"… as if I would tell him."

"You mustn't talk with this man."

Shohreh reached out into the air until she found Saeed's shoulders and grasped him. "He kept waving his hands in front of my face. He's very strange."

"How do you know he was waving in your face?"

"I could feel the air. I could hear the rustling of his suit. He was waving his arms like this…" She made the motion.

"A suit? How…"

"They sound different. I can tell."

"Ferdowsi trying to look pretty. He drives a taxi now. Or pretends to."

"I gave him a glass of tea and he wouldn't believe me when I told him I had made it myself. Then he stole the glass – plunked it in his pocket – took it with him right out the door!"

Saeed was stumped by this tidbit. He knew Ferdowsi was capable of anything. But, a tea glass? Saeed said nothing of this. He spoke: "You want to know who he works for now? Our beloved spiritual leader, the holy Abol Fazl himself – when he isn't playing taxi."

Shohreh sat upright with a start. She moved herself so she was fully apart from Saeed, out of arms reach, but she turned and faced him squarely, her aimless, dark wandering eyes confronting his fixed ones. "Mr. Ferdowsi works for Abol Fazl?" She paused. "I saw him, Saeed. I saw him. He burned the cinema. I saw him."

Saeed drew his head back in shock and let out a gasp. Even twenty years on the incident remained wrenchingly infamous. There were rumors in the press that the investigation was being reopened. Only months before the Shah had fled in January of 1979, someone had set fire to the Cinema Rex in the southern oil city of Abadan, during a matinee performance. It was an inside job. The rear exit doors had been chained and padlocked from the inside. Hundreds burned alive. Opposition leaders accused the *savaki* of having set the fire to sow fear among the population. The government accused the opposition of having set the fire to spread chaos. What scared Saeed the most was that that both scenarios were equally plausible, though the odds on bet was that it was the clergy working with the *mujahedin*.

"Ferdowsi?" Saeed said, disbelieving. "How could you…"

"No, no. Not Ferdowsi. Abol Fazl. I saw him…"

"But…"

"Sometimes I see things."

There was another long silence while each seemed to absorb the enormity of what Shohreh had said. Saeed recalled the arson investigation. He had been in Abadan at the time. He was there to inspect the books of the oil refinery, but each afternoon he took lunch with his niece, Shohreh, at her friend Mahine's house, slipping in through the chained gate in the rear to save a half block walk around to the front. They had never found the culprit. The investigation had dissolved in the chaos of the Shah's departure and Khomeini's return. But, Shohreh had been placed at the scene. She had been invited to Abadan for a week of concerts. She had been alone at her friend Mahine's house, which had a sitting porch above the alley behind the Cinema Rex. She testified she had not heard anyone in the alley after the matinee crowd had entered. And, of course, she was famous then, famous for having skyrocketed in popularity as a folk singer – famous for being famous as a blind folksinger. Everyone knew she could no longer see – had tragically lost her sight at the tender age of sixteen. And only through gossip whispered sotto voce had they heard the cause of that was her rape by unknown assailants. Saeed never knew if Shohreh understood the Shah's family had promoted her career even more than he had. The support from the royals (composers, lyricists, sound engineers, photographers, journalists and most of all, admen – all hired by the royal family and instructed to be grateful for the talent they had discovered) had been the fuel for her popularity's skyrocket. The royals had undoubtedly costed it out as just recompense. *They* were like that. But, Shohreh didn't understand all this. She thought her success real. Saeed never had the heart to explain the truth to her. He had betrayed her once by delivering her to the drugs party and even though she had not understood his role in that, he could not now devastate her. After the fall of the Shah, her popularity had waned. Khomeini prohibited musical performances. He ordered Western style instruments destroyed. Many of the performers had been associated with the former shah's cronies and had been imprisoned, all on flimsy evidence. But, Shohreh e'Kashani was popular and the public still held great compassion for her tragedy. So Khomeini had to tolerate her. The rumors that the royals had raped her had helped her case. Without the Shah's composers and lyricists and sound engineers and photographers and journalists and admen, her meteoric rise fizzled. Twenty years later she was still a tragic blind icon – but just that. And now she says she can see things – some things.

Shohreh, shaking, broke the silence: "I see them tearing at me, Saeed and I see them holding me open. I'm screaming and they're laughing – whiskey breath – hot – cocaine powder on their lips – like petrol fumes – like snow wolves – and they're cutting it with razor blades – and they're looking at me. They're fumbling at me and twisting my legs to make them hurt – a pack of them – it hurt – it hurt – Saeed – cutting it with razor blades – that's all I remember. But, sometimes I see things. I saw him, Saeed. I saw Abol Fazl. He came to get the padlock and the paint cans they'd filled with petrol. He came out of the cinema door. He looked up at me. He said, "*Allahu akhbar!*" And I saw him. But, he didn't know it. He took the padlock and the paint cans and went back inside. But, he must have needed a chain. They didn't think of that. He came back out and took the chain from Mahine's gate, the one I would unlock for you when you when you were coming for lunch. Nobody knew him then. He was dressed in blue jeans and a black t-shirt. He wore a sports hat from America. I saw him later at the end of the alley, by the front of the cinema, wearing dark glasses – before the sirens. He had his thumbs in his pockets – like a tourist – Saeed, I could hear them beating against the doors and he was strolling at the end of the alley whistling to himself like an American tourist…"

"You saw this? You saw all of this? You never told anyone?"

"I was the contact, Saeed. That was the password: '*Allahu…*'"

The sound of the front door latch shocked them into silence. Immediately there billowed into the house the lilting calls of women returned from shopping: "Shohreh, dear, we're home!" Tajmah and Pari were holding Nargess gently under each shoulder, helping her in the door. Saeed reddened with embarrassment at being alone with Shohreh. He knew they all distrusted him. He didn't want them to think there was anything between him and his blind niece. But, he reasoned they were sitting a respectable distance apart. He made an effort to remain seated to prove the innocence of their sitting together. Then he rose to his feet, affecting leisure. Soon he took refuge in the omnivorous gossip and the cultural ritual of pastries and tea. But, he was only pretending to relax. He couldn't wrest his mind away from all that Shohreh had told him. How could she have been connected with Abol Fazl without knowing who he was? What had she been hiding? What would happen to her if they found out? And arson? Shohreh aiding and abetting the burning of the Cinema Rex? Ferdowsi circling like a wolf. Princess Ashraf's party. Petrol cans. Padlocks…. Then it was as if amongst the entire cacophonous chattering of a city, the noise about him had become lost to him, disappeared in a crunched circle around him, like crickets hushed by a footstep:

"Father burn!" he shouted, dropping his tea glass and saucer in a crash, and ignoring the slack-jawed silence he had wrought upon the gossiping. "Fingerprints!"

℃

"Did you have to embarrass me like that?" Tajmah was getting into it when they were alone together. "Getting drunk with my blind niece in front of the family behind my back?"

"What? Who… I wasn't… Why do you make these things up?"

"As if I wouldn't know, my dear," Tajmah said bitterly, ignoring him. She removed her glasses and let them hang by their chain from her neck, looked off into the distance through the window and rolled her wrinkle-lidded eyes skyward. "Do you ever think of anything besides yourself and your own pleasures?"

"I caught an early flight…"

"Dropping your tea on the floor like an imbecile – You could have called."

"It was just a flight. Just an airplane flight back from Tabriz. Dumb stewardesses with small tits and no air. You knew I was coming back. So what if I caught an early flight? Do I have to have the CIA call and tell you I'm on an early flight? You could have just checked with them, you know." He made a cradle with his right hand and held one finger to his ear, the other to his mouth. 'Hello! CIA? This is Mrs. Tabrizi. Is Mr. Tabrizi on time?'"

"Huh!" Tajmah sniffed, signaling the end to the conversation.

❧

Saeed knew it would be trouble when Rasheed pulled him to the *bazaar* along with Javad. They were riding in Rasheed's used Peugeot diesel, which made noises like tumbling garbage tins every time the tire hit a pothole. In the rare moments of decrescendo between potholes they could hear the constant woosh of tires pushing through the winter slush, strapped by the indefatigable pinging of the engine. The women rode behind in a taxi.

Javad, from the back seat, was saying, "They can't deny you your birth certificate – even in Tabriz. We can sue them. I have friends there, clients..."

Rasheed flicked a quick glance at Saeed. He was still hostile, if softened over the years. But, in the eye flash Saeed detected a certain tired sympathy, as if the eye of a whale or a giant squid had blinked at him from beneath the gray froth of a cresting wave.

As if he entirely understood the camouflaged exchange between his cousins, Javad continued without inflection: "Of course, it's better to check with Rasheed's people first."

Rasheed's "people" were the Sarabis, father and son rug merchants in the *bazaar*. Saeed knew nothing about them other than they were *bazaari* and friends of Rasheed and could "do something." This told him pretty much what to expect. He was not disappointed.

The elder Sarabi was a petite, gray, feeble, mustachioed sort who wore a fez cap and walked like a featherweight prizefighter – though with a cane. He was possessed of a wiry arrogance incongruous with his size. But, the younger Sarabi was an eyesore. The son to the father was a comparison which questioned the honor of the mother. The younger Sarabi was a corpulent, sea squirt of a man, as perfectly round as a watermelon, but with a tiny undulant mouth as delicate and as pink as a girl's.

The *bazaar* brimmed with family businesses like these. The clerestory windows starting two and three stories up basked the giant hall in a soft, meandering glow that wafted along miles of similar corridors. The tradesmen, in stalls along the sides, stacked and hung their goods as high as two stories, variously leaving either a brief defile of bare stone and plaster to the bottom of the higher windows, or towering glassed, third floor store fronts rising to even higher windows. Row upon row of stalls debouched upon one another: bolts of silk in beetle-brilliant colors; stacks of gray rope and canvas; red and green and yellow pickles in glass jars; strings of beaten copper and tin jugs; trays and samovars; molded plastic strainers; open bins of laundry bluing; tiered displays of Sony Walkmen; bubble wrapped chrome corkscrews; sandals; kabobs, live chickens, dead chickens, grilled chickens... The *bazaar* offered more than you could possibly want, it offered more than you could even imagine. The sheer abundance thrilled Saeed, much as did Sam's Club Warehouse in America, except that you didn't have to buy everything in an army size twenty-four pack. And the women shoppers didn't have butts begging description in astronomical units. (Saeed considered it a cruel, if minor irony, that in America, where women had SUV buttocks, they were allowed to display them in thong-sized spandex or cutoffs – obscene marmalades of excrescent flesh. In Iran, where butts were trim, taut by even Hollywood standards, women had to hide them inside *chadors* as titillating as Hefty lawn bags. If he were president he would arrange a switch.) The *bazaar* harbored a maze of sprouting side corridors – narrow, crowded, shadowy, evocative. Opening onto these, or hidden at the backs of the stalls, were invariably musty, windowless, cave-like offices. These were illumined by shadeless incandescent or circular fluorescent bulbs hung from knotted electric cords, surrounded by stacks of inventory and receipts heaving up to the ceiling. They were the seed-roots of the *bazaar*, the collective womb of the *bazaari*. Here was where the Rashidian brothers, in the second world war, plotted on behalf of the British to deny Iranians suffrage and wheat, and in the process rewarded themselves with gold rings, natty suits, Swiss watches and sleek American automobiles – while the peasantry starved. And here was where, in 1953, the same Rashidian brothers filtered the money from the CIA's Kermit Roosevelt (grandson of Teddy) into the hands of their followers, who staged a "popular" uprising against the democratically elected, oil-nationalizing Mossadegh, for one tenth the cost budgeted by the American government. So, it was an appropriate venue for the Sarabis, "*pere et fils* – purveyors of fine carpets," and for the business at hand: to slip a wad of American dollars into the pudgy hand of a pink-lipped, wheezing, sea squirt of a man who offered Saeed's only hope for obtaining a copy of a birth certificate so that he could obtain his retirement salary and return to Philadelphia.

"You see, Mr. Tabrizi," the younger Sarabi said between labored gasps, "my father and me, we buy many of our carpets from Tabriz. We have our friends there."

Saeed twisted and looked over his shoulder uncomfortably. It was just himself and Rasheed talking to these *bazaari*, sitting in the office beside a pile of folded and rolled prayer carpets. Balanced on top of a sheaf of receipts was a copper tray with four glasses of tea summoned from the teashop next door. Saeed could smell the freshness of the wool of the carpets. He wondered to himself if Rasheed were going to get a cut of this. Probably. They had taken a while to separate themselves from the women, particularly because they kept running across Pari. Saeed knew that she was only pretending to shop, was stalking him, had left Tajmah to tend to doddering Nargess while she waited for a chance encounter to slip her hand in his, exchange longing glances, endearing whispers – all in the anonymity of the crowd. Annoyed Pari had managed to evade the other women and keep finding him, Saeed busied himself with Rasheed like a tail with its cat. He and Rasheed had sneaked around a corner and into the carpet store when Pari had her back turned, lingering beside a bolt of red and gold silk. Gossip spread through extended families like wildfire. After that, who knew where it would go? The fewer who witnessed this, the better.

"And if your government friends are on holiday?" Saeed said.

"I have some printer friends, if we need. Costs me more, though." The younger Sarabi waved his pudgy hand in the air.

Saeed squirmed in his seat, then tried to sit bolt upright. He was afraid to speak his mind least he be charged more for it. But, pink lips beat him to it: "I understand, Mr. Tabrizi: Time is of the essence?" While Saeed said nothing, pink lips became silent, leaning back in his squeaking swivel chair with both hands affixed to a bulbous stomach as if he were clutching a greased medicine ball: "Days?" He burped silently through his nose with such practiced grace it appeared to the others only as a legitimate exhalation. "I've heard you need a passport, too, no?"

Saeed choked. He wished Rasheed had not divulged so much. "No," he said. "Just the birth certificate." He glanced angrily at Rasheed, who had remained outside the office, standing guard.

"Better safe than sorry?" pink lips gasped. "I could…"

"No. No passport. Just the birth certificate, thank you."

"As you wish, Mr. Tabrizi. Just let me know if your situation changes. Heh! I may even do it on spec." He raised one eyebrow, doubled the bill, allowed the second half on delivery and struggled to gain his feet. With a parting gasp he added: *Allahu akhbar.*

☙

"Don't count on it," Ferdowsi's probing voice caught Saeed unexpectedly, as he lingered at the coin dealer's stall. Saeed was slowly fingering the glass case, vaguely pondering the purchase of some *Qajar* era gold coins as gifts for the next *Noruz.* The ones he could afford looked like they belonged to his granddaughter's Barbie doll. But, he wasn't really shopping, just trying to look as if he were. He was avoiding Pari and hoping to rejoin the women – *en masse.* And now Ferdowsi had to spoil it.

"I don't see a taxi line here, my general," Saeed said, fondling the coins with his eyes.

"Must be over where the shop assistants are hauling your carpet," Ferdowsi said.

Saeed began to sweat, despite the cold. He drew tight the rabbit fur collar of his overcoat. With numbing fear he listened to Ferdowsi continue: "You can get jail time for bribery – worse, even." Ferdowsi removed a pair of reading glasses from his breast pocket, breathed on them and cleaned the fog with his handkerchief. He donned the glasses and bent over the counter, pretending to inspect the coins. "Forgery too..." he said.

Saeed said nothing. He remained bent over the counter, inspecting what was now a tarnished blur of glinting gold.

"... Not a nice crowd, those Sarabis..." Ferdowsi continued, "... rug merchants."

"I thought they had a good stock," Saeed said in deadpan.

"I wasn't talking about their carpets."

"You didn't think I was referring to their breeding, my general, did you?" He was beginning to recover himself. He reasoned that Ferdowsi would have had him arrested already, if he really knew he'd slipped a thousand American dollars cash to the Sarabis, so they cold solve the problem of his birth certificate – a problem that was increasingly obviously manufactured by Ferdowsi on behalf of Abol Fazl. Ferdowsi was simply continuing the hunt – spooking him to break cover. He could be working just from the Sarabis' reputation. Even just that could present difficulties, though. So Saeed would have to be careful. He figured he could brush off Ferdowsi by ignoring him. But, what he heard next drove him to panic:

"We could avoid all this, Mr. Tabrizi, if you could tell me more about your cousin Shohreh."

Saeed pondered his response in a flash. Too quick or too slow, too cooperative or not enough – almost anything might raise Ferdowsi's suspicions. And why was he asking? Ferdowsi not only knew her history, he was complicit in it. "My cousin is a retired folksinger, blind since her tragic violation. I don't need to remind you..."

"Is she really blind?"

So that's it, Saeed thought. Abol Fazl is worried he'll be identified. But, who would take the word of a hysterical woman? She hadn't been blind before the drug party with the royals when she was sixteen. There were no medical reasons, no blows to the head. It was obviously hysterical blindness. And there were other questions: How did Shohreh know that Abol Fazl was the name of the man in the alley? How did Ferdowsi know Saeed was visiting the Sarabi rug merchants in the *bazaar* today – and the ministry of registry in Tabriz the day before?"

"We've unearthed physical evidence from the archives," Ferdowsi said, as if he were reading ahead of Saeed's train of thought. "I think you should know that. The case is being reopened."

"Evidence of what, my general? What case?" He hoped he sounded convincingly ignorant.

Ferdowsi paused for dramatic effect, as if to intimate Saeed knew perfectly well what case. "The burning of the Cinema Rex in Abadan."

Saeed raised a cautious eyebrow. This would be big news for anyone. If he showed no interest he would be perceived as deliberately hiding something. They would think he was hiding his own guilt. If he said anything too quickly, it could suggest he was nervous about the issue. Things would get messier.

"We know it's the *mujahedin*." Ferdowsi said.

Saeed maintained a poker face. He was learning something: Abol Fazl was going to put the blame squarely on the *mujahedin* – in court, no less. That is, they thought of it as a court – well, called it a court. They had already convicted and executed several for the crime. But, everyone knew they were most likely innocents. Now they probably thought they could make a better show of it. But, why was Ferdowsi telling him? To scare him? To lure him into a false sense of security?

Ferdowsi continued: "We have Shohreh e'Kashani's fingerprints on the padlock and chain used to lock the doors. We always figured someone from the inside sneaked out the back and retrieved them from an accomplice…"

Saeed betrayed nothing.

"… after all, you can hardly walk into a theater with chains and padlocks and petrol cans. We can place Shohreh at the scene. It's well known. She testified to it. Now we have her fingerprints on the evidence. We don't know why they never checked her prints in the first place. Of course, no one would ever suspect – a pitiable, blind folksinger – or…" He allowed himself another prolonged pause – an inquiry? – a threat? "… a sympathetic police – or maybe ministry of justice – could I? – should I say it? – 'conveniently' forget to suspect her?" He paused again, then continued in a clipped fashion, "She *had* experienced a rather meteoric rise." Ferdowsi abruptly stopped talking, to let this all sink in. "You don't think anyone is going to believe you helped in this all because you were a kindly old uncle, do you?" He eyed Saeed with menace.

Saeed was wondering why they hadn't arrested Shohreh if they had her fingerprints on the padlock. Which meant either they didn't have them, or they wanted to snag someone else, or they feared Shohreh would identify Abol Fazl – or all three. He remembered the case well. It wouldn't be a surprise to find Shohreh's fingerprints on the chain. It had been established the chain probably came from her host, Mahine's house, where she lived while in Abadan. They discovered it missing after the fire and immediately reported it. But, the padlock used on the inside of the Cinema Rex was from somewhere else. The padlock that belonged to Mahine's father was found in the gutter by the gate. They had immediately theorized the chain had been stolen by whoever set the fire, out of unforeseen necessity. Indeed, they determined in the investigation that the padlock used, though unusually large, was too small to secure the door by itself and could only do so with the aid of a chain. But, Saeed kept these thoughts to himself. All he said to Ferdowsi was a bland, "I remember the case, of course, my general. I remember her testimony."

"Doubtless you're wondering why they haven't brought this up before?"

"I haven't thought much about it. But, I will say, my general, I'm astounded at the privileged insights into the internal affairs of the Ministry of Justice now afforded me by a common taxi driver. And yes, my general, why now?"

Ferdowsi leaned back off the counter and faced Saeed squarely. "Doubtless, Mr. Tabrizi, you can explain your own fingerprints on both the padlock and the chain used to lock the alley door of the Cinema Rex of Abadan on August 20th, 1978"

Saeed recoiled at the threat. He straightened, backed away from the counter and faced Ferdowsi in pale shock. His prints couldn't be on the padlock. The chain, yes. He'd unwind it from the rear gate beneath the sitting porch when he took lunch with Shohreh and Mahine. There was nothing sinister in that. Men often took their lunch break with the closest residing relatives. It would be an insult to be visiting Abadan at the same time as Shohreh and not join her for lunch. But, the padlock? It couldn't be. He had had no residence in Abadan from which the *mujahedin* could have taken a padlock – nor one in Tehran. He had never even owned a padlock, except for the miniature ones on his luggage. Ferdowsi must be bluffing. But, bluffing how much? Did he have any fingerprints anywhere on the evidence? He must have something. Maybe he would just lie to the "court" and say the fingerprints lifted from the passport were on the lock as well. Otherwise he would never have gone to such lengths as stealing the tea glass from Shohreh. But, exactly which items had which prints – Ferdowsi was a liar. Even if Ferdowsi weren't lying this time, Saeed knew his (Saeed's) only recourse was to pretend he believed he was. His knees were buckling. He didn't have much time.

"As you can understand, my general," Saeed said, trying to speak in a monotone, "my family relies on me for advice in legal matters. In this case, I'm going to tell them..." He paused, for a dramatic effect of his own, then continued, "... you're just passing gas through your anus. As for me..." He held his wrists together in front of himself, palms upward. "... go for it!"

Ferdowsi glared at him like an angry bull, a flash of uncertainty tracing momentarily across his eyes. Then, without warning, he arced his bloated hand across the space between them and delivered an open slap to Saeed's cheek. The force sent Saeed tumbling backwards into a bypassing dolly of green and pink vinyl suitcases tended by a dark skinned, white robed stock boy. As Saeed struggled to lift himself from the tumbling mélange of colored plastic and the surprised face of a stock boy now grasping an empty, diverted dolly, Ferdowsi cursed at him, "You think it's going to be that simple, Tabrizi? You have no idea what's in store for you."

Saeed regained his feet. Still reeling, he held his hand against the red welling on his cheek, waiting for the pain the way you wait for a freight train to arrive from down the tracks: you wait and wait and wait, watching it in the distance, and then, all of a sudden, it engulfs you with thunderous steam and squealing brakes and tremors like miniature earthquakes that ping through your knees. He felt the sting and throb as he watched Ferdowsi turn the corner into a dark side alley. Saeed drew his hand from his face and, to his relief, found no blood. But then, his temples began to throb in fear. He knew what was coming next.

He raced to find Rasheed at the tobacconist.

"Rasheed," he cried, tugging at Rasheed's lapel, "give me your mobile!"

"It's expensive," Rasheed said, handing him the mobile. "What happened to you? Don't waste..."

Saeed rushed into the hustle of the crowd, where he knew no one could overhear him – at least without his noticing. He felt his chest pumping as he counted the rings. He saw Pari and Tajmah holding bent-backed Nargess, assisting her to a bench at the teashop beside the tobacconist while they flagged Rasheed to join them.

On the seventh ring Shohreh answered.

"Shohreh, who gave you..." Saeed started to say, but then he caught himself. They could have bugged the line. "Shohreh, get out of the house. Get out now!"

"Saeed, dear, what?" Her voice was clipped by the bad connection.

"Shohreh, we have to meet. Where..."

"What?" Saeed could hear her voice clipped again by the bad connection. Saeed shook the phone as if that would make it work better. Then Shohreh said, "Saeed, dear, someone's at the door, knocking. I'll call you back."

"Don't answer it," Saeed shouted into the phone, drawing stares from passersby. "Shohreh..."

"What... "

"Roshanie's. Meet me at Roshanie's," Saeed shouted into the phone, as if that would overcome the bad connection. Then he immediately regretted it. If the line were bugged, it wouldn't take them long to figure out where Roshanie's was.

"Saeed?" Shohreh said, partially clipped.

"Get out the back," Saeed said sternly, hoping the connection would last. "Shohreh, who supplied you?" he asked. " – the stuff." But, the connection was broken.

&

"Amini," Shohreh said. "The *mujahedin* – Saeed, I worked with them. It was the only way I could get back at them."

She didn't have to say more. Saeed couldn't blame her for revenge. Her violation had been smeared across her life. She might as well have had "whore" branded across her face. Blind made it pitiable. And certainly none of the lower level *bazaari* on whom Rasheed had tried to pawn her off would put up with her having an independent career – particularly as an entertainer, even if a respectable folksinger. Saeed knew she would have been a safe go-between for the *mujahedin* because she was blind. She wouldn't have known to whom she passed the padlock and paint can, only that it had been arranged by Amini, who had been convicted of being a *mujahedin* and shot shortly after the revolution.

They were whispering in a corner at the back of Roshanie's, a convenience store two blocks from Abrahim's house. They huddled beside stacks of rice bags and lavasch bread and racks of orange and lemon soda, and ginger, all suffused with the aromas of cumin and fenugreek and coriander and cloves. Roshanie, his waved gray hair making him look like a doddering American Mafiosi, manned a cash register at the front, nodding sleepily beside the racks of cigarettes and gum and sunglasses and magazines. Saeed had grabbed a taxi at the *bazaar*, leaving Rasheed without phone or explanation. All the way to Roshanie's he worried the police would get there first. If the line had been tapped, at least he hadn't said anything incriminating. And now he could give them Amini's name without being caught in a lie, if they knew more than they pretended they did.

"*Allahu akhbar*,'" Shohreh said. "Hah," she laughed in a brief puff. "That was the password. They told me to drop the padlock and the paint can to whoever gave the password. I didn't know what it was for, Saeed. I didn't even know petrol was in the can. What's this all about?"

"Did he see you? Did he see that you saw him? Abol Fazl?"

Shohreh faced Saeed with an air of despair in her wandering eyes.

"Can you see me now?" Saeed asked.

She shook her head, no. "But, I saw him at prayers in *Mosque e'Zaneb* after the revolution. I saw him then. It was the same voice at prayer – That's when I knew who he was – I looked at him, Saeed. He knew. He saw me look at him. I saw him with his entourage on the way out – when they passed the women's section. I tried to hide it, but I couldn't. Just one glance, Saeed. He knew. He knew…"

They both heard the squeegee sound of Roshanie's front door opening, the noise of traffic. Saeed said nothing as he watched the uniformed police-man enter and exchange words with Roshanie. Then the policeman turned to the back of the store and caught his eye. He approached along the linoleum aisle, halting between the jars of pickled garlic and olives on one side and the bin of chickpeas on the other.

"Shohreh e'Kashani?" he said.

*

Rasheed paced the room like a caged weasel. His brow bulged. His face boiled. The floorboards buckled with his lurches. Saeed swore plaster dust filtered through the cracks in Abrahim's old ceiling at each blind lunge, but nobody else seemed to notice – or care.

Rasheed was shouting at him: "I take you into my house…"

"Rasheed…" Saeed said.

"… and this is what you give? I take you to my friends and this is the way you thank me…?"

"Rasheed. Dear Rasheed…"

"… My own daughter? My own daughter!"

Saeed's own head began to throb in fear. What had Ferdowsi told Rasheed? He felt everyone watching him now. Tajmah glared at him with a tight-shouldered astonishment, like a boxer who has just missed an opening for a knockout. Javad, in his worn Italian suit, sat cross-legged on a pillow. Javad pressed his hands together, as if in prayer and held them to his chin, trying to appear judicial. Pari, by the carved trelliswork of the spiral staircases, brittle with unease, silently beseeched Saeed from the end of the room. The cracks in her cheap make up, the scraggly muss of her rust-dyed hair, the loose threads of her blouse, her puckered breasts, all exuded a despair that begged him: if only they could have run away together; it could have all been so different – all those years with drunken Mahmoud – then Akhbar… And had he done to Shohreh what he had done to her? She had to be wondering. Silken-haired Fahti, her arms languid in her lap, watched with bewilderment – vacantly staring, half aware. Morvareed, shadowing her husband's every step like a monkey, hunched her shoulders forward and squeezed her hands together nervously, as if she were coaching him. Of the women, only Nargess was absent, upstairs in her room, rocking back and forth in endless prayers. And the crippled twins were upstairs in their litters. And Gholam Ali prayed for forgiveness in his back room.

"I knew it would happen," Rasheed shouted. "My sister not enough. Now my daughter. Do you stop at anything? What's your business, Saeed? What's your business?" It was a plea. It was a threat.

"There's nothing between me and Shohreh, Rasheed. You know that. I helped her with her career. That was all. I have no idea why they arrested her. Addle brain Gholam Ali and his big mouth…"

Then, Morvareed stopped her pacing and placed her hands on her hips. She bent forward, angrily, in Saeed's direction. "What did Gholam Ali do?" she protested. "He said what he heard. That's all. She said Roshanie's. Why should he lie? To the police? My husband works hard all day long. He's a god-fearing man. Have you ever seen him mixed up in anything? In anything? He never had a line of limousines out the door wanting to fill his pockets with lucre. And of course, no, we're too good for that. No, we have to stay here and be poor and rot so we can be proud and everyone can look down on us. So my husband doesn't expect his servants to have to lie for him. Should we have retrained Gholam Ali for the return of the great Saeed Tabrizi – the hidden Imam himself? What were you were doing at Roshanie's? That's what my husband wants to know…"

"'Borrow my mobile,'" Rasheed shouted. "That was just a coincidence? You knew something." He stopped pacing and leaned forward at an intimidating angle.

"Shohreh called me on your mobile," Saeed said. He felt cornered, nervous. Would they know he was lying? He didn't know how much Ferdowsi had told Rasheed. "I don't know what she wanted. She said to meet at Roshanie's…"

"I'll get the bill, you know," Rasheed said. "We'll see who called whom." He continued his pacing unabated.

"… The police arrived when I did."

Rasheed spoke angrily, mimicking Saeed: "'The police arrived when I did.' That's why I have to be told by a taxi driver? A taxi driver, for God's sake! How does a taxi driver know all this?"

"He's not a taxi driver," Saeed said.

"Then what is he? Who is he?"

"I don't know," Saeed said. The brazenness of Ferdowsi, he thought: jumping out of his taxi and accosting Rasheed outside the *bazaar*, where they had parked. "He can't be a taxi driver…"

"You see?" Tajmah said. "They're following you. I told you so." She held her head up – almost with satisfaction. She seemed more proud that her husband was important enough to be followed than she was worried about the consequences.

For once Saeed welcomed his wife's expressing her worldview. Right now he needed to look like the victim, not the criminal. He continued: "They're cooking something up. I know it. Right from the time they seized my papers I knew it. Why did you tell the Sarabis they seized my passport, Rasheed?"

Rasheed looked over, surprised. "Passport? I never told them anything about a passport. I told them you needed your birth certificate." Then he returned to his anger: "That man – that taxi driver – You're the only one who can 'set things to right,' he said."

"What?" Saeed said.

"He said it. He said 'Your brother in law Saeed's the only one who can set things to right.' His exact words. What's your business, Saeed? What's your business with this Ferdowsi character?"

"That's all?" Saeed said. He said nothing about his surprise that Ferdowsi had given his name.

"That, and they've taken her to Evin Prison. Isn't that enough?"

ℭ

Evin Prison was a gift of the American government – and a codicil to another of its gifts, the SAVAK. The Eisenhower administration had brushed up these organizations as part of its program of international political hygiene some years after the CIA-sponsored coup against Mossadegh, convinced the best course was to deal with the Iranians as if they were children. After all, the population they had hired through the Rashidian brothers had proved to be incorrigibly shiftless natives during the overthrow of Mossadegh. What better tonic for the feckless than prison? Nestled on the side of a gentle swell in the foothills of the Alborz Mountains, Evin famously entertained prisoners with solitary confinement, sleep deprivation, interrogation and torture. The Ayatollah Khomeini apparently saw no irreconcilable evil worthy of destruction in Evin (either the institution or the symbol). So he retained it, absolved it of its former sins, and restaffed it with his own, tastefully preserving its offerings. Saeed dare not go there directly. He could be imprisoned just for showing up. Access was through the Ministry of Justice. But, no one in the Ministry of Justice would grant him an audience. He spent two frantic days calling on one official after another, sitting on wooden benches in chilly, tiled hallways muddied by wet boot marks, while the officials kept other appointments, went to lunch, kept more other appointments, went home to dinner, broke for prayers, postponed him to tomorrow. Rasheed and Javad fared no better. They all even tried scanning the taxi lines at the airport, the mosques and at various government ministries in the hopes of at least contacting Ferdowsi, but the search was fruitless. If the government didn't want to say it had Shohreh, it didn't have to.

Evin existed as much to extract confessions and sow terror as it did to imprison. But, only Saeed knew that Abol Fazl needed a confession from Shohreh, to keep his role in the crime from coming out at trial. If he learned she had seen him behind the Abadan Rex and could identify him, he would lose leverage over her. Their mutual complicity would be a stalemate – if she didn't decide to get religion and confess publicly to their mutual crime in a ruinous fit of confessional zeal. And time was running out. They could be torturing her. They could be tearing her heart apart with lies. They could be telling her Saeed had implicated her and they would go easy on her if she confessed. They could be telling her they had evidence against her and Saeed both, and would drop charges against her if she confessed first; or would drop charges against him if she confessed first – whatever they figured would work. There were countless ploys, but the lone, frail, slender hope to which she must cling was denial. If she confessed, she would be lost. Would she understand this on her own? Somebody had to tell her. A friend. A lawyer. Even a servant. But, she was being held incommunicado. And, then, there was the question of why they hadn't arrested *him* as well. Prints or no prints, it didn't matter to them. Maybe they thought the prospect of Shohreh in prison, while he, Saeed, ran free, would be too wrenching for him to endure, even more wrenching than mutual imprisonment. Maybe they were just making him worry that he would be next, or maybe they were waiting for him to make a mistake, implicate another *mujahedin* by contacting him, try to exit the country illegally, compounding his transgressions. You never knew.

The entire family was frantic. While the men fruitlessly canvassed the bureaucracy, the women withdrew to their rooms and prayed from dawn to dusk. They filled Abrahim's house with tears and plaintive murmurs. In between prayers they would take turns passing through the rooms of the house with a small charcoal brazier, burning esfand seeds. Emptiness filled the decayed rooms with shadows and damp from the winter rains. Slinking around the edges of this funereal despair, Saeed consumed himself with guilt – and fear.

Of the women, Nargess was the first to break the ranks of mourning. Bent-backed, shuffling, massaging her pain-wracked elbows between steps, she had worked sideways half way down the spiral staircase, one step at a time, before her daughter Pari discovered her.

"Mother?" Pari said, padding down the bare second floor hallway. "What are you doing?"

"We're going to the Mosque – the *Mosque e'Sepahsalar*. We're going to give money for Shohreh. I'll pay Mullah Fahrabi to pray for her."

Saeed, seated fretfully alone on a pillow in the receiving salon, overheard this with a mixture of pity and despair.

"Mother, you can't go out in this weather."

"Huh!" Nargess grunted, working her way down to the last step. "I've got my overcoat. Tell Rasheed I'll wait in the car."

"But, what are you going to pay them?"

Nargess halted at this; attained the ground floor; clasped the staircase still. After pondering a full minute, during which Pari joined her at the foot of the staircase, Nargess spoke with uncharacteristic confidence: "War Minister built that mosque. A whole mosque ought to be enough. After all, she is War Minister's wife's granddaughter – They won't have forgotten." She turned and faced the front door. "Where's the car?"

"Outside, Nargess, dear," Saeed said.

"Tell Rasheed I'm waiting," Nargess said.

Pari looked at Saeed with a mixture of helplessness and fear. They both watched Nargess with a sense of pity as she worked her way through the front door and pulled it closed after her. It took her three tugs from the outside to get it to latch.

Now was the moment Saeed had dreaded: he and Pari alone.

Pari stared at him, her eyes glazed. She held her shoulders backwards, her hands clasped beneath her rumpled blouse, massaging the palm of her left hand with the thumb of her right. She held her head back slightly, like a pigeon in reverse. Her cheap make up cracked at the corners of her eyes as she drew her lips into a smile of fear.

"You better call Rasheed," Saeed said.

"Is it true?" she said.

"I don't know what's happened to her. No one knows."

"Saeed, is it true? About you – and Shohreh – did you?"

"Of course not. You know it's not true. I was just helping your family out by making connections for her and getting her gigs at prominent weddings. And that's all I did after she went blind, too. Rasheed's just paranoid insane."

"I never asked for anything," Pari started to weep. The tears stained the cracked make up and created muddy rivulets of it. "Not for anything, Saeed. I only wanted to be loved. I only wanted for there to be some meaning for it all. Are those such awful things? I only wanted Akhbar back. Only for someone to say it would be OK. Only for someone to talk to. Oh, God, forgive me, and you couldn't come from tea..."

"I didn't know anyone, Pari, dear. They were all dead... The revolution... What could I do?"

"Dead," she said. Then she hung her head. "Or partying in Paris or Geneva – or Philadelphia – I just needed someone..."

"Pari, dear..."

"And you..." She couldn't finish the sentence.

"Pari, dear, what..."

"You didn't have to pull him from the body wagon, Saeed – Akhbar. He had no legs. None of them had bodies..."

"Pari, don't..."

"...just blood leaking out of their noses. – the ones that had faces. You weren't a woman dressed in black, waiting for the telephone to ring and them to tell you when they would deliver them. You didn't have to wait in line while the drivers pulled their prayer rugs out and placed them on the sidewalk and made you wait while they prayed, and you didn't have to pull your son out yourself from under the others. They smelled like rancid meat and shit, Saeed. Some of them were just heaps in bags – with tags." Pari collapsed on the bottom stair. "Oh God, Saeed, what did I do?"

"Pari, dear, don't!"

"You and Tajmah with your wonderful life..."

"Pari..."

"...gallivanting in America – And my son..." Her cries were like a bleating animal. "He didn't have to go to war, Saeed..."

"I didn't do any of that," Saeed said. He wanted to put his hand on her trembling shoulder, but he was afraid to. He was afraid her cries would summon the household. He was afraid of her cheap make up. "I'm not an American..."

"Why did I get stuck here, Saeed?" She paused and then continued: "You're a citizen now, right? No more green card?" She paused again; continued again: "And you have grandchildren and I have..." She paused in terror. "... I have what?"

"You have Fahti."

"Fahti? Fahti doesn't have Fahti. No one has Fahti. You've seen her. She's been like that ever since she was fourteen and figured it out, Saeed. Do you care about her? Do you even care about Akhbar? I never asked for any of this, Saeed. I never asked for it."

Saeed felt sorrow as he watched Pari weep quietly. "Do you want me to help you get to America?" he said.

Pari spent some time trying to compose herself, clasping her elbows with her hands. Then she spoke: "Your friends aren't dead any more, Saeed? Aren't stuck in Paris and Geneva? Now you can do something – twenty years too late?"

"Well, it has been twenty years, Pari, dear."

"It's always that way with you, isn't it," she said. "Not your fault. Nothing you can do. Nothing for you to suffer for. You're like my mother, *Khanoum*, always expecting someone else to take care of it. What does this Ferdowsi character want from you, Saeed?" She was crying again, now. "He didn't just come out of thin air. He isn't just following you for amusement."

"The guy's a crazy. I have no idea what he wants." Saeed tensed with the realization that she knew he was lying; that the whole family knew he was tied up in this somehow; that the whole family knew he was the solution to Shohreh's problem.

"Whatever he wants, just give it to him, Saeed. Shohreh's still young. She can have a life. Get her to America, Saeed! Get Fahti out of here. Get Shohreh out of Evin! Oh, God, Saeed, there's nothing left of us. We're all dead here."

❧

Mullah Fahrabi was the head mullah at the *Mosque e'Sepahsalar*. Nargess bade Rasheed to approach his assistant after prayers, to request an audience. It was common for supplicants to request a brief audience to ask the mullah to say prayers for them or their beloved in exchange for a small tip. Wealthy families would ask for a private audience, usually later in the week, at their own residences.

The busy assistant seemed to size up Nargess and her family by the decrepit state of their shoes (excepting Saeed's). "I can call you within the hour," he said to Rasheed. "We've had a lot of requests today."

"My mother is the widow of War Minister," Rasheed said to the assistant.

"*Sepahsalar?*" the assistant said, raising his head. "You are *Khanoum e'Sepahsalar?*" He bowed unctuously. "Forgive me. I have not had the honor. I am new here." He sidled over to Mullah Fahrabi, who, busy with a lesser supplicant, glanced in Nargess's direction and nodded his turban respectfully. Then the assistant swept back to Rasheed. "Thursday next," he said, "if Mullah Fahrabi may visit you then."

Thursday next, Nargess received Mullah Fahrabi privately for an hour. Mullah Fahrai expressed his deep gratitude to War Minister, whom he knew only by reputation as the mosque's founding benefactor. He promised to pray for Shohreh, next week, as he prepared for next week's Friday services. Declining the pittance Nargess offered at the end of the audience, he asked only that she prepare a tray of food for the poor at *Behesht e'Zahra* (Paradise of Zahra), the main cemetery in Tehran.

On the Thursday that Mullah Fahrabi was saying prayers for Shohreh, the family visited *Behesht e'Zahra*. They had to order two taxis to supplement Rasheed's aging Peugeot. Acre after acre of war dead dominated the cemetery, started in Khomeini's time. Grave after grave displayed miniature shrines: photographs of the deceased with artificial flowers behind glass, fresh flowers laid before the ones who had not been forgotten. Many of the photographs were of young children, with inscriptions announcing they had died in battle. At various stations cemetery keepers said brief prayers and announced food for the poor. Nargess donated the trays of *halvah* wrapped in bread to the keepers, in the names of her grandchild, Akhbar. The family prayed and wept together at his grave.

"I want to go to Qom," Nargess said, as they waited afterwards by the taxi line for Rasheed to get the Peugeot. War Minister's mausoleum was in Qom. He had reserved a space for her beside his other wives.

"There's no room for me there," Pari said to her mother, objecting.

Nargess shrugged. "Better for you to be here with your children." It was unclear if this was a veiled reprimand, or an innocent observation. But, nobody said anything.

Saeed absentmindedly helped Tajmah into the second of the two orange taxis, with the same mellow sadness that now suffused them all. Unlike the Sunni Muslims, the Shiites were suckled and weaned on sadness – sadness for martyrdom. A prayer service was not successful if it did not bring the congregation to tears. Despite two decades in America and a modern, agnostic contempt for gods and their impedimenta, Saeed could not avoid the despair that warmed within him at the echo of calls to prayer, or at the weeping within a cemetery. It was like an old friend come to comfort him, even though he was here to humor his aging mother in law.

But, his comfort changed to fear when Tajmah used the privacy of the taxi to pry: "Who is this Ferdowsi?" she said. "Another friend of Pari's?"

"He's a crazy," Saeed said. "I don't know who he is."

Tajmah flushed with anger. "Pari said you were the one who knew him. I think she's lying. I think you're both lying. Yes, dear. As if I wouldn't know Pari's trying to steal you."

"Oh, have it your way: Ferdowsi's CIA. Can't you tell?"

"You think you're so funny. You think everyone else is so stupid. You're always fooling everyone, and nobody knows you're running around with Pari. As if I wouldn't notice..."

"Running around? Pari here, me in America? That's a neat trick!"

Tajmah retreated into silent anger. She jammed herself back into the far corner of the taxi and stared out the window at the crowds of chador-clad women shoppers looking like penguins. She stayed silent till the taxi deposited them at Abrahim's house.

"Rasheed's made inquiries," she said when Saeed had paid the driver. "He said the Sarabis could get us passports under different names. He asked if we wanted them to go ahead."

"What?" Saeed truly panicked now. "When did it become Rasheed's business to talk to you? He can come to me, you know. You want to get us arrested? You'd think he'd be the last person to mix fool women up in this..."

"What's 'this,' Saeed? Is it Pari? It doesn't matter what it is..."

"What? – Nothing! – You're the only person on Earth who could conjure it up that Shohreh's going to Evin is a plot for me to run off with Pari. But, if you figure out how it works, let me know. I might just take you up on it."

"Rasheed talked to *Khanoum*. He went to Sarabi. *Khanoum* told me. I told her..."

"Your mother? Oh, God, another fool woman!"

"... to tell them to go ahead. We can have passports the day after tomorrow, Saeed. Mr. Sarabi called and left word with Rasheed. You can pick them up Saturday."

"Except that now Mullah Fahrabi knows about it and tomorrow all of Tehran."

"We can pick the passports up the day after tomorrow and can get out of here. I don't care what it is, Saeed. If they don't care about the tape, let's just get out."

There was another long bitter pause. Then Saeed spoke: "They've done with their *taghouti*. This has nothing to do with my government position; nothing to do with Pari. Ferdowsi's another Khalkali. He just wants people to go to jail dead – the more the merrier."

"Well, if Shohreh did something, it's her business. What if you'd never come back? Whatever it is he wants over you, he doesn't have it. He'd have arrested you by now."

Saeed eyed Tajmah suspiciously. They'd been battling for something over forty percent of an entire century. He knew her thinking.

"My retirement salary's that much to you?" he said.

"Huh! Your retirement salary! At the official rates it's nothing, my dear. You think you can live here to spend it? I don't think so. Forget about it. Get out."

There was another long silence while Saeed felt again the sadness he had felt at the grave of Akhbar. He thought of Shohreh when he'd taken her to the *Kloop e'Shahanshahee* as a fifteenth birthday present, along with the crisp white tennis dress he'd given her. She was embarrassed at not knowing how to play, and refused to join him on the court, but he'd enjoyed parading her around, had enjoyed the lewd thoughts of colleagues who would refuse to believe he was just her niece – and he had seen no need to disabuse them of their suspicions – had enjoyed glimpsing the tightness of her thighs, the swell of her breasts, had wondered if she had any feelings for him besides just uncle, had wondered what would happen if he touched her, kissed her... And now Shohreh was entombed in Evin, alone in a green tiled cell with a door with a small window and a slot for food, or lined up in the barracks with the peasant women and the whores.

"You'd abandon Shohreh – just like that?" he said, waving his hand backward like wind tossed chaff.

"You have a family to support, Saeed. She doesn't."

Saeed turned from her and started walking towards the front door, shaking his head. "How can you ask me to have the heart to do that to her?" he said.

Tajmah ran after him and caught him by the elbow, spinning him around. "What about me, Saeed?" she said. "You don't mind doing it to me."

❦

The failing light of winter closed in on Saeed as he made his way to Sarabi, *père et fils,* purveyors of fine carpets. He felt nervous. If this were a trap, Ferdowsi could not have picked a better time to either arrest him or rob him. He was not used to carrying such large sums in cash. The bank cashier had raised a suspicious eyebrow to see such a large quantity of travelers checks cashed at one time. He had even entered a back room to confer with his supervisor before handing over the money. Now, merchants were beginning to shutter the shops in the *bazaar.* Some heaved downward corrugated metal roll doors till they clanged against the pavement, each in turn arrested in a funereal thump by a ham handed padlock and a click. Others drew shut telescoping steel gates that closed with cold metallic snaps. As the sky, glanced through the narrow clerestory windows, gave to frigid shades of rose and purple, the remaining shopkeepers huddled together by the tea shops, as if to hold at bay just a moment longer the cavernous echoing silence of the darkening hour.

Saeed found Sarabi, the son (AKA pink lips), alone in his office, thumping his pudgy fingers on the waxy oak desk, the crease of his double chin drooping into its own oily, opalescent smile. A single circular fluorescent light, hung from above by its power cord, made a buzzing sound. It reminded Saeed of a library – or a jail. Saeed joked to himself that Sarabi would look the perfect American gangster, if only he had a green eyeshade. On the silver-framed, frayed green blotter on Sarabi's desk were two steaming glasses of tea, each in a saucer with three cubes of sugar.

"I took the liberty of ordering us tea," Sarabi gasped. He leaned heavily forward from his chair, removed the sugar cubes from the saucer, plunked the first cube into his lips, poured the tea into the saucer and began greedily sucking tea from the saucer through the sugar cube. Saeed, cautiously accepting the hospitality, similarly sipped his tea through a sugar cube, but took it directly from the tea glass, and in small sips. Sarabi pushed two passports across the dirty green blotter, towards Saeed. "For your approval," he said.

Glancing over his shoulder to make sure the office door was closed, Saeed pulled out his reading glasses from his breast pocket, and then picked them up carefully with his handkerchief. He held them up to the light.

"You're sure these will work?" Saeed said.

"Ferdowsi will kill me if they don't," Sarabi said.

Saeed froze. His temples clenched. He reddened. Was this an arrest? False passports would be enough to throw him in jail – maybe even as a spy – He could be executed. No amount of bargaining could save him – or Shohreh. They could threaten him with imprisoning Tajmah – the whole family if they wanted. How could he have been so stupid? Trust Tajmah's competence? Rasheed's veracity? Father burn, he'd blown it this time!

Saeed struggled to speak in a tone of anger, but he choked. His words then emerged in a desperate wheeze: "You bastard." He flung the passports on the blotter and stood up, ready to run. "I'll have nothing to do with this!" Thank god he had handled the passports only with his handkerchief, he thought. He might be able to make a case out of it. Deny it. Say he was only asking if his reading glasses would work in the light. "Is that what this is, Sarabi, a set up? You and Ferdowsi?"

Sarabi looked up at Saeed blandly. He placed another sugar cube in his mouth and gulped more tea from his saucer.

"Nay, Mr. Tabrizi. Pray, sit down." He watched without comment as Saeed obeyed stiffly, with an arched back. "This is how I get Ferdowsi." He kept his eyes on his hands, which he now held clasped together on the torn blotter. "I don't like the dog any better than you do. But, I have to stay in business, no?" He paused, then continued, "Ferdowsi knows about the passports…" With surprising speed Sarabi darted his hand across the table and grabbed Saeed's wrist before he could back away … "Easy, my friend!" He tightened his grip. "Sit!" He guided Saeed back to his chair. "Ferdowsi thinks they're arriving Monday night. That's two days from now. I've arranged it for him."

"That's supposed to reassure me, Mr. Sarabi? I have two days of freedom?"

"Hah!" Sarabi grunted. He loosened his grip on Saeed's wrist, but did not let go. "While you're stepping onto the airplane, Ferdowsi and his thugs will be setting up next door to spy on you. There!" He pointed to one side of his shop. "And over there!" He pointed to the other side. "While you're changing planes in Frankfurt, they'll be wondering why you're so late to pick up your forged passports from me." Sarabi now laughed and let Saeed's wrist go completely. "Come," he said. "Let us finish with your tea."

Although Saeed's temples still throbbed, it was less with fear and more with a thousand calculations. It didn't look like a set up. At least not an immediate arrest. Ferdowsi's thugs would have barged in by now. Maybe he and Tajmah could still escape. Over the mountains into Turkey? Maybe the passports would work after all. Could they get a flight on such short notice?

Finally Saeed spoke: "And what will Ferdowsi do to you when you don't produce the passports?"

Now Sarabi leaned back in his desk chair, making it groan. "Tomorrow Ferdowsi will invite you to his office at the SAVAMAH (Khomeini's kinder, gentler SAVAK)…"

"So that's where he works when he isn't driving taxis!"

"Huh! I don't think you're surprised. My friend, Ferdowsi will warn you that you're in imminent danger of being arrested. That way he'll be sure you'll come to me on time. As for the passports, I'm having a second set delivered Monday. Ferdowsi doesn't know about this set I've given you. Heh! I did them on spec. Remember? I had the first set done by a printer he doesn't know about. He'll figure you gave both of us the slip." He winked, like a toad on a lily pad.

"Is he going to tell me why he's doing this?" Saeed asked.

Sarabi burped through his nose, again so silently it was almost – but not quite – indistinguishable from a normal breath. "He wants to make you testify against Shohreh e'Kashani…" Sarabi hung his head, as if shamed by having to say this. "…for the burning of the Cinema Rex in Abadan in 1978 – We all know she didn't do it, Mr. Tabrizi. Not an innocent woman like that. She couldn't have. How could a blind woman torch a cinema? They're up to no good, I tell you."

"And you want me out of the country just to make sure?"

Sarabi gave no immediate answer. He pulled a tape player from his drawer and pressed the start button. "Do you hear that?"

Saeed listened to the plaintive voice and immediately recognize it as Shohreh's. She was singing a Joan Baez song, in English. He nodded to Sarabi. "How could I not?"

"Not a day goes by when I don't listen to that. My wife and I..." He stopped to compose himself. Then he continued: "She was pregnant when she was killed in Evin prison. It was early in the war. She wasn't a *mujahedin*, I tell you. They were lies. They were all lies. They knew she was pregnant, Mr. Tabrizi – seven months..." Then he released a long sigh. "This is how I remember her, Mr. Tabrizi, through your cousin's singing – and when I think of what they did to her..." He struggled again. "... They ought to just leave her alone. Whatever they want you for, it's to hurt her. I won't let them do that." Sarabi stopped and fell into a dark silence.

Saeed waited and then rose. "I'm sorry for your loss," he said.

Sarabi shrugged.

"Please, how much do I owe you? I've brought cash."

Sarabi shrugged his whole body. "No, Mr. Tabrizi. It's on me. Just make sure they see you still have the cash on you tomorrow – lots of it. I don't want this coming back on me."

Sarabi sighed and then said, "You loved her too, didn't you, Mr. Tabrizi?"

Saeed recoiled in shock at the statement's truth. He recoiled that it was so obvious to a stranger. Maybe everyone had known all along, but himself, and that's why they'd been suspicious. And to think he had always thought it just lust.

"Yes," Saeed said. "I loved her too." He hung his head in sadness. "It all could have been so different."

❦

Ferdowsi played his hand almost exactly as Sarabi had warned. The very next afternoon Saeed found himself in a small SAVAMAH office building in downtown Tehran. Ferdowsi had one of some two dozen desks on an expansive third floor.

"You've been hard to find," Saeed said.

"My apologies, Mr. Tabrizi," Ferdowsi said, rising and motioning Saeed to the facing chair beside his desk. Ferdowsi was wearing a western-style black jacked, charcoal gray flannel pants and no tie.

Saeed was scared by the formal politeness in Ferdowsi's voice. "Not bad quarters for a taxi driver," Saeed said, taking in the other desks and their busy occupants, and then seating himself.

Ferdowsi shrugged. "I live. I don't complain."

Saeed wondered if Ferdowsi meant that his role in the former Shah's government guaranteed him no spot high enough to let him be out of earshot or eyesight of his fellow workers. It would make sense. It was better than being executed.

"My general, I demand to see Shohreh e'Kashani…"

"You should not call me general, my friend. Not here…"

"Yes."

"…And I am the one who called you here, you remember."

"Where is she? Is she alive? I'm her lawyer. I insist on speaking to my client."

"Oh, please, Mr. Tabrizi, I've seen American detective shows too. Have you been an American citizen so long you don't know it doesn't work like that here?"

"She's done nothing. Let her go. Haven't you done enough to her life?"

"May I order you some tea?"

Saeed sighed deeply. He was getting nowhere. "Why did you ask me here, my … Mr. Ferdowsi?"

Ferdowsi leaned back in his chair and propped his feet on his desk. "I understand you've been engaging in large financial transactions – yes?"

Saeed was unsure what to say, so he did not answer.

Ferdowsi continued: "I hope you haven't spent the money illegally." He raised an accusing eyebrow.

Saeed reached into his breast pocket and held open his wallet, fanning through the bills. "All here," he said.

"Please put that away, Mr. Tabrizi. They could arrest you for attempted bribery."

"I haven't spent the money at all, as you can see. I have a lot of presents to buy."

"Planning a trip?"

"No. I have a big family here – as you know. Are we going to talk about my niece Shohreh? Or shall I just leave?"

"I wouldn't advise that."

"Are you keeping me here under arrest?"

"No, you're free to go at any time. But, you may want to talk to me first."

"I don't know anything about Shohreh's involvement in any kind of crime, if that's what you're asking – including the Cinema Rex."

"I'm not asking you for that," Ferdowsi said. He flicked a piece of lint from the knee of his trousers." We have enough to convict her – fingerprints – her association with the *mujahedin* – her friend Amini who bought the petrol and the padlock – her presence at the scene. In America they call it a …" He searched for the words and then said in English, "…a slam dunk?" He seemed pleased at his arcane knowledge of an American sport.

Saeed began to wonder if Sarabi had slipped him a fast one, or if he had been misinformed himself. This wasn't going the direction he expected.

"Why me, then?" Saeed asked.

"We have your fingerprints too, remember," Ferdowsi said.

Saeed began to sweat, but he recognized the bluff as a clumsy one. "My fingerprints on the chain? So, I would let myself in through the back way. I would have lunch with family. You going to arrest every man in Iran for that? I wouldn't put it past your *Mullah Nasr al-Din* friends."

Ferdowsi silenced Saeed by holding up his hand. "We will get you, Mr. Tabrizi. You know that. One way or another we will get you…"

Saeed wondered if he were intimating that they would manufacture some key evidence. Buy some fake testimony. Of course, in Ferdowsi's mind, they had already caught him the next evening with the phony passports.

"… and when we do," Ferdowsi continued, "now or next week or the week after – or after that – you will give us what we want." Ferdowsi folded his arms and stopped speaking while he cast a knowing glare at Saeed.

Folding his own arms, after a pause Saeed said, "And that would be?"

"That would be your confession, Mr. Tabrizi."

"My confession to what?"

"To the torching of the Cinema Rex in Abadan."

So this was how Abol Fazl was covering himself, Saeed thought. "And why should I confess to that?"

"Because if you confess, we won't execute her. We won't even charge her. The government doesn't want to execute a popular singer – if we don't have to. The people are tired of sufferings and executions…"

"You mean Abol Fazl doesn't…"

"We already have her confession, Mr. Tabrizi. I can show it to you."

"You forged it. I know your type. Either that, or, if I don't give you what you want, you'll burn her with cigarette butts until *she* does. No, she never would have confessed. I demand you let me speak to her!"

"It won't even go to trial. But, if you were to confess: Ahhh, then we would let her go, burn the confession; forget all about the whole matter. No one would ever know. I promise you this. I will even put it in writing."

Saeed thought briefly that Ferdowsi was trying to say they had done her no physically obvious harm – yet. But, he knew that would change if he didn't comply. They cut off ears, burned genitals with electric shocks and fire pokers. "Why would I confess to a crime I never committed?" he said.

"You're going to be convicted and executed whatever you do. I've got you for bribery, you know. I still have the photostats of the bank records and Purushahni's confession."

"I don't think so, Mr. Ferdowsi. The SAVAMAH would have used them long ago."

"I could arrange to have them reappear – an anonymous tipster. No sense two of you going down together. Maybe you just don't want to see two people die instead of one. Maybe you love her enough to sacrifice yourself for her. Maybe you feel bad that you arranged for her, an innocent virgin, to be delivered to the royals' drug party like a plate of pastries and destroyed for the rest of her life. I don't know, Mr. Tabrizi, you can confess now and save her, or walk out of here a free man today and get arrested next week and have the both of you go to the gallows together. Your choice, Mr. Tabrizi."

Virtues
Thursday, November 6, 1997

T he last Shohreh remembered of Saeed was the cold fear in his voice in the back isle of Roshanie's, as he asked the policeman if he had a warrant, and then where he was taking her. Something happened because the beefy hand that was gripping her wrist and forcing her towards the front of the store jerked her to a stop against a stack of glass jars which rattled ominously. There followed a silence, except she could hear the stretching of wool jacket and leather belt and a sound of rubber sole against linoleum, as if the policeman briefly twisted around to look behind himself and then another silence. Saeed said nothing. Then the vice grip of the hand jerked her forward again, making her stumble, past the smells of cumin and fenugreek and coriander and ginger and through the squeegee sound of the door, still stumbling. Then there was the slippery leather of the springy seats and the smell of congealed dust and stale cigarette smoke of the first car they put her into and the whine of the transmission straining every time the driver shifted gears, making the car lurch against her shoulders. Every time the car came to a stop she wondered if they were going to start beating her. They transferred her to a second car near a market, where she could hear vendors calling and peoples' feet clip-clipping hurriedly before the door closed with a latch sound almost as solid as the brakes of a lorry. The second car had plush, firm seats and was solid. It did not rattle or sway when it hit the bumps, and the engine noise was muted, so that you could hardly tell when the gears shifted – and you had no idea of what was outside. The car reminded her of the Mercedes limousine that had delivered her to the princess's party when she was scared and had begged her uncle Saeed to come and he couldn't and... She did not want to remember it. She smelled someone beside her – a man – Yardley aftershave, cloves on his breath. After a brief wait the man opened something with two snaps – a briefcase, from the reverberations of the latches. Suddenly he leaned his body against her, pressing her into the corner and then there was a painful jab in her shoulder and after that she couldn't remember.

She awoke handcuffed, in a stuffy room, with distant institutional sounds – sounds of doors being closed in bare hallways, hard-heeled steps on linoleum, lock clicks that echoed, latch clunks like slaps. Evin prison.

She began to weep. It was happening all over again. After the drugs party she'd woken up alone in a hospital room to sounds similar to the ones she was hearing now, but there were medicinal smells and she had bruises and a cut lip and a soreness between her legs and there were the voices of a nurse beside her talking to her mother and the only steps were squeegee sounds of soft rubber soles against linoleum. Later there were detectives who said they wanted to help – but there was no one who could help her from being alone, and no one who would believe her when she cried that she could not see – except for the detectives, who seemed relieved. And her father, Rasheed, came in shouting, "How could you go with that crowd? How? Running around behind my back like your dirty aunt. All I work for and this is what you do to me?" And her mother Morvareed was weeping. The doctors insisted there was no physical injury which could account for it – her blindness.

This time she would be lucky if she were only raped. They did that to you in prison. Khomeini's liturgy. She was ferociously thirsty. No one answered her calls for several hours.

For a couple of days they kept her blindfolded, chained to a bench which was fixed to the floor, facing a wall only inches away. They fed her bean soup and water, but would not unchain her, so that she had to wet herself – and later soil herself. Late on the second day she heard someone ushered in through her door. Stiff, man shoes. She heard the creak of the bed as he seated himself, settled into the bed, made himself comfortable, waited, as if to see what she would say.

"This is the rest of your life," he eventually spoke. She heard the door locked, wondered why they bothered. She knew the voice from somewhere, but could not place it. "Or possibly just the next twenty years – if you're lucky. You'll be what?" He rustled some papers. "Almost sixty?"

She recognized the voice as Ferdowsi's.

"What's the blindfold supposed to do?" she said.

There was a silence. A thinking silence.

"I happen to be of the opinion that it's useful," Ferdowsi said, "but…" he reached over her head and lifted the blindfold. "… if it makes a difference – I can humor you – I'm here to help…"

"Please, Mr. Ferdowsi, call my mother. Let her know I'm alive."

"She knows what she needs to know. You can call her when you give us what we need."

Shohreh waited until it was clear Ferdowsi was not going to say anything more. "It's just a phone call," she said.

Ferdowsi reached over and unlocked her handcuffs. "You won't run out on me, will you?"

"What am I here for, Mr. Ferdowsi? I haven't done anything? I want a lawyer."

"Saeed Tabrizi?" Ferdowsi said tersely. "I don't think so."

Shohreh heard the metallic snaps of briefcase locks. Then the sound of string being unwound from an envelope clasp, papers sliding out, the soft clap on the bench of papers.

Shohreh faced him with blank, questioning muscles on her face.

"Look at these."

"You know I can't."

"Do I?"

"Yes, you do. Please, Mr. Ferdowsi, please, I just want to go home. Please, let me call my mother…"

Ferdowsi let her beg until she tired of the endeavor.

Shohreh stopped talking and hung her head. She heard the tapping sounds of Ferdowsi straightening the stack of papers. Then she felt him lay the stack beside her on the bench.

"We can talk after you've had a chance to read these." He knocked on the door and called for the guard.

"What are they, Mr. Ferdowsi?"

"Huh!" Ferdowsi allowed himself a brief snort. "A statement. A somewhat long and detailed statement."

There was the sound of a key unlocking the door, and then the door opening.

"A statement of what?"

"A statement from Saeed Tabrizi – concerning the Abadan Rex – and concerning a bribe he took for signing off on a bogus contract for the Shah's cousin – back in the days. You'll only really know when you read them.."

*

Shohreh's heart leaped. What did Ferdowsi want with Saeed? How was he connecting her to him? Was he under arrest too? Had they forced him to divulge her role in the Abadan Rex? Her hands shaking, she felt along the bench till she came to the sheaf of paper. She grasped the papers, haltingly, fingering them to determine which side was which, wondering if they all faced the same way. Was this a test? Was there a man watching her behind a mirror? Was Ferdowsi lying? Oh, God, if only she could see! She wanted so much to see Saeed, to hear from him. Were these letters telling her what to do? He would know what to do. Saeed always knew what to do.

Saeed had been a god in the family. He was the connection to the smart set, the ones who partied in black tie and miniskirts – men and women together – in manicured gardens with Japanese lanterns hanging from trees, and music tapes from England and Johnny Walker from America, all purchased out of obscene oil profits. It was a vibrant world, that Shohreh could only view longingly through Saeed, her suave, engaging uncle. Through that world swirled the scions of Big Oil: university deans, diplomats, developers of dams and petrochemical plants and oil fields – ministers who partied in Paris and Geneva, elegant couples who sent their children to *Lycée Rahzi* with the Shah's children. The legacy Shohreh had inherited from her grandfather, Abrahim e'Kashani, was threadbare carpets and shabby plaster – doddering old people from another century – a name that had faded to a yellowed oblivion. Shohreh attended public school with the masses. Her mother was a former house servant, her father a resentful used furniture salesman.

Saeed and Tajmah had a house of their own in fashionable Shemiran, with gardens filled with the Persian violets for which Shemiran was famous. When Saeed and Tajmah visited Nargess, Saeed would breeze smartly along the dowdy hallways with his brusque moustache, pinstriped suits, Bally shoes, Monsieur de Roche. He would sun himself in his shirtsleeves by the cistern pool in the garden, smoking Havana Monte Cristos, sipping Remy Martin, sampling Belgian truffles. Shohreh spied on him through broken window blinds. The thought of how she used to shiver when she imagined what her Aunt Tajmah must do with such a man behind closed doors made her nervous - fearful. She willed the thought away. But, she clung to the memory of longing for his protection – the safety, the belonging, the shared discussions of subjects other than dusty furniture deals and dubious sales leads and fake restorations. Saeed discussed law and policy and justice and foreign affairs – how the Shah's police state was soon to come under international criticism, now that Nixon was gone and America was getting out of Vietnam. When Saeed talked, people listened. He was already a high judge by the time Shohreh started high school. She was just starting to sing to school assemblies. At the instigation of Empress Farah, the schools were eager to westernize their programs, including the performing arts. So they encouraged her. Soon Shohreh was composing her own songs and singing them at weddings of family and friends. Mostly, though, she sang plaintive songs by the famous Persian singers, Hayedeh and Delkash, as well as songs in English by Joan Baez and Judy Collins.

In her third year of high school, after a considerable row with her father, she started a band, inviting one of the senior boys to sing backup. Her father, Rasheed, thought the whole affair scandalous. But, her mother intervened, hoping Shohreh would become a movie star. Seeking the family's final approval, Shohreh's band held its first rehearsal on a warm June evening, dressed in sequins and jeans.

The elders endured the rehearsal with stone-faced stoicism and dismay, except for Morvareed, who beamed. Angry Rasheed started shouting that he would never allow it: "This is what she had in mind? She should get a stoning... performing like a harlot..."

"She's a prodigy," Morvareed shouted back. "You have a problem with that? The teachers say it's OK."

"OK? The teachers say OK? What would those ignorant fools know? They're really no better than servants…"

"Baba, please!" Shohreh shouted, embarrassed in front of the other band members. "Can't you take this upstairs…?"

"… That's why they make them teachers," Rasheed continued, red-faced and sputtering, "because they can't do anything else. I…"

"Of course they're not smart enough to be store clerks," Morvareed shot back, hotly. "No, they had to spend it all and end up with nothing. At least my family knew how to work, I can tell you …"

"What was your father, that you're so special, dare I…?"

"Aieeee!" Shohreh shrieked. "Stop it!" She burst into tears. "Please, stop it! Just stop…" Shohreh shook her head in a violent fit.

Morvareed and Rasheed continued bickering. The other band members skulked away around the edges of the family fight, like cats slinking around the barks of a dubiously chained dog. Eventually everyone abandoned the courtyard and only Shohreh remained, her head buried in her elbow, weeping in the June heat as the sun set beyond the walls.

Saeed first touched her in the shadows.

"Shohreh, dear," he said, placing his hand on her forearm, as an evening breeze freshened, "don't listen to them. You're a beautiful young woman."

"I'm not, Uncle. I'm ugly."

"No you're not. Not ugly." I have friends," he said, "friends who can get you gigs. But, you've got to get rid of that pimply-faced backup boy – if you want them to take you seriously."

Shohreh felt hot in the shadows. "I need someone," she said. "I can't go out there alone…"

"Shohreh, dear, he's just a boy. You're a woman… a beautiful woman…"

She was tongue tied – red-flushing. No one had ever told her she was beautiful or clever or destined for a life other than waiting on a family of moldering relics. No rakishly handsome man had pressed her arm, romanticized her on a bounteous spring evening with Venus glimmering in the evening sky.

"… You need more than that…

> *If anyone asks how the clouds uncover the moon,*
> *Untie the front of your robe, knot by knot, and say, 'Like this.'"*

She kept her head down shyly. She wondered if he would kiss her, wondered if she should half turn, if she would accept. Her heart ached, raced. Her face reddened. Was this what it was like? Is this how it happened? Did men just take women when they wanted? If he would kiss her she would open herself to him entirely, she would…

Saeed released her arm and disappeared into the shadows.

There followed weeks of band practice in the tiled fountain room in Abrahim's basement. During breaks, while she composed, she would dream of passionate kisses, self-conscious handholding, when the others weren't looking. She waited alone evenings in the courtyard for Saeed to come again and touch her arm, but he never did. He would find her gigs with prestigious families he knew, but he always sent the invitations to her in a note delivered through her mother, Morvareed.

Shohreh played the first gig to a wedding across town for a family none of them knew. She dreamed it would be a chance for stolen moments during breaks or after the performance when they would join the guests, stroll the grounds, a chance for Saeed to touch her breasts in the garden, fondle her knees, move his hand upwards, take her in his arms, take care of her, lead her with his elbow crooked for her hand, support her head with his man's chest. But, there was no place for them to be alone together – star crossed lovers.

At later gigs he would still always be there, sometimes hiding in the shadows. If only he would come see her, emerge with her from the shadows, whisk her away in an emerald carriage – touch her…

Aunt Pari became suspicious and began spying on her. She had a stern talk with her, warned her to be careful, now that she was growing into womanhood, warned her that she shouldn't put herself in a compromising position, that her Uncle Saeed, had a reputation, that men could never be trusted – should never be tempted. It was the woman's honor that would be ruined. Shohreh pretended she had no idea what Aunt Pari was talking about. She'd heard the rumors about Pari and Saeed and wondered…

Shohreh wanted Saeed for more than just romance… She longed for the safety, the arrival at adulthood, the rescue… If only Saeed would touch her, take her, she would yield and they would travel Europe together, be invited by the royal family to their retreat on Kish Island, dine together at the *Kloop e'Shahanshahee*, where everyone would envy them. They could sneak away from her gigs at hotels and lie together as the wind blew across their naked bodies – the scents of jasmine and roses and honeysuckle. And he would order gin and tonics sent up and would wait, watching her as she sat on the desk, swinging her legs like the school girl she was. He would take her in his arms, then take her to the couch, and she would say, "No, Saeed. I cant." And he would say, "I love you. I love you…" And she would say, "No, I can't. No…" and she would only half push him away – silk curtains wafting in the wind and smells of jasmine and roses and honeysuckle and her breast bared… And he would say," Marry me, then. Marry me, and we'll go to America and leave it all behind…"

What other hope did she have – back then? To be married off barefoot to a *bazaari*? Chained in a kitchen by some bespectacled, bearded cleric who didn't want other men ogling any wife of his – especially not on stage? There could be a better life for her than that.

Saeed had promised to take her to a party given by a cousin of the Shah's. He said there would be people there from radio and television – friends of his who would help her – powerful friends. It was time to move up, a chance to escape from the decay of her grandfather's crumbling mansion. Saeed delivered her to a matron, a servant of the royal family, who took her to *Charles Jordan* to buy shoes and a purse, who took her to a private seamstress for a silk dress, who took her to a private hairdresser that Thursday afternoon. All this attention. She knew Saeed had something planned, something special. Would this be the night he would take her hand on a carved marble balcony in shimmering moonlight, make love to her beneath a bronze fountain in an emerald garden? As she entered the limousine, he told her he could not go; it would be better for her to be on her own and she had turned to him, shocked, devastated, still clasping her dress to keep it from brushing the ground as she entered the limousine and she was saying to him from the still open door, "You won't be there? Why, Uncle? Why?"

He had closed the door on her, a soft, firm, limousine scrunch sound coming from the latch. She watched him through her tears. He was looking at her through the charcoal-shaded rear window, receding into the rain-slicked distance. But, he had said it would be OK. It would happen later for them. It had to be. Now she only had to overcome her fear of not knowing anyone and being so much younger than everyone …

Afterwards, when she woke up in the hospital, she could not see. It was quickly hushed up. A couple of newspaper editors arrested and released. She cried for three months. Then the television and radio people showed up. Her suffering would strike a chord in a nation of professional mourners, they said, "…if you know what we mean." Her voice was sweet and doleful, they said. These were things they could sell. Better than justice, if she didn't mind them suggesting. She'd need some coaching, though…

So she could have a career, but never a husband.

❧

A week. Maybe half a week. Alone in her cell, Shohreh lost track. Periodically they opened the door and placed a tray on the bench where she was chained.

Bread and water, sometimes cheese, sometimes vegetable soup. The room seemed to swirl around her. Disinfectant smells from the hallway. Smells of her own body odor.

She begged for help, begged for there to be a god to give her sight. Just a glance of Saeed, of what he had written. She fingered the papers Ferdowsi had left and held them before her eyes, but they did not reveal themselves. It was all blackness. She crinkled the papers to make noise, as if that would make her brain notice them. But, all was still black. Had they turned out the lights – a trick to torture her? Why wouldn't God let her to see? Saeed was writing something she desperately needed to hear and God would not let her see. She began to weep. Then she wept without stop.

After she had been weeping for several days Ferdowsi returned.

"You've done your homework?" he said.

"What did he write, Mr. Ferdowsi? Please..."

"Hmph!" he grunted. "I'd thought you'd have read it by now."

Shohreh said nothing. She felt embarrassed to have a man in her room while it reeked of her excrement and body odors.

Ferdowsi exhaled a long, annoyed sigh. "Saeed Tabrizi was being black-mailed..." He picked up the sheaf of papers, waved them before her, and then let them drop back on the bench. "You see, he didn't pass you on to the royals to further your career. He didn't introduce you to them to meet a better sort. He handed you over to them to save his own ass." Ferdowsi paused again to let the humiliation sink in. He was being blackmailed for having accepted a bribe to sign off on a waterfront project in *Bandar e'Pahlavi* for the Shah's cousin, the one whose party he delivered you to.

After a long silence she stammered, "No, Saeed wouldn't do that. He's the only one of you who never took a bribe. If there's only one thing I trust in the world, it's that. He couldn't..."

Shohreh was afraid to say more. If she didn't betray anything, she couldn't become a victim of Ferdowsi's game, but she wouldn't find out what was going to happen to her – until it was too late. "It was twenty years ago," she said. "More than twenty years ago."

"Yes, and it's a lot more serious, now – than it used to be. This government doesn't look fondly on the Shah's *taghouti* – particularly when they can prove they were stealing from the people."

Shohreh hung her head in shame. She could feel the grime in her hair as it swung forward around her face. "What do you want from me, Mr. Ferdowsi?"

Again he made her endure an agonizing silence. "I want you to confess to arson in the case of the Cinema Rex in Abadan, on August 20th, 1978."

Shohreh was speechless. Her thoughts raced. "But, that was solved years ago. I had nothing to do with it."

"Bah! Everyone knows there were others."

If she weren't in so much danger she would say that everyone knew the old convictions were phony, too, but she knew there was no sense challenging Ferdowsi. "I didn't do it," she said. "You know that."

"Your fingerprints were on the chain that locked the door..." Shohreh could feel him leaning into her face, could smell his breath, feel its heat. "...

and on the paint can that carried the petrol. You were sitting on a porch above the alleyway right behind the theater. You had the means. You had the opportunity. You had the motive." He drew away.

"Means, Mr. Ferdowsi? Opportunity? I'm blind. Are you accusing me of feeling my way across the alley to the theater, and pouring petrol that I couldn't see, and lighting a match that I couldn't see, and then feeling my way out again through the flames after chaining and locking the door? Motive? Kill three hundred innocent people I didn't know? What did they ever do to me?"

Ferdowsi was tapping his fingers on the bench. After she finished, he waited, as if he expected her to answer her own questions. Then he spoke with feigned patience: "You were *mujahedin*. You wanted to destabilize the Shah's regime. You wanted to sow fear and dissension. You wanted..."

"Me?" she shouted. "Me? Look to your mullahs, Mr. Ferdowsi. That was their trick. If I did what you said I did, I should be some kind of heroine under this regime."

"I wouldn't go around saying that if I were you."

"What have I got to lose?" All she had was Saeed, she thought. He was the only one sharp enough to get her out of this mess. The letter was a trick. It had to be a trick. Ferdowsi was lying. And he had said the statement concerned also the Abadan Rex, but he was saying nothing about that now. Was that another trick?

As if reading her thoughts and deliberately twisting them, Ferdowsi said, "You have Saeed Tabrizi to lose."

"Saeed Tabrizi? Who has Saeed Tabrizi? Saeed Tabrizi's only here to visit – to get his retirement salary. Then he'll go back to America – where they don't have mullahs."

"Sign the confession, *Khanoum*, and I'll let Saeed Tabrizi go free. There's no sense two of you dying."

"Free of what?"

"Bribery, for a start. Fraud. Misappropriation of public funds."

"And let them stone me to death, for a crime I didn't commit? Do you want to live with that, Mr. Ferdowsi, stoning a woman for something you believe she did as a girl, before she knew any better? How do you know he wasn't forcing me to do it – a grown man in a position of power? What if he had something over me? I was only sixteen, a helpless dependent, and he was a powerful *taghouti* under the Shah. What do you know..."

"You will testify to that, *Khanoum* – under oath?"

"Testify? I testify to your conscience..." She paused. "... if you have one. Did you ever love a woman, Mr. Ferdowsi? A mother? Hold a baby in your arms and kiss him – let him kiss you back?"

She could hear Ferdowsi's body tense in the brief quiet that followed.

"I had a wife…" he said, slowly, carefully. There followed a long delay. "…and three children murdered by *mujahedin* – a bomb…" He stopped.

"And this sets that to right?"

"Yes, *Khanoum*," he said, without hesitation, the tension departing from his voice, "this sets that to right. And now you have a decision to make."

❧

The days grew confused again, fetid and blurred into squalor. She had to sleep on the bench because the chains would not reach the bed. The corridor sounds came and went and came and went again and again. She tried to think. They never gave her enough water. It was hot. Always hot. It was a trick. It was always a trick…

After the rape it had been a full year before Saeed had talked with her alone. Until then, he had always visited her with Tajmah. They would bring her almond pastries and chocolates. They would bring her flowers to smell, *sharbat* to drink. They would read to her. Her mother, Morvareed, had no suspicions. Saeed had been with her and Rasheed the whole evening of the rape. And Tajmah was always there. Shohreh's days were otherwise busy with performances and recording sessions and interviews. She did not need to see to sing. She was accomplished enough that she quickly relearned how to play the guitar and compose.

Then one evening she and Saeed were alone, while the others were downstairs. And she talked to him, in despair:

"You're like the others, now, Saeed: Shohreh the hysterical rape victim."

"Shohreh, dear, don't…"

"Well, it's true, isn't it?" She lifted her hands and waved them in the air as if she wanted to feel his face. "Saeed, I didn't ask for any of this." She gestured wildly towards the paraphernalia strewn about her room, guitars and tape decks, wireless microphones and trophies and gold framed pictures she could not see – of her performing for the Shah and Empress Farah. "I don't want fans and performances. I want a life."

"You can have a life, Shohreh, dear. It takes time."

"With who, Saeed? Who wants me, now – like this?" She pointed to her eyes. She pointed to her violated hips.

"The doctors say you'll recover. Are you taking the medicine?"

"Taking the medicine? Everyone wants that, don't they? Do you know what it's like, Saeed, thorazine? They give it to crazies and psychos – crack addicts in withdrawal. What kind of life is that…?"

"Shohreh, don't…"

"… I can hardly think anymore. It's all a big buzz – everyone telling me what to do, what's best for me. 'Shohreh, don't!' Of course, 'Shohreh, don't!'

Everybody wants me to go away – like it never happened. 'Shohreh, don't!' as if Shohreh's threatening their lives. Except Baba and *Madar* – they're all 'cash is king.' Baba hates me, because I 'went with that crowd,' – because I've 'dirtied his name'– and now I have to bring him money to atone..."

"Shohreh, no..."

"... My own father, Saeed, he's pimping me..."

"No, Shohreh. No. It's not that way. You're lucky to have the money. Think what it would be without that. God knows..."

"God knows, Saeed? God knows? What does God know about me?" She fumbled for his shoulders and pulled herself towards him. "I want to be clean, again, Saeed. I want – I want to be wanted..."

Saeed took her in his arms and kissed her. Then he wrested free.

"It's not right," he said.

He brushed his clothes straight and took several deep breaths.

Shohreh wept.

Saeed returned downstairs, as if nothing had happened.

Then the revolution, caught Saeed in Philadelphia, where he decided to remain, lest he, too, end up on the cover of Time, in his Jockey shorts. The mullahs largely ended musical performances, though Shohreh's abuse at the hands of the previous regime served enough of a purpose that she was occasionally allowed to sing at hospitals and schools. Over the ensuing decade she gradually faded into oblivion, her brief intimacy with Saeed censored by their not being able to write each other. Saeed was the lucky one. He had escaped to America.

❧

Ferdowsi appeared again, interrupting the haze of the days. He said he felt sorry for her, living like this. He said he understood how she felt, how hard it must have been on her, abused as she was – a young girl with no protector. But, it was out of his hands... higher authorities... greater good... "*Khanoum*," he said, finishing, "I can understand it if you need him punished too. He deserves it – a girl, like you – I will have them remove the chains. You can shower – move to a fresh room..."

Shohreh began to wonder if this were another trick, if Ferdowsi would watch her showering, take advantage of her when she was done. A part of her wished he would just get it over with, so she could go home and be free. "How do I know you'll let him go...?" she said. "– If I confess?"

Ferdowsi paused, seeming genuinely surprised. "You have my word, *Khanoum*."

"That's not worth very much, Mr. Ferdowsi."

"*Khanoum*, I can understand you feeling that – but, if you pardon my saying so, do you have anything to lose?" Hardly missing a beat he continued, "I'll need a video tape. I can't have you recanting..." His voice was becoming official, now. "... claiming you didn't know what you were signing. You'll have to say it in your own words..."

"And he'll go free...?"

"... And there'll be no implications of anyone living in your confession. No Abol Fazl, no Khamenei – and no Khomeini or Khalkali or Donald Duck..." His voice was regaining its stern anger. "Just you and your friend Amini. You can call your family afterwards."

Shohreh finished writing the confession in a large, awkward scrawl, voicing it as she wrote before a video camera in a nearby office. Ferdowsi rewound the tape and played it to make sure it recorded properly. Then he switched off the camera and picked up the confession.

"God have mercy on your soul," he said, putting the paper and the video tape into his briefcase.

"Do you presume to speak for Him, Mr. Ferdowsi?"

Ferdowsi did not answer.

"He'll be pleased at your promotion."

He snapped the latches of his briefcase smartly. "I'll still get Tabrizi on forgery."

It was a trick, she thought. Always a trick. Why had she believed him? But, then, she sighed to herself, with an inner resignation: What did it matter? Nothing mattered.

"You said he'd go free," she said.

"It's not what you think, *Khanoum*. Heh! Not at all. You have acted in good faith. You have done nothing to implicate him. You have maintained your honor and integrity. But, this will get you your freedom."

Shohreh let out a long exhalation. It was all spinning around in her head. She didn't care any more. She wished it were over. Just over. Everyone was going to die. It didn't matter who went first. The mullahs were running the country and they would kill everyone whom they hadn't been able to trick into martyrdom in the war.

"May I go, now?" she said.

Ferdowsi didn't answer her. He began talking as if he hadn't heard her: "I don't really want your confession. It's Tabrizi's I want. He's already scared of the bribery charges. But, he's a sharp one, that father-dog. He may just figure I won't use the bribery. No, I've already told Mr. Tabrizi you've confessed to the Cinema Rex. In case he gets skeptical, I now have proof. I've offered to drop the charges against you – even though you've already confessed – if he confesses to the crime himself. After all, no sense executing a national heroine. They'd all suspect we made up the charges. Not good for business, you know..." Ferdowsi sounded in a good mood, now, as if it were all a merry game. "…And, of course, I'll have him on forgery charges to boot – And where does that leave Mr. Tabrizi, you ask…?"

"Please, Mr. Ferdowsi, just let him go. He didn't know about the royals. He had nothing to do with the Cinema Rex. He never took a bribe…"

"… It leaves him with a choice: save Shohreh by confessing to the Cinema Rex, or get out of town and save himself. Except that right now he's being arrested…" He paused while he looked at his watch. "… Make that an hour ago. My men, by now, should have arrested him for possession of forged documents…"

"You're a liar, Mr. Ferdowsi."

"… and should be interrogating him at SAVAMEH headquarters – as we speak. So, now he doesn't have the option of fleeing. I guess, now, it's confess and save Shohreh, or not confess and have both of you die in jail – one way or another."

"I don't believe you."

"I'll let you convince him yourself, if you like. Here…" He picked up the heavy office phone. "My mobile doesn't work here. What's your father's mobile? Saeed's been borrowing it – as you know. I'll dial it for you. My men will have confiscated it by now. Ask for sergeant Rajabi. He's expecting you."

Shohreh accepted the heavy, old-fashioned receiver when Ferdowsi had finished dialing. She listened to the rings with fear and trepidation, a hot pulsing in her temples. Please, she thought. Please, God, let it be Saeed who picks up the phone. Please, let Ferdowsi be lying. Please, let her warn him. Please…

She heard the familiar voice: "Allo!"

"Baba? Baba?" she cried. "Baba, is that you? Where's…"

"Shohreh? Shohreh dear? God bless, you're alive! Are you OK? Have they hurt you? Where are you? Shohreh…"

"I'm OK. Baba, I'm OK. Baba, where's Saeed? I have to speak to Saeed…"

"Saeed? Shohreh, dear, what have they done…?"

"… Saeed, Baba. Where's Saeed? Did they let him call from prison?"

"From prison? Shohreh, dear, they flew out this morning. Saeed just called from Paris…"

The Room Above
Martyr Imam Hossein Street
August, 2002

They're out there – hiding in the corpse-like silence – taking turns peering through the keyhole – making no more noise than scorpions, I tell you. Moving things all day long into Fahti's old room, creaking up the stairs with sweat-stained grunts of exhaustion and now going quiet, hiding – spying. They're out there, waiting. For what, though? For me to fall? To remove the ivory handle from the silver hand mirror? To tell them where I've hidden it...

"You won't find it," Nargess said, addressing Morvareed through the locked door. She wondered if Morvareed had told Rasheed, or had been too scared, wondered if Morvareed were really out there, wondered if she were really alone. Wondered if they were scared that Tajmah and Saeed would come back from America and have them put in jail. Because both of them had to be in on it. "Not ever. And don't expect me to forget. See if I don't!" Then Nargess realized that she hadn't said it quite right, so she added with diminished confidence: "Tell, I mean. See if I don't tell." Then she finished the thought silently to herself: ...as soon as I get out. She had trouble remembering things. Others mumbled. She reached over to the brass door handle and tugged to see if the door were still locked. The door made a futile rattle of unyielding. Then she went silent. She hoped it would goad them to betray themselves. They were surely just waiting for her to fall asleep, before they sneaked in and gave her a bath – no respect for her at all – just like they'd cut her hair – those rope-stiff, plaits – gray and resistant –so patiently braided by her granddaughter, Fahti, now moldering. More likely Rasheed had sold them to a wig maker and pocketed the money for himself. No one but Fahti, with her frail, uncomplaining delicacy had been allowed to touch Nargess's hair for half a decade. And now they had cut it away. They want to make me into a crazy.

As much as she strained her ears, however, all she could hear was the occasional creak of the house groaning beneath the assault of the late afternoon sun. They shouldn't leave her up here like this, not in summer – storing her upstairs like so much junk. Her daughter, Tajmah, had fled to America – had written her that in America they could put you in jail for locking a dog in a hot car. And here she was in Tehran, the family matriarch, royalty, and they were treating her worse than they treat dogs in America. They should take her down to the aqua-tiled room in the basement, seat her beside the pool and the lilting fountain; fan her; serve her mint *sharbat* with sugar and ice – but Rasheed had said the fountain was broken for years now. But, that was just an excuse, she was sure – as if she could ever trust him again. Just see if they would ever get her out of this room! Her own son…

"Your own son?" Morvareed had said, astonished. Then she had repeated the question: "Your own son? Who would believe you, crazy old woman?"

"I've got a note, I tell you. She left a note."

"Bah! No one found any note. Did the police say anything about a note? Who'd you get to write it for you? That's what I'd like to know. And what I'd really like to know is, why?"

"If you're not careful…" Nargess started to say, but stopped, not knowing what to say.

"If I'm not careful, what?" Morvareed said. "Where would we be without Rasheed? I don't think you're going to take in laundry at your age – Your highness – Huh! 'Note.'"

Feeling cornered, Nargess had glared at her in the sweltering heat of her third floor apartments, as if to say, unlike her, she had lots of family to take her in. She was Khanoum e'Sepahsalar, *after all, Qajar. And what was Morvareed but a scheming Arab servant who had latched on to their family by marrying her spoiled son? Oh, why had Zahra ever vouched for that hooknose? Yes, she had family who would take her in.*

"I'm the widow of War Minister," Nargess said with guileless pride. "I've got lots of family who'll take me in."

"Not now, they won't," Morvareed croaked. She brushed beads of sweat from her dark forehead with her hairy forearm. She was always like that. For a lifetime, in front of others, she pretended to be so kind, so selfless – her servant upbringing. But, now that no one was left, she had let loose the dogs of her cruelty. "An old crazy like you. Not if you start passing around your 'notes.' And don't think your old friends are going to help. You don't know what I know. You…"

Morvareed hadn't said any more for a while after that. She just brushed away the lunch crumbs which had fallen on Nargess's breast, wiped Nargess's parched lips with the soiled napkin after wetting it with water from the kettle, and then gathered up the remnants of the food she had brought up to Nargess's third floor bedroom on a tray. She worked with a slow, angry, perfunctory inattention to her charge, as if every motion were a brusque dismissal. On the way out she added, "We'll have to cut that hair. Don't expect me to wash it like this. What with all I've got on me now I've got to bathe you too!" She departed with a tired sigh.

Now, waiting in the sweat-stained afternoon heat, Nargess sat on a low bench by the window, fanning herself by alternately lifting and letting fall her light cotton chador. In between lifts she would lightly massage her elbows, which these days were inflamed half way to her wrists and shoulders, with large, sore splotches of flaking skin surrounding dark scabs, with occasional bleeding cracks. She leaned part way out the window to gather what little she could of the inconstant air flashing up from the street noises below. She braced her shoulder against the window frame to avoid the pain of touching anything solid with her elbows. There had used to be a courtyard below her window, with the three pools Abrahim had built just for her. Khomeini had turned it into a highway shortly after the revolution; had named the road after a martyr. Which one she couldn't remember. All of Tehran was now named after one martyr or another. It was like living in a battlefield graveyard.

If only she knew how to get out, had the strength like her granddaughter *Fahti tilting in the wind. She found Fahti, tilting in the wind before the sunlight... Frail, anemic, flat-chested Fahti, waif-like Fahti who had been so faithful. Fahti had brushed her hair for twenty years. Only Fahti.* Who would have thought? *dark odors, dress stained...* Fahti hadn't fled to America. Not like Pari, her mother... Should have. Could have, but for the cost of an airplane ticket. But, Rasheed wouldn't pay... And now she knew why... *lintel creaking: tick... slow... slow... tock... neck nestled in silk... soft silk... slippery silk... gentle, silk-fingered lavender silk... smells like sewers...* Fahti could have children. Could have had children... Nargess shuddered. Oh, Rasheed! She could no longer pray. Who could possibly save her now?

Nargess drowsed feverishly into the rhythm of her chador: lift and release... lift and release... lift and release... each pass briefly cooling her chest and drying her underarms like a dying breeze... swaying in the hot wind – back and forth... *her stocking feet traced a pendulum swing... the stain still spreading, socks wet, drip... slow... slow... drop – fetid smells...*

She awoke with a start – in fear. She wondered if they were there, again – Rasheed and Morvareed – spying from the mausoleum of the hallway. It was the seventh night tonight and they had made no plans – at least none that included her as far as she knew. They would have Fahti fallen into a gray oblivion, faded into the moldering obscurity that clouded the rest of Abrahim's old house, *Abrahim alone on his back, eyes closed, "Khanoum will you say goodbye..." at peace at last...* rooms and floors and hallways and stairways that were foreign to Nargess now. Anonymous, they had not suffered her in years. How many years she no longer knew. Five? At her age it seemed a lifetime – a minute. But, it had been at least since the first letters came back from Pari in America. Poor Fahti...

"How can I go without Fahti, Rasheed? You..."

"Go get Saeed to pay for her..."

Pari slapped him, slapped his face. A big red welt repelling up past his voice.

"Of course, you've still got marketable skills..." His hand grabbed hers like lightning, twisting her towards the door before she could hit him a second...

"I'll send for you," Nargess heard her call called backwards to Fahti as Rasheed pulled her to the door by her arm. "I promise – I will. As soon as – Fahti..."

Fahti had cried. Collapsed in a bundle as frail as soiled lingerie.

Rasheed had said, "Not to worry, dear niece. Your mother's as good as her word." The front door had closed.

And now she knew. Her own son. Her own son.

She was the one who had found the note, a small sheet of ivory colored writing paper with delicately muted roses and chrysanthemums at the top, folded with a sharp crease beneath her pillow. At first she had thought it a note from Fahti that she'd gone out, taking no wonderment that she hadn't left it against the bedside lamp. She had taken her time sitting up in bed, fumbling for her pharmacy reading glasses with the chrome beaded chain, unfolding the note, propping it in her lap, surprised at first only by the extent of Fahti's dutiful girl's scrawl. Still a girl's scrawl at thirty-five. Then the words wrenched her into temple-throbbing fear. "Fahti, what is this?" she croaked, hardly able to form the words into being. "Fahti?" Her voice was shrill now, agitated. Her eyes raced over the letters. She jumped from her bed. Then the room started to spin hotly. She kneeled and vomited, and, then, wiping her mouth with the sleeve of her nightgown, she forced herself to finish. She jolted up again, screaming, "Fahti!" her voice hoarse, "Fahti! Fahti!" racing into the hallway screaming, and then an infinite suspension of time as if her legs were moving like on a bicycle but not her body as she heard Morvareed calling up from downstairs, "What is it, Khanoum? What?" And she knew she had been here once before. Please not again, she thought. Because Abrahim had gone peacefully and she told herself she would never have to lose again the way she had with War Minister. But, she knew it was happening. But, it couldn't be a gun. How could it be a gun? Weak with desperation and age, she flailed through the door to Fahti's rooms, and there, before her, she beheld her granddaughter's frail swinging shadowed by the lilting bright backlight of the window, swinging from the lintel in her bedroom doorway, tilting slowly back and forth in the fetid breath of the dead hot afternoon making creaking sounds in the lintel and then she smelled the stench of Fahti's excrement and the reek of her urine that traced a crescent ellipse beneath her as slowly she swayed back and forth and then Nargess felt a warm hollow smell in her sinuses and was going over backwards...

❧

She awoke to Morvareed's screams and saw her grasping Fahti's thighs. Vainly she tried to lift her upwards. But, every time she lifted, Fahti's tethered head would flop around to one side or the other like a broken marionette, refus-

ing in death to cooperate as she had in life. Until Morvareed relinquished her grasp and blundered downstairs to call the police, leaving Fahti swinging alone again in peace. Tick... slow... slow... tock...

It was when Rasheed had come and after the police had removed the body – leaving in an abandoned lump at the side of the room the silk wrapped cord and the meat hook from the kitchen by which Fahti had affixed one end to the lintel – and were asking if there had been a note, if she had been jilted by any lovers, if she had taken drugs, if she were pregnant, that Nargess remembered back across the three quarters of a century to General Z.'s soldiers in War Minister's hallway of crushed mirrors, their avoiding eyes, their feigned disinterest in the painted scenes of turbaned picnickers and turquoise mosques, the frames of filigreed ivory, the pumice-sharp mirrors... General Z.'s greedy deferential bow and glinting monocle. And she remembered the faces of Vali's servants, as Vali convulsed on the cold cobblestones in the arms of his father. And to her horror she recalled for the first time in over three quarters of a century the face of her cousin Zahra's father, her father's physician, solicitously attending at her father's deathbed. And after a gasping reflection she understood why she was remembering all those faces now, why they erupted into her memory like bats bursting from a molten cave – the creases on the brows and the furrowed chins and the wavering averted eyes, the terrible, shameless looks – shameless looks of... and she could do nothing, she was nothing...

"Don't you see it?" she cried, tears welling hotly on her cheeks. "Morvareed, don't you see it?" Trembling with weakness she lifted an accusing finger at Rasheed. "Don't any of you see it? Look at him! Look there! Look!"

But, they looked at her, not Rasheed. And Rasheed nodded sadly, twisting his head sideways, back and forth.

She grew desperate. "My own son! Look at him! Can't you see?"

In her failing desperation she watched them regard her piteously – a crazy old woman. She was too old. Hallucinating. Suffering the heat and the shock that her granddaughter had hung herself from the lintel with a meat hook and an electric cord wrapped in silk not twenty steps from her bed – and while she slept! All except Rasheed...

"It's him," she cried, her voice garbled and parched. "He did it. My son. My own son..."

And as they surrounded her one of them stepped forward and forced a syringe into her shoulder and Morvareed was saying, "He's been at the shop all day. You can check with the owners. Nobody's seen him here since breakfast. And why would he want to? His own niece..." and Nargess screamed in helpless, forsaken, throat-galling terror because all the hideous faces taunted her: the faux-blank faces of General Z. and his soldiers, Vali's servants, Zahra's father, the face of her own son, Rasheed...

When she awoke she was unsure where she was, what day it was. There was only the insufferable heat and the imperceptible swaying of the tattered cotton curtains patterned with faded hyacinths, swaying to the sounds of traffic from below, the rush of tires and motorbuses, the jazz of motorbikes and horns. And then the worry they had searched her room while she slept. Her throat felt constricted by the blue exhaust fumes – oily. Her eyes stung. Where was she? There was a thickness in her tongue, a pain in the back of her neck. Slowly she moved in the bed and recognized the curtains as her own.

How could she have not known? How could Morvareed have said nothing? Fahti. The strange creaks at odd hours. *Fahti's face flushed: "It's only the heat. Go back to bed,* Khanoum." It wasn't natural for a woman to languish like that, not at thirty-five, not in her own room. But, there was no one to arrange a marriage anymore. Everyone had died or gone to America or Geneva or London. All that was left was *mullahs* and the Revolutionary Guards who had become the *taghouti* of the new regime. And Rasheed wasn't going to go out of his way for his sister Pari's daughter – not after Saeed and Pari. "… just the heat…" And of course…

Nargess crawled to the open window, gasping in the fumes. Her heart was battling in her throat. She swayed back and forth in the hot air, steadied herself. She wondered if she should… Wondered if anyone would believe her. Feared what they would do if they did. That Arab, Morvareed, would do something. Poison her. Cut her hair to make her look like a crazy, jealous that she had no children of her own to braid her hair for her in her old age, no grandchildren, no furniture other than the worn shop models she said Rasheed's employers allowed him to take if they didn't sell and none of their own children wanted them…

The words bubbled inside her throat, but she didn't know what to do with them. Indeed, she scarcely recognized them. There were people in the street, not two floors down, shopkeepers, teenagers out of school, young men out of work, tie-less middle aged clerks with tattered jackets and inconstant jobs, women in black *chadors* carrying stacks of bread and bags spilling cabbages from the top, shop boys in blue jeans pushing bicycles chest high with flat bread and fabrics, and mullahs with big paunches and gold spectacles in Mercedes. These were the people who had once filled War Minister's coffers, who had lost hands for stealing from them, who, like sheep, had fled the sulfurous thunder of Iran's first smoking carriage, the one from America, and now trod roughshod her sacred private pools. These were people born to serve. But, peasants were always unruly and needed a strong whip, and she was not born to do that either. She was not even born to ask them, to plead with them, to beg them, only to have a War Minister to tell them. And now she had come to this – prison. So what could she expect? Why couldn't Abrahim have lived? He'd grown simple at the end, but the family obeyed him. She was still *Kha-*

noum – or had been. And now, what was she? She forced herself, and nothing came out. Only a blood rush to the inflamed vessels of her face. She forced herself again, but again nothing came out. Only her tongue thickened in the back of her throat. Finally, she forced it out in a violent heaving agonizing throb: "Help me!" she cried, shocking herself at the sound of her own voice. "Help me!" She leaned out the open window, gasping desperately. "Help me," she called to the strangers in the street, beginning to feel dizzy from the thrill of it. "Help me! Help me! Help me! Help me!" Her face inflamed with excitement. "God help me! Help me…"

She yelled this way for several minutes, attracting a small crowd of curiosity seekers, even though her voice barely rose above the sound of the traffic. She wondered why none of them got a ladder, no one went to the door of her house, no one called for the police.

Until she heard Morvareed throwing open the bedroom door behind her: "Stop that, you old…" She didn't finish. "Do you want them to lock you up? Put you away?"

"Stop!" Nargess said.

"You old loony." Morvareed was pulling Nargess away from the window, holding her wrists to spare her inflamed elbows. Then she slid the sash firmly shut and latched it, drew the shabby cotton curtains.

"It's hot in here," Nargess said. "You can't…"

"You old…" She paused to stop Nargess from her attempts to raise the sash. "Here, you can't do that."

"I can too!" Nargess struggled, but the sash was unyielding. "He did it, I tell you. He killed her. She wrote it in the note."

"Show me your note," Morvareed said. She seated herself wearily on a straight-backed wooden kitchen chair. "I'll take it to the police."

"No you won't. You'll burn it. I know you."

There ensued a silent stalemate, exaggerated by the heat made more sweltering now by the closed window.

"I'll tell them you're killing me," Nargess threatened, beads of sweat staining her gray-patterned chador.

"How could he kill her? He was out all morning at work. The police checked."

"I didn't mean that way?"

"What way?"

Nargess did not want to answer.

"What way?"

Nargess hung her head in shame. "A dirty way…"

Morvareed slapped her.

"Owwww!" Nargess wailed – like a baby. "Owwww!"

"You big mouth old crazy!"

Nargess shrank into herself and held her scabbed arms up for protection. "*Madar!*" she cried piteously, longing for her long dead protector. "*Madar,* save me!"

"Some kind of mother you turned out," Morvareed said with a confidant sneer. "Two grandchildren dead by suicide. Another a mass murder…"

"That's not true, you vile – grasping… She was your daughter. What else could we expect…"

"…. of course," Morvareed continued, interrupting, "Akhbar died in war…" Her black eyes seared Nargess with contempt. "… a 'martyr.' Huh! You think my daughter, Shohreh, would have done anything like that if she hadn't grown up in your family. God forbid, I tried to stop it. But, no, you had to let in that Saeed – that 'scholar.' Too good for the likes of me and mine – and look what he did to Pari. Couldn't even call from America…. And Akhbar? Akhbar was the smartest of the bunch, wasn't he? – Got himself blown up playing soccer with Sadam's mines – a boy of twelve. Of course, I can't say as I blame him, what with Pari for a mother…"

"Stop it!" Nargess cried. "Stop it!" She was helpless. She knew where Morvareed was taking this. She backed from the window and lowered herself into a lump in the corner, against the wall, covering herself with her chador to hide against the crumbling plaster, crying.

"You think Pari's husband, Mahmoud, hadn't counted? You think maybe he wasn't happy to do whatever he wanted with Saeed's bastard? You're so hot to blame my husband for pulling his pants down? Well, you can believe that worthless drunk, Mahmoud, started it all – and we all knew who brought him into the house."

Nargess did not answer. Morvareed's cruelty pounded on her temples like sledgehammers. She felt like vomiting. She cried for her mother.

"You think I don't know about my husband," Morvareed said, now lowering her voice and venturing a conciliatory, though still angry note. "You think I don't know why he wouldn't pay for Fahti to fly to America with her mother? Why he wouldn't give her permission even when Pari sent the money and Fahti scraped her nose along the floor at his feet? You thought he was just being mean and that's OK, since he's your son, your only son?"

Nargess began sobbing in words: "I want to go home. I want to go home."

"You *are* home," Morvareed said. She now spoke with a firm voice, part nurse, part controlling daughter in law.

"No, I want to go to my home. I want to go to the house that War Minister built."

Morvareed did not answer her. Nargess was an old woman – harmless. There was no more need to hurt her. She decided to speak kindly, if noncommittally: "Fahti's gone. I'll give you your bath." The words came out awkwardly.

Nargess shrugged, still shrunken within herself against the wall. She barely noticed Morvareed exit her room and lumber down the stairs, couldn't possibly hear her rumbling around through the kitchen drawers two floors down, but when she returned, her heart skipped at the scissors in Morvareed's hand.

"Please no!" she cried.

"*Khanoum...*"

Nargess held her hand up to ward off her attacker. "Please!" She began to squirm away from the wall, tried to stand up, but was too weak. She had no choice but to succumb as Morvareed sat beside her and wedged her to the wall with her body. She struggled, shaking her head to not cooperate, but it was no use.

"If you do that," Morvareed said, "it'll just look worse."

Nargess ignored the warning and continued to squirm her head and wrestle free. She looked like a giant stick bug wedged against the wall, struggling. Morvareed worked the dull kitchen scissors through the scraggly gray braids of her hair. They were thick braids, and it was slow going, until Morvareed pierced them with the sharp point of the scissors and teased out small plaits to cut individually. By the time she finished, Nargess was no longer fighting. Her hair looked like a mangy dog's, hacked into uneven clots, no strands longer than the width of two fingers, some as short as the width of a child's crayon. She looked as incongruous as a newly shorn ewe. When Nargess finally saw herself in the hand mirror, she felt like a patient in the hospital cancer ward.

See if I give you the note, she muttered to herself. Then she cried out loud: "You dirty Arab!"

❧

Through the sticky, insufferable heat of the days that followed, Nargess agonized over what to do. Were she to call for help again from the window, Morvareed would just have Rasheed nail it shut. Indeed, Morvareed reminded her of this every evening when she brought her food up on a plastic tray and then gave her a sponge bath before bed.

Morvareed would say, in the high tone of a cheery nurse, "Now, we're not going to cause any more commotion, are we?" She would draw the faded curtains and wipe a fine sheen of perspiration from her dark brow using the back of her hairy forearm.

Nargess would not answer. She would withdraw into herself. Hide. She was appalled at Morvareed's darkness. Appalled at Fahti and Rasheed. Poor Fahti. Fahti had paid – paid her debt to God. But, what about Rasheed? She decided to say nothing more about Fahti's note. She hoped that would make them less suspicious. But, she could not let it all just go: Shohreh, even if she was the offspring of the likes of Morvareed; and now Rasheed; and poor Akhbar who had paid too. She never heard from Pari anymore. She wouldn't put it past Rasheed and Morvareed to be stealing her letters. Only Tajmah seemed to have escaped, though living with Saeed could be no joy – even in America. Saeed, who wouldn't help Pari find her son Akhbar who'd gone to the front, who wouldn't even send legal advice for his wife's niece, Shohreh, when they sentenced her to death – Saeed who slipped away in the middle of the night without even his suitcase, only calling from Paris late in the day. Too intellectual for Kashanis. Too intellectual for War Minister's family. Too intellectual even for God.

"You can't prison me here," Nargess objected one night, as Morvareed drew the curtains. She had to get out. Get to the phone. Mail a letter, if she could learn how to write one. She would have to keep it simple. In her day, women had only needed to be able to read, and mostly the *Qaran* at that. But, they had never been taught to write, for fear they could exchange letters with lovers. She could write some basic words, a simple sentence at best, but the writing would look awkward and untrained, like a child's. And she might make a mistake which would render the message uninterpretable – or worse, a joke. She should have given the police Fahti's note when they came to take her down. She would have, but for the shame of it. Now, it was too much shame to bear alone – and no one would believe her.

Morvareed looked at Nargess blankly. "You're free to go if you like," she said, flipping off Nargess's table light and slipping neatly through the door.

Nargess took little note of Morvareed's statement. She always said what would sound nice, what would cast her in a favorable light. But, what astonished Nargess was that this time Morvareed had neglected to lock the door. Was it an oversight? No, she had clearly invited Nargess to leave. Was she expecting her to fall down the stairs to her death? Maybe. Maybe she'd tied a trip rope at the top of the stairs. But, then, that would be her own fault. And, as grasping as she was, Morvareed would not be one to push her down those stairs. No, Morvareed's tone had been that of a confident nurse who knew Nargess was feeble and unstable, who knew that at one hundred and eight years of age she moved with the speed of a sarcophagus and the strength of a spider's thread, who knew she had not been out of her rooms for half a decade now, ever since her granddaughter, the famous blind folksinger, Shohreh e'Kashani, had been tied in a canvas bag and led to the local stadium and publicly stoned to death for torching the Cinema Rex in Abadan.

Nargess had died then, knew she had died then. They had sent *basij* in the night to arrest them, Nargess and Rasheed and Morvareed. They led them into the stadium, handcuffed together, and chained them to the front row. They pushed Shohreh out of the back of a white Toyota pickup truck. She was fully enclosed in a heavy canvas bag. One of them unlaced the top of the bag and pulled her head out by the hair to show she was alive, to show she was Shohreh e'Kashani, to let her own mother, her own father, her own grandmother savor the last red look of fear, the last tears of hers that they would ever witness, to let her last vision on Earth to be a howling mob and sobbing family. Then they laced her back inside the bag. Abol Fazl delivered a sermon on justice wielded by the Holy Fist of God Almighty, while Shohreh's bag heaved from weeping, bulged with futile attempts at crawling – but crawl to where? They led several rows of spectators to the pile of fist-sized stones they had piled beside the truck. Abol Fazl cast the first. The bag jerked in surprise – in fear. Then the spectators threw and soon the bag stopped jerking. They had all died then.

Nargess spent a sleepless night worrying about how to take advantage of her new situation. She had to pretend the unlocked door was as inconsequential as a hangnail, lest they get suspicious and lock it again. If she ignored it, they might simply forget about it indefinitely. At least long enough for her to get out and get word to the police. Besides, what could she do that one night? She had no plans, no preparation. She had no idea how to find the police. And if Morvareed and Rasheed caught her, they would claim she was a wandering old crazy, and smuggle her back to her room, wrapped in an old carpet – with the police and neighbors shaking their heads in sympathy.

The next morning, shaking from excitement and lack of sleep, she spent an hour ferreting children's coloring paper and a stick of drawing charcoal from Fahti's old room. It was rough going, working around the boxes Morvareed and Rasheed had lugged up the stairs and stored there – they had hardly even waited a week to do so. They had left Fahti's things behind, simply surrounding them with the clutter of boxes. The only thing they seemed to have unpacked was a row of books, which they neatly aligned at the back of Fahti's old desk between two bronze Buddha statues fashioned into bookends. Most of the time she spent working up the courage to enter the closet, fearful it still hid the silk covered cord. She eventually found what she was looking for on the top closet shelf.

When Morvareed had removed the lunch tray, Nargess placed a sheet of the thick, dusty, yellowed paper on her dresser. Perched on a high stool, she held the upper right corner of the paper by reaching around with her left hand and tried to write the words with her right hand, moving leftwards. She knew how to read the words, "Help me," but when she tried to form them with the blunt charcoal they smeared into an incomprehensible smudge. She started again, "Rasheed..." but fared no better. She didn't try to complete that sentence. Then she tried "in my mirror handle," which was just as unreadable and she gave up with a sigh. The words just didn't look right when she tried to write them. Even writing them very large, to overcome the thick smudge made by the charcoal stick, didn't seem to work.

Just then she heard the stairs creak under Morvareed's plodding and she thrust the smudged paper and the untouched stack and the crude charcoal stick into her dresser drawer, closing it with a jumbling noise as Morvareed entered through the door.

"I'm going out," Morvareed said.

Of course she was going out. She always went out at the same times each day for shopping. Once in the morning, once in the afternoon. What was so special about today? Nargess's heart beat wildly, but she said nothing, as Morvareed lumbered back downstairs. Again, she hadn't locked the door.

Now was her chance. Writing a note was too complicated. She would call the police. She had probably a couple of hours before Morvareed returned. She could call the police and they could arrest Rasheed when he came home that evening, maybe even track him down at the furniture store. For the better part of an hour she listened carefully for any sounds that would betray the presence of anyone hiding, anyone left behind to spy on her. But, there was only silence and shame. She worked her way slowly down the narrow stairs to the second floor, and then down one of the coffin-dark spiral staircases that flanked the front door, the only noises coming from the creaks of her own weight on the stairs, and from the traffic outside.

The house was shadowed and unfamiliar to her. More crowded than she recalled. She had not remembered so much furniture. But, the straw shades hanging outside the windows to block the fierce summer sun left the house darkened and it was difficult for her to see well around the glare. At her age she needed bright light to see clearly, but not so bright that the glare blinded her. She scanned the unfamiliar scene and remembered the telephone was in the hallway, by the jack. Searching for the hall table she sighed in despair when she realized she did not know how to call the police. She tried to remember the number of her old cousin Zahra, but then remembered she had died years ago. By the time she realized that she could call the operator, which she knew how to do, she had discovered the phone table now held only a small lamp, which, when she clicked it on, proved to have been made from a surprisingly nice yellow and gold Chinese export cloisonné vase.

She did not at first understand the eerie sense of familiarity that haunted her as she scanned the room, looking for the phone's new location. The objects, large and small, a few in sagging boxes of brown corrugated cardboard, some stacked on top of one another, registered on her fleeting eyes only dully as "not phone." She worried briefly that they had gotten rid of the phone, now that everyone had mobiles. Or maybe they had hidden it: another trick; a prudent precaution. She decided to see if she could find a wire leading from the jack. There was the old wire, brown, of some kind of rubberized woven nylon, covered with broken layers of paint, and a new, hard plastic khaki-colored wire leading along the hallway, which she reasoned must lead to the handset and which she followed until it disappeared, like a cockroach, underneath the hall closet door. It was just as she was tugging fruitlessly at the door and realizing that it was locked and remembering that it had never had a lock and there had never been cause to want it locked, that the front door opened and cast into the room a splay of light and a diffuse cacophony of traffic and commerce from the glare-bright street. Morvareed stood silhouetted in the open door.

"Where's the phone?" Nargess called. Her voice was a frail, gray gasp.

Morvareed replied to her, only half cheerily, "What are you needing a phone for?" She entered and worked her way down along the hall in confidant strides. "You should be up in bed, not wandering around in the dark. What with all…"

"Why's it in the closet – the phone? You locked it there. Why did you lock it? This is my son's house…"

While Nargess was complaining, Morvareed moved deliberately from window to window in the main salon, raising each sash and then raising each shade half way, to admit only diffused light.

"…I don't want my son's phone locked up…"

"Well, we can't have all the blind and bald calling long distance, can we?"

"I'm not blind, and I'm not bald," Nargess said, now with an air of self-righteousness.

"And who are you going to call at your age? Besides, Rasheed's head of the house…"

"My house, too," Nargess said, but she knew it was a weak objection.

As Morvareed ignored her and moved about opening the windows in the other salon, Nargess began to inspect the unexpected clutter of furniture.

"What is all this?" she said. "These are antiques!" She picked up a delicately carved alabaster savory bowl from its silver holder. "Where did you get…" She let her shaky voice trail off in astonishment. She had not seen such finery since – she couldn't remember – since before the war? There were Chinese lacquered jewelry boxes and ornate silver trays and jade carvings and yellow and blue Delft vases – as densely cluttered as a store. These couldn't be the furnishings Rasheed was selling in the shop. Certainly they wouldn't be giving it away to him. Maybe she was mistaken. Maybe her fading eyes were playing tricks on her. Maybe it was just junk artfully made to look like antiques – more of Rasheed's fakes. Could he be stealing it? While she was rubbing her hand along the backs of a row of ivory colored French Empire chairs decorated with gold leaf and upholstered in purple velvet, she noticed something familiar in a collection of a dozen or so blue vases as high as her chest, double stacked against the rear wall. "I've seen these before…" She hesitated, then thought, then blurted, "No. They can't be." She could just make out the sparkles of the gilt fleur-de-lis decorations. She tested one of them

with a bare knuckle and the sonorous chord washed across her consciousness as if she had tasted a petite Madeleine, and unleashed a flood through
her soul: she could feel herself, her heart thumping, chasing after gold coins
among the towering blue vases in the hall of crushed mirrors... She gasped,
"These are War Minister's. These are all War Minister's. We had them in storage... How ... how did you get them? This was all War Minister's. General Z.
stole them – Mansour was storing them..."

Morvareed seemed to be paying no attention to her. She bustled about
opening the windows and drawing the shades, oblivious to Nargess. Then she
started to walk towards the kitchen, no doubt to make tea.

"Morvareed," Nargess called, mustering the closest she could to a shout.
"Morvareed, how did you get my antiques. These are mine. I had them.
They're mine..."

Morvareed stopped suddenly in mid stride, bringing Nargess's sentence
to an abrupt halt. She turned and put both hands on her hips and glared at
Nargess. She shook her head angrily and brushed her hair to the side with her
forearm.

"Yours?" she said. "Your things? I got them same as you. They were my
father's, and his father's before him. What makes you think you're so special?
You and all your kind going on like I'm your servant or something."

Nargess watched Morvareed turn her back and start again towards the
kitchen. She hobbled after her, calling at her back: "Your grandfather was our
servant, I'll have you remember." She held a shaky hand to her forehead to
shade herself from the blazing sun as she stepped warily into the courtyard
in pursuit of Morvareed. She finally caught up with her in the kitchen at the
back of the compound.

"If he had this stuff, he stole it," Nargess said, again at Morvareed's back.

"That's not the way I heard it, *Khanoum*," Morvareed said. She was preoccupied with making fresh tea and did not turn to face Nargess. "My grandfather said Mansour Khan gave it to him – the husband of your cousin Zahra.
That's what I heard. He worked for Mansour."

"Your grandfather worked for War Minister, Morvareed, not Mansour.
He was his chauffeur. He swept the garage. If the car had been a horse, he
would have shoveled its shit."

"Until War Minister up and shot himself, *Khanoum*. After that he worked
for Mansour. Grandfather said they were so poor they could only pay him in
furniture."

"Pay him in furniture? There's more here than a hundred lifetimes of pay
– back then – the kind of servant your grandfather was. Mansour may have
been a fool, but he'd have driven a harder bargain than that."

Morvareed shook some tealeaves into the teapot as the water slowly started to boil. Then she said curtly, "Well, I'll guess you'll have to take it up with my grandfather, *Khanoum*, won't you?"

Nargess's temples throbbed with anger to have Morvareed talking smart to her like this. She knew no one would have paid a servant anything near that much. But, why did Morvareed's grandfather say he worked for Mansour, who was nothing outside of War Minister's household? And why did Morvareed's family get War Minister's furnishings? And why through Mansour? Zahra had never said anything about this.

Nargess spoke bitterly: "You think I'm going to be joining your dead grandfather any time soon? I'll tell you what kind of grandfather you had: War Minister used to have him whipped for the humor of it. Cleaning was too good for him. Always putting on airs – let that chauffeur's cap go to his head, he did. He was only cleaning one side of War Minister's Ford, thinking he'd never notice the dirt on the other side since he always entered from the right. Until War Minister heard about it. He had his guard deliver your grandfather a double whipping for that one. We entertained guests on stories about your grandfather's whippings."

"Yes, well, he didn't put a shotgun to his head, either, did he *Khanoum*? And he didn't let his best friend sell him down the river, either, did he – *Khanoum*?"

"What do you mean?" Nargess raged, in impotent fury. "What do you mean?" Not only was this Arab insulting her, she wasn't even looking up from her tea to do so.

Morvareed poured herself more tea and returned, Nargess in tow, to the main salon where she helped herself to one of War Minister's stuffed chairs.

Nargess knew it was all calculated. But, why had Morvareed chosen now to do it? And the furniture: she had wanted Nargess to see it; had wanted her to behold this sizable hoard of her long lost riches. Why now? It wasn't enough to put on airs for guests. She had to show off to Nargess as well. Before Fahti's death she could have gone to Rasheed to make her behave, but now, *her own son, her own son…*

"Help me upstairs," Nargess said without inflection.

"You got down when you wanted to, *Khanoum*," Morvareed said curtly, still not looking up from her tea.

"I'm tired. I need to rest."

"Well, get my grandfather to carry you back up, then – if you're finished whipping him."

Angry, Nargess turned her back on Morvareed and braced herself for the stairs. She placed one foot carefully on the first step at the bottom of the circular staircase and grabbed the handrail. With a forward lung she pulled herself onto the first step. By the third step, her heart was pounding and she was sweating. She grasped the handrail with both hands, while she regained her breath, leaning forward to keep from getting dizzy.

"What do you mean about War Minister being sold down the river by a friend?" Nargess said. She was panting. The words sounded as if she were breathing through a reed. "It was Amir e'Doleh, wasn't it? Amir e'Doleh because Vali abandoned his daughter Moulook at the altar – for that dirty-ass Christian, Rakshandeh?"

"Not the way I heard it, *Khanoum*." Morvareed laced the honorific with sarcasm and gently sipped her tea. "It wasn't just Vali they were after. It was the whole family. And it wasn't that little tart, Rakshandeh, either. At least not all by herself..."

"Who, then? How do you know?"

"She had help, she did. She *was* a little Russian spy – that Rakshandeh – just like everyone said she was. They didn't take too kindly to losing their oil to the British. But, your own little Zahra, what I heard, was the one what got her into it. Little Zahra had it in her head that War Minister had ruined her husband. Got him back good, I guess she did."

"That's nonsense. How would you know? Mansour ruined himself by sending out his caravans all together. Everyone knew that. Just begging for thieves to grab them. Zahra wasn't even born back then."

"Well, I guess it doesn't much matter, now, does it, *Khanoum*?" Again she delivered the honorific with sarcasm. Morvareed finished her tea and returned to the kitchen.

Nargess spent the better part of an hour laboring up the stairs. She would stop every four or five steps, seat herself on the stairs, wait for her heart to stop pounding and her breathing to slow, and then take another several steps. Why had God cursed her with such an inattentive and disrespectful daughter in law that she should be reduced to this? And the lies that woman told, trying to make her think that a devout man like Mansour, husband of her own cousin Zahra, had stolen War Minister's possessions! Trying to make her think that Zahra and Rakshandeh were friends – coconspirators. 'Paying in furniture,' which could only have been a bribe in the scenario painted by Morvareed, a bribe to keep quiet about something and that was supposed to be – what? Quiet about Zahra and Rakshandeh? To think that Zahra had vouched for Morvareed and now look what that hook-nosed Arab was saying about her, the ingrate! Oh, that black-skinned Morvareed and her lies!

If there hadn't been so many servants about, Nargess could believe that Morvareed's grandfather had stolen the furniture, but not under so many watchful – if only competing – eyes. A small curio here, a miniature lamp there, maybe yes. But, two dozen blue vases the height of her chest? An equal number of gilt Empire chairs? Matching settees? Bronze braziers? Walnut tables? Those were too big to not attract attention. Too big even to move without help. The sheer number was a sizable portion of what she'd had in storage. God knows what jewelry Morvareed had hidden away! That odious liar! Why didn't God punish those sorts? If only Zahra and her husband, Mansour, were alive. They would force that scheming Morvareed to return the furnishings.

But, what could she do? She could call the police and even if she could prove the antiques were hers and the police would say they were in her house, in her son's house, so what was the crime? No, Morvareed had wanted her to discover the antiques, had wanted to humiliate her – but why this way?

Nargess suffered another fitful night in the summer heat, assaulted by the sounds of traffic and crickets. They told her she was too old to sleep on the roof; might wander in the night and fall over the ledge. So she had to sleep in her stifling room on the third floor. Her knees and back ached from so many stairs. Her wrists were pinched with pain from having had to cling so strongly to the handrails. Her elbows were inflamed from rubbing against the sheets, and were bleeding.

In the tepid morning, which only hinted at the onrushing oppression of the day, Nargess awoke and soon recognized where she was. She wondered if she should close her window to keep in the only slightly bearable air against the overpowering heat that was soon to come, or enjoy as long as she could the slight press of wind, tainted with exhaust fumes, to dry the film of sweat sticking to the pores of her skin.

Morvareed resolved the issue for her by closing the window when she brought in breakfast: "We don't want the heat any sooner, now, do we?"

Nargess fled into silence and waited for Morvareed to leave. An Arab possessing her son. A servant calling War Minister's antiques her own, accusing her cousin. But, *her own son, her own son she must suffer the sacrilege, beneath the shared illicit roof, the squalid scents clung to the walls, her walls, not twenty feet apart... permeated rugs and curtains, the oily perfume oppressive and soiling, the unfading fetid imaginings... "It's just the heat," Fahti said... red-faced* abominations fouled the nostrils of her memory. And they had not even cleaned it. Did not even want to. There must be a plan to all this. An ultimate torture devised by Morvareed with her lies. And Nargess had no one to help her rid herself of their sins. And if she rid herself of their sins, she must endure the disapprobation. One or the other, she could not have both...

She spent the next several days practicing to write the words "Help me," so they would not look like the scribbling of a child. At each creak of footsteps upon stairs she would hurry the writings into her dresser drawer, and shift to the bench beside the window. She retrieved a ballpoint pen from Fahti's room, and, one by one, the line of the books Morvareed and Rasheed had stacked on Fahti's dresser between the Buddha bookends. Progress was slow. Her writing continued to look like a child's. Who would ever believe that, and on children's paper too? She searched the poems of Bahar for model words, for help, sin, death, murderer. Sin and murderer were hard to find, but the other words she needed were not to be found at all. She practiced on the ones she did find until they looked as good as the book's, filling up several pages of the yellowed, dusty children's coloring paper. "Rasheed" and "Fahti" she would just have to do on her own as best she could. Her temples throbbed as she practiced , "Rasheed, Rasheed, Rasheed, Rasheed…" she wrote in anger. "Rasheed" *her own son…* She trembled when she tried to bring herself to write, "Fahti." The mere thought of reducing her life to a pen mark upon the page brought tears. They dribbled along her nose and spotted the yellowed paper, making it pucker. Then she vomited. She begged Fahti to forgive her. Fahti was gone, now. Nothing could hurt her. She had to do this. But, she couldn't. Couldn't betray her beloved Fahti. Couldn't put her name on the condemning page. Maybe she should just forget about it. She would die soon. The dark secrets would be swallowed up by unsentient history, forgotten, absolved, expiated. Then no one would ever know. No one would ever again endure the shame…

In the suffocating afternoons, too hot to practice writing, she began to page idly through the books from Fahti's room, Sa'di, Khayam, Rumi. She would read sections randomly, no longer looking for model words to copy, half-heartedly seeking direction. They were mostly old books, many covered with gold embossed, tooled Moroccan leather, from the beginning of the last century. They too must have come from War Minister's library. She avoided the *Qaran*, thinking that, so far, despite her devoted perusal of it for over a century, it had in the end only betrayed her. Maybe betrayal was too strong. Maybe it had just forgotten her, talked about a world that didn't exist for her. She settled upon Hafez, with the intention of fanning the pages with her thumb, more out of boredom than a search for love, more to cool herself briefly with the air than illumine the icy recesses of her soul. To her surprise, immediately she drew her thumb across the pages, a letter fell out, and scudded across her knee onto the floor. She almost laughed at the thought: a sign! This was the stuff of what even she now accepted as too innocent a girlhood: flip open Hafez and read your future. Well, she mused half-heartedly, at least I didn't have a parakeet pick it. With almost the supercilious air of a scientist reading tealeaves, she retrieved the yellowed letter from the floor and began to read.

September 11, 1948,

R. We just received your letter today with excitement, and are delighted to hear you and your wonderful daughter and husband have returned safely to Tehran. Our house is open to you any time and we expect you to stay with us for as long as necessary to settle your affairs and find another place or move on. All has been kept safe for you and we look forward to an amicable division.

Zahra.

Nargess at first felt only surprised to stumble upon a letter between two of the central people in her life. Immediately she thought of calling on Zahra for an explanation, but then, she recalled again, Zahra had died. But, as she read and reread the letter, she became more stunned than surprised. Zahra had never mentioned any connection with Rakshandeh. Indeed, she had known little about her, besides some juicy gossip, after she had left War Minister's house and General Z. had seized the last of his belongings. She had reported seeing her only occasionally – at family weddings and what not. And here was a letter from her to Rakshandeh! And they were close enough for Rakshandeh and her family to live with Zahra and hers? And what did she mean by an amicable "division?" Did she mean separation, as in a separating of their ways? Or distribution, as in distributing possessions? Was this a trick? It would be just like that Morvareed to have planted the letter, knowing Nargess would sooner or later peruse War Minister's books. Had Morvareed forged the letter? Nargess didn't think so. The edges of the paper were dusty and yellowed with age, like Fahti's childhood coloring paper. The corners were slightly, though significantly, worn.

Then Nargess's temples throbbed in anger. She upended the volume of Hafez and fanned through the rest of it. Letters and telegrams tumbled forth, a small treasure trove of she knew not what fluttered out and fell to the floor – some seven in all. She fanned the book several times, until no more papers fell out and then she opened it towards herself and fanned through to make sure there were no more.

There was a note, dated August 2, 1953: "Dear R., P's note slipped to S. Love assured. Z." It meant nothing to her. Obviously it was from Zahra, to Rakshandeh, but what was it doing there – especially if it had been sent to Rakshandeh? And why did she use initials instead of names. The oldest was dated January 13, 1920, and written in a young woman's dutifully persistent scrawl: "I have met him, R." A set of notes between Rakshandeh and Zahra over a span of at least thirty years? It could not be. It was Morvareed's trick. That scheming Arab! Furiously, Nargess devoured the others, some not even addressed or signed: "January 22, 1923, We have arrived in Paris safely. R." And, then, a telegram to Paris: "October 12, 1924, War Minister to remarry. Suggest same and return." And then a note: Nov 7, 1929: "General Z. on the 12th. R." Then one from August 10, 1941: "The 25th is a good time for J. to meet M, R." And, "August 8, 1946, J traveling to finally marry your M in Tabriz Monday, Z. Huh."

"Morvareed!" she called angrily. "Morvareed, come up!" She would force her to confess – to planting the letters, to forgery. She pulled open the door with the brass handle and called into the hall and downstairs: "Morvareed! Where are you?"

Then she waited for a response, which, after a delay, was forthcoming: "What?"

Nargess did not answer. She waited while Morvareed labored up the creaking stairs in the insufferable heat.

"What is it? Are you sick?" Morvareed called to her from the stairs.

Nargess remained silent. She hid the letters and replaced Hafez neatly into the line of books so as not to arouse suspicion.

"What is it?" Morvareed said, breathless, finally entering Nargess's room.

Nargess stared at her in reddened anger. She turned her face out the window. A whole lifetime of being duped by crass upstarts came crashing upon her heart, suffocating her resolve. It was then that she realized it was not anger she felt towards Rakshandeh, and even Zahra, but envy. "Nothing," she said in a blank voice.

Morvareed released a sigh of frustration. Nargess tried to spy on her from the corner of her eye, to see if she were inspecting the line of books for clues. The two waited in silent, mutually assured despair, each expecting the other to speak first. Then Morvareed turned and lumbered back down the stairs, grumbling only half to herself, "As if I've got nothing better… Old looney…"

How could Zahra have kept this quiet? thought Nargess. No, it could not be! It was Zahra who had kept her alive so long, who had supported her through War Minister's death and the loss of his fortune, Zahra, who had found for her Abrahim, Zahra, who should be alive now to take care of her – who had always taken care of her. But then, she remembered it was Zahra who had arranged for Morvareed to marry her son, Rasheed, when he was only eighteen, after he had ruined Tajmah's wedding and demanded a spouse of his own. True, Nargess had begged Zahra for help. And also true, Rasheed could only have been a catch for someone who had neither class nor money. But, Zahra had promised that War Minister's old chauffeur had sired a god-fearing family, respectable at least at the level of servants, and, so what if Rasheed took as a first wife what in times past his ancestors would only have taken as a fourth wife, or a temporary wife? Men took wives to satisfy their lusts and only needed one respectable one to extend the line. But then, Nargess suffered a pang of anxiety: Why had Zahra been the only one to know about Javad and Maryam, Rakshandeh's daughter – or at least to tell her about them? And more, the furtive notes from Maryam, the notes that had lured Javad into a hopeless love affair, which any rational man could only have recognized as pure fantasy, the first of those notes had arrived in Zahra's hands. Her story of finding the beret perched at the entrance upon her ar-

Nargess could hear the silence

"Your diapers," Morvareed sa

"I'll be alright."

Then after another long silen

smell your *jish* for the rest of you

"I don't want help."

"Well, I'm coming in in the

or not. See if I don't." She rattle

remove the hinges."

Nargess didn't answer. She

to Morvareed lumber downsta

would wake late and Rasheed

would have removed it from

would search the room. Take

the bedside table she retriev

mattress.

Nargess spent a feverish

time. The dawn air would b

street. Every hour or so she

the ticking clock. Sometim

remembered. She alternate

who had been lucky to die

what remained of his fami

years. At the end he slept

one morning, on his back

one who had closed his e

say goodbye to him befor

When, finally, first

again, she retrieved the

copper coins and wortl

to have – around whic

about with the other lit

She waited, eyeing the

able. Finally she spied

style suit, walking wit

seemed curious to se

into the gray dawn, a

each other, he with n

range, she tossed the

window, watched hi

He unfolded it and

---

rival seemed so unbelievable now. Javad had confessed the whole story of his romance – at least, as much as he knew of it – to his Aunt Nargess on his deathbed. Zahra had told Nargess only that Javad and Maryam were seeing each other. The story of five years of exchanged notes without a single actual meeting subsequent to the time he had bicycled to Maryam's house the day the Russians bombed Tehran – in response to an invitation secreted in the sweat band of his beret; a fiancée whom Javad had never met again, not even at the planned rendezvous in Tabriz. These were shocking to her. Towards the end, Javad had lost weight; become a skeleton; suffered a series of infections; mold infections in his lungs, the doctors said; purplish cancers on his face. Even in Iran everyone knew what that meant. Fleeing to the seaside one night, he had swallowed a bag of opium pellets, enough to kill a man three times his weight. Then, clutching a pistol, he hung himself from the dock and while he was dangling, before losing consciousness, he held the pistol to his head and squeezed the trigger. They found him next morning in the surf along the beach, a glancing gunshot wound to his head, a severed noose hanging from the dock and its bruise around his neck, and he, dazed and incoherent, mumbling like an addict. The police suspected foul play. It was only to Nargess, as she prayed by his hospital bed, that Javad confessed he had tried to commit suicide three ways at once. But, the gunshot had severed the noose, and the salt water he swallowed made him vomit up the opium pellets. That night, after he had confessed to Nargess, he pulled the IV line out of the saline bottle to let the reverse flow finish the job he had so ineptly started. He was found by hospital staff and revived, only to die a week later from an infection of flesh eating bacteria that had spread to his blood stream from the puncture wound from the intravenous needle, the closest he ever came in his sad life to actually accomplishing anything he had set out to do. Had Zahra been the one to write the notes and sign them "Maryam?" Nargess would never know. Zahra could lie behind anything now. With a quaking pang, she realized Zahra had told her that Rakshandeh had told Karim Mirza about her chronically inflamed and swollen elbows and destroyed her hopes of a marriage to royalty. No one knew about her elbows other than Zahra. And with a deep pain that constricted her stomach like a knife wound, Nargess recalled the look she had seen on Zahra's father as he attended her own father's bedside. Her father had been old and failing. Zahra's father had given him herbal supplements to boost his strength. When Nargess's father became sick, for three weeks Zahra's father had stayed at his bedside, sleeping beside him on a cot when he could no longer stay awake, spoon feeding him his herbal elixir to fight the strange infection that afflicted him, an infection so unusual that Tehran's most famous doctors had been unable to diagnose it. Towards the end, he had begun administering the elixir to Nargess and her mother to protect them from contracting the father's infection, which was fortunate,

because they shortly came down
father's death, Nargess had cast h
both food and medicine. Her m
then intervened and spared Na
Nargess recalled so vividly nov
he attended her parents on thei
steadfast, resolute, impregnabl
ters of a century later, for the fi
she had seen on General Z. a
suicide in his hall of crushed
servants as he vomited his liv
had seen in Rasheed after the
tionless, horrifying, terrible

And she was helpless be

There was no getting a
hiding it. Indeed, there wa
ning light by the window, t
writing materials – Bic ba
composed as best she coul
Rasheed, Fahti." Then, fo
before regret and self-dou
doorframe. Then she ret
couldn't make herself w
wind, against the bright
determination: "Sinned
to say. And now she wo
high chair she dragged
placed her footstool. A
she crumpled the note
just as the note left h
and it lodged in the n
entrance and the ext
threw it too, but this
into the street, wher
in the traffic, indisti
it had grown dark, s

"Nargess!" Mor
without Nargess he

"I've gone to b

"Open the do

"I'm in bed."

looked upward, straining to see her through the sky reflection in the window. As if at a loss for what to do, he waved. Then he went quickly to the front door and she could hear him knocking.

She retrieved the cord from beneath the mattress. It would take them a while to figure out what to do. A while for them to wait vainly for her to answer their calls through the locked door, even longer to break the door down. She placed her hand mirror where it could be easily found on her dresser, before the mirror. She was scared as she contemplated climbing on the footstool – nervous. She hadn't climbed anything since she was a girl. The footstool was stable, and so was the stuffed chair, but she was old and afraid of heights and the vanity chair was frail and wobbly and made a clacking noise on the floor as she shuddered. She might fall before she could place the hook on the lintel. As she tested the cord she heard the beginning of the plaintive echoes of the morning's call to prayers and she remembered one last time back across three quarters of a century to the morning of General Z.'s first visit, and she remembered the way prayer calls sounded then, because back then they were called directly from the minarets by men without electric speakers, and their voices sounded naked, sad and gentle, like shepherds calling to their flocks in the night, and she knew that after the rude harsh pinch of the cord jerking tight around her neck there would come a gentle wavering feeling of fainting, and a shimmering, distant memory of a coal black back fading into the darkness at the end of the hallway, and then a deep forever forgiving sleep. And then she remembered the last words her husband Nahdeer had spoken to her, savored those words, as the death of a martyr, and finally understood them: "I will be alone now."

Wheel of Fortune
Philadelphia,
August, 2002

drip... slow... slow... drop...

Pari's half of the hospital room was darkened. She was waiting for Saeed. The patient in the bed beside her, behind the curtain, was watching television. From behind the nylon and acrylic flowered curtain she could hear Pat Sajak finish the introduction, and she tried to imagine if this time Vanna would be touching the blue screens to reveal the letters, or if she would just stand back and wave while the screens sequentially filled. Silent, velvet-slender, blond Vanna White. God loved Vanna White. American women loved Vanna White. American women thought she, Pari, was weird. American women hadn't fled their homelands in vain pursuit of love. American women weren't cast as misshapen hags spawning scraggly-bearded fanatics.

Vanna White, she thought, not a very imaginative name, even by the standards of American TV. Poor Vanna had just gone through a divorce. It was the beginning round, so, yes, Vanna had only to smile from the side as letters appeared without her intercession.

❧

Pari had fled nineteen years too late. She'd suffered Khomeini's gray theocracy of dead children and asphyxiated hope, where the adolescent progeny of powerful clerics now prospered with parties of their own – domestic drugs and American Scotch and Western rock – behind high walls and locked gates. Those same children had built their own empires smuggling opium and cocaine beneath prayers swelling from their parents' lips – prayers to please the people.

Pari had buried her only son, Akhbar almost twenty years ago. For years afterwards she had pretended to eke out an existence selling flowers from a store whose rent Rasheed quietly paid – invariably and begrudgingly late.

Every morning, six days a week, she had assembled a lunch of walnuts, cheese and bread and had trudged through the morning calls of vendors and corrugated shop doors rolling open to the store, and every evening she had trudged home – sad, wondering, hoping for she knew not what. What did any of them dare hope for after seeing Rasheed's daughter Shohreh stoned to death before a stadium of angry peasants?

A year after Saeed's visit to Tehran Pari had begged Rasheed for airfare to America.

Rasheed said, "What do I care whether they're getting divorced or not? One less rent..."

Pari had wanted to slap him then, but dared not, because he was going to keep Fahti in Tehran. She had not known why, had not figured it out, had assumed he needed someone to care for *Khanoum*, that he wanted to have his whip hand over her, that he had just wanted to be mean.

The airplane journey to America was exhausting, emptying. What kept her going was the thought of seeing Saeed again, waving to him at the airport, embracing him, kissing his cheek hello. But, only Tajmah and her doctor daughter greeted her at the airport. America was a busy place, they explained.

Nevertheless, Tajmah received her with a great fanfare in Philadelphia, even though she knew Pari had come to America in search of Saeed – despite so many years. Tajmah invited friends and family from as far away as Washington and New York to the welcoming party. Tajmah found Pari a store with an apartment above, in West Philadelphia, where she said the university professors lived. After several months Pari realized the closest university professor lived four blocks away, the other side of a Chinese wall of condoms and needles and empty plastic motor oil bottles. None of her fellow expatriates wanted to brave all that, even for a cursory visit. They maintained sunny apartments and houses on the Main Line. The poorest of them had duplexes in Havertown, which were still more than Pari could afford. They felt uncomfortable surrounded entirely by blacks. Invitations for Pari dwindled. So, Tajmah had succeeded in keeping her isolated – particularly from Saeed – while honoring her obligations to be welcoming.

There seemed no sign of Tajmah and Saeed seeking a divorce.

Once again, Pari pretended to make a living selling flowers. Rasheed paid her rent in Philadelphia too – again begrudgingly and late, keeping her in permanent arrears. Saeed ventured her a month's rent to get the landlord off her back, but Rasheed found out about it and skipped a month's payment to put her back in permanent arrears. Such was the reach within the diaspora.

So Pari lived by herself above a drab flower shop in West Philadelphia with a crumbling Victorian façade and forest green paint peeling from decayed window frames, in a dingy apartment with yellowed wallpaper, peeling linoleum and a chipped porcelain stove with two broken burners. And she lived at least four blocks away from anyone she might hope to talk to – but with no right, no entrée to do so, for what university professor would seek company in a common shopkeeper?

For the first couple of years – before their divorce – she was afraid to phone Saeed lest Tajmah answer, and afraid to phone Fahti lest she suffer the frail, lost, empty, vacant voice. Every evening she would wait for the sun to set and the skies to darken and then she would pull the blinds and wrap herself in a worn blanket and wait for the phone to ring and bring Saeed's voice. And every evening Saeed failed to call. She would pull the blanket over her head and press her eyes into its folds and weep.

☙

Pari's attention wandered to the processive drip... slow... slow... drop... through the clear plastic cylinder of the intravenous line beneath the hanging bag that sagged like a deflated breast implant. She could hear the silent ticking measuring out her life, as the first contestant told Pat Sajak he was a bartender from Minneapolis and wrote poetry in his spare time. Poetry. How could he admit it? In America, the land of engineers and war planners, writing poetry was about as close as you got to perversion without actually going to jail for it.

"Is Saeed coming, Tajmah, dear?" Pari asked. She was afraid to ask, because it would be a touchy subject, but she had no other connection to the world outside the hospital. She could try phoning Saeed, but Tajmah was always there. Besides, he wouldn't answer. She would only get his message.

"I wouldn't know, Pari, dear." Tajmah said. She spoke brusquely, in Farsi, with a tinge of annoyance.

Tajmah, older than her half sister by nine years, but looking every bit five years her junior, fidgeted beside Pari's bed in a steel and aqua blue vinyl chair. She was there to make sure nothing happened between her ex husband and her half sister. There would be no deathbed rapprochements, if she had anything to say about it. Tajmah was positioning herself so she could watch *Wheel of Fortune* through the crack in the curtain when Pat and Vanna would return right after the advertisement: *Mr. Clean gets rid of dirt and grime and grease in just a minute. Mr. Clean will clean your whole house and everything that's in it. Mr. Clean, Mr. Clean, Mr. Clean...* Another American TV name. In America, women liked to purchase carpet cleaners and laundry detergent from muscled men with tank tops, tight pants and haggard scoutmaster/drill-sergeant/sex-offender crew cuts – and this one even had an earring in his left ear and had had it for far longer than earrings had been acceptable. What were they thinking? That this is my big, safe, gay friend? And Americans thought Iranians weird!

Pari was annoyed Tajmah spoke Farsi to her. When Americans heard

Farsi, they stared, as if the words were dog droppings to be avoided by their feet. They conjured bent-backed women in black robes, like nuns, or toiling witches, goats and donkeys in chaotic market places seething with scrabble-beard fanatics, suicide bombers, angry mobs chanting, "Death to *Amrika!*" Of course, some of the Americans on the self-conscious Main Line embraced them effusively, like negroes. That was worse.

Pari envied Saeed. He could knowledgeably discuss law, politics, international affairs – and do so way above the heads of the provincial Main Line Philadelphians who mostly talked about the weather, tennis, skiing, sailing and trips to Jamaica.

❧

When Saeed and Tajmah sold their house and moved into separate apartments they pretended nothing had happened, that they wanted one place in town, another in the suburbs. But, everyone knew – or thought they did. Pari knew. When they attended large Iranian weddings, Saeed would drive forty minutes from his high rise on Arch street in center city out to the Main Line to retrieve Tajmah, then forty minutes more back to West Philadelphia to retrieve Pari, then another forty minutes back to the Main Line so they would arrive together as one family. Pari always sat in the back seat of Saeed's age-creaking BMW – the back seat another of Tajmah's arrangements, or was it Saeed's? Pari would join the other women doing Persian dances for the men, hoping to attract Saeed's eye, but none of the men noticed any woman over thirty.

The entire Iranian community had witnessed the *scandal du jour* – Monika Lewinski – unfold with dismay. In Iran it just would have been a temporary marriage, a ruler's trifle. In the Sodom and Gomorrah of the Great Satan it was a scandal that could topple the most powerful man in the world. How had such a simple people ever come to rule the Earth? And if the American president were setting the tone for the country, why couldn't Saeed find room in his day for Pari? Did he have to keep his divorce a secret? He could see her and keep that secret too. She knew she could rekindle the flame between them, if only they had time together.

"He said he would come –" Pari said, " – Saeed." But, she knew he had lied.

Saeed would return her phone calls, but always a week late. He made excuses of having been in Beverly Hills, visiting his wealthy cousins, or spending the week in Chester Springs, outside Philadelphia, with Iranian bankers he knew who had mansions there, with pools and Italianate gardens. He would brag about his "arch-millionaire" friends and complain bitterly that they were *bazaari* crooks whose children were addicts and store clerks. Pari would take the bus to center city and spend whole mornings in the Starbucks across from Saeed's apartment, hoping to catch him, letting the flower shop take care of itself. She would call him from her mobile phone and hang up when she got the answer message. Once she saw him sitting by himself at a coffee shop in spiffy Liberty Place on 17th St. She hid in the shadows and watched him for three hours. Nattily dressed with a dark blue Ralph Lauren suit that had grown too large for him and a crisp, yellow Ferragamo tie, he nursed a single cup of coffee, casually watching mothers and children pass with overflowing shopping bags and strollers. From time to time he would chat with Iranian friends who would join him for twenty minutes and then depart – as if they were keeping appointments with him. A week later he said he'd spent the entire week in California. Two months later Pari discovered the lump in her breast.

☙

Beside her bed Pari watched her heartbeat scurry across the other screen – the small flat black one – miniature identical cathode green ridges like the ribs on Playtex "living" gloves noiselessly filing one after another across the Windex-clean glass, silently falling off the end of the screen into nowhere. Waves of failed hope. And every so often a scrambled one would intrude upon the succession of identical ridges, announcing its struggle with an audible buzz.

She could not afford a private room, had no one to help her at home, had no choice other than to die in a strange bed, in a strange country, beside a strange, elderly Jewish Sears floor manager's wife, whose family visited every Sunday dressed in black, just as the lunch trays were being collected, and who liked television. They had been voluble at first, bubbling about bar mitzvahs, nephews in professional schools, unmarried nieces, successes who were Jewish. Once they had learned Pari was Persian, though, they huddled darkly, whispered in hushed, conspiratorial tones.

It was no time in her life to have another foreign culture crammed down her throat. Pari longed to be home in Iran. She longed so deeply not to be alone. She wanted Saeed to arrive. She yearned for the brush of his moustache along her cheek, the stroke of his hand across her breast, the comfort of his smile. If only he could be here for her… Life would have had meaning had Saeed loved her. There was no other god but love, no other love but Saeed. She had come to America for him, had abandoned what little life she had left for him. She would still give up everything for him. But, she had nothing left to give now.

She raised her head and searched for Saeed, then lowered her head to her pillow and thought of Hafez:

All the false notions of myself,
That once caused fear, pain,

Have turned to ash,
As I neared God.

What has risen,
From the tangled web of thought and sinew,

Now shines with jubilation
Through the eyes of angels,

And screams from the guts,
Of infinite existence itself.

Love is the funeral pyre,
Where my heart must lay its body.

&

In the four years she had spent in Philadelphia, Saeed had only visited her alone once. She had called and asked him to pick up her prescription. The cancer had already spread to her lungs by the time she'd felt the lump. She could have picked the prescription up herself, but she didn't want to. She wanted someone to take care of her. She wanted Saeed.

She had fluttered when he'd arrived with groceries and flowers along with the prescription. He busied himself warming Campbell's chicken soup for her, so she knew he had called one of his doctor friends – or his cousin in Beverly Hills – to explain the medications. She stayed in bed even though she felt well enough to prepare soup and tea herself.

And for the first time in forty years of loneliness she felt joy. Because Saeed was caring for her. Because Saeed was alone with her and making soup for her and sitting beside her bed talking to her and comforting her.

She nestled backwards into the bedcovers, in a delirium of happiness, savoring the moment: They were old friends. He would regret the past, confess, hold her, love her. She would lift her hand and he would clasp it to his heart; lift her in his arms; hold her to himself for their last remaining moments on Earth together...

But, Tajmah arrived and brusquely mounted the creaking stairs with more flowers and groceries and herbs and spices to make a body well – and to make sure there were no tearful, deathbed reconciliations. So Pari knew that word was out and by the next day – probably even already – the entire Iranian diaspora would know. It would take another day or two for news to spread to Tehran – if there was anybody left there to care. Pari wondered who would tell Fahti. She didn't have the courage herself. Would it be *Khanoum*? Who would tell *Khanoum*? Would they let her be buried beside Akhbar? Fly her body back to Iran wrapped in white linen? There had to be a place for her – somewhere.

☙

At the Cancer Center Tajmah hung over her like a vulture. Tajmah wore a lime green, cabled sweater from Talbot's, with matching shoes and a crisply pressed, light gray flannel skirt and a light yellow cotton shirt. She wore a modest necklace of woven gold strands. Her hair was immaculate, in fashionable, if stiff, salt and pepper curls. Rose red lipstick perfectly edged to her lips. Manicured nails painted pale pink. Her whole appearance as tightly coiffed as a Teddy bear. She had modeled herself after the women in Philadelphia who lived on the Main Line and vacationed in Nantucket and Maine (or pretended to when they knew the listener had no entrée into those enclaves). She was proud of her daughter, who went with that Ivy League crowd and avoided expatriate Persians like drain odors.

No matter how hard Pari had tried, she couldn't match her older half-sister. Her sweaters always sagged like misshapen Filenes leftovers (which they were). Her lipstick always smudged over her makeup as if she'd applied both hurriedly in a gas station restroom. Her makeup caked around her frown lines like packed earth at the edge of a sand lot. Her hair, what was left of it, was dyed the color of rust and scattered in a sparse frizz with gray roots even before she had entered the Cancer Center three weeks ago. Her skirts were brown and misshapen, with zippers that jammed and protruded in prominent fault lines. She always looked like the women from the Greater Northeast, home to the Cancer Center, with husbands who were welders and bus drivers, and fantasies that Mr. Clean made them as good as the wives whose husbands were doctors and accountants and lived in Chestnut Hill, who knew, as she did, that, but for the grace of God, any one of them could have been Vanna White, because they knew that, but for the grace of God and their bitter rotten luck, they too could stay slender (well, maybe not that – that was a tough one), wear flowing gowns, and every workday afternoon glide across a stage, not too obviously drunk or hung over to wave at colored boxes which were controlled by a hidden stage manager. Like Vanna, they too could have parlayed these accomplishments into publishing a bestselling autobiography and marrying a hedge fund manager – but for the grace of God. Pari was glad to be in a hospital gown so she couldn't be blamed for her shabby clothes and her makeup. She couldn't fault Americans for thinking the way they did, the way she looked: Persians *were* misshapen old women and scraggly-bearded fanatics.

She was glad, too, to be where she couldn't be blamed for anything, where she couldn't be condemned for not being the prim, proper, demure, little goodie two shoes perfect daughter that every mullah wanted to bless with a temporary marriage and his own manhood. She'd had enough of that from her brother Rasheed, from her grandmother Ashraf *Khanoum*, from her mother *Khanoum*, from her stepmothers Golnar and Masumay, from her cousin Javad and aunts Afsar and Tahereh… the list was endless – gossiping, staring, disapproving, lecturing. Persians were like Catholics in a Monty Python movie, a thousand to a household, spilling out of closets and armoires. Wounding each other.

Why couldn't she just have a grandmother in Flushing, and a daughter who taught at Julliard, and a son who wore a white coat and cured people's throats? Why couldn't she have Saeed – just the two of them? She hated being Persian. Hated being Moslem. Hated being henpecked by *mullahs*, ignored by Americans, scorned, alone… Saeed could come to the hospital, couldn't he? Just one afternoon? Just one evening? She thought of calling him, but then she decided she could not face another message machine.

"I want to go *Fahti's* grave," she said, in English. "I have to go to her grave before I go."

Tajmah said nothing. Pat Sajak let the bartender-poet purchase a vowel and when there weren't any "U's" he took the free turn token and let the bartender-poet spin again. There was a brief clackety-clack and the pointer stopped on "BANKRUPT." Vanna's screen read: "FO--TH--O--OF---RCY." The next contestant, a buxom Chinese girl from Chicago, who was a real estate agent with degrees in city planning and food services, spun for $300 and called for "M." Vanna strode across the stage and touched the sole "M" box, which had been lit up in blue by the hidden stage manager to help Vanna perform her task: "FO--TH--O--OF-M-RCY." The Chinese real estate agent from Chicago, with degrees in city planning and food services and tight thighs, who seemed to spill out of her thigh-length leather skirt, jumped up and down in excitement, as Pat Sajak asked her if she wanted to make a guess. "For the love of mercy," she cried. It was a squeal.

While the Chinese real estate agent from Chicago, with degrees in city planning and food services, jumped up and down in celebration, and the audience clapped congratulations, Pari spoke again to her half sister: "I want…" She stopped in mid sentence. I want Saeed, she wanted to say, but didn't. Because Tajmah was there. She would lift to his embrace. Saeed would sweep her in his arms at Bridge over Tajreesh, weep for her beneath the red cedars, wrap her in the canvas sleeping bag where he used to make love to her in the snow of the frozen courtyard, while others slept unaware – those dozens of prying eyes. She longed for Saeed to stroke her hair; draw her close within his scent of cigars and brandy and Monsieur de Roche…

Mussed hair, smiling lips, drunk;
Torn blouse, wine cup held...

... and with loving lips gently close her eyes.

If only she could reach for him, she would find him and he would be there.

But, Tajmah was there. Tajmah was perfect. Tajmah had the second floor studio apartment by the Main Line railroad station. Tajmah had the doctor daughter. Tajmah had the doctor son in law. Tajmah had the American divorce, which gave her half. Saeed could not forgive her for that.

"Why?" Pari said.

Tajmah turned her attention from *Wheel of Fortune*: "Pari, dear, don't... Fahti... Nobody knows why. It's just that – Fahti couldn't help it, Pari, dear. She didn't know..."

"Why?" Pari said again, not listening. "Why couldn't Fahti have called? Why did she have to ..." Pari stopped in mid sentence and tried to compose herself. "... like that – to a mother...?"

Poor Fahti had entombed herself with *Khanoum*. Fahti had combed *Khanoum*'s hair. Fahti had read the *Qaran* to her. Fahti had bathed her on the third floor in her uncle Rahseed's house, that had once been her grandfather Abrahim's. Pari had sent money for her. But, Rasheed kept it, refused to let her go to America, said, "If it weren't coming out of the rent I pay, I'd let her do with it what she wanted." Ugly Rasheed...

Pari recalled Fahti, in tears, on the floor – right after Akhbar – clutching at the bedroom wall, pressing her eyes against the crumbled plaster. And Rasheed: "Some kind of mother..." "What about your own daughter?" Pari had cried. "Her and that Shah crowd. Is that what you want for Fahti?" "Well, I'll say, at least Akhbar had more manners than to stick around with a whore for a mother...." Pari slapped him. Rasheed's eyes bitter, his sneer red: "I guess we could make that two less mouths to feed, if you like..."

Akhbar and his boy prayers on the battlefields of Khoramshar and plastic keys to open the gates of heaven for martyrs and virgins. The clerics who thought of everything – except what to do about Fahti.

But, that was Fahti's mother's, wasn't it – her punishment? Everyone knew. Maybe it would have been different, if Pari had had a mother herself – someone to shield her from Rasheed, someone to do better for her than the drunken husband, Mahmoud, that Saeed had foisted upon her, someone to shield her from the likes of Abol Fazl. But, what could she expect from her own mother *Khanoum*, who just watched blankly from the sidelines – like a cow chewing its cud beside the road? In America, even the Episcopalian mothers knew enough to cheer from the bleachers as their children did battle. In Iran, every mother plotted and schemed for her children – all of them – making connections, introductions, arranging good marriages. But, not *Khanoum*! All Pari could remember of *Khanoum* was her praying alone in her room, emerging to boast of her *Qajar* blood, her *Qajar* marriage, to consume food and tea and to complain – mostly about her. Until she relinquished all hope of her wayward daughter's salvation and stopped even that. Other daughters had mothers even unto their deaths. Pari had nothing. Pari was nothing.

Rasheed had been happy to get rid of Pari by sending her to America. Pari, who still ached shamefully for Saeed, her half sister's husband. Pari, who'd sullied the good name of a furniture store clerk in south Tehran. Pari, who would pursue Saeed past the ends of the Earth, even unto Philadelphia. Pari, who'd grown up with Rasheed in a morbid house of crippled twins who had moldered alone in their bedroom for seventy years, a failed lawyer cousin who'd squandered his patrimony on a foolish attempt to elope with a communist he'd barely met twice over fours years earlier, a mother, *Khanoum*, who was third permanent wife to a wealthy *bazaar* merchant, with two children by him, and a daughter by her first husband, the *Qajar* War Minister, to whom she had been third permanent wife also – though at the time only second concurrent permanent wife – to say nothing of where she had stood with respect to the innumerable temporary wives of his insatiable appetite...

Maybe she shouldn't blame *Khanoum*: How could anyone survive all that?

There was a pause, while the TV advertised a fund for the firemen of New York who had lost their lives on 9/11. Pari was nervous that this would remind the elderly Sears floor manager's wife in the next bed to be angry with her.

"Tajmah, dear, I want to visit *Khanoum*." She paused as a wave of nausea passed along her body. "It was Rasheed, wasn't it – why *Khanoum* never called?" She felt a fluttering and another wave of nausea. The heart monitor buzzed another misshapen mistake. "Is it too much to ask of a mother? Just a call? Rasheed could dial it for her. Does he hate me that much? He's supposed to be taking care of her. My own brother..." Her voice trailed off.

"*Khanoum* hasn't woken up yet. She will..."

"They should let her go. What does she have to wake up for at a hundred and eight? All she ever did was pray. Pray, eat and complain."

"You shouldn't talk that way..." Tajmah said. "... Pari, dear." Both of them knew she had been about to say she shouldn't talk that way about the dying. But, it was too late. At one hundred and eight and in a coma, *Khanoum* would not live long. They were waiting for the phone call. Rasheed would doubtless enjoy that phone call, much as he had the last. The house would be his, then – fully his. Just let Tajmah and Pari try to get their shares from half way across the world – as if it made a difference, given the official exchange rate and the American banking restrictions.

"She wouldn't even make Rasheed send Fahti to America."

"She was old, Pari, dear..."

"I sent Rasheed the money, didn't I? I told *Khanoum*, didn't I? She could have made him. She's *his* mother too, after all. There was no life for Fahti there. Why wouldn't he send her?"

"Pari, dear, she'd gone simple – simple and old, locked in an old room on the third floor. What…"

"Simple? I guess she wasn't so simple she couldn't blame me for Akhbar every time she called." Then Pari thought to herself: God knows what *Khanoum* thought about Fahti – now. But, she wouldn't betray that thought to Tajmah. She had enough. She had everything.

"God knows what any of us know about Fahti. Poor Fahti…" Pari said, picking up her thought from a moment ago. "You know, *Khanoum* wasn't too simple to walk out of that house and tell them all to go to hell…"

"She didn't say that," Tajmah said. "You know that."

"She said she was free, didn't she – just before the motorbike hit her?" Pari felt angry: *Khanoum* had it so easy. No long, nauseous hospital procedures for her, just bang and you're out, painless and simple. Her whole life had been like that, locked away from pain – cloistered.

❉

Tajmah turned again from Wheel of Fortune to peer into Pari's eyes to see if they would betray anything, if Fahti had given any hints in her letters, any indications, any warnings, any pleas, any fears. Tajmah knew Pari had spent a lifetime resenting her, keeping things from her, trying her patience the way she ran about – all of their patience. Slick squirts with loose pants strings. Powerful Clerics with venereal diseases. God knows… as if she didn't care who knew, wanted everyone to know, flaunted it over Abrahim's crumbling walls. God knows what she was searching for in her life.

Rasheed would certainly never say anything. Only last week he had called with the news about *Khanoum*'s accident, and that was a week after he had called Tajmah about Fahti saying only, *"I have no idea, Tajmah. None of us did. Please, you have to tell Pari. It's too awful. I can't…"* That was Rasheed, no more willing to tackle the unpleasant than their mother, *Khanoum*. She had a simple life – no appetite for family squabbles.

And when Rasheed called about *Khanoum* only a week ago, a week after Fahti, it wasn't any better: *"Who knows what she was up to, Tajmah? Will you tell Pari for me? – It's another long distance – Khanoum just creeps down the stairs bent over like she's in pain and I ask her, 'What's wrong?' And she walks right past this stranger she'd thrown a note to – a silly , note – 'Help me!' it says – Like a child – crumpled – I didn't know she even knew how to write, did you? – Then she says she's going out and I say, 'I don't have time to take you out.' And she says, 'I don't need you.' And I say, 'You can't go alone.' And she says 'I*

don't want you.' – Old looney – And I say, 'You'll get run over. See if you don't!'
And she says, 'You think I don't know about you? You think I don't know?' And
I say, 'You're not dressed. You want everyone to see that? You know how long
they'll let an old woman walk around Tehran in a nightdress?' And she says, 'I
don't care. What's left for me? What's left for any of us?' And I say, 'You want
to embarrass me? Is that it? I sweat all day long for those awful people and you
have to humiliate me at my very own door? Humiliate yourself?' And she says,
'I don't care. Don't you see?' And this stranger she'd thrown the note to is saying,
'Please, how can I help, Khanoum? How can anyone help?' And she's saying
back to him, 'It's alright now. You can go. I'm free, now.' And I say, 'You come
back. I'll make you come back.' And she's walking right out the front door and
I'm following right behind her, and I don't' want to grab her, because I'm afraid
I'll break something and she's standing there and I'm thinking she'll get scared
of the traffic sure enough when the light changes and she'll come back then and
then she's turning her head towards me and she's stepping out into the street
and I'm saying 'Don't!' because who waits for a light around here? And I'm just
reaching to grab her and she says, 'You see, I'm free now. I don't need...' and
that's when it hits her – this dumb stupid kid on a motorbike – She's not going
to make it, you know. Not at her age..."

"Rasheed," Tajmah had said, "what did she mean by, 'You think I don't
know about you?'"

But, Tajmah could guess. Rasheed had sold his daughter Shohreh to that
Shah's crowd – admen and songwriters – for an easy life for himself, hadn't
he? Rasheed was capable of anything. And why else would Rasheed imprison
his own niece – another mouth to feed? Ugly Rasheed. Poor *Khanoum* for
having married to such a family – *bazaari*. And now it was Tajmah's burden,
this knowledge. Because Rasheed had said nothing and she could guess and
what she wondered most was whether he did it because it was his nature or
because he wanted revenge.

☙

"Tajmah, dear, why?" Pari asked. She spoke in Farsi now. "What was it all
for? Children dead. No grandchildren. Me, alone – here in America..."

"Pari, dear, you're not alone," Tajmah said. It was unconvincing. She was
still sneaking glimpses of *Wheel of Fortune* through the crack in the curtain.

"...I have no one, not even in Iran..."

There followed an awkward silence, broken by game show sounds. The
nurse came and gave her medicine. She knew it would make her feel dizzy,
nauseous –wondered why they bothered...

"They never tell you when you're little. It's always just God says this, God
says that. God never says he's going to kill your children and take everything

away from you and leave you all alone your whole God damned life, with nothing to hold on to, nothing to look forward to, nothing..."

"Nay, Pari dear," Tajmah said. "Don't do that to yourself."

There was another awkward silence.

"I'm supposed to seek Him out? I'm supposed to beg His forgiveness? I'm supposed to reach for Him? What did He ever do for me? Did He ever reach out to me? He could have, you know, just once..."

"Pari, dear, don't. That's all *Khanoum* – all baggage. Look where it got her. You did what you could."

Tajmah and Pari looked into each other's eyes silently, Tajmah's eyes with pity, Pari's with doubt.

"You were a mother to your children, Pari, dear. You were a wife to your husband..." She stammered, paused, wrung her matted paper napkin with her hands, daubed her eyes with it. "...You loved when – when you were loved – when you could. There was joy..." She stopped in mid sentence and they both looked away from each other.

After a pause Pari said, "Do you mean that?"

Tajmah looked back into Pari's eyes. "Yes, Pari, dear. You were loved. We all loved you."

Pari closed her eyes, holding back tears. She wanted Tajmah's pity, but didn't want it. Wanted to embrace her, but didn't want to. Wanted to believe her, but didn't want to. What did it mean? All those years she failed them. All those years she'd lost. Tajmah was perfect. What would Tajmah know? Tajmah had everything.

Pari tried to pull herself together. "What was in the note?" she asked.

"Note?" Tajmah said.

As the time neared 7:30, Pat Sajak was just starting the bonus round. It would end soon.

"*Khanoum*'s note –" Pari said, "– the one she threw into the street."

"Nothing. Rasheed said it just said, 'Help me!' Did you know she knew how to write? I didn't. Rasheed said that was all there was. He..."

"He's lying. I know he's lying. I want to see the note. Make him send me the note. I know there was more in it. I know that Rasheed. *Khanoum* would have put it in the note – Fahti..."

"Pari, dear, don't..."

"No one said why? Neither one of them? My own brother..."

Pari leaned to the side and grabbed the green plastic kidney shaped bowl to catch her vomit. But, all she had were dry heaves.

"He's not going to come, is he – Saeed?" she asked Tajmah, recovering.

"He'll come, Pari, dear."

But, Pari didn't believe her. She lay a long time without speaking, letting

Tajmah return to *Wheel of Fortune*. After a while she began to feel dizzy. She spoke in a mumble: "They think we're weird here."

Tajmah didn't answer. It was just as well. It was not the kind of statement Pari wanted answered.

Pari felt sad. In Iran there would be someone to sit beside her bed at home while she died. A host of nurses: aunts, cousins, nieces, daughters, friends. In America there was hardly anyone – just Tajmah. In America they were all too busy wailing at their pet cemeteries. Even Tajmah scarcely had the time. She did night work for a nearby motel, keeping the books. Nobody had time in America. Nobody had time to reach out for anything – except money.

Pari wanted to go home. She wanted to grasp what she knew, what she understood – cling to it.

"Don't let them burn me, Tajmah." She closed her eyes to keep the room from spinning. "Don't let them put me in a box…"

"Pari, dear, don't…"

"… I want a white sheet and I want them to lay me on my side, shake my shoulder in the grave to remind me of the catechisms…"

"Pari… You'll get better – *Khanoum* too…"

"I don't care. She never cared about me. She never cared about you. I don't think she cared about Rasheed – or War Minister or Baba. It was all about her…"

"She loved you – us – Pari, dear. You must believe that…"

"You, maybe…"

Pari kept her eyes closed. What did she want? Would she ever know?

"I want Saeed," Pari said. "I want Saeed to come and say goodbye." She knew she shouldn't have said it out loud, not in front of Tajmah, but she couldn't help herself. She'd had to say it. She had to cling to what little truth, what little hope, what little meaning remained to an empty life going dark. She could love herself in Saeed, she thought, love herself if he loved her. He would set her to rest in the earth and flee with her to Bridge over Tajreesh, pass languorous afternoons touching her where no one could see, sultry summer evenings where the household slept and Saeed stole to her room and made sweating love to her. Passionate throbbing silence against the distant calls of street vendors and the fading clop-clop of donkey hooves on cobblestones. These were the sounds she wanted to ease her from life, not American TV. She had lived only in those long-fled moments with Saeed, those scant, scarce, sacred, stolen, selfless moments when no one saw them, fleeting moments over forty years gone. She knew that.

She felt the first light begin to swell within her, and wanted to reach for him.

"I love," she would say, and he would say it back. He was standing over her, bending in the light. She lifted an arm, trembled, lifted into the air, longed for him…

He would take her home. Everything would be right. He would lead her one last time to taste whitefish from the Caspian, *gaz* from Isfahan, honey from Mount Sahand; smell the fragrant carpet of rose petals before the tomb of Hafez, the Persian violets in Shemiran; stroke the red-frothed sea of poppies at the foot of Mt. Damavand, the snow necklace of the Alborz Mountains; the golden tomb of Imam Reza; behold the turquoise domes and crystal water channels of Isfahan; savor the poems of Hafez, Sa'di, Khayam, Rumi, Shams Tabrizi, Sabzewari, Bahar, Khaqani, Shaykh Abu Sa'id Abi'L-Khayr, Sorush Esfahani, Ansari, Khwansari, Awi, Attar, Qazwini, Razi, Shaybani, Beheshti, Farrokhi, Nezami, Darrabi, Samirza, Esmail, Ebn Moqaffa, Talb Amoli, Rabe-e'bent Kab, Mohlavi, Jami, Tusi, Ferdowsi, Rudaki, Ghazzalie – a thousand years of poets…

But, Saeed was letting her die here to the rhymes of Mr. Clean and *Wheel of Fortune*, which was ending

> She sensed love draw nigh,
> Paused, raised, waited,
> Searched, longed, lifted,
> Her eyes to the shadow-flickering ceiling:
> "Tajmah, dear," she called, "turn my bed to Mecca."

> She reached,
> Wavered,
> Reached again,
> And knew,

> *When no one is looking,*
> *I swallow deserts and clouds,*
> *And chew on mountains knowing,*
> *They are sweet bones.*

> *When no one is looking,*
> *And I want to kiss God,*
> *I just lift mine own hand*
> *To my mouth.*

Glossary of unfamiliar names & terms.

andaroon women's quarters

baleh – conversational assent: "yes," or "really"

birouni men's quarters, typically offices at the entrance to a large compound

bonyad – an organization or company

gaz – a natural taffy made from the syrup of a special root, similar in color and texture to nougat

Haj – Moslem pilgrimage to Mecca, where they circle the Kaaba

hashtee – octagonal entrance room

Hoveida – Mohamed Reza Shah's longtime prime minister and political eunuch, replaced shortly before the revolution.

Imam Lit. – "he who sets an example;" used by the Shiites to denote successors to the prophet Mohamed

Khalkali – A Himmleresque member of Khomeini's inner circle known as "the hanging judge."

Khan / Khanoum – Honorific for Sir / Madam.

korsi – A heating arrangement consisting of a large charcoal brazier placed beneath a blanket covered table used for heating in the winter. It would typically be placed in the center of a room. People would sit and often sleep with their legs under the blanket.

majlis – parliament

polo – steamed rice, often includig meats, fish, vegetables, herbs, etc. according to a variety of recipes

Rashtee – Lit., man from the province of Rasht. Men from Rasht were humorously regarded as having wives who cheated on them, and for denying it.

sephahsalar – war minister

Reza Khan Shah – first Pahlavi shah

Mohamed Reza Shah – son of Reza Khan, second (and final) Pahlavi shah

taarof – An intricate set of rules governing the giving and receiving of offers in polite situations

taghouti – derogatory, post revolutionary term for the ruling elite under the Pahlavi Shah

temporary marriage. In Shia Islam, men are allowed four permanent wives at the same time, but they may have an unlimited number of temporary wives at any time, each lasting from minutes to a lifetime.

vaqfe – a church association for holding and distributing lands donated or forfeited to the church